Visions of Isabelle

Visions of Isabelle

William Bayer

DELACORTE PRESS/NEW YORK

Manufactured in the United States of America

First printing

Designed by MaryJane DiMassi

Library of Congress Cataloging in Publication Data

Bayer, William S
Visions of Isabelle.
1. Eberhardt, Isabelle, 1877–1904—Fiction.
I. Title.
PZ4.B3563Vi [PS3552.A859] 813'.5'4 75-30770
ISBN 0-440-09315-5

FOR PAULA

Contents

AUTHOR'S NOTE

This book is not a biography. It is a novel, a fantasy, based on the life of Isabelle Eberhardt. Though it contains distortions and inventions devised to serve the telling of a story, many of the events took place, and many of the characters lived. The names have not been changed, except in a few cases.

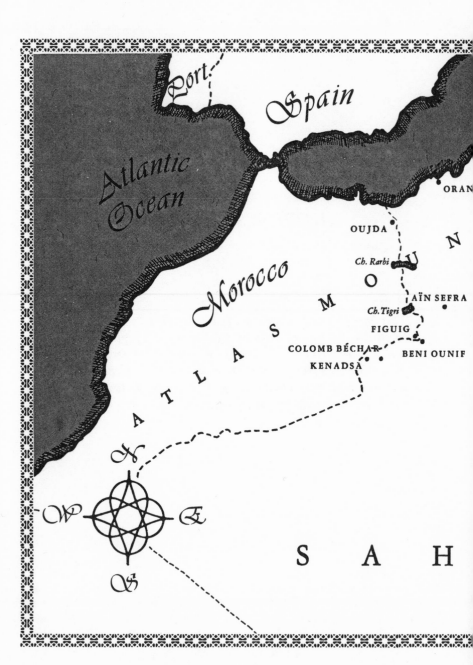

Prologue

To Major Édouard De Susbielle

Sir:

It has come to my attention that after a memorial service organized under the auspices of the Resident-General, Commander in Chief, General Lyautey, in honor of the memory of my late friend, Isabelle Eberhardt, also known as Si Mahmoud, you were overheard to make certain disparaging remarks in the officers' mess at the garrison in Fez.

In particular it has been reported that you made reference to certain erotic episodes in her life of which you could have no first-hand knowledge, and made other vicious slanders, among them that my late friend was a "drunkard, an addict, and a syphilitic" and that "she slept with most of the Foreign Legion."

I find such statements insupportable. Mademoiselle Eberhardt was a person of the highest moral character, she was a devout Moslem, and her activities during the time of the border war in the Sud-Oranais were of inestimable value to France. She was one of the great personages of her time, and any imputation to the contrary, by you or anyone else, must be considered an intolerable lie.

It is possible that the reports to me of your comments have been incorrect. I sincerely request, sir, that you affirm this in writing, or else be prepared to meet me on the field of honor.

With my most distinguished sentiments,
Major Eugène Letord

Part One

Everything in my childhood and adolescence prepared me for the fact that peace and good fortune would have no place in my life—that I would be doomed to a maddening struggle, and would become, if you like, a scapegoat, bearing the burden of all the injustices and misfortunes that hurled my family to ruin.

Mes Journaliers,
January 18, 1900

The
Cracked Piano

Nathalie De Moerder was the illegitimate daughter of a German Lutheran named Eberhardt and a Russian Jew named Korff —a fact unsuspected by her husband, General Paul De Moerder of the Imperial Russian army, until several years after they were married. In the early 1870s, Madame De Moerder ran away from her home in St. Petersburg with her three children— Nicolas, Nathalie and Vladimir—and their tutor, a former parish priest named Alexandre Trophimovsky. A fourth child, Augustin, was born in 1872, and he, too, bore the De Moerder name. In Geneva, on February 17, 1877, a fifth child was born—sired by Trophimovsky or perhaps by someone else. She was named Isabelle Eberhardt.

Spring of 1888 in Meyrin—a town outside Geneva. The sun shines brightly upon the tropical plants, the cacti and bamboo, rubber trees and miniature palms that grow, bloom and perfume the air in the garden of the Villa Neuve. Two children, a teen-age boy and a girl eleven years old, wield axes against a pile of logs. They chop for a while, then sit down together to rest. A dog barks, another answers from far away, and then a distant scream rends the air.

In the villa, a vast, high-ceilinged, noble-looking house, sobs and cruel laughter echo through the rooms. Vladimir, a boy of twenty, lies upstairs on his unmade bed, his arms rigid by his sides, his bare feet extended between the brass rods of the baseboard, and turned so that his legs are locked in place. He stares at the ceiling with crossed eyes and listens to the sounds below. At each scream he winces; at each sob moisture gathers in his eyes; at each trail of laughter he curves his mouth into a sarcastic smile.

After a while these contortions take on a pattern of their own. He begins to twitch, to vibrate his head, and then to arch it back so that the tendons made hard in his neck pulse with his rapidly beating heart. When he can stand this no longer, when perspiration has risen upon his whole body and matted his long blond hair to his forehead so that it nearly covers his eyes, he springs up, grasps a violin off the floor, and begins to play rapid, high-pitched scales. He swoons with his music, presses down his bow as hard as he can, bends back and forth like a Slavic gypsy. Still, no matter how rapidly or piercingly he plays, he cannot blot out the cries and wails that fill the house, and have filled it for as long as he can remember.

In the garden Augustin and Isabelle hear Vladimir's fiddling, try to find his rhythm so that they may fit their chopping to his beat. They cannot succeed; their axes become embedded in the wood and must be wrenched free. Still chips fly about, and after a quarter of an hour Isabelle has produced more firewood than her brother.

The scene in the drawing room has only begun. The black and white squares of the marble floor provide an arena for the combatants who pace about. The room is spacious, luxurious, flooded with light that pours in through a row of glass doors on one side, but it is furnished with junk: a table made of a single unfinished plank supported by wooden packing crates and covered with stains of food and paint, the cheapest overstuffed chairs bought in secondhand shops from the estates of retired British civil servants, an old black and green Turkish samovar set upon a battered steamer trunk. Everywhere there are piles of mildewed books. A legless piano crouches in a cobwebbed corner. Gardening tools, hoes, rakes, picks, shears and ceramic pots clutter a section of the floor, and a paint-spattered ladder leans against a wall where may be seen an extraordinary sight.

This is a vast disjointed mural, crudely but passionately painted—the work of a lunatic perhaps, or a child in a rage. Figures are superimposed, perspective is distorted, limbs turn the wrong way at vital joints. Colors clash and run together. Mistakes have been stricken out rather than erased. The mural depicts a grotesque crucifixion in which a diabolic Christ wails in ecstasy upon a bejeweled cross, surrounded by sneering saints and wild dogs with lascivious tongues who look up at Jesus or else out of the mural and into the room.

Various monetary symbols—signs for dollars, rubles, sterling, francs—are emblazoned upon the foreheads of popes whose villainies are listed in angrily painted slogans that curl about their heads: "CHRIST THE DEVIL"; "PETER THE BETRAYER"; "OPPRESSOR POPES IN LEAGUE WITH ROYAL DOGS"; "THE GREEDY CHURCH STEALS FROM THE HUNGRY POOR." To one side, covering part of two walls, is a gigantic woman with a beatific face who holds a saw-toothed sickle and threatens to sweep away all these villains with a single swipe. This avenger is labeled *The Revolution*.

If anything is more bizarre than the contents of the painting, it is the anger impacted within—an anger that shows in the way it spills off its wall, turns corners, makes no distinction between wall and ceiling, wall and floor, extends onto the marble mantelpiece, is smeared across several panes of window glass, attacks mirrors and even the nearby furniture, running across the velvet of the chairs, incorporating an ancient Russian icon that leans against a trunk, then spills out of the fireplace and onto the hearth where, one can imagine on a winter day, flaming logs would provide a blazing inferno, which in league with the avenging revolution in the corner, would threaten all organized religion with an enormous auto-da-fé.

Alexandre Trophimovsky, affectionately known as "Vava," a huge, bearlike man with mercilessly piercing eyes, a thick black beard, wild locks of graying hair, is the author of this stupendous mural and also of the violent scenes that take place in this room. His stepdaughter, Nathalie De Moerder, has just announced to him her intention of marrying an apprentice watchmaker in Geneva. These two move around the room—Vava with the swagger of a village priest, young Nathalie, like a trapped and flustered bird, awkward, alighting here and there, placing all her weight on one foot, then on the other. Madame Nathalie Eberhardt De Moerder, or "Old Nathalie" as she is sometimes called, sits watching her daughter and her lover from a filthy brown velvet chair, her sweet-natured eyes pouring parallel rivers of tears. Young Nathalie and Vava have been hurling insults at a tempo that exceeds the feverish fiddling of Vladimir. All three ignore his music: it is merely background, part of the blend of barking dogs and twittering birds that fills in the spaces between their cries.

"Disgusting pig!"

"Bitch in heat!"

"Monster!"

"Whore!"

"Drunken goat!"

"Shrew! Witch!"

To Isabelle and Augustin the exchange in the drawing

room which wafts to them garbled, in the garden below the house is but the prelude to a climax which they know, in time, will be punctuated by flung bottles, kicked vases, even threats of suicide and murder in the form of frozen gestures with rakes and shears.

Augustin flings his ax away, Isabelle sets hers down, and together they creep toward the house to share the drama—the only thing that relieves the boredom of life at Villa Neuve.

"You want to keep me here—locked up! You'll do anything to ruin my life!"

The children see Young Nathalie standing in front of the broken piano, feet apart, hands on her hips, her head extended so far back that they wonder how she can keep her balance.

"On the contrary," bellows Vava, "I have ruined my own life for you."

Now he, too, steps into sight so that from where they spy in the garden Isabelle and Augustin can see the combatants framed in separate windows like portraits on a wall. There is another window between—here sits their mother, twisting her head abruptly from Vava to Young Nathalie and back again like a spectator at a game of tennis. Isabelle barely listens to the argument—she is more fascinated by this trio of living paintings, framed and glassed.

"Yes! By making us slaves! Insulting everyone we bring home! Destroying our friendships! Filling our heads with hate!" Spittle shoots out of Young Nathalie's mouth as if she is pumping venom from a reservoir within.

"Ungrateful! Bitch! I taught you everything you know. You and your brothers were nothing but cold-assed little snotnoses until I—"

"Drove us insane!"

"Taught you what the world is! Taught you languages, mathematics, history, science, sketching, how to live!"

"I'd do anything to get out of this asylum."

"Anything? Fine. Pack your bags and get out. You'll be the laughingstock of whores. The daughter of General Paul De Moerder married to some tradesman scum! Your brothers will die of shame. Your mother will be snickered at by bakers. And I shall be defeated, too. So be it. But," and as he says this Vava leers at Young Nathalie with withering scorn, "you shall suffer the most—saving thread and pennies, skimping on soap, buying cheaper and cheaper cuts of meat. I can see your dinner table—pieces of bread mixed up with watch springs. I can see your body widening as your children take over your life, puking and crying and demanding this and that. I can see you mending their ghastly middle-class clothes, vulgar dresses garnished with disgusting frills, and I can hear the endless arguments over money—Christ, how I know these people!—money, money, money. 'We must cut down here, dear; mustn't spend too much there, dear.' Sickening! You won't last a year. And one winter day you'll come around here with a sniffling baby in your arms and say, 'Vava, Vava, let me in, you were right. I've come home.' But I won't let you in. I won't look at you. You'll have to go back to your stinking life and that'll be my sweet revenge. Because, I promise you, if you go off with this idiot, you'll never enter this house again!"

"Oh! The slimy way you twist everything! We're already the laughingstock of whores! My brothers are already dying of shame. To think that the wife of General Paul De Moerder is living with a flabby old drunk, a defrocked priest who squanders our inheritance on some half-brained scheme to raise cacti in Switzerland and turn them into perfume! We must be mad to put up with you and your drunken fits. Mother—get rid of him. Listen to me—look at me when I talk to you—"

Old Nathalie now is staring straight ahead, as if she were looking into the eyes of Isabelle and Augustin crouched side by side by the hedge outside. They are shivering, trembling in each other's arms. Terrible things have been said inside the house—they have heard many fights before; have screamed, too, at times; have stood up to one another and to Vava; have shouted out words that later they wished they hadn't said; but never, at any time, has any one of them implied that it is their mother who gives Vava the power by which he holds them in thrall, that it is because of her weakness that they have become his slaves.

In the window on the left, Isabelle can see her sister pleading with Old Nathalie to send Trophimovsky away. In the window on the right she can see Vava, certain that this ploy of Young Nathalie will fail. And in the center window she can see her mother who stares with the look of a person who refuses to listen to things she does not wish to hear.

For a moment the tableau freezes, the characters held against the swirling scenery of the mural that riots across the background wall. But a moment later it all comes apart, the combatants hurl themselves against one another in a frenzy of slaps and screams. Vladimir is playing wild and dissonant arpeggios as Young Nathalie purses up her lips and lets fly with an enormous glop of spit that sails across the three windows and lands on Vava's leg. He gathers up his own spittle and lets fly at her, hitting her squarely between the breasts. Young Nathalie rushes at Vava with a scream. They meet, eclipsing Old Nathalie in the center window. Here Vava grabs Young Nathalie by the hair and with his other hand begins to slap her face. She kicks at his ankles until he falls upon his knees. The fiddling upstairs has become a screech.

"I'm leaving, I'm leaving," Young Nathalie screams at him, and Vava screams back, "Get out, get out!"

"I'll never come back," she yells, yanking herself free.

"Never come back," yells Vava, and turns away.

Augustin has fled. But Isabelle remains crouched by the hedge—she hates Young Nathalie, adores Vava and her mother, cannot understand how her sister can do such a terrible thing. To marry a watchmaker's apprentice—it is madness. She has seen the young man, and then listened to Vava dissect his middle-class values to bits. "Make love to anyone anytime you want," Vava has said, "but never renounce your dignity nor give up your soul." Young Nathalie, upstairs now packing her bags, is throwing her life away. *I should speak to her*, Isabelle thinks, and then, *If she won't listen to Vava she won't listen to me.*

Vava is pouring Old Nathalie vodka from a flask. He pours one for himself, swallows it in a single gulp, dashes the glass against the floor. Isabelle's mother does not even quiver at the sound. Seeing that peace has fallen again upon Villa Neuve, Isabelle wanders back into the garden to look for Augustin. She finds him sobbing behind the woodpile. To comfort him, she kisses his cheek.

The evening comes and with it chaos. Nicolas arrives back from Geneva. When informed of Young Nathalie's departure he says, "Good riddance," and retires to his room. No dinner is served. The children wander into the kitchen, grab what bread and vegetables they can find, devour them on the spot, leaving a mess. Old Nathalie sits cross-legged on the floor, playing polonaises on the ruined piano. Vladimir has long since put down his violin and disappeared to a secret part of the garden where he sits, arms curled about his legs, staring tearfully at the moon.

Playing hide-and-seek with Augustin among the hedges near the house, Isabelle hears the perfume of Chopin give way to Tchaikovsky's "Marche Slav." She peers through the drawing-room window, watches Vava dance around, vodka flask in hand, jumping and twirling like an Armenian peasant. "Faster, faster!" he yells, but Old Nathalie cannot meet his demand. He jumps upon the piano and dances there; Nathalie becomes stuck on a chord. Vava, angry, pounds his foot on the piano top and the musicale ends with the sound of splintering wood.

While Isabelle has been watching, Augustin has crept behind her and placed his hands over her eyes.

"Guess who?" he whispers.

"Vladimir Petrovitch."

"Yes, Zinaida."

A week before they stole off to an obscure corner of the garden and there Augustin read Turgenev's *First Love* aloud. Both of them loved the story and decided to take its characters' names. Now Isabelle laughs in Augustin's face as she imagines Zinaida would have done at Vladimir Petrovitch. Together they run off around the corner of the house to peer in another window and spy on Nicolas. They find him posing in a tight pair of riding pants and nothing else, his hand resting on his shoulder, holding an imaginary revolver. He makes several paces across the room, pauses, then turns and lowers his arm so that the weapon is pointing directly at his image in the mirror.

"Puff," he says, in a hoarse and masculine whisper, as he squeezes off a shot.

Isabelle begins to giggle. Startled, Nicolas turns and glares at the window. Isabelle and Augustin hurry away.

❖

Long after midnight Isabelle is awakened by terrible noises downstairs—curses, shouts, gardening pots hurled against walls. She moves to her door and opens it a crack. A thud. Isabelle peers down the hall. Her mother's door is closed. She can hear Vladimir whimpering in his room, then the sounds of creaking floorboards, as if people are moving in the hall. She goes to the landing, makes out Nicolas and Augustin creeping toward the drawing-room door in their underwear. They pause, then enter. She waits a moment then tiptoes down the stairs. The stone is cold against her bare feet. At the bottom she discovers the drawing-room door is closed. She inches her way across the hall, kneels at the keyhole, presses her eye against cold brass.

She sees her brothers standing beside Trophimovsky, muttering together in muddled tones. Vava is lying on his back, extremities spread, snoring loudly, twisting in his sleep. Saliva trickles from his mouth, oozes into his matted beard. The room is a shambles—broken glass and shards of pottery are scattered about. The mural is disfigured by gashes of red, as if cans of paint have been hurled at the walls.

"How I hate him!" Nicolas' whisper is furious and cold, cuts to her ears through the heavy wood. He plucks a hoe from the pile of garden tools and raises it above his head.

"I could kill him now and set us free," he says, and turns to Augustin as if for consent. The eyes of her brothers meet; Isabelle trembles with fear.

"Shall I kill him?"

"Could you, really?" Augustin asks.

"It would be easy. I could make it look like he fell on his rake. In the morning when Mama comes down she'll think he killed himself by accident."

"She'll weep—"

"Nothing new."

"What would happen to us?"

"We'd go home! To Russia!"

Augustin ponders the problem.

"Don't do it," he says.

"I will," says Nicolas. "Someday I will."

He heaves the hoe into a corner and the two of them start toward the door. Isabelle presses herself back against the wall, is nearly crushed as her brothers come out.

Later, when they have gone and all is quiet upstairs, she slips inside and looks down at Vava raging in his sleep.

Eclipse

On the morning of April 15, 1893, Isabelle Eberhardt rises from her bed and makes her way to an austerely framed mirror that hangs in an alcove off her room. This room, in the back and on the second floor, is strangely shaped as if made up of all the spaces left over after the creation of the other rooms of Villa Neuve. Isabelle likes it—the odd corners, alcoves and diagonally slanting walls are always a feast for her wandering eyes. She spends hours here, reading, studying, dreaming of distant lands.

She is sixteen years old, her hair is cut short like a boy's, and her ears stand out a little from the sides of her head. Looking at herself she is pleased—she appears intelligent, youthful, brave and, when she chooses, severe. *A young person not to be trifled with*, she thinks, *a person who can hold his own in a duel.* She is particularly happy about the way her eyebrows are set—slightly off-center, each one curved into a different arabesque. She gazes at her reflection a long while, wonders for a moment how she may look in ten or twenty years, and is in the midst of a fantasy in which she sees herself dancing, the center of attention at a great ball, when she hears a sound, glances to the side and catches a flash of Augustin's hand pulling her covers over his head.

He hasn't seen her, is too busy hiding in her bed for some ambush he evidently plans to spring, perhaps when she changes into her clothes. She smiles at the mirror, finds it charming the way her smile breaks the brooding, intelligent cast of her face, and then continues with her fantasy, a dizzying waltz in which she is swept around and around at dazzling speed by a tall lean nobleman wearing elegant white silk gloves (she cannot see his face, but can feel the texture of the gloves) until the room, the gilt, the crystal, even the jewels of the women blur into sparkles and streaks of light.

Fantasy concluded, she sets about for a way to properly deal with Augustin. She begins to hum a Russian folk song abstractly, hoping to deceive her brother into confidence that he has not been seen. As she hums she moves closer to her bed, and then, with the speed and energy of a panther, she leaps, landing directly on Augustin's back. Quickly she pulls a blanket over his head, wraps it down about his face. She holds on tight as he begins to buck, so that his yells and pleas are muffled by heavy wool.

She laughs as he struggles, and when he raises his body she presses her knees against his flanks as if she is taming a runaway horse. For a moment they fight, and then, when he begins to weaken, she lets him go. He comes out from the covers gasping, red-faced. She looks at him quizzically, and when he regains his breath, the two of them begin to laugh.

"You *surprise* me, Nastasia Filippovna."

"You were *trying* to surprise me, dear Prince Myshkin."

(In recent weeks they have read together from *The Idiot* in their rooms, lying across each other's beds.)

"What were you admiring so assiduously in your mirror?"

"Myself, of course."

"Of course. But what part of yourself? Superficial exterior or subterranean soul?"

"Both."

"Any conclusions?"

"Many."

"For example?"

"For example—let me see." She sinks her chin into her palm. The two of them are sitting cross-legged on the rumpled bed. "I saw the face of a woman irresistibly attractive to men—a face that will haunt the dreams of a whole parade of youths unfortunate enough to cross her path. I suspect, Augustin, that I shall be a breaker of many hearts."

"What conceit!"

"I don't think so. You asked me to tell you what I saw and I told you—objectively, too." She pouts a little, but he knows she is not displeased.

"There is something else in your face, Nastasia Filippovna, but I wonder if I should tell you what it is."

"Please, please, Augustin. I must know. I simply have to know."

"I wonder—"

"No, Augustin. That's not fair. You have to tell me."

"Well, all right. But don't be cross if you don't like it."

"What is it?"

"Something—two-faced."

"What are you talking about?"

"There is something doubled—"

"I don't understand."

"Something in you that shows two aspects—just a minute, damnit, let me explain." She is practically on top of him, panting into his face. "I would say something soft and something hard, something warm and something cold, something—" And as he says this, he peers at her closely, studies each feature, then tightens his lips as he searches for the right words. "Some side of you that will be hurt and another side that will hurt."

"Go on! Go on!"

"It's hard. Let me see. Something of Mama and something

of Vava. A part of you that's a girl and another part that's a boy. A romantic and a revolutionary. A peasant and a scholar. A person who is simple and a person who is complex."

"A sister *and* a brother?"

"Yes. A nice nuisance. A bothersome cat."

"Well, I like all of it except the last two." Her fingers explore the sides of her face, stroke her cheeks as if she is sculpting them from clay. "Yes, Augustin, I think you have grasped something of my nature. And you are the only one who does."

Their faces move together, their lips meet. Their mouths press, glow, tingle. For a moment they feel they may succumb to forbidden desire. Augustin presses in closer. Isabelle shuts her eyes, feels her head grow warm as her lips begin to part. Augustin draws away. There are droplets of sweat beneath his nose.

A few minutes later, dressed in a boy's shirt and pantaloons, Isabelle goes to the garden. She finds Vladimir on hands and knees, weeding among the cacti, and Vava, leaning on his rake, speaking with bravado of his future gardening plans.

"We shall put the Arizona rhizomes in a row over there," he says with a wild flourish of his arm.

"This plot will cost me thousands, but I'll get it all back by spring. In Paris they're paying a fortune for anything that smells good. It's the same all over the world. People stink, women find themselves turning foul, and something must be done. Even in Argentina—imagine, Argentina!—there are fools who will pay anything, five, ten, twenty pounds an ounce for a new smell. It's madness, like paying a fortune for a hat or a dress. The idiots give bottles of the stuff to their mistresses, *but*, and this is the *point*, a different aroma to each one. Otherwise they couldn't tell them apart. In circles where people devote themselves to fornication, the motto should be 'Follow Your Nose!' "

Vava gives out with an enormous laugh of cynicism and spite. For more than fifteen years he has poured money into his majestic scheme to be purveyor of odors to the world. He has dreams that bottles of his preciously distilled aromatics will find their way into the boudoirs of the Faubourg-St. Germain and the palaces of St. Petersburg. He has engaged a printshop in Geneva to make up ten thousand labels embellished with an imaginary coat of arms. A fortune's worth of crystal bottles lies in crates in the cellar where former owners kept casks of wine. Every few years he travels back to Russia with a trunk containing samples of his wares. The bottles that aren't broken by the time he arrives at the Finland Station are left off at expensive shops to encourage extravagant orders that never come. The Persians (and how he curses them!) have beaten him at this game. He has not the salesman's easy wit, nor enough sense to offer his clients jars of caviar. He must look, thinks Isabelle, like a lunatic, flying down the streets of St. Petersburg, screaming curses against Persians under his breath, coattails flying, hat blowing, his pockets filled with those ludicrous bottles whose labels have been pasted on askew by Vladimir.

On his last trip, discouraged and broken, he spoke with a lawyer about suing the Persian representative. The man began to laugh.

"His practices are unfair," said Vava.

"There is no law against that," he was told.

When he returned home he was nearly in tears. "Nothing means anything," he wailed as he rode back to Meyrin in a hired coach, Isabelle and Vladimir on either side. "Impossible to do business with these horrible Russians. They are intoxicated with religion and money and they stink like hell. I tell you, though, this garden is a fortune. We must plow under the old plants, bring in new ones from America, Australia. Damn the cost! Someday we'll have a scent that will set them reeling, and then, ha! We can spit in Mother Russia's face. We'll refuse to sell to them. All contracts with our concessionaires will carry one nonnegotiable clause—if one bottle, one drop, ever finds itself inside Holy Russia, then the penalty will be ten times the royalty, and the concessionaire will have ninety days to liquidate his stock. I can see them now, plotting ways to make me relent, and, when I refuse, to steal away the formulas. On the train down from Warsaw I was thinking about how we'd work. We must have a warehouse in Geneva, an old home, perhaps, totally secure, bars on the windows, one set of keys, with Nicolas— he has a head for business—keeping track of everything from an office above. I hear that workers in the South African diamond mines must pass a physical search before they're dismissed from work. A good idea! By the way, did the retorts come from London? I've thought up a new combination we must try at once. . . ." On and on, raving like a maniac, all the way back to Villa Neuve, while Vladimir searched Vava's face with his usual dutiful expression, and Isabelle stared straight ahead and wondered how long it would be before the old man would totally crack up.

She is thinking of that mad ride, and the nights he spends in his "office" converted from a sitting room for servants (whom he refuses to employ), pouring over his manuals of chemistry, boiling up new concoctions. Sometimes, so exhausted by the time he locks his precious notebooks away, he confuses flasks of his half-made perfumes with his always available flask of vodka, and has to spit out the horrid oily substance in a stream of curses against competitors he is sure are plotting to steal his work.

She loves him, though, in spite of his insanity. He has spent hours teaching her languages, has made certain that by the age of fifteen she is fluent in Russian, German, Arabic and French. He has taught her how to ride like a jockey, to work out massively complicated problems in trigonometry and algebra, to recite Pushkin until she can do so without a pause in a deep, sonorous, masculine growl that always leaves her exhausted and her clothing soaked with sweat.

For all his terrible displeasure with the world, his conviction that conspiracies are everywhere, his insults about everyone or anything that is accepted or acceptable, his morose nihilism, his scorn, his sarcasm, his drunkenness, his insane demonic rages, he is capable, too, at times, of great good humor. He tells stories with riotous climaxes, anecdotes filled with double meanings, and plays rough practical jokes such as putting a mouse inside someone's chest of clothes.

It is this sort of thing that makes him impossible to hate despite the fact that Isabelle believes he has crushed her mother's spirit. For though he shouts at Old Nathalie, curses her, shows her contempt, there are times, too, when he makes her laugh, breaks through her blank staring into space and makes her sweet face wrinkle with glee. Obviously he adores her, and just as obviously he finds it difficult to demonstrate his adoration—in fact he usually demonstrates it by acting as if she's the most loathsome object in his sight.

Except for Vladimir, her brothers seem to detest him, yet they are careful to act meekly when he's around. He can beat anyone of them at riding, running, wrestling and any and every feat of strength, and his intellect, though applied to the ridiculous scheme to produce perfume, is massive in comparison with theirs.

Vladimir seems to adore him, to hang on his every word, though he, too, has his moments of rebellion. But he is a strange boy, full of sideways glances and whimpers and bowed-head obedience. Though Isabelle loves him well for his tenderness with her, and the way he seems to soothe their mother, who can often be seen stroking his hair as he lies on the floor beside her, head resting like a dog's in her gentle lap, still she does not really feel she can speak to him beyond the everyday matters that concern people who share the same house.

Nicolas—he is mysterious, constantly away in the city, with friends who, she understands from vague references and overheard whispers, are Russian students, members of anarchist groups. They plot acts of terror and treason against the czar, and in their cramped rooms in the place Bourg-de-Four, smoke opium, make licentious love, and are moved to tears by the thought of the Russian peasant masses so oppressed. She wants to know him, he fascinates her, she needs to penetrate his mystery. But he remains aloof, evades her questions, and she is reduced to spying on him, hovering about outside his window as he chats in whispers with Vladimir and Augustin, or scribbles away in notebooks which, when he is out and she discovers them, she finds have been inscribed in code.

Augustin is another matter altogether. She looks at him now, slinking out of the house, trying to evade Vava's eye for fear he, too, will be handed a rake and forced to spend the day in the garden. Although he is five years older than Isabelle, he is her best friend, the brother for whom she feels both sisterly and brotherly love. But he is weak—she sees that, knows she can always bend him to her will. They have sworn everlasting love, have even signed papers, elaborate detailed contracts, in which they swear they shall never be parted in their lives.

Their kisses are erotic and they like to touch. She especially likes to feel the hardness of his body against her own, and enjoys the times they visit each other's rooms to exchange messages, long deep probings of each other's flesh. On these occasions she peels off her shirt like a boy, making no effort to hide her small firm breasts. Once he touched them and they both laughed. She touched him back, laying her hand for a moment between his legs.

"Ssss. Ssss. Nastasia." He is trying to get her attention from behind a corner of the house. She decides to ignore him—it will amuse her to watch him risk exposing his position in order to entice her to speak. She moves a few feet away, hears him whispering again, louder, more frantic, and then a quick shuffling of footsteps as Vava turns, looking for the source of the hiss.

"Joining us today?" he asks, frowning at Isabelle, taunting her with his finger crooked. "You've been standing there too long—if you'd given us that time we'd already be finished with the row."

"I'm going inside to study—there's some verbs—"

Vava shrugs, then joins Vladimir among the new Arizona rhizomes. She starts around the other side of the house, but before she is gone Vava turns to her and shouts: "Send out Augustin. That boy is lazy and today he promised to work."

She runs into her brother a moment later, starts to exclaim, but he puts his finger to his lips.

"Shhhh."

"But it's your turn today."

"The hell with it."

"Come on, dear Prince. Your services have been demanded."

"Let's go for a walk."

"Where?"

"Beyond Chancy. To France. To Bellegarde."

She thinks a moment. "Yes," she says, "let's leave at once." They slip down the drive, cross the moat that surrounds the garden and then are off down the road, walking side by side, swinging their arms, analyzing, as they often do, the strangeness of their family.

"Sometimes I think Mama will collapse." Augustin, who loathes physical exercise, is already panting as they mount a modest hill. "She seems so calm, so impassive in the middle of all the storms, but if you look closely you'll see a slight trembling—her eyelids, sometimes her lips."

"She hardly touches the piano."

"Especially, notice, since Vava's had it fixed."

"She doesn't resent him—that's what I don't understand.

Nothing upsets her. The angrier he gets at some imagined slight, the more she smiles—so gently that it enrages him more."

"I've heard him crying in their room. And when she barricades the door, he whimpers outside, begging to be let in."

"Do you suppose they—you know—?"

"What? Oh—that. Well, probably. Doesn't everyone?"

"I don't know, of course."

"Well, don't ask me."

"Come on, Augustin. You know all about that."

He laughs.

"Well?"

"Well what?"

"Haven't you?"

"Haven't I what?"

"You know—"

He clears his throat. "If you must know—yes."

"Tell me about it?"

"Absolutely not."

"Were you afraid?"

"Nothing to be afraid of."

"What did it feel like?"

"Impossible to describe."

"Try."

He ponders, then smacks his lips. "It felt very, very good."

"You're ridiculous."

"I know."

"Who was she?"

"Which one?"

"How the devil do I know which one? Any of them. Tell me how it happened."

"That's very personal, Isabelle. A gentleman doesn't talk about things like that."

"But you're not a gentleman."

"Ha! You're right!"

"A whore I bet."

"Never!"

"I suppose you're so handsome you don't have to pay."

"My dear Nastasia Filippovna—I have never had to pay for a woman and I never shall."

"Tell me about it."

"Find out for yourself."

"Gladly. Find me a lover. Introduce me. I want to be taught. Find me an experienced man who will initiate me into everything. That's the least a brother can do."

He laughs, and she stalks off ahead. By the time he catches up, he hasn't enough breath left to speak.

They move along the banks of the Rhone, following cow paths and horse trails, sometimes cutting cross country on their own. The atmosphere is bucolic, the light shimmers on everything. They pass cows with bells hanging from their necks, milkmaids poised outside chalets, ponies trailing mares in meadows, old men fishing from rocks on the banks. They see butterflies, bees, robins, sparrows, hear the croaking of frogs. The countryside is so peaceful, so far from the tensions of Villa Neuve, that Isabelle and Augustin feel elation, join hands, swing their arms in what is at first a mock imitation of rustic fraternal affection but becomes, by the time they reach the frontier, an unashamed demonstration of joy.

The road toward Collonges is white clay, a rolling ribbon shaded by tall straight poplars evenly spaced. This road, soft in the brilliant April sun, seems to draw them along to a place unknown. Horizons change. The river widens and slinks. Someplace between Chancy and Collonges they find themselves alone—there is not even a hay wagon, a scarecrow in sight. They stop at a farm when they are hungry, and pay a few centimes for a loaf of bread. Then they are off again, through Collonges, to the outskirts of Bellegarde, where suddenly a huge vista opens up. They see miles of land split by the river, a silver trail in the afternoon light.

They sit down and stare toward the south. Each is thinking of escape. The Alps, which to tourists are such an exhilarating sight, seem to them at this moment like fortress walls which close them in.

"Oh, Augustin, how are we ever going to get away?" Escape—it is painful, impossible. All of them, Nicolas, even Vladimir, spend hours staring at ceilings or off into space, dreaming, plotting ways of leaving home.

Augustin shrugs.

"We must," Isabelle insists.

"Yes. I suppose we must."

"There has to be some way."

"Yes . . ."

"Or otherwise we are doomed."

At this moment an extraordinary event occurs. In the last few minutes the afternoon sun which had been brilliant has begun to wane. Isabelle and Augustin, immersed in thoughts of escape, have not noticed this ebbing of the light. Suddenly they both realize that the sky is becoming dark. They look up, see the sun reduced to a crescent nearly covered by a dark brown disk. They look at each other with the same word upon their lips: "Eclipse!"

They are amazed. They have read of this thing, understand perfectly how it can occur, have seen it demonstrated by Vava with croquet balls and a candle set before a mirror. But this is their first experiencing of it, unexpected, unforewarned.

Augustin begins to shiver; he feels cold. Isabelle embraces him tightly and they peer around at the strange soft light that plays upon the trees, draining all their green away. The Rhone, far below, goes rapidly from silver to deepest black. The snow on the mountains of Haute-Savoie loses its brilliance, turns to chalky gray.

They press together, touch for warmth. A tremor passes through them, a single charge that links them to this cosmic change of mood. The eclipse binds them into one, and as they huddle, cold, superstitious, amazed and moved, it occurs to Isabelle who is fond of finding equivalents in nature for her own psychic states that this incredible sight is a prophecy of familial doom, an omen of the darkening cloud that hangs above Villa Neuve.

The Brown-Eyed Levantine

By the end of November of 1893 Lake Geneva was frozen deeper than it had been in years—some said to a depth of two meters. The cold weather came in a flash, swirling down overnight from the Alps in a frosty wind, petrifying everything, including the juices of Alexandre Trophimovsky's precious Arizona cactus, killing whatever chance he might have had of recouping the fortune he'd put into the earth the previous spring.

The air of that winter was extraordinarily clear, the mountains seemed painted, and the trees were coated with crystals of snow so delicate that they looked unreal. Children fought duels with icicles, dogs shivered and their barks turned hoarse, and as Christmas came upon the city, some of the owners of the larger villas ordered sculptures of the birth in the manger carved out of blocks of ice.

A group of students from the university got together and constructed, according to an engraving in an old American book, an Eskimo igloo with a mathematically perfect dome. This was such a great success that the students were able to charge a nominal fee to curious passersby who could not believe that such a house was warm inside. Isabelle was one of those who paid, or rather she was the guest of her three brothers who escorted her on occasion into town. After the visit to the igloo she went to a café with Augustin while Nicolas and Vladimir disappeared on a mysterious errand. When Nicolas returned he was with someone new, a friend from Turkey whom he introduced as Rehid Bey.

As the three youths talked, of politics, anarchism, Michelet, Bakunin, she studied the newcomer with extreme curiosity. He was slender, about her own height; his neck was wrapped in a long embroidered scarf; and his hair, or what she saw of it creeping around the sides of a matching Alpine cap, consisted of dark brown silky locks. But it was his eyes and eyelashes that she found most extraordinary— the eyes huge and soft dark brown, and the lashes lengthy, arching upward and downward with attenuated and, to her, delightful grace. However it was far more than these soulful eyes that interested her—really, and she said it to herself at the time, it was a very special aura, an almost sublime radiance that surrounded this young man whom she dubbed at once "the brown-eyed Levantine."

At one point in the conversation, to which she barely listened, being bored by politics and particularly by what she considered the absurd intensity of her brothers and their extremist views, the eyes of Rehid Bey came to rest upon her own. She could not be certain if he was really seeing her. He acknowledged nothing, but at the same time gave off such a warm and mellow glow that Isabelle suddenly gasped as if she had been struck. At that moment of contact between their eyes, a flash of heat swept across her cheeks, moisture broke out upon her brow, and a tingling spread from a point at the base of her neck coursing in waves of delicious sensation to the tips of all her limbs. The cup of black coffee she had been holding slipped from her fingers, crashed upon the cobblestoned walk below. Though people in nearby chairs turned around, her brothers barely glanced at her, for they were in the midst of making important points.

Rehid Bey offered her a cigarette from a thin, elegant silver case.

"Thank you," she said.

"You are extremely welcome," he said, and this time, when his eyes met hers, she was certain she filled his sight.

This encounter with the "brown-eyed Levantine" ricocheted in her mind through the Christmas holidays which were, in this particular year, even worse than she remembered from before. Old Nathalie wanted a Christmas tree—she timidly broached the subject on one of those rare occasions when the family ate together at one time. "It will warm the house," she said, but Vava dismissed the idea with a snapping of his jaws. She brooded for a few days then brought the matter up again.

Isabelle was amazed; she had never seen her mother in such an insistent mood. The clash was frightening, for the more violent Vava became, the more he pounded down his fists, kicked at chairs, threw pots against the walls, the more tranquilly Old Nathalie repeated her demand.

"But this is against everything I've been saying to you for twenty years," Trophimovsky said.

"I don't care," she said. "This is what I want."

Finally he shrugged and Vladimir was dispatched to cut an evergreen from the back of the house. When it was finally set up, decorated with candles, little wooden images of angels and stars and a crèche at its base arranged in a bosom of boughs (a bizarre sight before the long-abandoned fresco which, due to age and dampness, had begun to peel), Vava refused to enter the room. All the work was done by the children who found the whole business laughable but wanted, more than anything, to see their mother pleased. So in the evening the five of them, mother, three sons and sixteen-year-old Isabelle, sat in boredom beside the tree and the precious De Moerder icon (finally dusted after so many years), reading, singing, playing chess, even helping Old Nathalie with her knitting of winter sweaters. Vava stayed secluded in his office where they could hear him shouting at the chemical additives and precious distillations, cursing them for not blending as he had foreseen. The tension was frightening. They all tried to stay out of the old man's way, but were forced inside by the chill, at times so cold that Isabelle's cheeks became numbed at the merest contact with the wind.

A break was bound to come, and when it did on Christmas Eve, it was with unexpected deviousness. Vava's eruptions were always public spectacles—he savored his performances and sometimes, in a joking mood, would remind them of a particularly fierce one and laugh with them at the memory. But this time he struck behind their backs. He slipped into the drawing room when they were all asleep, stripping the tree of all its ornaments, singeing and then scraping away the needles until all the branches were bare, painting the denuded tree an angry red, hoisting it up by its stump to the ceiling and from there allowing it to hang upside down, decorated with ornaments of his own— grotesque little figures crudely crafted out of paper and cork which appeared to be devils, monsters, ghouls.

Old Nathalie, unfortunately, was the first to find it in the morning and she began to scream. The others converged upon her and stared, amazed, at the incredible sight.

Vava had disappeared; at least they could not find him. Finally, after their initial horror, and after the boys had dragged the ruined tree out the back door, Isabelle saw him walking across the snow, looking haggard and a little scared, timid about coming too close to the windows to see the effect of his terrible prank. She never forgot that sight of him, for he appeared most vuluerable then—the nasty demon skulking with fear and shame in the Christmas snow. When he finally did come in, and with a grand smile asked how they liked his little joke, Old Nathalie turned her face and fled upstairs.

"What's the matter with her?" Vava asked, and indulged in a meager laugh. Later, thinking about it, discussing it with Augustin, Isabelle was horrified at the amount of anger in his act, the treachery, the scheming, for the plan must have taken him the whole night to carry out. Just considering the meanness and rage that it would take to sustain an attack like that made her depressed and also worried about his sanity.

By January the mood of Villa Neuve was dark. The three boys were constantly away on errands in town that seemed to Isabelle to be the flimsiest of pretexts for something else. Old Nathalie had taken to her room with a debilitating cold and Vava was wracked with a ruinous cough. Isabelle immersed herself in the darkest works of Russian literature: Dostoevski's *Notes from the Underground*, Gogol's *The Overcoat* and *The Nose*—books and stories that doubled her gloom. She felt cut off from everything, even from Augustin who would not, no matter how longingly she pleaded, tell her about his activities in Geneva. There were hints, of course—he could not resist feeding her inklings of depravity, suggestions about strange people, plots, conspiracies, women, drugs, but he refused to be specific about any of these things, and she found him, on the rare occasions when he was home, deep in whispered sessions with Nicolas and Vladimir—conversations which would cease the moment she came near. Vladimir's behavior confused her the most, for he had always been a lonely boy, without outside friends, and devoted to Vava and his grandiose gardening schemes. Now he evaded the old man with a craftiness that defied her conception of his character, and she saw in his eyes the special gleam of a man who has secret knowledge and from that takes strength.

On February the seventeenth, Isabelle turned seventeen.

Augustin took her into town, brought her to a Viennese pastry shop and there she was surprised by the appearance of her brothers and a fabulous confection ordered especially by them—a cake embellished with scallops of frosting and chips of candied fruit, her name emblazoned at an angle in an elaborate cursive script. Below it was a symbol of her life, an ax (for she was known in the family as the best of them at chopping wood) and a quill pen (since they knew she loved to read and longed to write). These two objects were crossed into an emblem, and the decorated piece was the one she devoured first. She was touched by this attention, and also by the way the boys included her in their talk, asking her opinion about politics and people, promising to introduce her to suitable young men. After tea they proceeded to a portion of Lake Geneva that had been cleared of snow and skated out among hundreds of young people, the three De Moerders clearing the way, mimicking trumpet flourishes and courtly bows as if introducing their younger sister to the grown-up world.

Isabelle's skating was excellent, though more forceful than balletic. She had a special walk, a gait that would remain with her all her life. It was a strong, sliding stride, similar in ways to the famous desert pace of the foreign legionnaires of France. When applied to ice with bladed shoes, it allowed her to sweep about, hands behind her back, to glide with a swiftness that had more grace than all the coquettish pirouetting of the other girls who came to the lake in pairs to meet young men.

With her brothers as a phalanx, on account of her special sense of herself at being seventeen, it was not long before she was a center of attention, and mobs of youths, students, soldiers, even young doctors and frivolous millionaires were trailing behind her, gliding at her side, trying, by various means such as racing ahead of her, sliding suddenly to a stop, then skating back past her, to catch her eye. She neither ignored them nor showed much interest. She set her face into a warm but abstracted smile and raced about as she saw fit, weaving in and out, cutting across their paths without much regard for their elaborate and mistimed attempts to intercept. Her brothers were delighted, cheered her on, took turns sweeping beside her, grasping her hand and leading her at racing speed far out to the edges where ice met snow. These mad dashes charged her body with a glow and filled her head with that special exhilaration obtained so easily by the limber and the young.

Gliding back from one of these wild forays she spotted a familiar form sliding across the ice. She was struck at once by this person's graceful ease, the way he skated among the others with the superior air of a champion racehorse amidst a herd of mares. He wore a red sweater and a pair of elegant riding trousers with leather patches at the knees. A moment later he was joined by Nicolas, and the two of them slid along while deep in animated talk. Then Vladimir swooped down to them and they skated up to her three abreast.

"Ah," Augustin whispered in her ear, "it's Rehid Bey."

A moment later he stood before her and she was struck by the tiniest ridge of frost that clung to the tips of his arched eyelashes. He greeted her warmly, and while her brothers tried hard to conceal their smiles complimented her on her magnificent carriage.

"You skate," he said without the slightest trace of irony, "like a Russian princess among Finnish serfs."

She glowed with pleasure but felt weak-kneed. Suddenly her ankles gave way, she tried to recoup her balance, but fell awkwardly upon the ice. Augustin began to giggle, but Rehid Bey knelt to help her up. While Nicolas looked on amused and Vladimir gawked and Augustin turned his face away, Rehid Bey gravely placed one of her hands upon one of his, and with a nod of his head motioned for her to step out. She did, then he swooped forward himself and bore her away.

It was as if wings had sprouted from her shoulder blades,

as if they were two eagles glinting through the sky, as if they were twanging through space, zinging on rosewood skis through powdered snow, darting faster than time, flashing forward on thunderous stallions, a pair of pebbles rolling over and over in a cascade of foaming glacier melt. Before, she had been one of the attractions for the other skaters, but now, with him, she was the single attraction on the lake. "The brown-eyed Levantine and me," she kept saying over and over to herself as they gleamed before a multitude of witnesses, twirling dervishes, her hand on his, their skates flashing the cold February light.

Strange, she thought to herself, *that the colder it becomes the warmer I feel, the more I flush, the hotter become my lips, so hot I believe they could sear.*

When, finally, after a wide-sweeping duet, during which they made ten great circles around the entire rink, perhaps fifteen slashes down its diagonals and several promenades down its central corridor, they shot together to a brilliant finale, all flashing blades and chips of ice which spattered the gaping spectators, embers burning flesh. Standing, then, together, their lungs heaving, their foreheads dripping sweat, they laughed, and Isabelle was seized with an unrequitable desire—to kiss the steam of Rehid Bey's frosty breath.

With her brothers they sat down to mugs of hot chocolate at a small glass-enclosed pavilion that adjoined the lake. There the four young men toasted her seventeen years and wished her many more which, Augustin noted, should be even more delicious than those she'd already endured.

This led to a discussion of the meaning of life, upon which each had his own opinion. Nicolas said that one should aspire to nobility, face each moment with bravery, believing it may be the last. Vladimir said that survival was the only purpose he could divine in human existence, and amplified this depressing thought with nothing more than an enigmatic smile. To Augustin life was a privilege that must be earned— the great sin, he said, is to let it pass one by, to sit while others run, when clearly the point is to lead the pack. Isabelle listened impatiently to these sentiments, for she had heard them all for years. She wanted to hear from Rehid Bey whom she noticed had been most attentive to the others and whom she feared had suddenly lost all interest in herself. She was about to turn to him, to insist on hearing his manner of coping with existence, when he turned, at the same moment, to her, and began to speak in serene and mellifluous French.

"It seems to me," he said, "—and I speak from a pedestal here since I'm twenty-seven years old—that the point of life is to perfect the spirit. Your brothers have mentioned some of the ways, and there are many more besides. I know mystics who devote themselves to contemplation so that they may rend the curtain that separates men from God. I know believers in man—humanists, they're called—who worship at the altar of human culture. And it seems that everyone I know is trying to express himself in a poem or a novel or a play. Then," and he glanced at her brothers, "there are the political revolutionaries who want to alter the social order by subversion and force—a popular mode, this season, among young Russian intellectuals of my acquaintance.

"But I believe in the senses—the pursuit of physical sensations wherever they may lead. For instance, Isabelle, our experience today—the way we felt when we skated the ice. It seems to me that a man must strive, as best he can in his limited tenure on earth, to hone each feeling to its sharpest point. Requital of desire, total satiation—by this route I hope to perfect my spirit, and avenge myself against the germ that will bring my death."

He stared at her, and her alone, the entire time he spoke, his eyes growing bigger, it seemed to her, in the dwindling afternoon light. When he was finished, he blinked and added that in his opinion the same theory held true as much for a woman as a man. There was a moment of silence and then the conversation shifted to something else. Vladimir started speaking in Russian, the three De Moerders were off upon one of their political disputes, and after a few moments Rehid Bey leaned toward Isabelle and whispered subtly into her ear:

"Have lunch with me tomorrow. Come to the Turkish consulate at a quarter after twelve."

She was in the city by eleven o'clock, and having nothing to do, amused herself for a while at the Maison Vacheron-Constantin where she watched the workmen, all of them old and wearing identical black cravats and light blue smocks, assembling watches in elaborate casings, including one, she was told, for the emperor of Japan. Despite the cold she strode around the old part of town, finding her way to the Russian church whose eight gold onion domes filled her with nostalgia for a homeland she had never seen. Finally, at the exact time, which she read off the giant clock in the tower of the Hôtel de Ville, she entered the lobby of a baroque mansion which housed the Turkish consulate. Here she paused for a moment before the concierge's grate, rubbed her hands to relieve the freeze, unwrapped her long white scarf which Old Nathalie had embellished with blue fleurs-de-lis, and quivering with excitement, entered the office door.

She found herself facing an empty desk. In another room she could hear muffled conversation, then, finally, an "au revoir." A serious-looking woman with thick black curls and an intense expression came out to the anteroom, looked Isabelle up and down and strode out the door. A minute passed, then another girl appeared. She asked Isabelle whom she wished to see.

"Ah, Mr. Bey," she said. "The new vice-consul is *so* charming!"

She walked back into the other room, but Isabelle could hear her speak.

"A lady is here, and I must say she looks quite young."

"Thank you very much, Mademoiselle, and you should feel free now to take your lunch."

The secretary walked out of the office without giving Isabelle a glance. Rehid Bey appeared a moment later dressed in splendidly cut pants of pinstriped wool and over his starched white shirt a gray suede vest.

"How marvelous to see you. How splendid you've come."

He took her hand, squeezed it, then brought it to his lips.

"I've been looking forward so much to seeing you alone. After yesterday's race across the ice—which was, positively, the best time I've had all winter—I felt we should come to know one another well." By this time he was guiding her out the door, and she found it odd that he was wearing neither jacket nor coat. "I'm very fond of your brothers—they're quite intelligent and very enthusiastic, too. But you—well—" At this moment he turned up from the crouch he'd assumed while locking the door. "—you strike me as being very special." The lock clicked in place.

"One hears a great deal about people from relatives and mutual friends and so often one is disappointed. Do you know what I mean?" She nodded—they were walking then across the lobby, though not, she noticed, toward the front door. Suddenly she became self-conscious. The concierge was looking at her and smiling and she could hear the echo of her footsteps on the marble floor. "But you, Isabelle, do not disappoint. And I have heard a great deal about you."

He paused then at the foot of stairs that curled out of the lobby in a spiral loop. "I hope you won't think I'm presumptuous. I had thought of taking you to an elegant restaurant for lunch. Then it occurred to me there would be too many distractions—waiters, other diners, that sort of thing. So I am asking you to lunch with me at my home, which just happens to be up this flight."

Isabelle was astonished and at the same time delighted by

the strange things that befall one in life. She had not really imagined what their lunch would be like, though she'd had a vague notion they'd sit together in a café. The thought of visiting his apartment, though it had never crossed her mind, seemed natural and appropriate to what she suddenly realized had been her interest all along. She had wanted, for more than a year, to be expertly seduced by a man. When she'd first laid eyes on Rehid Bey, she'd thought him entirely suitable for the task—his charm, his ease, his radiance were all she'd ever imagined her first lover would possess.

"Yes," she heard herself say, "to lunch with you upstairs would be very nice."

The landings were decorated with elegantly proportioned mirrors in gilded frames. Cherubs crafted out of malachite supported balusters which supported a railing of burnished bronze. As her eyes swept the mirrors, she was struck by her youthful appearance—her short cropped hair, her innocence among all these glittering refinements and in the company of so sophisticated a young man. She paused before one of them and then, to her amazement, spoke of her own unease.

"I overheard your secretary saying that I look very young. And she was right. Just look at me. I'm a child of seventeen. Whatever am I doing here with you?"

Rehid Bey laughed. "Isabelle," he said, "you are not a child at all. You are a stunning young woman who at this moment just happens to be dressed like a boy."

"But this is how I always dress."

"I know, I know," he said. "What I mean is that it seems to me you can be anything you want."

He led her to a lavishly bordered set of doors, opened them and showed her in. She was delighted with the apartment which had once been, he explained, the private chapel of the house. The living room was a miniature nave arched by a series of groined vaults. There was a fireplace where the altar had been, ablaze with crackling logs. Before the fire a table was set, and beside the table there stood a silver bucket, glistening with moisture, icing a bottle of champagne. Rehid Bey called out a name, a servant appeared in pantaloons and fez, and a few words of Turkish were rapidly exchanged.

While they waited for lunch he showed her his library which was filled with religious and poetic texts. The books were in all languages, but the ones that fascinated her were written in Arabic, a language which interested her enormously and in which she was quite well-versed. She had read the Koran with Trophimovsky, because, Vava had explained, despite its "superstitious nonsense," it was a great work of literature which every educated person should know. Rehid Bey owned a large collection of ancient Korans, some of them enclosed in leather boxes and locked by jeweled clasps. He took one of these out, and they sat side by side to study the elegance of the Arabic script.

Isabelle became so enraptured by the interweaving of the border designs that she tried to trace a line around a page but soon became hopelessly lost. Rehid Bey then placed his index finger back at the beginning of the design, placed the same finger of her hand on top of his own, told her to ride him "piggyback," and carried her through the border without a fault. She was delighted, suggested they do it again. He turned the page, and this time her little finger rode his thumb. They were so amused that they did it on the next page, and on the next, until they drew so close on the velvet divan that Rehid Bey had no choice but to pull his head around and press down his lips.

The kiss was long. Their fingers slid off the book and began to interlace. The precious Koran started to slide to the floor, and would have landed there if the Turkish servant hadn't accidentally jarred one of the crystal glasses with a fork. At the sound they both snapped around and Isabelle caught the book just in time.

As soon as lunch was finished (partridge "en chartreuse,"

floating island), their embraces began again. And again they used their fingers to trace, but this time upon each other's flesh. An hour went by (though both, by then, had lost all track of time), and Isabelle, heated by his tender kisses and tickling fingers and strong arms and flattering words, found herself slipping into a novel mood. A sweetness filled her that she had not known before. She felt suffused by a blush, a glow, and felt that for the first time in her life she was being tended with the care that old Vava only lavished on his fondest plants. It was the "brown-eyed Levantine's" attentiveness that made her feel this way. It was as if each and every one of his caresses was a delicate stroke of a master painter's brush—a lick here, a lick there, until she felt like an image on a canvas glowing with life.

There came a time after they had thoroughly embraced that Rehid Bey led her to the balcony above his drawing room nave and there to a great four-poster canopied in paisley silk. Here, dazed and flushed, she opened herself to him, ready to endure what she guessed would be nearly unendurable pain.

Ah, such pain! No drill puncturing brass, no searing rivet probing into steel, no immovable object attacked by an irresistible force—none of these images suited the case. She felt neither the sting of the bee nor the sharp pain of vodka poured over a gushing wound. It was not like a spark in the eye, a splinter in the knee, or a piece of flesh opened by a gnawing rake. But what was it like? At the very moment it was happening to her, she was struggling to define its nature. More like a filling of soft rich cream. More like a swallow of chocolate soufflé. It was as if she had a tongue down there and was licking at something with a sublime soft taste. This food (or whatever it was) was so delicious, in fact, that she lost completely her self-control. So good it was that it inspired an unquenchable hunger, and she was forced to eat at a faster and faster rate so that all that was offered she could more rapidly devour. This desire to pin down the essence of the experience was soon abandoned, obliterated by the joys of the experience itself. She gave way to it entirely, lost all sense of what was going on, until she woke herself out of the whole frenetic dream by a cry that flew in soft whisper from her lips.

"Archivir," she said, and without knowing quite what she meant by it, or by what process the word had come into her mind, repeated it several times, trying it out with various mellifluous intonations until she achieved a pronunciation combined with an affectionate gasp. It was, she decided later, a splendid word that had been locked for many years inside her heart. Finally she had found something that deserved its caress. And that was how she happened to give it as nickname to Rehid Bey, whom she never called again by his Byzantine name, and, only rarely, by that phrase she'd coined for him the first time they met. Forever after he would be "Archivir" to her, and only on occasion "the brown-eyed Levantine."

In the middle of the afternoon Rehid Bey escorted Isabelle down the stairs. He asked her to wait in the lobby a few moments while he picked up his jacket and coat inside.

"I'm going out," she heard him say to the secretary.

"But the consul wants you to finish those reports before he returns from Bern."

There was a silence and then she heard Archivir's reply.

"Let the consul be hanged."

He took her to a little photographer's shop around the corner from the Cathedral St. Pierre. The photographer, a stubby little man who sucked on the stump of a cigar, greeted him like an old friend. He ushered them into a back room where a wall was painted neutral gray. Facing it, mounted on a stand, was a Beaulieu camera, mahogany with fittings of brass and a magnificent set of bellows that reminded Isabelle of the ruffled collar of a clown. Archivir flung himself upon a sofa, lit a cigarette and peered about.

"Jacques," he said, "we must dress this young lady up. What do you suggest?"

"A sailor suit?"

"A little young don't you think?"

"It's really quite splendid—the latest thing from Britain."

"Well, give it to her then, and after that we'll try something else."

Isabelle was shown to a dressing room that smelled of camphor. A huge variety of costumes were displayed on hooks. Obediently she put on the sailor suit, and when she reappeared in the studio, Archivir gasped.

"Marvelous! I love the name on the hat. 'Vengeance.' Jacques, take her just like that. And be sure to catch the confused expression—she's just been pressed into service, and though she doesn't know it yet, she's going to have a great career."

Isabelle was shown to a decaying cane chair, seated there by Jacques who disappeared behind the camera and then came out again to adjust the angle of her head.

"Now you must sit very steadily," he urged her. "Frown a little—I think that's what Monsieur wants. Your ship, you know, is called *Vengeance*, a powerful British man-of-war. There's no fooling aboard her. The English flog disobedient sailors. That's right—hold it—don't blink—" and he lit the powder that ignited in a flash.

After appearing as a sailor she was photographed as other things: a Syrian banker, a Turkish gallant, a Bedouin warrior, a Spahi sergeant. The session took up the entire afternoon. Jacques and Archivir coaxed and admired, and by the end she was posing like a professional, assuming studied stances, glaring with Tartar eyes.

Finally, when she grew impatient with all this changing in and out of clothes, she cut the whole thing short with a flamboyant challenge, a race on skates with Archivir, twenty-five times around the rink on the lake.

He won the race, but not by much. Afterward they went back to his apartment, and again made love in the balcony above the nave. She did not return until late to Villa Neuve, and when she did no one asked her where she'd been.

Over the next weeks she met Archivir every day for lunch, and after each repast (each more elegant than the one before—lamb in pastry crust with *pommes dauphines*; duck breast filets with green apple puree), they indulged in new ecstasies upon the four-posted bed. Never in her life, she thought, had she learned so much so fast, not even during the most oppressive years of Vava's tutoring when it seemed he wanted to convey to her everything he knew.

Archivir, she discovered, had studied in Paris, was extremely well-educated and cultured in the literature of half a dozen lands. A lover of poetry, he could quote her vast texts by the hour, including most of the great speeches from Shakespeare's plays. He was extremely tough on her favorite Russian authors, especially on Nádson whom Isabelle adored. "He's smooth and lifeless," Archivir said, and when she mentioned the name of Pierre Loti he launched into a diatribe of scorn. Isabelle and Augustin had read Loti over and over. From him they had acquired a longing to visit the Middle East and an attitude of romantic gloom haunted by premonitions of death. Archivir would have none of this. He called Loti a dreamer and a fake whose romanticization of the lives of simple people was erroneous and in poor taste. "I could hardly believe it," he told her, "when he was elected to the Académie Française. But that particular body has always been a haven for overrated fools."

She listened to him with great attention, and occasionally argued back. But usually he overwhelmed her with his superior knowledge, and since he was teaching her so much about the requitals of the flesh, she was attentive to his views on everything else. Sometimes he surprised her by flinging himself down, after one or another of their bouts in bed, and stammering melancholy oaths at the uselessness of everything except the satiation of all physical desire. "Divine food, great wine, expert love—they are the only important things in life," he said after a particularly violent session during which he taught her the sweet pleasures of the giving and taking of moderate pain. "I wish I could feel—only feel. I despise my education. I hate the curse of being intellectual, the need to impose words upon experience. If I could only just feel—FEEL!" And at that he beat with his fists upon the linen while Isabelle watched him, puffing on a gold-tipped Turkish cigarette.

His moods were unpredictable—he could slip from joy and laughter into long morose silences and then back again in a few moments time. When he felt like spending money, he would take her to the finest shops, order her custom-made pantaloons and capes of melton wool. He never bought her dresses—he said she was too unique for clothes like that, and since she'd never worn women's clothes in her life, nor anything that was not a hand-me-down from her brothers, she did not protest. Archivir had a special fondness for leather of all types, suede vests, alligator belts, calfskin wallets, boots made in Morocco whose softness, he assured her, was attributable to the leather having been chewed in its makers' mouths. Once when making love he had covered both their heads with a tent of leather things. Then they breathed in the warm smells which he promised would increase his potency and her desire. She was fascinated by such bizarre escapades, believed he was teaching her the refinements of life.

There were times, too, when Archivir had no desire to leave his flat. Reluctantly he would go down the stairs to work, but when he felt so withdrawn, he would not go outside. Then she would wait for him in the nave, reading books about Turkey, Persia, Arabia and Egypt, all the countries of the Levant and the Maghreb. She longed, she told him, to visit these places, but he told her that in his opinion she was less interested in where she went than in leaving the place she lived.

"You're going to tell me that the things I want to escape will follow me wherever I go?"

"That may be true," he replied, "but then it's interesting you have no desire to go to Russia. Not like Nicolas—that's his dream. You're interested in the warm countries. You're a sensualist and the gray northern cities, the lands that are cold, repress your nature. Isabelle—you need warmth, a lush place where you can grow."

He was both extravagant and parsimonious, funny and melancholy, sensual and intellectual, European and Asiatic. She had never met a person so complicated, so mercurial. And yet she recognized that his overriding trait, the arch that covered all his facets and moods, was his unrequitable hunger for new experiences, his desire to perfect his spirit by becoming a sensual connoisseur. They tried everything together, every sexual position he knew, and, when he ran out of these, new ones he uncovered in ancient manuals of love. Each time they ate, they sampled different foods. A Chinese restaurant hidden away down an alley off the Quai du Mont Blanc provided them with strange and remarkable dishes, gelatinous soups, exotic sauces, fishes prepared in spices they had never tasted before. He had joined the diplomatic service, he told her, so that he could spend his life traveling the world. He wanted to taste women of every race. He spoke of sleeping with one-legged dwarfs, and a cross-eyed whore whose eyes uncrossed when she was satisfied.

He believed in anal intercourse and practiced it upon her, urging her not to restrain her tears. Later, when she was still quivering from the pain, he assured her that by yielding to him that way she had given him proof of her submission. That night he bought some opium from an Indochinese in a café, and they smoked it together in ivory pipes, and again, the following night, through a Turkish hookah.

Through March and into April their passion raged. She defied Trophimovsky's anger and spent whole nights away from home. Her brothers knew what she was doing, but when they pressed her for details she refused to talk.

"Unless you tell me what you've been up to in town, I won't tell you a thing," she said to Augustin. He grinned at her shrewdness and bowed his head to show his esteem. Each morning she looked at herself in the mirror. She found it remarkable that she was so intensely desired, and searched her face for some clue as to why this was so. It seemed to her, though she thought it was probably an illusion, that her cheeks were more filled out, her flesh had acquired a more mellow glow, her lips had taken on a more sensual curve. Certainly her body felt good—she had always adored physical exercise and that winter, between skating and the making of such ardent love, every muscle had become limber and lithe.

There came a time, however, not six weeks after the affair had begun, when she began to suspect Archivir of deceit. One day after one of their magnificent feasts (Corsican blackbird pâté; lake trout with walnut sauce followed by *pudding diplomat*), he told her he had been neglecting his work. This in itself was perfectly understandable—she had wondered for some time how he managed to get by with the consul. So she spent the afternoon taking a long walk by herself with the understanding that he would spend the same time catching up on the papers piled on his desk.

The bitter cold had lifted from Geneva, and it was a pleasure to walk about without fear of an icy wind swooping down and blowing her off her feet. She wandered far down the Quai Gustave Ador and then out the Jetée des Eaux Vives to the lighthouse that marked the limits of the channel of the left bank. Looking back toward the Pierres du Niton, she observed people in bright clothing strolling on the Promenade du Lac. The ice had begun to break up, and pieces of the skating rink, polished and deeply grooved chunks, were floating away from the quais. Feeling nostalgic for those afternoons when they had skated like dervishes among envious boys and girls who'd hoped to find a winter lover but had spent the season skating alone, she was seized with a yearning to revisit the café where Archivir had first announced to her his philosophy of life.

Slowly, dreamily she made her way toward the place. Workmen were already dismantling the glass screens, preparing for spring. Suddenly she saw Archivir sitting with a young woman, a girl with thick black curls whom she knew she'd seen before.

Her first thought was of pleasure—Archivir had finished work early, and now they could spend the rest of the afternoon in bliss. She was about to join his table, having dismissed the dark-haired girl as either a client or one of his business friends, when she observed a certain animation in the way they spoke, and an intensity on his part that she imagined he reserved for her. She stopped, and her heart began to pound. Thinking it better to keep an open mind, she decided it would be amusing as well as wise to watch this pair from a concealed place.

She bought a newspaper, then slipped into a seat at a table behind a pillar. Here, with the paper held high enough to hide her face, she observed Archivir and the dark lady with a cunning she did not know she possessed. She could not hear their voices above the babble of the café, except for an occasional squeal of laughter from the girl. But as she scrutinized them she felt a mounting horror. Archivir was fondling the girl's hand, running his fingers up and down hers in a way that brought back the memory of that first afternoon when *their* fingers had played together upon the borders of the Koran. Yes, he was stroking her fingers the same expert way he stroked with his tongue. At first she could not believe what was perfectly clear. Rapidly she began to fabricate excuses. The girl was an ex-lover; Archivir was merely being kind. Then she remembered where she had seen the girl before—the first time she'd come to his office; the girl who had walked out while she was waiting in a chair. She wanted to tear herself away, to walk away someplace and cry, but she was fascinated and could not leave the café, could not stop watching their flirtations despite how cruelly she felt hurt.

When they left she followed them, keeping the newspaper near her breast so that she could raise it if they turned around. They marched toward the Place Bourg-de-Four with Turkish cigarettes dangling from their lips. Her heart beat faster as she tracked them through narrow streets, watched them turn corners following an inevitable route to the mansion where Archivir lived. From across the street she saw them enter the house. Peering through the front door she saw them pass the consulate office and mount the stairs. She could not believe it. After they disappeared she paced about outside, arguing with herself. *I've been with him every moment*, she thought. *He's had no chance to meet someone else.* But as the minutes went by she was struck by the truth. *Of course*, she thought, *he has an unquenchable thirst for new adventures. How stupid of me to doubt it. It's part of his nature that one woman cannot be enough.*

She suffered a difficult night at Villa Neuve, trying to work out some way to deal with his deceit. Should she share him? Had she bored him? If she avoided him could she rekindle his ardor? She was tormented by a thousand questions, but when dawn came she could think of nothing better than to confront him with what she'd seen.

At first he was amazed. "Why didn't you just come up and say hello," he demanded, "instead of sneaking around behind us like a third-rate spy?"

"Who the hell was *she*?" she shrieked.

"None of your goddamn business," he screamed.

They fought for an hour, then he grabbed her, kissed her.

"You're a maddening female creature," he said, but she would not let it go at that.

"The thing that disturbs me most is that you'd carry on with somebody else before you were finished with me. I understand your philosophy, but to start one thing before finishing another—that I don't understand at all."

She was the first, she told him (and he was amused since he could not forget she had just turned seventeen), not to care a whit about the stupid values of the bourgeois class. He wouldn't find her trying to trick him into a marriage, or speaking about the verities of eternal love. But there was such a thing as personal honor. One did not sneak around behind another person's back.

"I have always believed," she said, "that a person has a right to sleep with anyone he wants. But to deceive a lover— that's a crime."

Their argument went on until suddenly, over a most sumptuous lunch (braised herbed hare in champagne sauce; omelets filled with Irish confiture), they both began to laugh. Yes, he admitted, he had committed an infidelity. But it was a momentary lapse and had no meaning. She was ridiculous to think she could ever be replaced.

After lunch they embraced in his bed, but later she decided that things between them had subtly changed. He began to make excuses for his absences, excuses so elaborate she knew they were contrived. Then she began to suspect that this was what he wanted her to think. He was operating on some level of irony that she could sense though not fully understand. He was deliberately erecting suspicions in her mind, and this was part of some esoteric game he was playing—to give her torment in a thousand small ways. She could not resist his little thrusts which reminded her of moves in a game of chess. Suddenly everything he did became suspect. Every woman she saw was a potential rival. The secretary for instance—she thought over the way they spoke and how their eyes met, and these things added up in her mind, became irrefutable proof that they were having an affair. Within a week her life became a misery. As spring came upon the city, trees turned green, buds opened, flowers bloomed, her mood, which should have been buoyant, turned dark, and she was paralyzed by fear.

What she feared was not some drastic scene so much as her own disillusionment with the sweetness of love. She was introspective enough to realize that she'd been experiencing emotions which, when they were over, she'd not be able to feel again. This, after all, was one of the great lessons she'd learned from Russian literature—the irretrievability of first love. *I deserve more*, she thought. *It's seeping away too fast. It should last a year at least.* But the longer she thought this, the more slender her happiness seemed, until, by the third week of April, she looked back upon that first exhilaration on the ice with the nostalgia she might have felt for an event ten years in her past.

It was then that for three or four days Archivir courted her with overwhelming charm. He was gallant, courteous, attentive, gentle with his embraces, generous with his time. He made love to her as if she were a duchess, was tender with her body, caressed her to ecstatic heights she had not known before. She began to forget her doubts, and decided it was true that a man who can give a woman satisfaction can have that woman forever in his debt. He satisfied her so splendidly that she wondered why none of the great authors had ever been able to describe such things in words. It even occurred to her to write a novel: "The Sexual Enslavement of a Russian Girl by a Violent Turk."

One evening, lying in Archivir's arms in the great four-poster with candles burning all over the room, listening to him sigh and whisper snatches of Arabic verse, she heard him mutter something about a book. She said that of course she'd be willing to look at any book he cared to show, and so he left the bed and walked to his library in the nave. Watching him walk away and then return, his body open to her without shame, she thought how remarkably her life had changed, how on that dreadful Christmas morning when she'd faced Vava's horrible prank, she could never have imagined that in a few short months she'd be watching a Turk with silky locks and delicate lashes approaching her naked in his bed.

Archivir nestled beside her, and by candlelight together they inspected the book. It was a portfolio of small engravings, beautifully made, of persons making love in esoteric ways. But the last few pages offered something new: these depicted combinations of persons numbering more than two, in the most imaginative positions.

"Have you ever tried this?" she asked.

He nodded. "Yes, and it's—incredible!" He glanced at her with a lascivious grin.

Very soon he revealed a plan. Since neither of them believed in middle-class morals, and since they were lovers for whom no sensation held any danger or emotional threat, why shouldn't they experiment, too, with some of these sexual situations that were titillating their desire? She was tantalized by his proposal, but a moment later a problem arose in her mind.

"How shall we find partners?"

"A very difficult thing," he agreed.

"Yes," she said, "since first off we demand enormous physical charm."

"And then," he added, "there's the question of discretion. She, whoever she may be, must have as much to lose as ourselves."

"I hadn't thought about another girl."

"Well, I certainly wasn't thinking we'd do it with a man."

"But in the pictures . . ."

"Damn the pictures. You just want to be fucked from both ends."

"And you," she said, "you want to turn this place into a

seraglio, with concubines all over you doing everything at once."

They both laughed, then Archivir turned serious. He did know some people, he said, who were experienced in this kind of thing. They were attractive and discreet and would know how to manage with grace and ease. He wanted to try it, slowly, perhaps the first time with only one person more. If she were willing, he would arrange it for the next night. But if she were too shy—then, of course, he'd understand.

She knew at once she couldn't refuse. He'd be disappointed, and that would surely be the beginning of the end of their affair. But even as she agreed and noted how joyfully he smiled, she felt a premonition of something bad, of some unhappy trap most cleverly laid.

Walking to the mansion the following night, she felt upset. The rendezvous was set for ten o'clock, and it was late for her to be hurrying through the streets. Her stomach quavered with fear, but she was excited, too—the anticipation of pleasure had been building the whole day. She was curious as to who their partner would be, and embarrassed already over the introductions, the small talk, the preliminary flirting, the first stripping off of clothes. She expected pleasure—she had never been disappointed by Archivir in that. But there was something unsavory in their arrangement that gave her pause. She decided, finally, that she feared the experience only because she'd never read of it in a book. A man loving a woman—that was a common literary theme. But three together in one bed—she assumed it happened but was something no author dared describe.

The concierge gave her a knowledgeable look, tinged, she thought, with a supercilious smile. The embers of the lobby fireplace provided the only light on the glittering stairs. She mounted them slowly, dreamily, feeling that she was ascending to her doom. At the chapel's double doors she paused a moment to regain her breath. Then with her face as serene as she could contrive, she gave the wood a forceful knock.

She waited a long while before Archivir opened the door. He grinned, then showed her a scene that had nothing in common with what she'd harbored in her mind. The girl of the café, the one with the thick black curls, was seated on the large divan wearing one of Archivir's gowns. He was in a loose Arabian robe, open from neck to waist.

It took her a moment to understand what was wrong. Everything in her mind had been the other way around. She and Archivir were to be together first; later a stranger was to come. The black-haired girl smiled, looked her up and down, and suddenly Isabelle was furious—she felt she was being inspected like a piece of meat. In her fury she grasped the significance of their clothes: the girl had been there for hours; Archivir had already had her in his bed. She was pondering this, wondering what to do, when she was surprised again by a shrill and piercing laugh. The girl, to whom she'd not yet been introduced, was doubled over, choking on her mirth.

"What's wrong?" Archivir demanded. "What the hell's so funny?"

"But she—she's—" The words were cut by another convulsion. The girl was wiping tears from her eyes. Her mouth was edged by a rim of foam. The laughter went on, out of control.

"This is preposterous!" Isabelle turned on Archivir.

"Please, both of you, stay calm ..."

"Yes Yes! Preposterous! So it is! Indeed it is!" The girl finally stopped laughing, wriggled in her seat.

"Well, what's so funny?" asked Archivir.

"But, my dear, she's so young. So incredibly young. How could you think ... ? She's nothing but a child." A look of amused pity swept her face. "But don't you see what I mean? My God, Rehid, you must be insane. We can't do a thing like that with her. If she isn't still a virgin, then she was when you skewered her last week. Look at her! She's absurd! She looks like a boy! I may be a hard old dyke, but this little piece is not for me."

She smiled again at Isabelle with a combination of pity and scorn. Archivir, too, was looking at her closely. They were both undressing her, deflowering her with their eyes.

"Yes," said Archivir, finally. "Yes. Of course. You're right."

"Well, of course, darling." And then to Isabelle: "Poor child. Can you imagine?"

"Who are you?" Isabelle demanded.

"Now don't be rude, dear. You were still in pigtails when I was fucking Swedish nuns. If anyone should be angry, it should be me. I came here, after all, in excellent faith."

Isabelle looked to Archivir. She could not believe he was allowing this woman to speak to her this way.

"Is this—this creature—is she a whore?"

"How dare you!"

"I think she's a whore. I think you wanted us to do it with a whore!" She was screaming at Archivir, but he looked away.

"Now just a minute, sweetie."

"Get out!" Isabelle cried, but the girl only settled back and broadened her smile.

"Get her out!" she shouted at Archivir, but he neither moved nor said a word.

The girl was staring at the ceiling, bored. Isabelle saw an expression on Archivir's face that reminded her of Vava on Christmas day. Craftiness and shame—she recognized the combination and felt a terrible disgust well up.

She stood there for a moment waiting for something to change. Nothing changed—the three of them were riveted in a *tableau vivant*. After that there was nothing to say. She left.

❖

On the first of May, heartbroken but unbowed, Isabelle Eberhardt went back by herself to the photographer's studio near the Cathedral St. Pierre. In the dressing room she pieced together an eclectic costume from odds and ends: Russian short jacket, Bulgarian blouse, Hindu cummerbund, Bedouin cape. She snatched up a string of Moslem prayer beads and tapped onto her head a ratty Turkish tarboosh. While the photographer set his lamps and prepared the slide, she suddenly jolted him with a stream of oaths in a mélange of all the languages she knew.

"Deceiving bastard! Stinking Turkish swine! Cock-sucker! Ass-fucker! Cunt-licking Levantine worm! Monster! Wretch! Hideous piece of shit!"

The insults toppled out in a venomous stream. When she was done, she pursed her lips, cocked her head and stared off into space with cold derision. She pretended that she was facing a firing squad, determined to go down with honor intact. The moment she heard the shutter click, she waved about at the powder of the flash and instructed Jacques to send the photo to Rehid Bey.

"When you deliver it," she said, "tell him I spit in his eye."

A week later there was delivered to Villa Neuve a huge box of chocolates bound in ribbons and bows. On a card she found the following words written in a familiar Arabic script: "You are magnificent and I shall always remember you well. Conquer the world! Your admiring Archivir."

She laughed; and then, much later, she wept.

Escape

In June 1895, depressed by Vava's latest gardening initiatives and still dazed by her adventure with Archivir, Isabelle bought a magazine filled with columns in which lonely persons advertised for lovers and friends. Over a weekend she wrote a score of letters under a variety of assumed names (Sasha, Vera, Eunice, Nadia) and within a month received back her first replies:

Dear Sasha,

> *I am a middle-aged banker in Hamburg, in an excellent position to give substantial security to an attractive young lady willing to relocate and share her life with me.*
>
> *It is best to tell you from the start that marriage is out of the question, since I am already married and the father of seven children, including one son who is a certified engineer.*
>
> *It will be necessary to arrange an interview, someplace equidistant between our residences. May I*

*suggest Darmstadt, which I shall be visiting on a
business trip in July? I know a hotel there that provides excellent lodgings. You will, of course, have
to travel at your own expense....*

Most of the others seemed to follow this line, though
some, with bizarre variations, gave Isabelle a chill. An English viscount was searching for a young woman with the
manner of a governess and "a strong hand." A fireman in
Milan who'd lost his sight in an accident begged her to be
his nurse. There was a sailor in the Romanian navy who
wanted to learn how to cut women's hair, and a Chinese girl
in Warsaw who solicited news of Geneva's "theatrical life."
The oddest of them all was from the representative of a
group of Bulgarian deaf-mutes who were raising money to
establish a Utopian community in Wisconsin in the United
States. It seemed to Isabelle that they had been badly mis-
informed, since they spoke of a tropical climate and of
friendly Indians who would take their handicrafts in exchange for food.

These letters gave her the feeling of being a scavenger, a
dustman rifling through the garbage of Europe. She was
about to throw away the rest, still unopened, when her eyes
fastened upon an envelope with an exotic return address.
She opened it and found a beautiful letter inside, which she
rushed to show to Augustin:

Dear Nadia,

*Thank you for your exceedingly pleasant note.
As I stated in my ad, I am a young French officer
stationed in the Sahara and bored to death. There is
no one here I can talk to. The other officers despise
the local people, have no sympathy at all for them
or any wish to improve the terrible conditions under*

which they live. I am most disturbed by the plight of the children—there are no doctors, disease is rampant, and most people seem stricken by sores and worms. Yet the doctors in my garrison are unwilling to share their knowledge, and all the men hold these poor people in the highest contempt.

I feel cut off in a way I never dreamed. When my assignment first came through I was looking forward to a life of action and contemplation in the great emptiness of the North African desert. I am from a literate family where music is a way of life. Our home has always been filled with books, but here, besides manuals of gunnery and a few volumes of military history, there is no literature at all—not even a volume of Montaigne. I don't wish to sound bitter about my lot. I know that bitterness is a contemptible state of mind. But I need a companion, even if she is a thousand miles away, who will exchange letters on a fairly regular basis, and will be sympathetic to my plight. I long for a correspondent with whom I can share my doubts about the path I have chosen in life, a young lady who can also keep me informed of the latest music and books.

Please, if you are interested, write me as soon as you can. Tell me about yourself, your family, your studies, your dreams. I promise I shall answer by return post.

Yours sincerely,
Eugène Letord

Augustin agreed that Letord's letter was magnificent and she should answer it at once. Together they burned the other letters, and then, over the signature of "Nadia," she wrote him ten pages about her life.

She also asked him for details about the Sahara, the hardships of the desert people and the process of "pacification" in which she knew, from the newspapers, the French expeditionary force in North Africa was then engaged. Six weeks later she received back a long reply in which he answered all her questions and ended with a paragraph of personal revelation.

> *I am fascinated, Nadia, by your family. I can tell that you love them, all of them, but to an outsider, your description would seem apt for a chamber of horrors. There seems to be something ghoulish about your brother V., and I feel pity for your mother and all the hardships she must endure. I understand your longing to get away. I volunteered for desert service to escape from a personal unhappiness. It's a long saga but suffice to say it involved my relations with a young lady to whom I was once engaged. I wanted to go as far away as possible. I could not bear to be in a place where the seasons changed. They reminded me of joys I had and would never have again. I wanted dryness, simplicity, an uninhabited land.*
>
> *Perhaps I thought that the terrible desert heat would finally dry my tears. But, alas, things are not so easily resolved. For the lonelier I become (and it is very lonely here) the more I brood about my unhappy past. Remember this, Nadia—the desert is a place where all one's ghosts reappear in a mirage. In the silent desert nights they come back to haunt one's tent.*
>
> *Surrounded by Frenchmen deprived of women (a situation that brings out the worst facets of my race) I feel the same sorrow I used to feel at dusk by the banks of the Seine. People crossed the bridges hurrying home from work, people together while I stood*

alone. And even when I walked with them pretending to have some motive in my stride, I felt a loneliness that here, the place where I've escaped, is doubled and redoubled each lonely night.

Write me more—pages more. I feel most fortunate, I never expected that my pathetic request, hidden in the columns among all those other pleas of unhappy people, would find the eye of one so tender and humane.

Eugène

Dear Eugène:

I am most touched by your letter. It is imperative that we be frank. Only then can we achieve the intimacy we both so clearly need. So I shall write you tonight about an unhappiness of my own, how a violent young man of enormous charm seduced me, lifted me to heights of romantic bliss, and then deceived me as cruelly as any heroine in any story I have ever read. But first let me tell you how I imagined you when I wrote you the first time. Thinking of you, a lonely young French officer stationed in the Sahara, caused me to break out of the firm wrappings of my reserve. I imagined a man tall and lean and deeply tanned by sun, wearing a tan kepi and desert shorts which showed off his strong young legs. I expected, too, a roughness that concealed a poetic nature. I imagined a man who wrote crude verse which he kept hidden beneath his linens in the bottom of his trunk.

Well, we misjudged each other. I can see now that you really are an excellent poet, that poetry is engraved upon your soul. And, my dear Eugène, you have misjudged me, too. I am far less tender than

*you think, about as soft and feminine as a mountain
oak. But enough of that—let me tell you of my own
unhappiness.*

Isabelle

The correspondence between Isabelle Eberhardt and
Eugène Letord grew over the summer months. Each wrote
lengthy letters and spent hours in replies. After the first
exchange of confidences, she wrote him of the books she'd
read, thoughts that flashed through her mind, adventures
that she dreamed. She told him more about her family and
introduced him to Augustin who began to enclose notes of
his own. Eugène, in turn, corrected their misconceptions
about desert life, but in his minute descriptions of the little
settlements he visited, the oases, the inner workings of
the Moslem faith, there grew in Isabelle and Augustin a
vision even more seductive and exotic than any they had
held in the past. Their dreams of escape, which had always
centered on the south, were now concentrated on North
Africa. Through the eyes of Eugène Letord they felt they
knew it well, could feel its dry sun, could taste the acrid
water of its closely guarded wells.

With each other now they began to speak more openly
of escape. They decided, finally, to write to Letord and
solicit his aid. Their letter went unanswered for many weeks.
When Letord finally did reply it was not, as they'd assumed,
to cut them off, but to apologize for being unable to help.

He'd been transferred to an even more remote garrison,
was isolated except for mail which reached him only every
other month. He begged them to wait. He felt that the time
was not yet right for them, that "Nadia" was still too young
to break away and that Augustin must stay with her, not
leave her alone in the "evil garden." They wrote back at
once expressing their gratitude. They felt, for the first time,
that they had an ally in the outside world.

The autumn was going well, it seemed to Isabelle, until one night, angry with Augustin for refusing to explain to her his even more frequent and mysterious absences from the house, she rifled his drawers and discovered that he was carrying on a secret correspondence with someone else. The man's name was Vivicorsi, he lived in Trieste, and as she read his letters she realized with horror that with him Augustin was plotting an escape of his own.

The evening of October 12 Augustin is dressing in his room. A knock on the door.

"Who is it?"

"Isabelle."

"Just a minute."

Quickly he gathers up all the incriminating materials that cover his bed: roll of money, packets of opium, bundle of letters from Madeleine Joliet. He stuffs them into a musette bag, then heaves the bag into his wardrobe.

"What's going on in there?"

"A minute, damnit!"

He pulls on a pair of trousers, then, when she knocks again, turns his back and rapidly buttons his fly.

"I'm getting dressed. I *am* entitled to some privacy, you know."

"There's something we must discuss."

He opens the door.

"This is serious, Augustin."

"Oh! Should I sit down?"

"Why don't you just put on your shirt."

Isabelle sits on the bed, watches Augustin thrust his arms through sleeves.

"I've been upset," he says.

"What's the matter?"

"Do you really want to know?"

"Yes."

A pause.

"I don't want you to get involved. It's my own problem and I have to solve it myself."

"What is *it?*"

He ignores her question, gathers up loose change and his watch, stuffs them into his pockets.

"Read this." She hands him a piece of paper. He glances at it.

"Oh! *That!*"

"Yes. *That!*"

"Well, what about it?"

"Yes, what about it?"

"Isabelle, please don't bother me with that sort of thing tonight. I'm nervous. I've got lots to do."

"Then this isn't serious?" She waves the paper about in front of his face.

"Child's play."

"I was afraid you'd say something like that."

"Well, what do you expect? Some silly contract—some silly pledge. We're too old for that sort of thing now."

"Read the date—September 21, 1894. About a year ago. Were we really so much younger then?"

He shakes his head. "I don't know. I can't think about it now."

"Listen, Augustin—I have premonitions. I feel something. I feel you're about to go away. And if that's true—if you're going to break the pledges we made—then all right. But at least tell me why. And tell me where you're going."

He sits down beside her on the bed.

"Things are very bad now."

"What's happened? Why all the mystery? Why can't you trust me?"

Silence.

"What's happened to Nicolas?"

"That's what *everyone* wants to know."

"Where is he?"

"I don't think he's coming back."

"Where did he go?"

"You know how he's always talked about going back to 'Holy Russia'? Well—that's where I think he is now."

She gasps.

"He escaped!"

"Yes. But ask yourself, Isabelle, how could he do it?"

"What do you mean?"

"How did he get there? Where did he find the money?"

"Yes. Well, where did he?"

"He has a list of names and I think he sold them to the police."

"What are you talking about?"

"Names of people here—students, activists—you know. His *friends*." His eyes meet hers, then turn away. "I think he sold us out—his friends, Vladimir, me, everyone."

"I still don't . . ."

"You want to know? All right. The three of us were up to our necks in the terrorist groups. We knew everybody. We went to all the meetings. We saw people off—people who went back to Russia to *kill*. We were the financial committee. We got them money—not very much really, a few francs here and there—not much at all until last winter. Then they began to really look at us, and suddenly they got suspicious. It never occurred to them that we were only dilettantes. They told us we'd better come up with some money fast, or be considered traitors and take the consequences for that."

She is stunned. Terrorist groups. Killers. Nicolas selling out his friends. She can't believe it.

"But how could you get money? None of you ever has a cent."

"It was hard." Augustin begins to pace around the bedroom. Every so often he dashes a fist against his head. "Of course we had nothing. But it was a question of producing money or ending up at the bottom of Lake Geneva. We borrowed from everybody. And when that wasn't enough, we bought things on credit and sold them, new, at half their value. Nicolas, you know, is a marvelous mimic. He goes into a shop and very grandly orders all the most expensive things in sight. Then he flings down some preposterous card —*Prince Pomerov, Grand Duke Stavrogin.* 'Send everything over to my hotel,' he commands, telling them he's in the 'Royal Suite' at the D'Angleterre. He grabs up a few trifles— some watches, a pocket telescope, a diamond bauble or so, and tells them to wrap these lavishly as gifts, he will take them with him, they can send over the rest, but he needs these little things at once. Then I step in assuring them, as the grand duke's *homme de confiance*, that His Highness always pays in gold. Their eyes begin to glitter, and we end up with several thousand francs."

"Unbelievable!"

"Wait! There's more!" As anguished as Augustin wants to seem, it is clear to her he relishes the story. "We could only manage that particular trick three times. The stores, of course, had notified the police, and we were afraid to go anywhere near Place de la Fusterie. It was then, around April, that we started with opium."

"What?"

"The drug . . ."

"Yes, yes, I know. I've tried it with Archivir. But go on—how did you get involved with that?"

"Vladimir loves gardening—you know that. He's the only one of us who's ever cared a damn about Vava's garden. Well, a few years ago he made friends with an Indochinese boy who cultivated opium in Paris. He got in touch with him, got hold of some seedlings and planted them in the garden late in spring. A few weeks later we had poppies. We set up a little laboratory in town equipped with things we stole from Vava, and Vladimir, who's been working with Vava for years on the perfumes, knew all about distillation and was able to get oil out of the seeds. We tried it. It was good, and we managed to sell quite a bit."

"I don't believe any of this."

"It's true, Isabelle. Those gray plants with purple flowers down near the moat—they *were* poppies. Vava, of course, didn't know what was going on. As far as he was concerned Vladimir was just experimenting with some new exotics."

"All right, all right, but what happened next?"

"Things got difficult. The Russians saw all this money coming in and they got greedy. No matter how much we brought them, they immediately demanded more. So we needed to expand our market, and that meant recruiting smokers. Nicolas and I concentrated on that, visiting the student cafés and selling the stuff wherever we could. It had to end, of course. We ran out of flowers, and then the police got onto us because some of the students talked. These last weeks have been dangerous. We've been afraid to go around Bourg de Four, and meantime the Russians have been clamoring for money. A couple of weeks ago the question came up—what were we going to do?"

"What could you do?"

"We decided that Vladimir was safe. The Russians didn't know much about him and he wasn't involved in the selling. But Nicolas and I were cornered—it was clear we'd have to pull out. Nicolas wanted to go to Russia and he came up with a scheme. We'd go directly to Count Prozov—the man at the Russian legation who's been sent here to get rid of the terror rings. We'd give him all the information we had, and in return we'd ask for transport back to Russia and some position there so we could be safe. But for me this was impossible. I didn't give a damn about Russia, and I didn't trust Prozov. He's got his thugs here stalking the terrorists, and he's killed a few of them already. What was to prevent him from killing us, too, after we talked? Then there's something else . . ."

"What?"

"Haven't you had enough?"

"I want to know it all."

"Well, all right, it concerns a girl. You know her. Madeleine Joliet."

"Yes, of course I know her. But you're not serious?"

"Very serious. We're engaged."

"If Vava ever heard . . ."

"But he hasn't. Nobody knows. It's a secret engagement. I didn't want to be thrown out of here just because he doesn't approve of her social position or some nonsense like that."

"So . . ."

"So I couldn't go to Russia and leave her behind. Nicolas and I argued, and we decided to go our separate ways. The three of us made an agreement. Vladimir would stay on here, working in the garden, never leaving the house. Madeleine and I would slip into France, and then make our way south where I would join the French navy. And Nicolas would go to Prozov with his list of cadres—he had everything down in code copied from its reflection in a mirror. That was the plan."

"What happened?"

"I don't know. The whole point, you see, was that the two of us would act on the same day. Well, when Nicolas disappeared a few days ago, I just assumed he'd lost his nerve —or something. It never occurred to me that he'd break his word. So I just went ahead with my own plans to leave on Monday night. But this afternoon I heard that ten or fifteen of the Russians have vanished suddenly, without a trace. I thought of Prozov, and then of Nicolas who's been gone, and then I thought that maybe Nicolas sold us out. I don't know. Maybe he had this in mind all along. He kept his little notebook for years. He always thought of himself as a patriot, and he's always wanted to go back and be the son of General De Moerder and be an officer in the Imperial army. I think he only started with the terrorists so he could get their names and then trade them off for a good position —show his patriotism and be honored in Russia as a savior of the czar. Anyway, whatever the reasons, I have to leave right away. I'm meeting Madeleine in an hour and we're off tonight for good."

"But this is mad, mad—absolutely mad."

"Yes. That's exactly what it is." He sits down, exhausted. He is panting and she is dazed. For several seconds they stare out into space.

"So, you will finally get away."

"Yes . . ."

"The navy."

"Yes."

"With Vivicorsi?"

"So you know about that, too."

She nods. Though he must realize she's been through his desk, he doesn't seem to care. It's as if nothing matters to him anymore.

"And Madeleine—do you really think you'll be happy with her?"

"I don't know. Maybe. Yes. I suppose I shall."

Another silence.

"When do you go?"

"In a few minutes, I suppose."

"No good-byes?"

"No. Impossible. I shall have to write Mama later."

"And you'll come back for me."

"Of course."

"Oh, Augustin." She throws her arms around him, holds him as he begins to sob. "Who could ever have guessed it would end like this?"

"It's all such an awful mess."

"Yes," she says, "but at least you'll finally have escaped. Your life begins now, you know. You're so lucky to be a man. You have the whole world."

"Yes, yes . . ." He smiles at her. "I'm glad I told you everything."

"But you've been so stupid, Augustin."

"I know. That's why I couldn't tell you before. I couldn't bear to face your cool judging eyes."

"Promise me you won't be stupid again."

"Yes. I promise."

She holds him for a while. Then, he gets up slowly. She watches while he puts on his coat, retrieves his bag from the wardrobe. He turns to her, is about to speak.

"No. Not here. I'll come with you to the door."

The house is silent as they pass through the halls. Downstairs it is dark. Vava, Vladimir, Old Nathalie—they've all disappeared. Augustin opens the front door. They both step out. The cool wind that blows down from the Alps shakes the limbs of the trees, blows colored leaves to the ground. They stand in silence on the steps, inhaling the damp pungency of this garden they know so well. Augustin carefully places his bag upon the stones. Isabelle opens her arms and they embrace.

Their kiss is long, tender, then slowly turns another way. Without realizing what is happening or why, their mouths begin to open, their tongues begin to dart, and Isabelle flings back her head. Suddenly they feel warmth, heat, fire. All the forbidden lust that has been stored inside them for years rushes out as they cling to one another and begin to sob. Their bodies press and twitch, they pant and moan, but it is too late for them. They have no time to consummate their love.

Finally Augustin breaks away, wipes his tears and places his moist handkerchief in her hand. She watches as he walks away, disappears into the blackness of the garden, and then, long after he is gone, she returns to his room and spends the night between his deserted sheets.

December 8, 1895

Beloved Sister,

Augustin De Moerder, soldier in the First Foreign Regiment, 18th Company, Serial No. 19686, at Sidi-Bel-Abbes, near Oran, Algeria.
There, my dear, is the whole unhappy truth. Still I dream of you and Mama.

Yours forever,
Augustin

Villa Neuve
Christmas Eve, 1895

Beloved Augustin,

The sky is sad and gray, and a blanket of snow covers the garden. It is Christmas Eve and I send you greetings from my unhappy heart. Who knows if we shall ever see one another again? Who knows if the kisses exchanged on the doorstep at 10:00 pm, Saturday, October 12, will have been our last? Where are all our dreams? Oh, Augustin—those papers we signed on September 21, 1894, in which we asked ourselves where we'd be the following year. . . .
A few days ago I received a letter from Vivicorsi in which, in reply to one of mine signed N. Podilinsky, sailor (I didn't know any other way to gain his confidence) he informed me that you'd joined the Legion. Then, yesterday, your confirmation. Have you really been such a fool?
No one knows anything yet. Impossible for me to mention these letters. And really, even without this latest fiasco of your's, I'm being absolutely destroyed by all the madness around the house. Two brothers gone, and Vava in a bewildered rage. I am con-

templating suicide, but have no fear—I shall resist.

I vaguely understand some insane scheme that has germinated in your over-heated brain: to become a naturalized Frenchman, thanks to the Legion, and then to join the Navy later. Let me know if that is really your plan. (Your notes from Marseilles were incoherent. What were you doing in Toulon? What was all of that about going to South America?)

Augustin, darling, do you remember the day we sat alone in the shade of white maples in the mountains above Collonges? To be together like that again—beneath that great silent shadow, that magnificent eclipse. That is my dream.

> *Yours, devotedly, near or far,*
> *Isabelle*

Nicolas De Moerder was not heard from again—it seemed to Isabelle that Mother Russia had swallowed him up. Vava stormed about cursing him and Augustin for their unforgivable stupidities, and then became even more enraged when Augustin wrote he could not bear the rigors and discipline of the legion and was scheming to cut short his enlistment on grounds of failing health.

"He's a weakling and a coward," Vava ranted. And then, to Old Nathalie: "It seems his yellow De Moerder blood has finally won the game!"

But Vava was pleased with Vladimir who stayed within the villa walls, head down near the ground, preoccupied with plants. For his devotion to the garden Vava lovingly named him "Cactophile," and said many times that Vladimir was the only one of the De Moerder children who showed signs of purpose and strength of will.

Through 1896 the atmosphere at Villa Neuve grew oppressive—with only a single brother still at home (and one she believed was slowly going insane before her eyes), Isabelle alone bore the brunt of Vava's rages, and of her mother's inconsolable tears. She spent hours on her correspondence with Eugène Letord, begging him for help, still dreaming of escape.

He'd convinced her now, and so had Augustin, that North Africa should become her home. She'd decided to become a writer and to begin her career there. But her problems seemed insurmountable. She was certain that Vava would never willingly let her go, and that, if she ran, Old Nathalie, without her presence as a defense, would crumble with the strain.

In February 1897, Isabelle finally decided to make her move. A friend of Augustin had a house for rent in the Algerian coastal town of Bône. She showed the letter to Old Nathalie, then proposed that they leave Switzerland together, if only to free themselves awhile from Vava's diabolic moods.

After some days of discussion Old Nathalie agreed, then together they planned their attack. They chose the breakfast hour to announce their plans, since Vava was always irascible at the end of the day, if not completely incoherent and drunk.

He glowered at Old Nathalie the whole time Isabelle spoke, grinding his breakfast rolls in his hands.

"And it won't be as if we were really leaving home," she lied. "Just a long vacation—a chance for all of us to calm our nerves. If we're away too long, you can always make a visit, and of course we'll come back here often to see you and Vladimir."

Silence, then, as Vava sprouted a crafty smile—a prelude, she was sure, to a horrible scene.

"So you're to live among the barbarians!" he said, finally, still looking at Old Nathalie though addressing her. "I'm sure you both do need the sun—your pallors have turned a sickly gray, doubtless the result of lack of commitment to productive work! And then you'll have your wretched brother close at hand, and this 'Eugène' you speak about, who's surely after what he thinks is virginal flesh and the illusive 'Russian Fortune' that all Frenchmen think we possess."

His lower lip was trembling, then, and she felt his sarcasm was about to give way to rage. But he kept his temper, and for a moment Isabelle thought she saw the gleam of moisture in his eyes. If there were tears, Vava drew them back. A moment later he turned serene.

"Ah," he said, as warmly as he could, "just as our little family has reduced itself to three—the three, I might add, whom I've always loved the best—you two decide you have to leave. I won't stop you. I'd even join you if I could. But please forgive me if I stay on here. The Cactophile and I are very close now to the formula for the ultimate perfume. After all these terrible years I feel the breakthrough is just months from my grasp."

And then, as if he sensed their talk of a "vacation" was a pretext for a more permanent escape:

"Ha! You'll always be welcome back, of course, even if you come back only when you've heard I've gotten rich!"

With that he gulped his coffee, stood up, threw the crumbs of his rolls onto the table, bent down, kissed them both, then marched out to the garden shouting orders at Vladimir, while Isabelle and Old Nathalie stared after him in disbelief.

The Warm
Shade of Islam

She is ravished by the sun. Her skin glows with its warmth. It gazes down upon the white city out of a sky of the clearest blue, radiating energy, illuminating life.

She buys herself a man's woolen robe, then strides through the narrow streets of Bône like a tribal prince. It is Ramadan, the Moslem holy month, and the fasting has made the Arabs irritable. But she doesn't care—she revels in their surliness, for it requites her expectation of a disturbing barbaric land.

The light glitters off white walls. Minarets, like affirmative fingers, point the way to heaven and sky. The sea is clear. The muezzin whine. The juices of the oranges run like blood.

She barters in the souks, then stands back to exalt in the clamor all around. The east wind blows with a faint and maddening howl, and everywhere there are smells, hundreds of them: incense, sewage, coriander, lemons, mint, donkeys, sea and death.

She discovers kif within the month. Of all the odors of

Bône the pungent smell of the drug caresses her most force-fully, snags her off the boulevards of the European quarter into narrow rooms on twisting streets. With kif, the notes of flutes become the harmonies of stars, the thud of drums becomes a cosmic pulse.

She walks through the streets of woodworkers, iron-mongers, copper-beaters, button-makers, men who work gold and make daggers, women who mold pots and weave cloth and rugs. Then, exhausted, she flings herself down upon the mats of a café, lies back against velvet cushions, nibbles at honey-soaked confections and sips mint tea.

She loves the way the tea burns her lips, and the sound of Arabic, so guttural, so much like grunting, so filled with "ach" and hiss, that wafts from the circles of men shrouded in hoods of dark brown wool.

She spends hours in cafés reclining with her pipe, inhaling pungent, acrid, beckoning smoke that penetrates her nostrils then crawls deep within to balloon her head. She stares out into streets striped by sunlight burning down through over-arching slats, and after blurred hours, she makes her way through the dark medina labyrinth, guided by oil lamps that glow like pinwheels. From there she wanders to the ramparts of the port where the sea, phosphorescent and still, seems to quiver at the pressure of her breath.

She trembles with anticipation as she prepares to meet Eugène. What will he be like? Will all the confidences they've exchanged make them awkward, shy?

Their rendezvous is set for the Café de France, central meeting point for travelers by the docks where the boats from Europe come in. Though they've long since exchanged photographs, they set up elaborate signals of identification which they then most scrupulously observe. He's to arrive in his uniform a half hour early, take a table, immerse himself in a novel by Dostoevski. When a tall young woman

in a cape of rust-colored wool sits near, he's to offer her a
cigarette.

He looks as she's always imagined he would—tall, straight,
blond hair cut into short curved locks. His face is sensitive
yet firm—the face of a man who lives a double life, spends
his days feigning excitement over maneuvers, his nights writing verse, humming Brahms, reading Aeschylus in Greek.

As they appraise one another (to him she's always been a
cipher, someone he's met by the sheerest luck, whose friendship he prizes but whom he dares not tell himself he's ever
really understood), they fall into an excited intimate way of
speaking that reminds her of a brother and a sister in reunion
after a term away at school.

"Good—you're happy," he says. "I can tell by your eyes."

"Oh, yes, Eugène, yes! Now I feel that everything begins."

"And you like it here?"

"I adore it! I think that I really am an Arab at heart—
born by mistake in a wrong country, you see, struggling all
these years to find my real home. Now I can't imagine being
anyplace else. The streets; the light; this African sun—look!"
She reaches down, touches the pavement beneath the table.
"These stones, even these stones! I feel as if I've known them
always, have dreamed of them. As if they're a part of me,
and have always been."

He stares at her, amazed.

"Really," she says. "You've given me the best gift of my
life." She makes a great circle with her arm. "This," she
says. "All this!"

"You *are* extraordinary. I can't get over it. I don't know
exactly what I expected. Someone very difficult, I suppose—
someone moody, tormented, dark. But you are just like your
letters. So full of life."

Tears come into her eyes. She searches his face for some
clue to the love that comes upon her so suddenly in this
ordinary café.

"People are looking at us," he whispers.

"I can sense it. Yes!"

"Listen. The tone of the café has changed. People are touched. They are watching us and inventing stories in their minds."

"Yes. Yes."

And to her it does feel as if the whole café terrace, the quai, the port, the coast are coated in dark shadow, while shimmering sunlight dances only upon them.

"All right," he says. "Now you've escaped. You're free. But what about the future? What will you do now?"

"I don't know. I'm still struggling with that. I want to be a writer—to shock people. And—a great *personage*, like a character in a novel. My life should be full of struggles and passions. Great moments. Ecstasy. Fame."

"Good. I like that. It's right for you, too. You will be a great heroine. Yes!"

She is moved and remembers: he's always been so delicate with her in his letters, so careful not to intrude when she's written him turbulent accounts of the maddening tensions at Villa Neuve. Gently he's led her to this strange land, where she feels now she's found a place to grow and live.

"I want to walk with you, Eugène. I want you to put your arm around my waist and guide me, show me everything. Tell me stories. Tell me about Arabs and Berbers, the blue men—the Tuaregs—and the oases of the south."

They walk, then, for hours. She listens as he explains. And when he begins to speak of himself, his own life, his loneliness, she is touched by something vulnerable in his soul.

"The nights are miserable," he tells her. "There are no women, of course, and I dream of these veiled creatures and feel deprived. In the Sahara sometimes the women shroud themselves completely—you see nothing but a single eyeball peering out from the hooded wool. It is torture for me there, and yet I love the desert, the emptiness, the cleanness of everything, and only wish I did not always feel so sad."

"Of course you are unhappy," she tells him. "Of course

you are. But let me tell you what I like about you—the marvelous way you carry your sadness. The fine way you endure it."

They come to the doors of an inexpensive hotel, and, without speaking, she motions for him to lead her up the stairs.

There is a narrow iron bed in the room they take, two old cane chairs, and a set of tall windows where they stand and look out upon the city and the port.

She leads him to the bed and they lie down, he in his cossack-collared tunic, she in her rust-colored cape. Carefully she undoes the buttons near his collar, stretches her arms around his chest and hugs him to her, kisses his cheeks, runs her fingers over and over through his hair. They rest this way for hours, just touching, loving each other like a brother and a sister until it is dark outside and time for him to catch his train.

They speak for a few minutes before he leaves. They will see each other as often as life permits, though both recognize it will be difficult to arrange meetings and the visits will be long between. But they will write as before and their letters will be lit by a new intensity, fueled by this meeting so glowing, so long forestalled and so sincere.

Old Nathalie has always been devout—even a quarter century with Vava has not extinguished her love of God. She wants to enter every mosque they pass, search out the deity of this strange land she's come to on a whim. At first Isabelle resists. Vava's imprint has been strong, his atheism has infected her. But then she begins to marvel at the way religion here is entwined with everyday life.

No separation, as in Geneva, she sees, between pious exhortations heard at Mass, and the way people speak in the streets. Here God is everywhere, upon every lip, evoked in the merest greeting, the slightest exchange.

Inchallah. Mektoub. Humdoul'lah. God willing. It is written. Thanks be to God. Impossible to be an atheist in Islam —impossible to speak or think without acknowledging that God is great and has willed every nuance of life.

Early one June evening she climbs the hill of the old quarter and enters, at its summit, the Mosque of Sidi Bou Mérouane. Wandering through the great hall of prayer and its seven hushed naves, she marvels at the tiles glistening beneath the hanging oil lamps. After a few moments she presses herself against an ancient Roman column to savor the mood of peace.

Her calm is shattered by a cry from the minaret, echoed by more distant cries from the towers of all the mosques of Bône. Listening to them rebound against the stones, echo and overlap, she is suffused with a feeling of mystery, of something ancient, veiled.

Then, like a sound in a dream, she hears the old imam begin his prayer. His voice, tremulous and distant, calls her to her knees. Without knowing why, she joins others in the echoing gloom, listening as the prayer begins to build.

The imam's voice rises, becomes fresh and strong, then swells at last to a powerful cry announcing the inevitable triumph of Islam.

Her throat dilates. A tremor of deep emotion races down her spine. A sense of radiance fills her, and then everything turns serene. She closes her eyes, listens to eternity. A cosmic power enters her body from deep within the earth. She feels a call and then a warm embrace. Stunned by the revelation, she leaves the mosque convinced.

By nature she's a skeptic. Vava has seen to that. For days she questions her experience, probing for any weakness in her character that has brought the feeling on. Perfectly proper, she knows, to be logical, but one must live by one's senses because they are the only things one can trust. She believes she has found God by the only authentic path—not by reasoning his existence to explain the mysteries of life and death, but by feeling his presence in a shudder of deep insight.

Old Nathalie, exhausted by a Christ whose crucified body comes too close, in its agony, to the miseries of her own life, becomes entranced with the idea that she and Isabelle should convert. Nathalie arranges instruction, collects books, corrals the finest Koranic scholars of the town. These men, delighted at the opportunity, spend hours at the house on Rue Bugeaud, leading the two infidel ladies through the Prophet's words. Isabelle has a mind for it, adores reciting verses from the Koran, and soon becomes fascinated by its intricacies, just as she is stirred five times a day by the wild calls to prayer.

Studying Islam, learning to submit to God's will, she and Old Nathalie become close in a way that was impossible at Villa Neuve. Here in their tiny house there are no unpredictable tantrums to spoil the serenity of life. No demons skulk the living room walls; no mad scientist works in the cellar. Here, suspended in the imbroglio of their neighborhood, they contemplate the mystery of their new shared faith.

Still Isabelle is restless and needs, every day, to plunge out into the streets. And it becomes clear to her as she walks the medina with her sliding masculine stride, that she is being accepted as something strange and formidable, a European woman who dresses as an Arab man, a Russian who speaks Arabic, a passionate person in whom female sensuality and male force are proudly forged.

She discovers that if she walks into a mosque and kneels down and prays with Moslems, then she becomes a Moslem, too. And that if she strides into a café among soldiers smoking kif, expecting to be accepted, to share the pipe and be included in the talk, then, indeed, she is accepted and welcomed and served.

It is a startling revelation, this ability she suddenly finds to create herself as a personality, then have her portrayal accepted by an entire town. Feeling like an actress who suddenly discovers she has the power to compel belief, she spends hours before a mirror practicing sweeps of the arm, enigmatic smiles, expressions of scorn, suspension of a cigarette between her lips. She wants to see how she looks when she prays, and learns to stand facing Mecca in the manner of a sherifian king. She practices walking with a book upon her head, so that she can sweep through the crowded streets with a straight back, conveying an impression of leanness and swiftness and primitive power.

When she returns from her walks, full of discovery and exhilaration, of deep thoughts about her destiny and life, she goes always to the terrace, gently wakens her mother, and shares what she has seen.

"Something's happening to you," Old Nathalie says, inspecting her slim and fiery form. "You're becoming wild, strong. There's something of Vava in you—something driven, willful, like steel."

"Yes, yes. I'm trying to find myself—uncover what I am."

"But, Isabelle, you frighten me sometimes. You're so like Vava, so *extreme*."

"Oh, Mama, you disapprove."

Old Nathalie shakes her head.

"God will show you the way—I'm sure of that. And I pray He pities your poor brothers, too, if they're not lost forever in atheistic gloom."

Tears come into her eyes. Isabelle moves beside her, kneels, takes her hand.

"I don't know," Old Nathalie says. "I look at you sometimes and see your father. Then I think back on all the wasted years."

"You mustn't say that. There was love in the house . . ."

"Not enough. Nowhere near enough."

"There were good times . . ."

"Yes. There were. Heaven knows the man wasn't dull! But they don't cancel out all the terrible things he did—all the violence, those awful scenes. I don't care about myself. I was grown up. But I'll never forgive the way he bent your young minds—twisted you, back and forth. Still, if you have a happy life, Isabelle, then all of it will have been worthwhile."

They sit in silence, Isabelle astonished, Old Nathalie a little ashamed of what she's said.

"Look!" Isabelle points toward the sea. "Maybe we'll see it tonight."

They search the horizon. The sun is only a millimeter from the water, smooth like a tile.

"There!"

"Yes!"

The "green flash"—the strange explosion between falling sun and darkening sea—fills Old Nathalie with thoughts of God, and Isabelle with a question: will she ever escape the past?

A handsome, teen-aged Tunisian prince named Tefik Saheb-Ettaba, rumored to be the heir to millions of acres of the richest wheat-producing lands in the Tunisian Sahel, sees her in the streets, follows her, then sends flowers to her house.

Isabelle feels nothing about this except slight amusement. She continues her afternoon walks, becoming used to the sad-eyed young man who tries so hard to keep up as she sweeps through the sun-filled streets.

But after several days her amusement fades—he is making a spectacle of himself at her expense. She makes her move carefully. She stops suddenly in a public square and turns upon him in annoyance.

"Isn't it rather silly for you to follow me?" she asks in French, hoping he'll be humiliated as she is overheard. "I don't like it. Please leave me alone!"

That night he hires flutists to serenade her as she sleeps. Furious, she drives them away with a few well-chosen expletives and a couple of well-aimed stones.

No longer able to bear her indifference Tefik demands an interview with Old Nathalie. Then, in her presence, he makes a proposal of marriage in florid Arabic couplets, classical and rhymed.

"Thank you so much," says Isabelle when he's finished, "but I doubt I shall ever marry, and I certainly won't consider it now."

The look of astonishment on his face is sweeter to her than any contrived serenade.

But later she thinks: *If I am a sensualist, if the world of sensation opened up to me by Archivir is the world that satisfies me the most, then I must indulge all my cravings and give myself over fully to desire.*

The next day she accompanies her mother to the prince's house. While his father enraptures Old Nathalie with a description of an esoteric Islamic rite, Isabelle asks Tefik to show her through the fruit orchard in the back. Alone with him at last she seizes his hand and brings it to her lips. Then she kisses him, begs him to take her to his room and ravish her with ardent love. Mesmerized by her impassioned eyes, he obeys her like a slave. Afterward, he is grateful, delighted and amazed, and redoubles his pleas for her hand.

"Out of the question," she tells him, fondling his organ to a spire.

Then later, recalling his perplexity and maddened tears, she thinks: *Now I can do anything I want.*

On September 17, on a clear afternoon, while the sun seems to stand still in the sky, shining down with a radiant gloss upon the city spread below, Isabelle and Old Nathalie stand together on the side of a hill near Bône, raise their right hands and make a solemn pledge:

"I attest there is no God but God, and Mohammed is His prophet."

Standing about them are all the friends they've made, the Koranic scholars who've indoctrinated them, the love-struck Tunisian prince, well-wishers, neighbors, friends.

After they say the fateful words, they clasp their hands together and embrace. Old Nathalie's eyes fill with tears.

"Who in Moscow could have known," she asks, "that at the age of fifty-nine I would find God again?"

As they kneel in proud submission, Isabelle looks at her mother and feels moved and sad. She prays that what she's heard is true: that those who come by choice to rest in Islam's warm shade are dearer to God even than those born to His faith.

In October Old Nathalie falls ill—chest pains, soreness in her bosom, headaches, lack of energy. She stays out on the terrace nearly all the time, absorbing the autumnal sun. Isabelle does the shopping by herself, then spends as much time with her mother as she can. But the pressure she has known all her life—the need to move, to explore, to lose herself in strange quarters—this pressure is redoubled under the duress of the illness, and the moment the old woman slips into sleep, Isabelle flees the house.

She wanders and marches, peering into people's faces, sitting down in cafés, smoking her pipe. Sometimes she does not return until dawn, and then, after looking into Old Nathalie's room, hearing the labored breathing of her sleep, she flings herself upon her bed, and dreams of adventures she knows will come.

She is waiting for something, a release perhaps—some trigger that will be pulled and will propel her into life. For the moment she is content in Bône, though she senses that in time she will want to move away from the shore. There are things in the south: people, places, ways of life awaiting her discovery. But for now Old Nathalie must be cared for; a return to Geneva and all the madness there is impossible.

On the evening of November 27 she goes out before the sun is down. The light is crisp, the trees green. It has been raining for several days and, as always after a shower, the sky is clear and the air has taken on an extraordinary glow.

She walks down the hill into the medina toward the port, choosing a long and tortuous route that leads her to a notorious café. This is a place where the kif is alleged to be the very best—cut with chira with belladonna added, a mixture guaranteed to dilate the pupils even as the vision is enlarged.

She lies here on mats made of rushes strewn over bales of hay. In the corner, behind a screen of candles, an Arab plays a flute. She stares about at the faces of the men, but as her lungs absorb the smoke, she loses her ability to concentrate and fixes her eyes upon one of the flickering flames, thinking of night and shade and death. She does not understand why she feels depressed. She has escaped, after all, and to a place she loves. But she senses that her life is soon to change—that something in it is flickering and will soon go dark.

The shadows of the other men, settled, immobile, reposed, seem stained upon the walls. It seems to her that they are, all of them, timeless and lost in the corner of an enormous cave. After a long while of being immersed in sadness, she falls into intoxicated sleep.

At dawn she wakes to find herself in a room of sleeping men. They lie, like cattle, in heaps covered by dark burnooses that give off an odor of cold damp wool. All the candles have decomposed to pools of wax, and outside, on the narrow cobbled lanes, she can hear the patter of rain, and somewhere farther off, the slamming of a shutter before the wind.

Slowly she pulls herself to her feet, checks to see that nothing has troubled her in the night. Then she makes her way to the streets. Rain runs in gutters toward the port; the cobbles are slick with mud and donkey dung. Few people walk the medina: some old women with heaps of twigs piled on their backs, some men in shabby skullcaps pushing wagons filled with fruit. She pulls up her woolen hood, and shivering, weary, aching in her bones, hunches her shoulders and begins to climb.

When she emerges at the top of the hill, an enormous gust twirls her against a wall. As she enters Rue Bugeaud the rain slashes down from all angles; she cannot protect her face and so lowers her hood and marches forward without flinching. By the time she reaches the house her hair is soaked, her face is washed, and rivers of water slide down her chest and legs.

She thrusts open the door, enters and slams it shut. Wiping water from her eyes she calls to the servant for a towel. It takes her a few moments to realize that there are others in the house: a doctor, a priest and a large fat woman she recognizes as a nurse.

They tell her what has happened during the night: the heart attack that struck as the sun went down; Old Nathalie discovered, unconscious, by a servant; the hours of waiting; the agony while desperate neighbors tried to search her out; the final crisis just before the dawn. Even as they are telling her all this, and eyeing her with reproach, Isabelle forgives herself and begins to mount a grief that, by the next few days, she carries to a frantic pitch.

Trophimovsky, hearing that Old Nathalie is sick and anxious to lure her back to Meyrin, departs before the arrival of the cable informing him that she is dead. He comes to Bône unexpected by Isabelle and not expecting to find a wreath upon the door. He realizes what has happened while still in the street. With the same steeliness that had made it possible for him to persist for years with his scheme to manufacture perfume, he takes firm grip. If a passerby had peered at him at that moment, he would have seen a strange and pitiful sight: an old man ravaged for the slightest instant, a human face reflecting the stun of grief between two moments of studied calm.

Men are shrouding Old Nathalie's body at the very moment that Vava enters the house. Isabelle is throwing herself wildly about, rushing up and down stairs, her robe streaming, her fingers clutched into her short and ungraspable hair. From her mouth comes a trail of sobs and wails. The body rests on a table in the small courtyard, a calm center in a whirling storm. As Trophimovsky watches she pushes back the men, then flings herself upon the corpse. The smell of pitch is in the air, and a chorus of sobs issues from the adjoining roofs where the women of the neighborhood stand looking down.

Appalled by Isabelle's vulgar demonstration, Trophimovsky, unnoticed in the gloom of the front arch, shouts to her as loudly as he can.

"What is this *farce?*"

Isabelle spins around, snapped by memory of the bellow that made her brothers tremble for years.

"Oh, my God! Vava! Vava!" She starts toward him, but his next words stop her cold.

"If she's dead then let's hurry and get her in the earth. Old corpses stink, and this spectacle must cease."

"But . . ."

Just the grayness of his pallor, the iron set of his jaws, brings back memories of the coldness, the hardness with which he stained her youth. Smitten by the reality that Old Nathalie, the single source of warmth and tenderness in her life, is gone, she flings back her arms and shrieks. Staring about, wondering what to do, she rushes to the table, kneels beside it, and begins to knock her head against the wood.

"Life without her—impossible! Please, God, take me! Let me die, too!"

Vava steps into the sunlight, squints at Isabelle writhing near the ground.

"Here," he says. "Use this."

She turns to him, through her rain of tears sees his offering hand, and the polished Colt revolver in his palm.

"Go ahead," he says. "Take it! It will provide you with the quickest and least painful death."

"Oh, my God!"

She screams, runs from him, scales the steps to the main level of the house. The rooftop audience has ceased to mourn, is now enraptured with the drama being played.

"What's the matter?" he taunts her. "Lost your nerve?"

She stares down at him, the shrouded body, the men, the servant, then up at the Arabs all around.

"Beast!"

"You really want to die?" he demands.

"Yes! Yes!"

"Good!" He runs past her, grazes her body, then mounts the stairs to the roof.

"Wonderful view from here," he shouts. "Come on up! A terrific place to jump!"

Looking up at him, poised against the sun, one arm extended to show her where to leap, the other dangling the Colt by its trigger guard, she finds herself suddenly relieved.

"Where on earth did you get that gun?" she asks him with a grin.

"I always carry a revolver," he replies. "I never know when I'm going to meet a suicidal girl."

Old Nathalie is buried in an Arab cemetery overlooking the port of Bône. Trophimovsky weeps during the entombment, but Isabelle remains calm, her face a gentle mask. Later the two of them return to the little house on Rue Bugeaud, drink vodka together and talk of this wondrous soothing woman far into the night.

"She never said a bad word to me in all the years," Vava says, "but her eyes—they reproached me for my sins ten thousand times."

"She was a pure flame, a pure spirit in a demon's nest." Isabelle lies upon a sofa, feet bare and hanging over the arm, smoking kif from a brier pipe.

"In all our years together I never gave her anything—not even a bottle of French perfume." Vava's eyes are moist. Isabelle glances at him, decides, sorrowfully, that he does not have long to live.

He stays with her for two weeks, trying to lure her back to Villa Neuve. But she refuses him every time, insisting she must stay in North Africa and find out who she is.

"I want to be a writer," she tells him. "And now I must try my hand."

In the end, when he sees she cannot be budged, he hands her a wad of money and wishes her good luck. She will always have a home in Meyrin, he says, and the villa will be left to her and Vladimir and Augustin when he dies.

On the morning he sails for Genoa she awaits a precious phrase. She wants him to acknowledge his paternity, but though he gives her a lengthy, loving gaze, the words never come.

On December 14, 1897, she leaves for Tunis to begin life on her own. On that same day, in Geneva, Vladimir De Moerder goes humbly forward to face his ordeal.

Cactophile

Since the first days of October 1895, he had hardly stepped out of the villa grounds. He was twenty-nine years old and had spent nearly two decades working in the garden. He had not taken a violin lesson since 1887, but in the ten years since he had continued to play, devising a special technique by which he could render the tremulous screech he favored most. After 1894 he devoted himself exclusively to the E-string, and for the past year had not played a single note below high A.

He found himself bizarre, but not so bizarre as the world outside. There, it seemed, people ran about speaking nonsense and defying nature. It was strange, he knew, to fondle the earth and speak to plants in a loving whisper. He knew it was mad to take the nettles of cactus and, hidden away behind some trees, use them to puncture bare flesh, imprint stigmata upon his palms. But was this any more strange than the pursuit of money, the desire to change a political regime, or belief in romantic illusions which one knew in advance would break one's heart? At least in his life there was order, a genius to direct him, a father to love and respect, and the glories of nature which he could nurture with his hands. A germinating seed was more exciting than a slippery kiss. Better to make things grow, make beautiful things flower, to alter and embellish the very shape and texture of the land, than to waste one's life in cosmopolitan pursuits.

The walls and moats of Villa Neuve did not make the place a prison. Rather they were its guardians, the guarantors of his security. The house was a fortress to him—from it he could defend himself against the enemies he knew were plotting outside.

Vava had pointed them out, and they were everywhere. The baker, the postman, the local women who washed people's clothes. They spied upon the house, tried to obtain information by appearing friendly, smiling, starting trivial conversations. But sooner or later the questions would begin, clouded at first in innocent curiosity, but becoming increasingly direct. "Where is your sister?" "Why does she go about like a man?" "Where are your brothers?" "Is it true they are wanted by the police?" "Your older sister who left years ago—where is she now?" "Where does the money come from?" "How do you live?" "Didn't your brother run off with a girl from town?" "Was your father really a priest?" "Is he really your father?" On and on, probing, demanding, trying to accumulate sufficient facts so that someone, somewhere, could put the pieces together and complete the dossier.

At first he agreed with Vava, that they were after information about the perfumes. But then he realized that Vava was not working on perfumes at all. Of course the old man would never say anything to contradict this well-known fact, but it was clear to him that all this effort, these years of work and this enormous expense was not on behalf of the sweetness of womankind. Vava was a genius and a genius did not waste his life on trivial things. No, Vava was working on something infinitely more important behind the smoke screen of perfume, and when Vladimir discovered by deduction what that was, all the odd things that had happened about the house over the years fitted together into a grand design.

Why, for instance, he had begun to ask himself some years before, did Vava carry a revolver, even when he went to his laboratory, even when he retired to his room to sleep? None of the others had seen it, but he had spotted it by accident some time before, and then by cleverly stumbling against the old man at various times and feeling it beneath his clothes, had learned it never left his side.

The revolver was but the first in a chain of seemingly random elements which when added together revealed a pattern that convinced him his deduction was correct. There was Vava's tension, the violent mood he created about himself, which could not be explained by the mere pursuit of a scent. He was always at a crisis of nerves because he was working on something dangerous, and that, too, was why he enforced seclusion upon the house. No one was allowed in, the gates were permanently barred—he had not wanted Young Nathalie to marry because he could not abide the presence of a stranger he could not trust.

Nicolas and Augustin—they might have sensed it, too, known that there was more to Vava's difficult behavior than mere hysteria and rage. Perhaps Nicolas had pulled a triple cross—pretended to the Russian students he was an anarchist, pretended to Augustin that he was a patriot, while all the time, having somehow discovered the true nature of Vava's work, it was that and not the names of the members of the Russian group that he had inscribed in code and sold. But was Augustin really innocent? It was strange the way he'd disappeared so fast, then turned up in the Foreign Legion. He had never shown any military inclinations. Why this sudden interest in soldiering and arms? Perhaps he, too, had information of value to a Ministry of War. And why had Vava sent Isabelle and Mama away? Clearly because things were getting too dangerous, the work on the botanically based explosives too close to completion, and their enemies, the agents of the nations that wanted the formula, were closing in.

That was the only explanation—an incredible scientific breakthrough—a way of creating explosions by means of naturally found and easily acquired substances. Even a child could see the potential—an army that could sweep into a country like Russia virtually without supplies, make its own gun powder out of plants and barks and leaves, lard the fortifications of enemy towns with materials that could reduce its walls to dust.

But having deduced the true nature of Vava's work, it was important that he never speak of it aloud. Of course Vava knew that he knew—how else explain those smiles and winks, those comforting pats on the back when they worked together in the garden? How else explain those strange half-uttered phrases, those lines filled with innuendo and *double-entendre*: "our perfumes shall knock down walls"; "our scents shall pierce through armored plate"; "capitalism shall yield before our odorous power"; "let the pope beware—the world will never be the same!"?

Before he left two years before, Nicolas had warned him to stay within the villa walls. Some lingering particle of fraternal affection had evidently entered into his elder brother's triple-crossing mind. He'd obviously been torn between selling out Vava's work and selling out his closest relatives at the same time. Nicolas did not want familial blood on his hands, even if he was prepared to destroy all the fruits of Vava's life. So Nicolas could be trusted to a point, and for that reason the note he'd sent became a matter of grave concern. It had landed suddenly at the greenhouse door— a heavy, cream-colored envelope tossed one day over the garden wall, tied by a black ribbon to a medium-sized stone.

He was down on his hands and knees packing black earth around some hibiscus cuttings he'd nurtured from a successful graft. Frost was on the garden, but over the years he and

Vava had constructed a series of glassed-in sheds heated by piped steam. This way it was possible to work with plants even though the harsh Swiss winter. He had not been in the greenhouse fifteen minutes when he heard Vava's bellow from someplace in the house. And then, just as he stepped out to heed this call, he noticed the envelope lying on the ground. It had certainly not been there when he'd brought the cuttings in. He picked it up, disengaged it from the stone, began to perspire when he read his name. Vava hollered again. He hid the envelope in a nest of pots and hurried to the house.

Vava wanted him to replace an emptied canister of gas that fueled the burners at the forward end of the distillery. Vladimir towed a new canister from the other end of the cellar, helped Vava attach the tubes and after finishing the job, fled back to the greenhouse to read his mail.

"Urgent we meet to discuss important matters. Friends will contact you outside Bureau of Alien Registration, December 14, 10:00 A.M. Nicolas."

It could not be a forgery. The handwriting was familiar, a script he'd known as far back as Moscow when Vava had tutored them together. And the meeting place had special significance, too. As Russian nationals they'd gone each year to the little bureau, housed in the census office on Rue Soleil Levant.

But should the rendezvous be kept? What "important matters," he wondered, were suddenly so "urgent"? He pondered the question through the night, and finally decided he must appear.

December 14, 1897, was a day of brilliant sunlight. The lake, not yet frozen, was as smooth as a glazed blue plate. The trees, bare of leaves, looked like hieroglyphs etched out against the Alps. The cold air burned the nostrils. The swans, all panoplied in winter feathers, glided among the toy sailboats of boys.

Walking across the Pont des Bergues, past the Monument

Jean-Jacques Rousseau, Vladimir felt no menace in the air. On the contrary, he felt elated to be away from the villa—he loved its enclosing walls, but realized he had shut himself in too long. Perhaps, if he were careful, he might come out now once every other month—walk on the quais with people, sit in a café, perhaps even try to skate again when the lake froze up. He was struck by the gay look of the girls, and one in a salmon-colored sweater caught his eye and twitched his lust. He felt happy as he crossed Place de la Fusterie; positively exhilarated as he aproached Cour St. Pierre. But then as he made his way around the great cathedral, a cloud out of nowhere crossed the sun, and as the census office came into sight he felt an intimation of danger and turned his head. Two men in belted overcoats and fur hats were bearing down on him from opposite sides of the street. He backed against a wrought-iron railing; the sun reappeared. He raised one hand to shield his eyes; suddenly he felt them take his arms.

"De Moerder?" The voice was urgent.

He nodded.

"De Moerder sent us—you know *who* we mean?"

He nodded again and they began to walk, Vladimir in the middle, a convict between two guards. He was tall and they were both short, heavy, strong, bearing down with their arms locked into his so that if he'd wanted to make a run he could never have gotten loose. Nobody noticed as they moved so closely linked, turned the corner right and then left again, emerged onto Rue des Granges at the Café Diabolique. Hurrying faster—there were fewer pedestrians here—they slid past a synagogue and the magic store on the corner of Boulangerie, and finally turned right into narrow Cheval Blanc. A vendor selling funeral wreaths gave them a knowing squint. They paused outside a horsemeat store; his companions looked about. Then they entered—there were no customers, no one but a fat woman in bloody apron cleaving intractable bones. They filed around the counter, then through damp sawdust to a room in the back. Here amidst the odor of fresh-killed meat, his guardians relaxed, lit up black Russian cigarettes and leaned against the doors with folded arms to seal off escape.

What was there to say? These thugs seemed to be avoiding his eyes, and in any case he'd resolved to deal only with Nicolas. He knew what to expect—an irresistible deal that he would most certainly resist, a bargain by which he might be offered the directorship of the Jardin Exotique in St. Petersburg in return for the contents of Vava's safe, perhaps even for Vava himself. After all, he thought, what good were the formulas without a genius to explain their use? But whatever the offered deal, and no matter how high the promised reward, he would take great pleasure in turning it down. He would prove to Nicolas once and for all that there were men on earth who could not be bought. This confrontation between them was long overdue, and if Vladimir remained sufficiently meek, it might perhaps result in Nicolas finally acknowledging his error.

The back room by then had filled with smoke, dark acrid fumes which pained his eyes. Then—the sound of footsteps on some hidden stairs, and a knock on the door away from the shop. Vladimir's stomach tightened. His guards became tense. One of them opened the door a crack, he heard a whisper, and then footsteps retreating back above.

"All right," said the one who'd spoken before, "time to see the count."

They guided him through a door, up some stairs and down a hall painted black. He could hear sounds from the rear of the building, a girl singing as she mopped the court, a child crying somewhere in a flat across the way. A sickening stench filled the air—when he passed a greasy window he knew what it was—they were burning old hooves and horse heads in the yard below.

He was pushed into a room, then into a chipped leather chair. His guards again stood smoking with folded arms, one before the door, the other before the narrow window that looked out on Cheval Blanc. A few moments later he heard brisk footsteps in the hall, the door opened, a heavyset man with full black beard and burning eyes appeared.

"Allow me to present myself—Count Igor Prozov, consular of his Imperial Majesty's Government, specialist in political sedition and crimes against the Imperial Russian State."

So this was Prozov! Vladimir feasted his eyes on the man. There was a sinister cast to the flabby face, something cruel, something dangerous.

"You, I presume, are Vladimir De Moerder, brother of the wretched Nicolas."

He neither nodded nor spoke. He would say nothing until Nicolas appeared.

"Your brother was very kind to prepare our summons. A touch of the knout can make even the strongest men beg to help us."

His throat began to throb.

"Nicolas?" he asked. "Is he coming here?"

"I doubt it. Still in Moscow I suspect—old Peter's prison to be exact."

"Then this . . . ?"

"An ambush, yes. But you have nothing to fear, poor boy. I am a reasonable man. I can guarantee your safety if you will help. I'm interested in information. There are a few lacunae in your brother's story. But later we can get to that. Suppose we start at the beginning—your role in the affair. You—am I right?—were the key figure, the one who introduced your brothers to that disreputable gang. . . ."

On and on he went, bearing down with precise formulations, entrapping sentences, assumptions of Vladimir's guilt. The questions flew at him like a thousand knives. It was not long before he began to scream. Then they manacled his legs to the feet of the chair and wrapped damp wool around his mouth. The more incisive Prozov's questions, the more incoherent Vladimir's response. To each specific query about certain events in 1895, he shouted back the name of a botanical phylum, muffled to a groan by his woolen gag. He became terrified, lost his mind. After an hour of tears and wails, all resistance crumbled; he began to speak. Prozov listened, fascinated, then pulled off the wool. Vladimir became excited, could not hold himself back. The more profoundly he understood he must keep silent, the more he felt forced by his inquisitor to tell. *I must confess, must confess*, he kept saying to himself, and in the end he told everything—all his suspicions, how he'd come to the conclusion they were not making perfume, the whole tortuous chain of logic, his deductions, step by step, then the revelation of the true nature of the work, his estimate of the value of botanical explosives to foreign powers, his belief that Vava was but days from final success—it all came out in a mad jumble, a frantic disgorging of all he'd stowed away those long silent years. When he was finally finished, awash in tears of shame for having broken down before those relentless drilling eyes, and smiling, too, on account of his relief at finally being unburdened of so many secrets, Prozov threw up his hands and sighed.

"The boy's mad," he said quietly, "a harmless, poor mad boy. Beat him up a little so he knows he must not talk, then throw him out and never return here again." He burned his pages of notes, crumpled the ash beneath his heels.

They beat him for ten minutes, methodically pounded his ears until blood ran out. Then they slapped his face, in shifts, until the sides of his jaw went raw. When they were done, they brought him tea and offered him a cigarette which he took with gratitude and smoked. They warned him sternly that he'd do well not to say a word, or they'd come after him at night and set his bed on fire. He blubbered his thanks for their good advice, stumbled down the stairs, through the horsemeat shop, out into the blinding, sun-filled street.

❖

The next four months were worse for him than any moment of physical torture he'd endured. He could not forgive his cowardice, his betrayal of the man he loved. Everything conspired to punish this treachery. The plants themselves with their grasping vines seemed to seek to strangle away his breath. All leaves seemed poisonous, and the needles of the cactuses were daggers stretching to puncture his heart. Insects and worms were conspiring to burrow into his body while he slept, and his nights were always frantic, filled with the fear that suddenly he'd be doused with oil, then lit and turned into a torch.

He took to his room, spent hours sobbing, and when Vava came to comfort him, to pat his head and whisper encouragements in his ear, he'd turn to the uncomprehending old man and beg forgiveness for his betrayal. Life became hopeless, and in his few lucid moments Vladimir knew it must end with his punishing himself.

Early in the morning of April 13, 1898, he turned on the gas valves in his room, locked the doors, played his violin for a while, then lay down to sleep. When Vava found him at 11:00 A.M., still warm, still damp, all breathing done, he moaned the eulogy he'd long rehearsed:

"Ah," he said, "ah—my cactophile is gone."

Red Boots

Upon arrival in Tunis, Isabelle presents herself at the tiny office of the Russian consul, where a balding young man with a walrus moustache suggests she leave at once.

"Unless you have business here," he says, "it is utterly pointless to stay. These people are fanatics, and have no morals at all."

Walking the huge medina Isabelle sees strange things: pickpockets led away by crowds of angry citizens to horrible punishments meted out in dark corners of the maze; packs of howling dogs rushing down the narrow streets at night before disappearing into fields of ruined stone to corner some poor rodent and tear apart its flesh. She hears strange stories of banditry, kidnapping, and the selling of whites as slaves. Terrible things take place in the dark labyrinth—unspeakable acts are perpetrated against the innocent bodies and virginal orifices of foreigners who wander where they do not belong. But Isabelle is undaunted. She has come to be a writer, and so sets out to find herself a place to live.

One day, soon after her arrival, wandering an old Arab cemetery on a hill near the Menara gate, she's attracted by the subtle colors of wild flowers and herbs beyond. Walking among them she comes upon a region of ruins: smashed lintels, free-standing chimneys, courtyards choked with decaying vegetation, archways split by unattended trees. She is struck by a sense of desolation and is about to turn away when she notices, across a garden of roses, an old domed Turkish house—grand, sullen, looming in the sun.

She approaches, knocks and after an interminable wait, sees a dark, wizened old face appear at a tiny window in the door.

"Yes! Yes!"

"I'm looking for a house."

"Yes!"

"I thought this one might be for rent."

"Yes!"

"Can I come in?"

After a few moments the door swings open, and she's confronted by an old black lady and a large black dog. The dog squints at her, pants then turns back inside.

"What's your name?" she asks.

"Khadidja."

"Well, Khadidja—*is* this house for rent?"

The old maid nods her head.

"In that case I should like to look about."

Khadidja shows her through a maze that puts the intricacies of the medina to shame. She is led through a labyrinth of passageways, then a series of interlocking rooms, all decorated with old Andalusian tiles, and plaster cut with intricate Arabic texts. At one point, when they enter a hall without windows, Khadidja takes her hand, leads her to a high-ceilinged octagonal room whose walls are embedded with rusting mirrors. From here they make their way up a spiral stairs, climbing finally to a great domed room in the turret where she finds stained cushions placed along the walls, a table and a row of arched windows overlooking the town. She goes to them, stares down at the sunlit ruins.

"What a fantastic place! I must see the owner at once."

Khadidja directs her to a bank which has seized the house in lieu of an unpaid debt. Its manager, a stylish young Frenchman named Pierre, at first tries to discourage her from taking the place.

"The rent is extravagant," he warns, "and the house is absolutely huge. It's really ridiculous if you're going to live alone."

"Irrelevant," she says. "I've come here to be a writer. If I can work in that tower room, then I may make myself a fortune, in which case the size and the cost won't matter to me at all."

Pierre is delighted with her, orders the lease drawn and quickly establishes himself as her friend.

"You'll love Tunis. It's perfect for a writer—one of the great places in the world. Here you can bring your fantasies to life. Nothing's forbidden; anything can be arranged."

"But I hear all these awful stories . . ."

"Don't listen! Tunis is a city of love. Only the prudes find it scandalous. The great gift of Tunis, you see, is the way that it shows their true natures to men. You can be sure that those who detest it are the ones who fear what they find here within themselves."

"Has it helped you, then?"

He looks at her, lowers his voice, confides.

"Yes, I found myself, and my own form of love. They call it 'the love that dares not speak its name' in Europe, but here it is quite acceptable, sometimes even admired."

His own special tastes are so deviant and bizarre they startle her. He lives, he tells her, in a delightful villa where he keeps a gracious garden and two large Dalmatian dogs. The dogs and flowers are his passion. At night he likes to dress himself in polka-dot clothing, paint black and white spots on his face and, with his canine friends, sneak about his neighborhood stealing exotic plants. Then, laden with booty, but still steamy from the risk of the chase, he returns home for an erotic romp with his dogs who glaze him sensuously with their tongues.

"I don't believe you," Isabelle screams, howling with giggles. "Impossible! You've made it up!"

Pierre raises his finger. "Ah," he says. "The vices of Tunis —they are magnificent, and without end."

They are all exhibited nightly, she learns, in a quarter near the old Roman slaves' prison and the cemetery by the gate called Bab El Gorjani. Pierre takes her there the next evening to watch the parade of the prostitutes. She marvels at the carnal pacing and the seductive gestures that sweep up sailors from a dozen lands into brothels for the night.

Pierre shows her little side streets choked with boys for sale. Some are mere children, ten and eleven years old.

"Luscious flesh," says the Frenchman, dabbing with his tongue at the corner of his mouth, "but too dangerous for me—they're nearly all diseased. Tunis," he continues, "is *cornucopia sexualis*. The Englishman who likes to be whipped, and the Russian who likes to whip. Japanese girl, Persian boy, Siamese cat. All three orifices satisfied at once.

"I've prowled here often and seen many strange things. Amateurs, noblemen, sometimes, or millionaires offer themselves to the meanest trash on the street. They take a sailor's coins, and then, at dawn, throw them to the beggars. But a man who likes women must watch out for transvestites— those fiendish boys will seduce him with phony female guile, then, later, in a pitch-dark room—it'll be too late—they'll have his ass!

"Fortunately that's not my problem, though I was once

tricked by a maiden I'd mistaken for a rough street boy. Her ass was sweet, but when I grabbed 'round front—nothing! We fought furiously over the money, then settled for half, which, as far as I was concerned, was all I'd got. Later I learned she was a Scottish marchioness. She'd come here to study the art of strumpetry which she hoped to practice back in London, in the style of Catherine Walters—whom, I believe, she referred to as 'Skittles.' "

Pierre looks around.

"The pandemonium here is about to crest, but, unfortunately, I must leave. Take care little sparrow—you look so innocent. There is love for you in Bab El Gorjani—I'm sure of it. But beware of evil."

Installed in the old Turkish house she quickly makes friends with the dog. Since he has no name she calls him "Dédale," appropriately, she thinks, for the creature seems quite happy in her palatial maze.

She also befriends Khadidja whom she presents with a new djellaba, a bottle of perfume and other lavish gifts. Then she gives her instructions.

"If anyone should call at the door and ask you who I am, you are to repeat exactly the following words: 'Mademoiselle Eberhardt is a Russian Moslem, and she devotes herself to literature.' "

Khadidja practices the phrase several times, then wanders off. But whenever Isabelle meets her in a corridor, or on the stairs, she repeats it with a solemn face.

Determined to be a writer, she tries hard to capture the experience of kif. But it is beyond her reach—she realizes she does not yet have the skills. Looking for inspiration she buries herself in her books: Loti, Nadsón, the Russian classics of her youth. And when these provide her with nothing she turns to the journals of the brothers Goncourt, if only to savor the essence of the literary life.

If I'm successful, she thinks, *my future is assured. I'll earn a fortune with my pen, and join the Brontës and George Sand in the elite sisterhood of literature.*

Knowing she must work, but discovering not a single idea for a story in her head, she forces upon herself a vast literary project, a series of tales about the destroyed people of Tunis—the beggars, cripples, lepers, syphilitics, dwarfs and other deformed specimens she knows so well from her marches through the town. Though before she has gone to great lengths to avoid them, crossing streets, darting down alleys, doing anything possible to escape their wails, she resolves now to make a point of hovering near, hoping that by wallowing in their foulness she may somehow learn to relinquish her disgust.

She tries a story, modeling her style on Loti, then shows the draft to Pierre. He reads it, and abruptly throws it down.

"No, Isabelle—no! You must forget about other writers. Walk, ride, explore until *you* have something to say."

He gives her a little book by an obscure author named André Gide. It is called *Les Nourritures Terrestres*, and she dips into it many times, feeling that it has been written especially for her.

This book, which urges its readers to sever themselves from all restraints, satisfy all cravings and live at fever pitch, implies that nothing can really be learned from books, even from *Les Nourritures Terrestres*. Watching the sun rise through the arches of her tower bedroom, she recalls an admonition from Gide's *Envoi*: "Throw away my book. Tell yourself it is but one of the thousand ways of confronting life, and seek out your own."

Seized, after a night of warring thoughts, by a new confidence that comes with the dawn, she takes the book, and the rest of her library as well, packs them up, rents a horse and rides out to Carthage where, from a high cliff, she flings them all into the sea.

"Now I am done with books," she says aloud. "I shall live my life and I shall write only of my adventures and myself."

❖

But if she is to seek inspiration in the streets, she has a problem, for though she speaks the language, is Moslem and even looks something like a boy, she is still a European woman in an Arab town. There is only one solution and she seizes upon it: *disguise*.

It becomes her passion, for it seems the only way she can fully penetrate the forbidden Arab world so dominated by men. Thinking of how she used to dress up for Archivir's photographer, she smiles and shakes her head. It is one thing to cut her hair short and wear men's clothes. It is quite another, she knows, to actually pass herself off as an adolescent boy.

This requires more than the affectation of male qualities. It requires their subtle display, a certain way of walking and standing still, of perching on the steps of a mosque, of holding a cigarette and hoisting a glass of tea.

The first few times she tries it, she fears the consequences if someone should see through her charade. But gradually she realizes she's in a land where she can have things both ways: from those who accept her as a boy she receives the insights she requires, and from those who realize she is not, she receives acceptance, too, on account of the polite Arab convention that one accepts a man on the terms he sets himself.

She begins, then, to do strange things, even to chance discovery by wrestling with boys on the streets. She tries to put herself in situations where bizarre adventures will occur. She rides about on a horse with a cigarette dangling from her lips, hoping to set off a confrontation or a fight. And there does come a moment one day when she wriggles with fear—in conversation at a café with another youth who suddenly suggests they relieve themselves in each other's ass.

When, finally, despite all her provocations, she still has no ideas for stories, and is about to give up looking for experiences in the streets, a strange adventure unexpectedly occurs. Recalling it later, she gives it a name: "The Incident of the Red Boots."

It begins one night when she's resting in her tower, staring at candles she's set up all around. She moves to the windows and peers out at the full moon—African, brilliant, washed at its center by a small drift of clouds. She stares out at the cemetery of Bab Menara, bathed in silvery light, then looks down at the ruins below her house where she sees a young man, wrapped in a white burnoose, sitting still as a statue, silent as a ghost.

And then, as she watches, he begins to sing a mournful Andalusian ballad that reaches her as if it comes from within a cave. When the song is finished, the figure glides softly into the ruins, then disappears behind a broken wall. She waits a long time for him to reappear at its other side, but he does not, seems simply to vanish in the night.

The next morning she asks Khadidja if she heard the young man sing. When she nods, Isabelle asks who he is.

The old maid shakes her head.

"No one can know," she says, and then, in a trembling voice, "no one but God, of course."

That evening Isabelle walks to Bab El Gorjani, and after an hour or so of inspecting the love market, she turns into a café to rest.

The place is not familiar to her—there is a certain roughness about the clientele, and a terrible aroma, too, that issues from the armpits of a band of Spanish sailors, mingles with the kif smoke and the smell of burning paraffin and threatens to make her sick. She feels menace in the café—flickering candles, strange sounds, looming bodies, erotic parade outside—and is about to leave when a boy brings her a glass of tea. She feels better the moment she sips, orders kif, stuffs her pipe, and settles back on the mats to dream.

After a while all menace is diffused. The stink of the Spaniards turns earthy, the candles tint everything with a golden glow. Isabelle begins to slip into a haze when she is seized by a sensation that she's being watched. Slowly she turns to meet the gaze of a thin high-cheeked youth whom she recognizes as the boy who sang beneath her house.

Their eyes lock. Isabelle smiles and then he subtly purses his lips. Someone in the café produces a guitar, and the Spanish sailors begin to sing. A Sicilian woman snaps her fingers. One of the sailors ties knives to the feet of a stool, while another strips off his shirt to make a cape.

Both of them are smiling now. Then the youth toasts her with his glass of tea. She raises her own glass, and, with her other hand, makes an elaborate gesture, a delicate rendition of flowing water, a desert greeting as she imagines it would be made by characters in the *Arabian Nights*.

The Spaniards now are lunging with the knife-legged stool, playing *toro* and *torero* to everyone's delight. Isabelle watches, and when she turns again the young man is no longer there. She dashes to the door, looks up and down the street. A matelot with filthy pompon lumbers by, stops, backtracks, then huddles with a prostitute beneath an arch. Someone in a room above pulls a curtain, and for a moment a shaft of light falls upon the pair. Isabelle peers around—the boy has vanished again.

Wondering then if he really was her singer, or merely a hallucination induced by kif, she wanders back through the alleys, finding her way by familiar sounds, the squeak of a public pump, the tune of a wheel turning before a sewer cascade.

At last she comes to the cemetery at Bab Menara and stumbles out among the moonlit stones. Approaching her house, she hears quiet footsteps, and then the rustling of cloth. She stops, looks around, sees the boy, dressed now in his white burnoose, sweeping like a ghost between two columns, then disappearing again behind another wall.

She is amazed, crouches behind the *murette* of a broken terrace, and moving cautiously, bent low and sometimes actually crawling on hands and knees, she creeps toward an archway that marks the side of a ruined court.

Here she stops, her breath clouded by heavy scented air. It is the perfume of roses, thick and rich, that presses like a soft cushion against her face.

The young man, seated now on a fallen pillar, raises a flute to his lips and begins to play. Clear, pure, the sounds vibrate in the aromatic air with a sadness that gives her the impression she's a secret sharer, a witness to a private movement. But then, as the song nears its end, she changes her mind. Something tells her the boy knows perfectly well that she's near, and is trying, like a Hindu playing for a cobra, to lure her out.

There is no time for this notion to catch hold. She watches, astonished, as her musician gathers up his burnoose and glides away. And, when he is gone, she walks out of the garden and up to her room, thinking strange thoughts of inscrutable cabals.

"But this is absolutely extraordinary."

Pierre is holding a delicately sugared crescent of pastry between his fingers, twirling it, examining it in the light.

"How amusing! How bizarre! Little sparrow—who would have thought you'd have such an adventure. A naïve like you. Such good luck! And there's something about your story that tantalizes me, though I'm not sure I can put my finger on exactly what it is."

They are sitting in a proper café in the French quarter of the city. Boys vending fruit and pastries are circulating about.

"Please try," says Isabelle. "I'm so confused myself."

Pierre bites into his pastry, releasing an aroma of orange-scented almond paste.

"Well, it's the convenience of the coincidence, if you see what I mean."

"I'm not sure I do . . ."

"The chain of events. It's rather too neat, and that final vanishing act! Ha!"

"How do *you* explain it?"

"Well, you've made quite a spectacle of yourself in Tunis, my dear—surely you know that your wanderings at night and your formidable disguises have not gone unobserved. There is even some talk, I understand, that you're a Russian spy! Ridiculous, of course, but there you are. What I'm getting at is that you might well be the victim of a complicated hoax, spun perhaps by someone wanting to use you for a fool. And I don't trust that maid. I think she knows more than she's letting on."

"Impossible!" Isabelle shakes her head. "She's devoted to me."

Pierre takes a swipe at a cookie seller who's been pulling at his sleeve. The boy jumps out of the way, sticks out his tongue

"Ugh! These children are verminous! This isn't a good place to talk. We'll meet tonight at the same café. I know the place—one of the most sordid around. Perhaps the boy will reappear, and I can help you analyze his tricks."

She is tense that night as she makes her way into the medina, plunges through the narrow streets, pushing beggars aside. New ships have landed at the Port of Tunis, and the alleys of the love market are packed with sailors on liberty, sweaty, husky men who surge through Bab El Gorjani, eager to release the tension of the seas.

Concentrating on keeping her burnoose clean, avoiding the moist walls and the windows overhead from which, at any moment, she might be drenched by a quickly unloaded basin of slop, she takes a wrong turn and becomes lost.

The more she struggles to find her way, the more confusing she finds the alleys. In panic she darts this way and that, searching for some familiar sight. Finally, exhausted, she stops to rest at the edge of a public well. Catching her breath, she finds her body sticky with sweat and her robe badly stained, caked with donkey dung.

She peers about the tiny square with desperate eyes. It is hopeless, she knows, to continue looking for the café. She must first find the cemetery near her house, then work her way back along the route she took the night before.

As she stumbles about, looking for the cemetery wall, she takes no notice of the other people around. It never occurs to her that a man is treading behind, stalking, pressing against walls, crouching in doorways, tracking her through the maze. It is only when she reaches the Menara gate and pauses to wipe her face that she has a feeling that someone is lurking near.

Suddenly she snaps her head around. A shadowy figure emerges from the cemetery, walks directly toward her with a familiar gliding gait. She feels puzzlement, and then extreme curiosity. The young man looks stunning in his brown and white striped gown, and even before she can see his face she is certain who he is.

"Good evening."

"You know me?" she asks.

"Of course. You're a Russian Moslem, and you devote yourself to literature. Is there anyone in Tunis who does not know that?"

They both laugh, then, and though she does not yet

understand his game, she had no doubt now that a game is what he plays.

"Strange we should meet here," she says. "Have you been following me for long?"

"Not too long. I saw you get lost, and thought I should help. Then I thought you might be insulted. But I followed you anyway, just in case. The medina is a nightmare, unless one is born in it, and even then . . . Do you know that often, if you ask a native the way to a certain place, he will send you in an opposite direction to make a joke?"

"What's your name?"

He stares at her, ignores the question. "Have you smoked tonight?"

"Not yet."

"Good. I don't think kif and absinthe mix. Let's go to your house and have a drink."

"*My* house! You *do* have a nerve. I don't even know who you are."

He shrugs. "It's not as if we've never met."

"No, but one must be careful here . . ." She remembers all she's heard of the dangers of the medina, those tales of kidnapping and being sold into slavery, forced penetrations, multiple rapes. There is a side of her that is wary and another that is hungry for life. Already she is savoring the promise of adventure, wondering how to frame the opening words of a short story that will recount this strange meeting in the night.

"How odd of you to want absinthe," she says. "You're the first Tunisian I've met who drinks."

"I didn't say I was Tunisian."

"No, but I assumed . . ."

"Ah—but you mustn't assume anything. It's much better not to think. One must take one's life as it comes, accept the odd meetings, choose the untraveled roads."

By one hand she leads him inside the house—in her other she carries a torch. When they reach the octagonal room, he grasps the torch away and brandishes it, causing whorls of light and swirls of shadow to dash across the mirrors. He laughs, the torch races faster, spattering embers on the black marble floor. In an infinity of reflections Isabelle sees her hazel eyes enlarge, catch fire, gash the silver glass with streaks of gold.

He pauses, moves close to her, holds the torch between them so it illuminates their faces from beneath. As they stand together, peering into each other's eyes, she feels a warmth rising in her loins.

They climb the spiral stairs, higher, higher, to her round domed room in the turret at the top. Here he extinguishes the flame, throws himself on her cushions and looks about.

"Ah," he says, pointing to her folding writing table covered with her papers, her pens and bottles of ink, "so this is where your devotion takes place. And there . . ." looking at her tiny prayer rug arranged with four candles, each set at a corner, stuck to the floor with a bead of wax, ". . . there is where you pray. Yes, I like your house. This is the room of someone interesting—an interesting personage."

"That's very kind of you to say," she says, uncorking a bottle, pouring them each a drink. "But, if you don't mind, I think you should explain yourself."

"My name means nothing. It wouldn't interest you, and besides I prefer to present myself in a different way. I've been observing you closely for some days now, following you about, discovering what you do and where you live. Your disguises caught my interest, and the way you run around in the medina, peering at people with that intent expression on your face."

"I've never noticed you."

"Well, that's the way life is—a person looks at everybody else, and never notices somebody looking at him. But sometimes," and he smiles, "there is an encounter, like a story, perhaps, or like a dream. The two observers meet, by chance or by design, and then something happens between them, and they remember it well although they never see one another again."

"Oh," she asks, amazed, "what do you suppose is going to happen between us?"

"It is written," he says, staring at her with devouring eyes, "it is written that we shall make love."

And at that he brings down his head and presses his lips against her mouth.

Suddenly, she does not quite remember how, they are facing each other, their bodies bare. He grasps her, moves his fingers slowly down her flanks, until she feels moisture begin to run between her thighs. Then she seems to be falling, shedding some part of herself. She senses a wildness in him, something powerful and strong. He is limber, lithe, slim, and his skin, white, pale like lime, is glazed with a delicate moistness that shimmers in the moonlight scattering around the room.

They lie now on cushions, on their sides. She has never felt so light, has closed her eyes, is dreaming of colors, sounds. Suddenly they begin to struggle, and then laugh as she tries to throw him off. But she can't, and when she lies beneath him, pinned, exhausted, panting for breath, playing with her palms and outstretched fingers, smearing the sweat about on his chest, she feels they've enacted a game of mastery and conquest, in which he's proved his strength and so can now take his prize.

Suddenly something warm and moist glazes her below, and she finds herself falling into a pit of wildness and violent passion. He licks her as he might lick a sherbet, in long even strokes toward a single point. She can barely stand it—his strokes are so delicate and fine. He probes on, deeper, deeper, until her whole body begins to thrash.

Then he is upon her again, an expert horseman controlling a new mount. One part of her wants to resist, but another side takes joy in being tamed. His face is radiant as he rides, and she loves his roughness, his limber strength. She has never fought a lover so hard, never sweated in embrace like this. She revels in the push and pull, moving harder, faster, even laughing as they blast.

At last: an explosion. She feels a contracting deep inside, spreads her thighs, arches back and thrusts. He gasps, she cries out, and then they fall. She feels him emptying—the flow goes on and on. She shudders, grasps his body. And then the odor of roses floods full in.

It makes her heady, this rich red aroma, fogs her mind. She rolls upon her back, her head down near his thighs, and gulps in air as if she's run a race. They lie like this, eyes glazed, and then she falls off to sleep.

She awakens occasionally in the night, once when she thinks she hears a flute. Long before dawn she hears the moans of the muezzin calling from the minarets of all the mosques of Tunis. Looking about a few minutes later, she sees her lover on her prayer rug, surrounded by lit candles, bent.

"God is great; There is no God but God; Allah is His name; Mohammed is His prophet."

She falls off and when she wakes again her tongue feels salty, her lips and body battered, bruised. She turns, looks about. The room is flooded with sunshine, and he is gone.

Confused, she inspects her things. The absinthe bottle is corked, the two glasses washed, dried and arranged together on the tray. The papers on her writing desk are arranged, too, the quills and inkpot set at right angles as if ready for a clerk.

She dresses, wanders down the stairs and corners Khadidja preparing coffee on her charcoal stove.

"When did he leave?"

"Hours ago."

"Did he say anything—when he'd be back?"

Khadidja shakes her head. Isabelle looks at her closely, forces her to meet her eyes.

"Tell me, Khadidja—tell me who he is."

The maid shrugs and fidgets.

"I don't know," she says. "He came here several days ago when you were out, asked me about you, and I told him the words you taught me to say. Then he left."

"But you'd seen him before?"

"No, Mademoiselle. He's not from Tunis."

Isabelle nestles herself by the old maid's side.

"In that case, Khadidja, tell me what you *think*."

Khadidja looks puzzled, as if no one has ever asked her opinion on anything before.

"I feel he is sad, Mademoiselle, and perhaps very rich. He could be a Moroccan. Maybe he is a prince—his words are fine, and so are his clothes. When I heard him sing, I thought he might be a ghost, perhaps the ghost of someone who lived here long ago."

"The music was real."

"Oh, yes, Mademoiselle. But a ghost is real, too."

Khadidja bows her head, and Isabelle understands. The gesture is an acknowledgment that there are things in the world that cannot be explained, things which happen, nevertheless, and to which people must submit.

She spends the morning pacing about her house. When her phantom lover does not return, she goes to the city, hires a horse and gallops out to the ruins of Carthage, followed by Dédale.

She watches the sun begin to set from the Baths of Antoninus, stumbles across the huge capital of a fallen Corinthian column, then looks out to the sea. Sweaty, dirty, smelling of her horse, she tosses aside her robe, and runs, followed by the yelping dog, into the spumy waves.

That night she sits for a long while among the rose bushes in her garden. Then she calls for Khadidja to join her outside.

"He *is* a man, Khadidja—that I know for sure. And a man cannot disappear. Come—we must find out how he leaves."

Grasping onto torches they explore the ruins. Finally they come to the wall where, they agree, he has disappeared three times. There are bushes behind it, and behind one of these is a niche. Inside they find the white burnoose, and wrapped in it the flute.

The next morning Khadidja comes running into the tower.

"Mademoiselle," she cries, shaking Isabelle awake. "A boy has come from the flutist and has brought you this."

She hands over a package which Isabelle frantically unties. Inside she finds a pair of Spahi riding boots, made of shiny red Moroccan leather, finely waxed.

"Was there a message? Did the boy say anything at all?"

"Just that his master is leaving Tunis, and will not be back again."

Days pass, and the young man sends no further word. His flute and burnoose remain untouched in the niche. Isabelle waits and waits, and the next time the moon is full, she watches the garden the whole night hoping he'll return. But he does not, and after that she takes him at his word.

Through the rest of 1898 she writes little, though she comes to know Tunis well. She becomes adept at assuming a male disguise, and begins to use a man's name: "Si Mahmoud."

Often she leaves the old Turkish house to ride in the countryside for days. Then she sleeps out in the open, in meadows or on the beach, listening to herself, her thoughts, trying to work out the meaning of her life.

Sometimes she does not leave her tower for a week, smoking, drinking, dreaming of herself in situations, her destiny, the real meaning of her disguise. Then she goes out to Bab El Gorjani, finds a lover, takes him to her tower, gratifies herself and dismisses him at dawn.

Sometimes, when she is prowling in the medina, she thinks she sees the donor of the red boots. But always, when she looks closely, the person turns out to be someone else.

In early 1899, she begins to receive disturbing news. Vava is ill, and Augustin (out of the legion, married to Madeleine, "in business" in Marseilles) writes her that the old man does not have long to live. She knows she must return to Geneva, but puts off the trip as long as she can.

Finally, when she receives an urgent cable, she calls at the bank to tell Pierre she will no longer be able to keep the house. She learns that he has not come in to work for several days.

She finally finds his home, a charming villa poised on a hill overlooking the sea. She walks through the garden and finds her friend running about his terrace in a rage. The two Dalmatians are barking ferociously as the Frenchman, forehead covered with sweat, scurries about throwing potted plants off his balcony into the sea.

"They're transferring me to Lyons," he shouts, as rose bushes, potted yuccas, rare bamboos and dahlias are heaved. "My life is over. I shall never survive in that hideous, heartless town. Seems some rumors of my inversion have filtered back. God damnit," he cries, as he holds a huge earthenware pot of violet hydrangeas above his head. "The brutes! The dirty swine!"

He thrusts the pot over the railing, and Isabelle watches as the petals break loose and glide, sprinkling a thousand shards of smashed pottery scattered on the rocks.

Later that night, the two of them drunk on wine, the Dalmatians snoring loudly at his feet, Pierre asks if she ever met up again with the mysterious boy who sent her the boots.

"No," she says. "The story was left unresolved."

"Still you should try and write it up."

"I've tried many times," she says, "but the words never come."

"Ah," Pierre shrugs. "Perhaps it was not such a great experience after all."

"He was the best lover I ever had."

"And the boots . . . ?"

"What about them?"

"You must use them, little sparrow. To march. March and explore."

A Garden Gone to Seed

May 1, 1899. There was no one
to meet her at 5:00 PM when she arrived at the Gare de
Cornavin. She was wearing her red boots and a hooded
cloak of pure white wool. Crowds thronged the station, the
smoke of the locomotives was blue, and the papers that had
come on the same train from Paris were full of speculation
about whether Captain Dreyfus would be retried. The
Affaire had been the talk of Tunis, and for that matter Bône
when, a day before Old Nathalie's death, Mathieu Dreyfus
had denounced Esterhazy as the true author of the *bor-
dereau*. But to Isabelle the Dreyfus case was confusing to
the point of boredom; she swept by the newspaper kiosks
and out to the street to find a carriage for Meyrin.

Moving down the Rue Voltaire she found it difficult to
imagine she'd once lived among the Alps. No camels plowed
these neat Swiss farms; no African sun beat upon these
verdant fields. Long past the outskirts of Geneva it struck
her that she'd reentered a museum—of European culture and
of memories from her past. As the wheels of her carriage

creaked, she recalled exchanges with disillusioned Europeans who'd complained of living in the Maghreb so far from opera, theater, concerts, museums. *They missed the whole point of North Africa,* she thought; *it is a place to escape the embalmed culture of Europe, to learn to live on a sensual plane.*

Traveling the road that day to Meyrin was reverse to her escape of 1897. The closer she drew to the pleasant little town, the more she felt stifled by its charm. Each chalet, each wall, each tree was familiar—she had often walked this way returning from the freedom of Geneva to the prison of Villa Neuve. Her body tensed; what vileness now lay beyond the moat?

She dismounted, waited for her carriage to go on, then stood alone on the silent road and stared through the gate. The magnificent garden was in ruins. The lawns and paths were confused, the flower beds had gone to seed, and the lattices of bougainvillea were twisted now and overgrown. No one had cleared away the undergrowth or broken up the earth—that ritual of her childhood's springs. The gate had not been painted, and when she entered she heard its hinges grinding rust. Even the little wooden bridge across the moat of darting trout was rotten with decay. *Faisandé,* she thought, as she wandered toward the house—the garden in its unattended state reminded her of half-putrescent rabbits hanging in Tunisian souks.

The villa was just as she'd remembered—its proportions perfect and grand. It had a look of deadness, though—all but a few shutters on the upper floor were closed. She sat on the front steps and waited for Augustin. It was here they'd embraced that mad night he'd fled three and a half years before.

He appeared a while later with baskets of groceries. She searched his face, found little left of his youth and fire. Their reunion was casual, almost embarrassed. She'd expected they'd run to each other's arms, but some new diffidence held them back. After a few exchanges of news, including the fact that Vava had been upstairs all this time and was actually on the verge of death, Augustin burst into a long harangue about shortages of cash, astronomical loans, difficulties settling Old Nathalie's estate and problems that would confuse the sale of Villa Neuve which they must commence, he told her brusquely, the moment Vava died. She felt as though she were talking to a small-time *commerçant*, not sitting with a dear lost brother amidst the ruins of their youth. During all his talk of money, litigations, wills, she asked herself why she felt no wish to smear kisses about his face.

". . . thank God," he was saying, "for Monsieur Samuel of Vernier. Without him Vava would have starved long ago. I talked to him this morning and he has agreed to loan us whatever we need to get by, even to handle our affairs here, and show the house. It seems Vava's been dependent on his loans for more than a year."

He stopped suddenly, saw the disappointment in her eyes.

"You know," he said, chuckling, "it's a good thing I didn't come to meet your train—I'd never have recognized you."

She smiled a little; he was beginning to sound like himself.

"Strange to have a reunion here," he said. "With the old man dying, and the garden in a ruin, and Mama and Vladimir and Nicolas gone. It depresses me enormously. I can't wait to leave this place for good."

Suddenly he took her hand, held it tight, brought it to his lips.

"I don't know what's the matter with me. I feel strange here. The night I left I thought I'd never come back. And I feel strange with you, too—as if I've disappointed you terribly. I realize, of course, that I'm sounding like an ass."

"No," she said, "you're just being Augustin. And that will always be fine with me."

At last an embrace. "I didn't come to meet you—well, it was on purpose. I was afraid."

"Why?"

"Of you, your being so grown up. And you are, you know. You're even bigger now. Your shoulders are—magnificent. I could tell by your letters that you'd grown. In each one I could sense it, a step, a leap almost—that your life was changing fast, that you were gaining so much experience, becoming a woman. I knew it would happen once you got away—that you'd be bigger than me—that you'd look at me and find me petty and ridiculous. . . ."

He turned to her, beaming through his tears. She smiled back as if he were an errant son.

They talked awhile longer, and when it was dark and time to go inside, she knew he was not the same brother she'd always adored. He'd changed, and, it seemed to her, for the worse.

Even as they mounted the stairs, she could hear Vava's wheezing cough. From the doorway of his room she saw a shrunken old man lost in a huge bed. His eyes were still ferocious, though hair and beard had lost their gloss. But of all the changes the one that frightened her the most was the weakness of his voice. He had cancer of the throat and could no longer bellow. Gone forever was that deep bass growl that was so essential to his vigor. Now he spoke in a grizzly whisper that, when she heard it, made her shrink with chill.

"I don't give a goddamn for anything anymore," he croaked. "I've wasted my life on stupid things. You children —learn a lesson from a ruined old man: it's better to die young than to live to an old age supported by a grand obsession."

"Vava, don't talk like that! You're looking for pity and that's contemptible."

She was surprised at her own harshness, but realized at once that she'd been right. His eyes glowed, first with fury, then with pride.

"Isabelle, Isabelle—as usual it's you who understand.

You're right, child. Now go away, both of you—I want to sleep."

He held on for two weeks more, but the pain was terrible and he could only find relief with increasing dosages of chloral hydrate. Sometimes, in order not to shriek, which he refused to do out of pride and also because the effort even further inflamed the torment in his throat, he'd distract himself by muttering the old obscenities against the Church, or whispering searing epithets against all his enemies, those evil corrupt people who'd tried to thwart him at every turn. But his greatest rage was reserved for Young Nathalie, whom he accused of breaking Old Nathalie's heart, and for Nicolas, who, he was convinced, had martyred Vladimir, and whom he held responsible for the torture that had made that sad, beloved boy lose his mind.

Isabelle and Augustin stood on either side of the bed and listened as he railed on; it seemed only just that this strange, vicious, maniacal man who had formed their youths should have an audience as he slipped away. It occurred to Isabelle as she stared down at his tortured face, all creased by years of drunkenness and rancor, that if it weren't for him she'd have been brought up to wear dresses and petticoats, to make dainty small talk and serve elegant tea. *Thank God*, she thought, *for the devil that possessed him; without it I'd now be everything I despise.*

Even if most of what he'd done in his long and grievous life had been informed by hate, the real motive was probably some twisted kind of love. Even the wretched incident with the Christmas tree—he had probably meant less to hurt her mother than to cry out with terror at having to live with a loss of faith. And for all his pounding on the table, all the flasks of vodka he'd flung against the walls, his vile epithets against religion, she'd emerged with a deep and unshakable faith that God was great and had willed her future and that to what had been written she would happily submit. *I was destined*, she thought, *to find Islam, even after he tried for twenty years to beat out of me any longing for belief.* She forgave him then, at the very moment that in his phantom wheezing voice he began again to cough out oaths.

On May 15, he could stand it no longer. He begged them to help him put an end to his pain. They did not quarrel with him; no false sentiment told them to resist. Together they prepared him a mortal dose of chloral hydrate, and by sunset he was dead after a painless sleep.

He left them everything, but even in his will he referred to Isabelle simply as the daughter of Nathalie De Moerder. Was it out of malice that he withheld recognition, even at the end? She didn't think so. Probably some obscure principle was involved—perhaps it was part of some compact with her mother, and, perhaps, too, some other man had been responsible for her birth. It didn't matter—Vava had been her father in everything but name—and, she decided, he'd wanted to spare her the sentimental tears he so abhorred. She chose to think this anyway, and when she read a special letter of instructions that accompanied the will, she grinned in the same admiring way she'd done at Bône when he'd ordered her to shoot herself or jump from the terrace wall.

"There should be no ridiculous expenditures," he wrote, "charged to the estate on account of my demise. The simplest pine wood coffin will do perfectly well, and everything should be managed so that the whole affair is cut-rate. For example, my body can be taken to the cemetery in a fourth-class hearse. . . ."

She and Augustin began at once to look for ways to liquidate the estate. They advertised the villa for sale, but within a month a representative of the Russian legation arrived with members of the Swiss police. They sealed up the house, informing the heirs that Trophimovsky's will was now in contest. He had a wife and children still alive in Russia, and still resentful at his desertion thirty years before. They'd learned of his death and wanted the property for themselves.

Samuel, the notary from Vernier who had lent so much to Vava in the preceding year, promised to handle the legal aspects of the case, since both Isabelle and Augustin were anxious to go away. They gave him power of attorney and received in turn a thousand francs apiece, enough for Isabelle to get back to Tunis and live awhile until a settlement could be arranged.

She spent her last day in the garden, exhilarated by its wild state. All the neat rows had given way to chaos, indigenous plants were crowding out the tropical exotics, and it was clear that within a year all of Vava's work would be permanently destroyed.

It seemed to her that in its ruin the garden at last had come alive. Nature was reestablishing its order, more real, more beautiful than the compelled order of Vava's deranged mind. And just as the garden at last was free to become itself, so now, she felt, was she.

There was nothing to hold her anymore—no obligations, no sense of guilt to keep her from the life she craved. Physically she'd escaped two years before. Now, with the ruin of her family—the deaths of her mother, Vladimir and Trophimovsky, the disappearances of Nicolas and Young Nathalie, the shriveling up of Augustin—her bondage was broken, and she was free.

There was a trip she'd been planning for over a year. She would make it now, into the Sahara, across the sand.

Part Two

If the strangeness
of my life were the result of snob-
bishness or posing then people
could say: "Yes, she got what she
deserved." But no one has ever
lived more from day to day or
more by chance than I. It's been an
inexorable chain of events that has
brought me to where I am—not
anything I did myself.

Mes Journaliers,
February 9, 1901

The Dunes

On the morning of July 8, 1899, Isabelle Eberhardt, dressed as a young Arab male, made her way to the railway station at Place Mongi Bali in Tunis and boarded a rickety passenger car attached to a troop train bound for Constantine. For hours she stared out the windows, oblivious to the people who moved in and out of her compartment. Sometimes she fastened her eyes onto a hut or a horse or the mosque of a distant town, but mostly she focused on a single spot on the glass, letting the passing countryside blur before her eyes.

She spent two days like this, sometimes slipping into sleep, eating fruit and bread she bought in half somnambulant states from vendors who herded each time the train stopped. At Constantine, where she had to wait two hours for a connection, the station smelled of the smoke of coal. She went to a café outside, drank cup after cup of coffee, furiously smoked cigarettes, and allowed a boy to shine her red leather boots.

The train for Batna did not leave until dark. The seats in the first-class compartment were covered with stained brown velvet, and the kerosene lamps, which hung from a wire, coated the ceiling near their smokestacks with a carbon crust. Every once in a while the train would stop in the middle of nowhere, and she would hear cries, the banging of hammers against the track, and see men walking outside swinging lanterns from their arms.

The next morning she boarded a coach bound for the oasis of Biskra, and began to scribble impressions in her notebook. She arrived late in the afternoon, checked into the Hotel Caid, then went to the Arab Bureau where she requested an interview with the commandant of the region.

When, finally, she was shown into his office, Lieutenant Colonel Fridel met her with a cold and curious stare.

"I have no intention," he said, "of dealing with a servant. If Mademoiselle Eberhardt is serious about wanting to travel farther south, she will have to appear here herself."

"But I *am* Mademoiselle Eberhardt!"

"*You* are Mademoiselle Eberhardt?"

She nodded, and when some younger officers in the room began to laugh, Fridel glared about.

"Mademoiselle," he said, "I assume you have your reasons for appearing here in such repulsive garb. I won't ask you what they are. I am sure that no amount of explanation will ever make them explicable to me. But I *must* have an explanation of your request to travel. This area, as you know, is a military zone."

"I'm a writer, making a study of the local customs."

"A good pretext for a Methodist!"

She squinted with curiosity.

"What?"

"One of those spying missionaries. One of those goddamn British troublemakers . . ."

"Colonel, I'm Russian. Look at my papers. And I happen to be Moslem, too."

The officers exchanged glances, but Fridel did not seem to hear.

"Can't stand Methodists—going to get rid of them all."

His face, now, was creased with rage. He snorted his words and pounded his fist upon the desk.

"This is absurd."

He stared at her quizzically.

"You're not a spy, you say?"

"Absolutely not."

"Very well. I'll consider your request. But, so help me, if I catch one whiff you've been making trouble, if you dare preach one particle of a sermon, then, young lady, you'll be sent back in irons to Constantine with an escort of my most rapacious legionnaires!"

More laughter from the officers as Fridel thumped his desk. Isabelle was dismissed.

An hour later at her hotel a boy told her there was a French officer waiting downstairs. She spotted him immediately—one of the captains who'd been lounging around Fridel's office at the end of the day—blond, proud, with a well-trimmed, haughty moustache, and narrow, hooded, demonic eyes.

When he saw her he snapped his heels.

"Édouard De Susbielle," he said. "The colonel has signed your permit."

He handed her a paper bearing an angry slashing signature and a red stamp.

"Thank you."

"Not at all, Mademoiselle. And please forgive the colonel. Few European ladies come to these parts. The old man has forgotten how to act with a woman of quality."

"Your function, I gather, is to make his apologies."

"It seemed an appropriate mission."

She didn't like him very much as he stood there eyeing

her, and was wondering how to get rid of him when he grinned again.

"Have you eaten?"

She shook her head.

"Would you care to dine with me?"

"All right."

They moved into the dining room of the hotel.

There came a point during dinner when she was not so certain about her dislike. He treated her with deference, asked her all sorts of questions about the latest happenings in Europe and confessed that it had been almost a year since he'd dined with a European woman alone. She intrigued him, he told her—there was something forceful in her personality, something adventurous that he could respect.

"My first impression," he said, "was that you were foolish to present yourself in Arab clothes. But I liked the way you stood up to the colonel. He's insane about Methodists, and became rather insulting toward the end."

She waved her hand with scorn.

"I know all about his sort. I've been corresponding for years with a captain who's served here a long time."

"Really? Perhaps I know him. What's his name?"

She was about to say "Eugène Letord" when she stopped herself and smiled.

"The letters were confidential."

"Of course. But you must understand that there are basically two types of officers: the ones who do their duty and represent France in the proper way, and the sniveling ones who fall all over the Arabs, fraternize, even take them as wives."

"I prefer the sniveling ones."

He bowed his head. "*Bien touché.*"

He tried various other tactics during the meal, was clearly bent on her seduction. But there was such a divergence of views that no matter in which direction he thrust he could not get close to her heart. Finally he threw up his hands.

"I like you. You're obviously an intelligent woman, and you know who you are, which is more than I can say for most members of your sex."

He twisted a bit in his seat, watching her closely, hoping his compliment might crack her hard defense. But she thought him sly, and was about to tell him so when he struck again.

"I'd like to help you. I'm leading a convoy tomorrow to Touggourt. If you're interested you could ride along. You'd be under my protection, of course. All I ask in return is that you dine with me each evening on the road, so that we can further express our disagreements and continue this evening's stimulating dialogue."

Suddenly she was won. Touggourt! When she'd started from Tunis she'd harbored a vague plan to go as far as Ouargla. But already it was clear she'd miscalculated about the time of year. It was madness to travel the Sahara in July. August would be even hotter, more brutal. She'd come on a hope that she'd somehow fall into something, find some situation where she could fit. Who could have guessed that this stiff and pompous young man, who represented everything she loathed, would take an interest in her, find her notions "stimulating," desire her company?

At least, she thought, *he's true to his type, and, no matter how tiresome, will lead me two hundred fifty kilometers deeper into the sand.*

Back in the lobby he kissed her hand. She found the gesture amusing though somewhat repulsive. His convoy would leave at sunset the following day. She assured him she would be there with a horse.

The moment De Susbielle was gone she felt relief. She couldn't bear the idea of arriving at a new place, dealing with officials, staying inside her hotel. She must explore, walk the streets, seek out a dark café from which she could observe the life of the oasis. Outside was Biskra. She must feel it, smell it, learn its sounds. She returned to her room to fetch her burnoose, then properly hooded and draped she stepped outside.

The summer moon shined brightly upon the cracked mud walls. Flute music burst from doorways as she made her way across the old quarter filled with people of all the races of the Sahara—Tuaregs, Mozabites, Negroes, Sudanese. The district of the Ouled-Naïls—that strange mountain tribe that sends adolescents of both sexes into prostitution before marriage—gave off an aroma of erotic power. Youths, their bodies supple and fresh, hovered in doorways, silhouettes against fires. As she strode leisurely through this great open-air love market, she felt their eyes upon her, burning, boring, trying to divert her from her path. The girls, bejeweled with silver earrings that dangled to their shoulders, and elaborate necklaces of heavy engraved silver triangles alternating with egg-sized amber beads, tried to lure her to them by rattling the bracelets on their arms.

Finally—a café, one sufficiently dark and secretive from which to observe this Saharan scene. She sat down with two young men, exchanged the usual Moslem greetings:

"Good evening."

"Thanks be to God."

"The night is good."

"God be praised!"

She introduced herself as "Si Mahmoud," a young Tunisian traveling the oases of the Sahara, visiting sacred tombs and monasteries to meet holy men and learn their wisdom. The young men, in turn, introduced themselves as brothers, Saleh and Bou Saadi Chlely Ben Amar, commercial traders, kif dealers and lovers of all women.

As they talked Isabelle could not help but notice the various transactions taking place around. A majestic Negro in snow-white burnoose with tribal scars on his cheeks purchased the services of a tiny light-skinned Berber girl; a blond legionnaire with Germanic features made arrangements with a curly-headed Arab boy. And so it went, people drifting in, taking stock of whomever they had found on the street, creating a relationship over a glass of tea, sealing a bargain over a shared cigarette.

She was fascinated by the tales of the Amars, their experiences in the dunes, their stories of various dangers encountered upon the sands at night. But when she chanced to mention that she had met Captain De Susbielle and was joining his column for Touggourt the following day, their faces fell, and they began to tell her of his terrible misdeeds.

"Once," said Saleh, "he struck a holy man, a Marabout, who refused to yield him a right-of-way."

"I heard," said Bou Saadi, "that he let his soldiers rape the fiancée of the sheik of Ouled Djellal."

"He spits into mosques!"

"He once kicked a sick woman near Sidi Rached!"

"He's rubbish," said Saleh, "the worst of all the French. To travel with such an infidel is to defile God."

They both stared at her, and she knew then what she had to do.

"Oh, my brothers," she said, "thank you for saving me from an ordeal. I cannot travel with this man now that I have learned the truth!"

Bou Saadi handed her his kif pipe, to signify their shared sense of outrage and hate.

"Have no fear, Si Mahmoud," he said. "God willing we will ride to Touggourt ourselves in several days, and you shall ride there with *us*."

Late the next morning Isabelle went to the Arab Bureau to tell Captain De Susbielle she would not be joining his convoy. She had just received an urgent telegram from home, she said, and would have to delay her departure for several days. The captain was disappointed, but took his disappointment in a gentlemanly way. He would wait for her at the post at Chegga—he had business there and could not imagine completing the full trip without her good company.

Relieved to be rid of him—an obvious hindrance if she was to gain the confidence of the Arab population, and a bore besides—she spent the day exploring the groves of Biskra, intricate gardens crisscrossed by little streams, tiny patches of vegetables fringed by date-bearing palms rustling in the desert breeze.

That evening she rejoined the Amar brothers at the Chéoui Café, and so spent the next few days until at 2:00 A.M. on the morning of July 18, she and the brothers began the trek.

They were in Bordj-Saâda by nine the same morning, and even at so early an hour she was impressed by the fury of the sun. It beat down with a menace she could hardly believe, scorched her hands, baked her face. At the tiny settlement she and her companions joined a group of Chaouiya tribesmen in a game of cards. Then at dusk they were off for Chegga which they reached, fortunately, before the rising of the sun. She drank coffee there with a group of legionnaires, was pleased to learn that De Susbielle had left the night before, and departed with Saleh and Bou Saadi for the oasis of Bir-Sthil.

By this time (and she had eaten nothing but bread since leaving Biskra, was already beginning to run a fever and to suffer from unquenchable thirst) they had entered a region of dunes. She split off from the Amars, charged out upon her horse, drove the beast to step through ripples of sand, laughed as the wind lashed at her face. Sometimes the air was like a wall, and as she charged against it, eyes squinting, hood tied closely under her chin, cloth wrapped over her nose and mouth as protection from blisters and cracking by the sun, she felt a mad joy, a strange otherworldliness in which fantasies and sensations blurred and merged. Then, for the first time since Vava's death, she felt she was alive.

There was a great splendor about the desert—deathliness, barrenness—that seemed to intensify the experience of being upon it. It made her wish, time and again, to be out of sight of her companions, to be the only live thing in this utterly lifeless place. And her feverishness, too, added to her exaltation. Glowing from the heat without and the burning within, she felt as though she were on fire, a moving, rushing flame, an incandescent blinding torch shooting across the sand the way a comet shoots across the sky.

She charged forward with one arm extended to cleave the wall of sand and wind. She pranced, she plowed, she dashed, she tore. The friction between herself and the sparkling air gave off currents that coursed through her body, sent shooting throbs down from her head to her heels and back up again, until it seemed she could feel energy surge out through the root of every hair. She was real, but the landscape she rode in was not, and her intoxication grew until at times she felt she might annihilate herself, that the faster she galloped, the more furiously she charged, the more likely she was to reach a point where she would blend with the wind, the sun, the sand, and disappear.

Yes, she thought, as her head reeled with this madness, *I might be here one moment and gone the next.* And dwelling upon so magical a notion, she was moved and felt the tragic aura of the desert, the intense, dry, hot song of sorrow sung by its lonely burning sands.

Finally, when her exhilaration gave way to exhaustion, and fever made her so dizzy she feared she could no longer maintain her mount, she reined in, climbed off and shrouded herself in her burnoose. She flung herself down and curled up in the shadow of her horse, pulled her hands inside her woolen cuffs and rested, dreamed, slept. The Amars found her, then, moistened her lips with water from their goatskin bags, and when she was revived, they helped her remount and led her forward between them like a wandering stray they must protect.

They were not dismayed by the strange mad fury of her forays. On the contrary, they were intrigued by them, in-

credulous at her energy, filled with awe. Her evident joy in
this wasteland, in the face of this hard and indifferent mani-
festation of God, drew their sympathy, for to them oases
were merely tiny stars set in the vast firmament of a great
sad emptiness, the desert which was the world. And on this
sand man could make no mark—it was the ether through
which he traveled and suffered, and by suffering came to
know himself.

They cared for Isabelle, huddled with her in the evening,
gave her warmth through the chattering chills of Saharan
nights, shared bread with her, taught her how to ride the
dunes, how to save her water, how to camp in the crevices,
cushion her saddle for a pillow, wrap herself up against
scorpions and wind. And even as they nursed her, calmed
her fevers, applied their mother's salves to her desiccated
lips, she quoted them verses of the Koran, and joined them
as they improvised desert poems. She sealed their comrade-
ship with the cachet of her love for the desert, her exultant
pleasure in its radiant pain.

They did not reach Bir-Sthil until 11:00 A.M., and by then
the sun was in a rage. They left again at nine in the evening,
joining up with a caravan of Chaamba tribesmen resting by
a telegraph pole a little beyond the post.

By 1:00 A.M., fascinated by the strange blue glow of the
dunes, she dashed off from the column to ride alone in sand
that was phosphorescent and sparkled strangely beneath the
moon. She strayed to the west of the track and was soon
wandering dazed and lost near the glistening wastes of a dry
salt lake. She was frightened but wise enough to dismount
and lead her horse on foot. Soon Saleh and Bou Saadi found
her and led her back to the caravan route and into M'Raier
before the dawn. She resolved, upon seeing the oasis, that
she would buy a good compass as soon as she got to Touggourt.

They were off again when it was dark, and soon met up

with a pair of nomads traveling under the armed escort of a huge black horseman, heading for a place near Ourlana where they were to be executed for unspeakable crimes. She and the Amars shared bread with the "condemned ones" who struck her as inexplicably resigned. When they broke away again to rejoin the Chaamba column, Saleh rode by her side.

"Will they really be killed?" she asked him.

He shook his head.

"Probably not, since their crime was committed against a deceiving woman—the sister of one, the wife of the other."

"But what, exactly, did they do?"

"Oh," said Saleh with a grin, "first they mutilated her, then they carved her up. A perfectly justifiable crime, Si Mahmoud, since her deceptions had put them into a frenzy of rage."

Isabelle was fascinated, wanted to ride back and gather material for a story. But it was nine in the morning, the first well of Ourlana was in sight and her need for water, then, was stronger than literature's call.

She rested all day in the Chaamba camp, her head burning, her hunger relieved by bread spread with honey, her thirst by a thick buttermilk she could barely get down. She dragged herself up at sunset, watched incredulously as the Chaambas spent an hour searching by torch for the only good well on the route to Moghar, then spent another hour watering their horses and filling their goatskin bags. By two that morning she felt dizzy and sick. The Amars broke off from the column, made a fire of camel dung on the freezing sand and then comforted her with stories of ghosts who resided in the dunes.

In the morning she was awakened by a terrible bang— Saleh used a pistol to light his cigarette.

They were doubled over with laughter as they rounded up the horses. Then they raced as fast as they could to the oasis of Moghar, barely succeeding in beating out the first broiling flares of the sun.

From there it was a short ride to Touggourt. They departed an hour before sunset and she was in bed before light in the best hotel she could find.

It was difficult for her to part from the Amars, who had decided to continue south. They recognized that she was too sick to go on, but swore everlasting friendship at the gates of the town, saying they would meet again if God willed.

As she left them she knew she had made the proper choice—it was far better to travel with Berbers, who accepted her as she presented herself, than with a French officer who could think of nothing but her seduction, disgusted her with false charm and had nothing to say that was true.

She slept through the day, ate her first decent meal since Biskra, spent the evening making notes on her adventures and her intoxication with desert life. She slept well again but was awakened early in the morning by an Arab courier bearing an official note. Her presence was demanded at once at the offices of the Arab Bureau. The order was signed by the acting commandant, Captain Édouard De Susbielle.

When she came in he did not stand up, but glowered at her from behind his desk. He didn't say a word until his orderly withdrew. Then came the onslaught.

"How *dare* you!"

"How *dare* I what?"

"Do you take me for a *fool?*"

"No, of course . . ."

"Do you think you can treat *me* like a buffoon? Do you think you can ridicule an officer of *France?* We shall see about *that!*"

"What on earth have I done?"

"*Done?* You haven't done anything, unless you think lying to a regional commander means nothing at all. I don't give a damn, of course, but the bloody rest of it is something else."

"Just a minute, Captain De Susbielle. Don't talk to me of lying. I changed my mind about traveling with you and gave you a respectable excuse. My conscience is clear, and I won't have you screaming at me as if I were a delinquent groom."

He glared at her.

"I offered myself as an escort. You spurned my aid, and then spat in my face, taking the same journey down the same route in the company of Arab scum."

"The Amars are my friends!"

"Ha!"

"You can't talk to me like this . . ."

"I most certainly *can*. I'm in charge here. And you're an illegal traveler. I want you out in twenty-four hours, and frankly, Mademoiselle, this time I don't give a damn how you go."

"I shall go on to Ouargla."

"Permission denied!"

"Why?"

"It's a military zone, there's fighting on the track, and you're suspected of being a spy."

"This is a joke!"

"Decidedly not, Mademoiselle. Not a joke at all."

"A spy?" She started to laugh.

"Why not? You identify yourself as a woman, a Russian subject, then travel about dressed like a man, speaking Arabic with people whose loyalties are highly suspect. As the responsible officer here I can't take a chance. I'm being lenient—considering the circumstances."

"What circumstances?"

"*Those I have just stated!* Fact is that Fridel never wanted to give you a permit, and it was only at my intercession that he did."

Isabelle stood up, pulled out a cigarette, lit it, inhaled

deeply, then blew the smoke toward De Susbielle's face.

"I've never heard such rubbish in my life," she said, approaching his desk, staring him in the eye.

"Tell me, Captain De Susbielle, is this a sample of the manners they teach at Saint-Cyr?"

Her eyes bored into him; her voice withered him with scorn.

"As you've been told, Mademoiselle, the Sud-Constantine is not a region for tourists. The officers here are not required to give strangers a courteous reception."

"I have a permit signed and sealed, and you know perfectly well I'm not a spy. Now that I'm here, that I got here on my own, perfectly safely, perfectly fit, you're trying to stop me from doing what I came to do, which is harmless as you perfectly well know. Isn't that the situation right now?"

He stared at her, silent, unadulterated contempt showing in his narrow eyes.

"Since you don't answer, I take it you agree. All right. If you say I must leave Touggourt, then doubtless you have the power to make me leave. But you tell me I can't go on to Ouargla, and since I haven't the slightest intention of going backward, there's the question of just where I should proceed from here."

"Where you go, I assure you, is not of the slightest consequence to me."

"Susbielle," she said, exhaling smoke again, turning away, her voice heavy with boredom and contempt, "you are a very tiresome young man."

She sat in a leather chair at the far end of the room, crossed one leg over the other, leaned back, stared at the dull gray ceiling and thought that she would rather spend a hundred years as a Berber peasant hauling twigs all day long on her back than five minutes in De Susbielle's tanned blond arms.

"You are entitled to your opinion, of course."

"Yes," she said. "Of course."

They sat for a while in cold silence, he thinking of some way to regain his injured dignity, she wondering if she'd left him enough room for maneuver without losing face.

She needed to be allowed a few more days in Touggourt so that she could recover her health and look around. But she wanted much more than that—the freedom to travel farther into the sand, to go to at least one of the fabled places where no other writer had been.

Her eyes fell upon a large military map of the Sud-Constantine. She began to calculate the alternatives since she doubted he could retract his prohibition against her continuing south. There seemed only one solution, and as she squinted to read the name of the place that lay to the east between Touggourt and the Tunisian frontier, she noticed him doing the same.

There was a cluster of oases probably no more than four days' march away. The main town was called El Oued, the region was called the Souf. He was staring at the same spot with resignation, she with a beating heart. For at that moment, for some reason she could not divine and would never really be able to explain, she felt an ineffable call, an overwhelming desire to travel there and explore. She must conceal it; she knew her plans would be doomed by the slightest show of enthusiasm. She glanced back at De Susbielle. He was playing with his tongue inside his mouth.

"I think it would be better for us if we'd forget all this unpleasantness," she said.

"I agree. It's been most unfortunate."

"And inopportune."

"Precisely. Inopportune."

"We're busy people. We don't have time for personal rancor."

"Mademoiselle," he said with a smile, "at last we are beginning to agree."

"Then I beg you to be reasonable. I can't possibly be out of here in twenty-four hours."

"Hmmm. Yes. I see your point. Well, then, let me see—three days—I think that would be a reasonable time."

"Most generous of you. And Ouargla? You will let me go there?"

"No." He shook his head. "Ouargla is out of the question."

"Then—?"

"Yes, well, let's see. There's nothing to the west, except Ghardaïa, and to get there you'd have to pass through Ouargla, too. No, I think your best bet is to the east. El Oued. I haven't been there myself, but I hear it's most interesting from the touristic point of view."

She shrugged.

"I suppose, if that's my only choice, I shall have to be resigned. Could you supply a guide?"

"No problem."

She stood up. "Thank you, Captain. I'm sorry to have troubled you so early in the morning."

"No need to apologize, Mademoiselle. It's my duty to assist."

Isabelle turned and, without a backward glance, walked out the office door.

She spent her days in Touggourt sleeping through the heat, writing in the afternoons and at sunset descending into the town, wandering the narrow alleys filled with sand. She searched out strange dark cafés, sat in them through the night, drinking, smoking, talking with other travelers. Then at dawn she'd wander to the main square where the caravans encamped.

Here men slept by brush fires, while others stood on guard and still others sang songs in soothing guttural whispers while exhausted Ouled dancers performed in slow undulating arabesques. At the cries of the muezzin from the minaret, men would rise from their blankets, and she would face Mecca with them and pray.

Then she'd return to her hotel to sleep as best she could, passing in and out of agonizing fevers that gave her the impression they were making her clean, were burning away all the encrustations of her upbringing that had corroded her for too long.

On July 30, at four in the afternoon, she departed for El Oued. Her guide, a black postman named Amrou, led her through the broken stones of ruined forts. Her fever that day was worse than ever, but she was determined to make the trip, not only to meet the deadline set by De Susbielle, but also to heed the strange haunting music she felt calling her to the east.

By sunset they reached the first dunes, magnificent brooding mounds of sand bathed in golden light. And when she turned she saw all of Touggourt spread out against the yellow sky.

By two o'clock that morning her fever was worse and she fell from her horse onto the sand. Amrou led her as far as Mthil, where she rested the entire day, grilling like a piece of meat.

On August 1, traditionally the hottest day of the Saharan year, she left with a new guide to cross a vast desert of great dunes marked by the wind into intricate ripples and parched rivulets. They arrived at dawn at Ourmès, where she lounged by a fountain in the garden of the sheik.

On the third day of August she left at five in the morning. It was possible for her to travel during daylight then, for she was in the immense complex of sunken groves that make up the inhabited region of the Souf. At four in the afternoon she stopped to drink at the wells of Kouïnine, and just at sunset, surmounting a vast high dune, laid her eyes for the first time upon El Oued.

She paused at the crest to stare down at the legendary city of a thousand domes. She was to its west, and at that moment its shimmering walls, its fantastic clustering of white domes and arches and vaults were lit up with such intensity by the setting sun that she was convinced she'd finally reached a place beyond compare. As she rode down, seeking refuge in the shadow of her horse, her fever subsided and was replaced by joy at having come so far, at having finally finished so hard and tortuous a journey across such an immensity of sinking dunes.

And so she rode down to El Oued, her shadow growing longer as the sun sank farther down, deciding, as she noted later in her journal, that her first vision of the place was the most complete and definitive revelation of the harsh and splendid Souf, so strangely beautiful, so agonizingly sad. And as she entered the town, her nostrils pulsed at the cool sweet smell of gardens which flourished behind walls that lined the sand-filled streets.

To her, coming out of the vast silent emptiness of the west, El Oued was an island of riches, a holy place of cool. She dismounted in the great market square, walked to a stand, bought a cup of water from a vendor and two handfuls of fruit. Then she settled down delicately on the sandy floor with other travelers, men of caravans and of the groves that ringed the town, to gorge herself on the soft rich flesh of dates.

She thought for a while of her adventure, the long trek that had begun at the railroad station in Tunis less than a month before, the exhausting journey and the encounters with De Susbielle which seemed to sum up for her all the insufficiencies of the civilized world. She'd finally reached the place she'd always sought, a different world, strange, mysterious, full of possibilities, where there lay perhaps a destiny that would change her life.

But how odd to feel this, sitting on alien sand, cloaked like a man, among people of ancient races, before strange domed temples built for the worship of a God who had written the adventure she'd just endured.

Mektoub—it has been written that I come here. And

thinking that, she smiled, wrapped herself in her robe and fell into a deep calm sleep.

Though feverish, she could not keep still. She spent the next days exploring the sandy streets of El Oued, then the sunken groves and endless dunes around. She was ravished by the way the light glittered on the sand, and by the faces of the Berbers peering from their encampments outside the town—black cloth tents, elegant pavilions.

El Oued, she became convinced, was the home she'd been seeking since she'd been a child. She had fled the garden of Villa Neuve in search of passes between the mountains that walled her in. Now at last, in the center of this vast Saharan emptiness, she'd found a place where she could feel free.

But there was confusion in her mind. What was she doing, twenty-two years old, alone in the world, pretending to be a man? Was this merely disguise or real transformation? Was she Isabelle or "Si Mahmoud"?

The question taunted her as much as the splendor of the dunes gave her peace. She knew why she wore men's clothes and called herself by a male name. It was the only way she could travel in this world she'd chosen to explore. But there was more—she was grasping for something deeper, a way to turn her disguise inward, remake herself from inside.

It was not, she decided, that she wanted to become a man, but that she wanted to *live* like one.

That, she thought, was the key. She was a woman, liked being a woman, would never try and renounce that fact. But she would embellish what it meant to be a woman by re-creating herself as something completely new.

No longer would she allow others to view her as a precious thing whose favors were coquettishly withheld until a seducer could charm them out. That, she knew, had been her problem with De Susbielle—after she'd rejected his hypocritical gallantry, nothing was possible, friendship least of all. No more infatuations, she decided, no more Archivirs. *I shall be Si Mahmoud, without explanation, and men will simply have to deal with that.*

There was forged within her, then, a wish to do battle with men, to win and stifle them with her being, give them experiences they could neither imagine nor forget. Or else, if they were strong enough, could accept her as "Si Mahmoud," a woman who could do anything they could do, who could savor physical adventures and the dangers of the road, then she would become their lovers and their brothers, both at the same time.

"Si Mahmoud," she decided, would be a creature of the desert—as strange, as undulating as its mirages and its dunes, as free as its gazelles, as open as its cloudless skies. And as for love she would accept any embrace, fraternal, powerful, painful, as long as its sensation was intense.

Having settled at last the question of how she was going to live, she decided with regret that she must leave the Souf. Her fevers were too much to bear, and people she met told of others driven mad by the heat—incredible in the summer of 1899, even by Saharan standards. She knew she would have to leave, but, much more important, she knew she must come back.

There was a letter waiting in Tunis, unhappy news. She learned from Augustin that the litigation surrounding Villa Neuve had grown unbelievably complex, and that Samuel, the notary into whose hands they had placed their affairs, was trying to cheat them out of their share of Vava's estate.

Impossible for her to remain in Tunis—she had no money, and after the splendor of the dunes, her house near Bab Menara seemed artificial, pretentious, raffiné. She sold off her belongings, the few precious rugs she'd bought with money she'd obtained for Old Nathalie's jewels, liquidated everything but her notebooks, a trunk of robes and capes and her worn red boots, and left for Paris, a place as different from El Oued as there existed on the earth.

She went there with one objective: to seek backing as an explorer, an assignment to write about the Souf, anything at all that would finance a return to the desert, and her new life as "Si Mahmoud."

Where Literature Is Supreme

April 1900. Isabelle arrived in Paris, found lodgings at a cheap rooming house near the cemetery of Montparnasse, then made her way as quickly as she could to the grounds of the Great Exposition. On the Champs de Mars she wandered among Kymer pagodas and Tahitian totem poles, strolled through a Japanese garden and a perfect reproduction of the Seraglio of Constantinople, saw Persian sword dances, a puppet show from Java, a Hindu charming a cobra, and a Kabuki play. She passed through tents filled with wax effigies, dioramas, acrobats and elephants, and visited an exhibition of machinery made in the United States.

Lost after many hours she came upon a Tunisian souk constructed of papier-mâché. Here workmen pounded out brass trays in stalls, veiled women prepared pastry leaves, and languorous camels sniffed at the air. Near sunset the crowds were pushed back so that a dozen Arab tribesmen could gallop on white horses across the grass, discharge their rifles, then rein back before trampling the gaping mob.

How marvelous, she thought, *to find a fantasia in Paris.* And then she thought: *how false!*

She stood in line for an hour, finally ascended to the first platform of the Eiffel Tower, and from there gazed down at the extraordinary scene below.

Paris glitters, she thought, *money flows in the streets, and literature is supreme. Here I shall make a success, take whatever I can get and disappear back into the dunes.*

Though the "City of Light" amazed her, it depressed her, too. Despite the wonders of its streets glowing with electricity, and the lavish displays in shops of all the things made by men from all the corners of the globe, despite the swirling mobs that pressed her on the boulevards, despite all of these things and a thousand things more, she became sad when she thought of the desert so far away. Then she longed for the solitude of empty sand, a night aglow with stars, the subtle sound of gently blowing wind, the warmth of a naked sun. Better, she thought, the fevers of that empty wilderness than the smugness of this city of a thousand dreams.

Her daytime walks back and forth across the Champs de Mars were followed by lengthy strolls at night. She would pass through the crowds that thronged the boulevards and mingle with the mobs outside the theater where Edmond Rostand's *Cyrano de Bergerac* had been playing for three years. Here desperate men fought for tickets to performances months away. She watched and scoffed at them for pursuing vicarious sensation because they were too cowardly to fling themselves into an adventurous life.

It was the vanity of Paris that struck her at these moments, the meaninglessness of all the efforts being expended on the gaining of wealth, the pursuit of power, the conquest of stunning lovers. She knew then that for her there would always be more satisfaction in beginning a long journey down an unknown road than in bringing this light-filled city to its knees.

Nevertheless she had come for a reason, and so set out on

a spring afternoon for the offices of the newspaper *La Fronde*, where she presented herself to its editor, the noted Dreyfusard, estimable friend of the trod-upon and oppressed, formidable heroine of European feminism, Séverine.

She was received in a small office cluttered with letters, manifestos, tracts. The walls were covered with drawings and cartoons which depicted the huge bosomed woman who bustled before her, a person with a classic Roman head surrounded by a halo of wild iron locks. Isabelle waited on a narrow sofa while this frowzy bull paced about issuing orders, scribbling her signature on scraps of paper and commanding an assistant, who appeared at her door like a jack-in-the-box, to "rip up this trash and write it again." Isabelle was amused until she caught sight of Séverine's eyes. Then she was stunned. They were slate-gray, and, when she squinted, they flashed fiercely like a pair of finely honed blades.

These eyes inspected her closely before the two settled down to talk.

"I approve of women who dress for comfort," she said, indicating Isabelle's trousers and blouse. "I'm only disappointed you didn't come to me in your desert robes."

"I've thought of wearing them," Isabelle replied, "if only to make a sensation. But with the Exposition, Paris is already too full of people in peculiar dress."

"Quite right, my pet. How very astute!"

She rifled through the papers that were piled on her desk, finally extracted a purple folder.

"I have read your desert sketches, and though I find them talented, I must tell you frankly they are of no possible use to me."

Isabelle lowered her eyes. For an instant she felt crushed. She'd worked hard her last weeks in Tunis, bringing her slender sheaf of writings to a high polish.

"Now you mustn't be hurt. You describe the terrain very

well, and the characters certainly come alive. But these are personal reflections, better perhaps for a volume of sensitive essays than a journal like mine that's engaged. My readers want to know about the scandals, the outrages, nepotism, corruption, who's taking the bribes. I need documentation of conditions in the prisons and the whole stinking Algerian mess."

She was excited now, pacing her small office, pounding her fist into her palm.

"If you can write about those things we can make a good arrangement."

The plump woman studied Isabelle again.

"You do cut quite a figure, my pet. I think it's especially daring that you don't wear scent."

Isabelle laughed.

"My father was in the business," she said, "so, naturally, I loathe perfume."

"How fascinating! And how Russian you look! Those Tartar eyes! I'm sure you'll have a great success in Paris."

"I have many letters. People are kind. But sometimes I feel lost in the salons."

"Ah, but you will catch on quickly to that little game. It's the 'real' Paris, of course. Not what happens in the streets— oh no!—but the talk and manners of a dozen drawing rooms. Unfortunately that's what's wrong with the 'real' Paris, and why I've decided to become the conscience of this cowardly town."

They talked on for a while, and Isabelle found herself intrigued by the quick wit and cunning irony of this impressive woman. As their interview ended, and she rose to leave, Séverine took her arm.

"Would you like to come on one of my weekends? A few close friends, good talk, country food."

She placed her fingers against Isabelle's ribs.

"Yes, my sweet—you could use some fattening up."

Grateful and touched, Isabelle accepted, even agreed to come in her burnoose.

She'd been busy since her arrival making calls. The secretary at the Société Géographique had been particularly kind, agreeing that her Saharan expedition entitled her to membership. But then he set her back when he told her the entrance fee was one hundred fifty francs.

She tried but failed to see the great explorers, Prince Roland, Count Leontieff, Prince Henri d'Orléans. And at the door of the residence of the Prince of Monaco she stood helpless before a footman who refused to accept her letter unless she could first present him with a card.

There was, however, one salon where she was politely received—the home of Maria Laetitia Bonaparte-Wyse, on the third story of a vast mansion on Boulevard Poissonnière.

This woman was known in Paris as "La Ratazzi," for though she was a grandniece of the emperor, she had been married to a minister of King Victor Emmanuel after turning down a match with Napoleon the Third. Now an old lady, deaf as a pot, she received in a series of boudoirs draped in blue satin, the walls and tables covered with Empire memorabilia which included everything from tattered Corsican handicrafts to gold plate bearing the imperial arms. She looked slightly Oriental, like an aging mustachioed Cleopatra wrapped in lacy garments, she was a poor shriveled old thing who welcomed absolutely everyone and thus had gained the reputation of running a "salon of junk."

Her visitors were not all undistinguished. The American, Isadora Duncan, who was then creating a sensation with her Grecian dances, came by several times. Maurice Ravel occasionally touched the keys of her piano. And a portly sad-eyed man with a pale complexion, who wandered in one day, was, Isabelle gathered from the whispers that greeted his entrance, none other than the infamous though failing Oscar Wilde.

Among the more scrofulous of the regulars was a young curly-headed poet who struck languid poses, wore powder on his face and edited the review *L'Hercule*. His name was Paul Durand and his magazine was a wastebasket for whatever refuse writers such as Daudet, Louÿs or Anatole France happened to have unpublished in the back drawers of their desks. It was a standing joke that he would pant at the merest mention of a baron, and would fawn before a duke. He would do anything for money, including sleeping with rich old ladies, but he never paid his contributors, and had a nasty habit of "borrowing" their writings and publishing them without consent.

Isabelle knew she was failing to make an impression until one day this creature presented her with a long-awaited chance. She overheard him describe her as a "Slavic hermaphrodite," and without thinking of the consequences marched up to him and emptied her coffee cup onto his lap.

He shrieked, stood up, called her an "awkward moose" and bellowed that he would send her a bill for the cleaning of his suit.

Suddenly the room became still. Everyone was waiting for her reply.

"It'll be the first time the stinking thing's been cleaned," she said, and turned her back.

At once she was surrounded, for such coarseness as she'd displayed was then in great repute. And since there were scores of writers chez Ratazzi, she reveled, for a while, in the literary life.

The Count and Countess de Triche pursued her. Fabrice de Triche, a facile journalist, had a swarthy complexion and the cruelest face Isabelle had ever seen. For years he had worked on a novel about his ancestors, but was more notorious for his rudeness than anything he ever wrote. His American wife, Clarissa, was an untalented poet, and bore the scars of nightly beatings at the count's vicious hands. She tried hard to win Isabelle's friendship, took her to lunch and confided that her husband, inspired by her example, wanted to change his name, too. Later, when Isabelle ventured the notion that he wanted to do this because he had come to loathe himself, both De Triches began to tell terrible lies about her and to turn their backs whenever she came close.

There was a Dutch journalist who wrote with great concern about Great Social Issues, but who could speak of nothing but treacherous servants, false friends and the expenses of constructing his house. Isabelle preferred him to his companion, a simpering, balding creature whose specialty was the literary crucifixion. This man would pretend to be kind in order to entice people to reveal their inner miseries, and then would skewer them in ironic short stories in which they would appear as fools, and he, the literary bystander, would be depicted as compassionate and wise. She learned wariness from these two and also an important truth: that some men who love men despise women more than anything else.

These regulars and the many other writers who dropped in at La Ratazzi's caused her finally to be disillusioned by the literary life. They were competitive, vicious, malicious toward one another and had nothing in common with her ideals. Writers, she learned, were likely to have ugly souls, the degree of ugliness often in direct proportion to the beauty of the prose. They were as mean about money as the most avaricious tradesmen and were quite pleased to forfeit all honesty for the sake of a cutting line.

The villa of Séverine was full of slopes and curves, *art nouveau* grills, embracing sweeps. The center section was set back so that the two wings of bedrooms reached out to hug the visitor, pull him to the heart. This was a splendid salon filled with bowls of flowers and soft cushioned sofas covered with warmly colored fabrics of floral design. The light, dappled by vines outside the windows, filtered through the branches of chestnuts giving everything inside a coating of sheen.

The grounds, too, were warm, embracing. Mysterious lanes meandered out of a lawn to secret nooks hidden behind ferns. In the center of the lawn two charming swans glided on a small lake. As the women strode toward it, Séverine told how in summer she liked to hire musicians to sit on the grass and play Chopin.

"Then," she said, "I can feel that I've actually escaped, left behind all my political burdens, my imprisoned anarchists and long-suffering Jews, to become the sensual being I truly am."

The garden had an aspect of a maze, but one without menace, built not to imprison or confuse, but to coddle, to assuage. Isabelle felt that around each corner she would find some sweet aroma or fragrant bush. The house and grounds were one long symphony of fabulous scents, and, as Séverine led her, Isabelle found herself becoming drowzy, and was reminded of the gardens outside her house in Tunis that flooded her room at night with the dizzying fragrances of roses.

There were a number of attractive persons in various places around the house and grounds—reading in the drawing room, playing badminton on the lawn or just toying with a *bilboquet* while reclining in one of the garden's hidden naves. As they strolled, Séverine made introductions. Isabelle was presented as "Si Mahmoud," and the others by their first names, too: "Evelina," "Natalie," "Odette," "Gilberte," "Lucie," "Albertine," "Eugénie" and several more.

All these young ladies were extremely elegant, with long blonde or auburn hair, in one case so long it reached to the girl's knees. Each comported herself with a regal, swanlike gracefulness, and wore a warm engaging smile that lingered upon the lips. In the end it was their eyes that struck Isabelle the most—grayish, steely, with the same cutting severity as Séverine's.

She was eventually shown to her room, and here, for the first time in ages, lay down upon a luxurious bed. She dozed off and only awoke when a servant rapped gently at the door. The guests were assembling; Madame requested her presence downstairs. She dressed in her finest outfit—red boots, Arab cloak, scarlet fez—and descended to the salon.

As she approached she could hear the chiming of silvery laughter, a soothing glossy sound that suggested pleasure. She entered to find the others already there, some in black smoking suits leaning against the mantel where they puffed on slender cigars, others, more daintily attired, ensconced in chairs or perched on cushions on the floor. All were arranged in a pattern around Séverine who, stunning in a riding habit, stood apart, turning this way and that, occasionally swishing for emphasis at the sides of her boots with a horn-handled crop. Her young audience responded to her monologue with glances of shared knowledge, for her subject was the vulgarity and ineptitude of men.

"Oh, my lovelies, they are awful hard mattresses," she was saying, as Isabelle found herself a place to lean against the wall.

"Their decorated canes and dashing uniforms cannot disguise their savage barbed cheeks, their primordial hairiness. And, as we know too well, their sentiments are as crude as their hideous pudenda. Who, if she had a choice, would prefer to lay her head on one of their roughened chests, when the world is filled with soft-breasted odalisques? Ignore them, I say. We have each other, thank goodness. We are all Gomorrhans here!"

Séverine stamped her foot. More silvery laughter, hands clasped together in glee. The young ladies began to look about, some, their gray eyes all devouring, upon Isabelle in her robe. As they searched her face for favor she sweated in her boots.

At dinner Séverine seated herself and Isabelle at opposite ends of a long baronial table, alternating girls in smokings and girls in dresses along the sides.

Looking toward her hostess, framed by these rows of "ladies and gentlemen," Isabelle was appalled. The charade was ridiculous, and there was also something vaguely sinister that she struggled to understand.

Staring at the girls again she found her eyes drawn to the finely chiseled Grecian features of Lucie Buffet. The high-cheeked girl caught and held her gaze. Isabelle in reply practiced, for the first time, one of those slatternly but devastating smiles.

Later, as they sipped Armagnac in the grand salon, the creature nestled herself by Isabelle's feet like a spaniel angling for a pat.

"How brilliant of you to wear hazel eyes," she whispered, holding up a match to light Isabelle's cigarette. "They go so well with my sash."

Lucie's hauteur melted in her laugh, and Isabelle, struck dumb for a reply, turned to face Séverine's steely eyes.

"Come, Si Mahmoud," she said, "let us stroll together outside. There are some delicate points to be explained."

Lucie was still smiling when Isabelle looked back, a moment before Séverine pushed her gently through the terrace doors.

The garden air was clogged with the aromas of night-blooming plants. Three-quarters of a moon gilded the edges of clouds, skimmed the waves that flowed behind the paddling swans. Séverine took Isabelle's arm, led her gently across the grass.

"I'm so happy you've come, my pet. You seem to belong with us. Such an Amazon you are, too—you have the hearts

of all my lovelies going pitter-pat. Little Lucie is thinking
you're a goddess—I can tell! She gets hot for anything in
boots, loves leather and the bite of the whip . . ."

Séverine slashed at her own boots again, then stuck her
crop into her belt.

"Look back at the house," she commanded, and when
Isabelle did she saw through the drawing-room windows that
the girls were beginning a graceful dance.

Séverine clasped her hands.

"Oh, such angels! Who can resist them when they dance
like that?"

She turned back to Isabelle.

"I just want to say again how delighted I am to have you
here. I adore it that you don't wear scent. Better to let the
natural odor seep forth to enflame the senses. You have a
sturdy figure, Si Mahmoud, a lot sturdier, I would say, than
your hothouse prose. There's a delightful suppleness about
your body. Truly, you bridge the gap between a boy and a
girl, with just enough of the finest qualities of both, I think,
and, thank goodness, none of the revolting qualities of a
man."

She reached over, drew Isabelle to her and planted a long
deep kiss upon her lips.

Isabelle gently wrestled herself away.

"Ah, Séverine—you said you were going to clarify some
'delicate points.' "

"Just so, my pet. In fact I was hoping that you would
clarify some points for me."

" 'Points'?"

"You seemed troubled at dinner, disturbed when we met
earlier for drinks. Just now I felt your body tremble. I could
not be certain whether out of passion or of fear."

"Surprise more than anything else."

"But surely you know my reputation."

"Only that you are a brilliant editor who has stood by
Dreyfus from the start."

"You flatter me, Si Mahmoud. And pretend to be ignorant of my well-known vice. I'm sorry to say that I'm now finding you dishonest, or," and she smiled, "most engagingly naïve."

Isabelle let out her breath.

"I think there has been a misunderstanding, Séverine."

"Not possible, my pet. Your clothes! Your flirtations! All the signals are clear. It's no use pretending you're not a daughter of Sappho—not, at any rate, with me."

"I've dressed this way all my life."

"And your masculine name?"

"A means to an end. In the Arab world a European woman does well to assume a disguise. I use the name 'Si Mahmoud' to signal the equality I expect from my lovers—who, it so happens, have always been men."

Séverine searched her face.

"Evidently," she said, "there *has* been a misunderstanding. Very well. I'm glad we've had this little chat. Your feelings will be respected, of course. I can only say that I feel sorry for you, for tonight you shall certainly sleep alone!"

They returned to the house, Séverine severe and cool, Isabelle still wondering how the situation had gotten so far out of hand.

She stood, smoking a cigar, watching the ladies dressed as gentlemen and the ladies dressed as ladies perform a perfect minuet. Every so often a couple would desert the salon. She saw Séverine whisper to Lucie Buffet who immediately departed with downcast eyes. Then, a few minutes later, Séverine followed her out.

The dancing continued, and when Isabelle became bored she excused herself and went upstairs. On the way to her bedroom she paused before a door, heard slaps and whimpers, reprimands and tears. *Poor Lucie*, she thought, as she made her way to sleep.

Lying in bed, she thought her feelings through. It was not that sexual inversion frightened her in any way. What she resented was the falsity, the notion that one could dress up in a costume and act out a fantasy as if it were real. It was the same thing that had struck her when she'd watched the events on the Champs de Mars and prowled the lines outside the theater where *Cyrano de Bergerac* was playing. Paris, it seemed, was a theater, a great stage where people dressed up, assumed roles and acted out dramas to satisfy their whims. The whole city seemed based on the notion that one could cut oneself a piece of experience from a great available bolt of adventure without having to pay for it in any way.

It meant nothing to visit the Tunisian souk erected out of papier-mâché. If one wanted to experience North Africa, it was necessary to cross the sea, make the trek, suffer the heat, endure the fevers and the thirst, just as she had done on the route to El Oued.

No, she thought, *it isn't lesbianism that's sinister, but the false posturing in this house. They call me 'Si Mahmoud,' but they don't understand what being 'Si Mahmoud' really means. They think it means I want to pretend that I'm a man!*

For a moment she felt indignant. Then she shrugged, penned a gracious farewell, packed up her bags and left.

By the beginning of June the "City of Light" which had mocked the hopes of countless other youths now began to mock her own. She was short of money, had barely enough to survive another month, and Paris was not paying her the slightest attention, although her little scandal with Séverine had been the rage of the salons for a day.

Then one night, tired of brooding, she dropped in at the salon of La Ratazzi, and there, by some miraculous stroke, which she later took to be the will of God, good fortune gently smiled.

She was introduced to a sour and yellowish woman who bore the name Marquise de Morès. She had a hideous pinched-up face, wore spectacular diamonds and spoke with an ugly flat accent which Isabelle easily placed. An American heiress who's exchanged money for a title—that was her immediate impression. But the creature had a personality of her own. She waved her arms about in the air to disperse the foul fumes of a giant Bavarian meerschaum clenched between her teeth, and when she laughed, which was often, she threw back her head, thrust out one arm with the pipe and regaled the ceiling with hysterical mirth.

She observed Isabelle shrewdly as she was describing her lonely trek to El Oued. Then, after a few sharp questions by which she extracted the fact that Isabelle was fluent in Maghrebi Arabic, she asked to speak to her alone.

They found a small room. Here, lit by candelabra fashioned by Osiris, the marquise opened up her heart. Her husband, the explorer Antoine de Vallambrosa, had been brutally murdered on the night of June 8, 1896. The place was a tiny settlement not far from El Oued, a crossroads called Bir-El-Ouadia. For nearly four years the marquise had been waiting for justice, but the Arab Bureau had given her no help at all, the government was indifferent, and the murderers, she knew perfectly well, were free and laughing behind her back.

"Do you think, Si Mahmoud," she asked, as tears began to stream from her eyes, "that you could help an old lady like me? I need a proper investigation. You know the territory. And I have unlimited funds."

"I shall certainly try to help," said Isabelle, as the precious words "unlimited funds" echoed in her ears.

The marquise gave a pathetic flourish with her pipe, then hardened her face.

"It's a matter of honor," she said, "that I not rest until I've had these hoodlums tracked down. When I finally discover who they are, I shall take immense satisfaction in having them killed. I can do no less to avenge my dear Antoine. Then my greatest satisfaction will be to spend an afternoon kicking their severed heads about, or, if that's not possible, at least to possess an album of photographs that documents the agony of their final hours."

Isabelle was amazed by the marquise's combination of sentiment and violence, venom and tears, but not so stunned as to hesitate in contriving a means of squeezing her dry.

Then, just as she was beginning to feel guilty about taking advantage of such a pathetic old thing, the marquise launched into a description of her "dear departed Antoine" that only redoubled Isabelle's resolve.

"He was the most splendid duelist," she began. "He practiced every day, then arranged things so that people he despised were forced to offer him a challenge. He killed one sniveling Jew lieutenant just before he left France for the last time. I was there and it was marvelous—the mists at dawn, the stern seconds, the little Semite trembling in his boots. He needed a good lesson and Antoine gave it to him. The field of honor was more than he deserved."

"Indeed!" Isabelle replied, incredulous at the lady's savagery, already savoring her own revenge.

"I remember," she continued, "going with him once to the slums. He had this brilliant idea, you see, that the workers wanted a restoration as much as the noble class. We rode in on a splendid carriage just as the butchers of La Villette were leaving work. We stopped among the slaughterhouses, and these great strong men, their aprons stiff with blood, stood about and cheered. 'France must cleanse itself,' Antoine told them, '. . . must wipe away the venomous snot that drips from the grotesque noses of her banker-Jews. Help me restore the throne and together we'll eat Dreyfusards off gold platters at the Palais Rothschild!' The workers were moved and yelled back, 'Long live Morès!' "

"What an amazing man!"

"Oh, Si Mahmoud, he was. Naturally I miss him as a husband, but when I think of all he might have done, I feel ever so keenly his loss for France."

As she continued with more endearing anecdotes, Isabelle could barely restrain herself from slapping the old lady across the mouth. Still she listened, calculating all the while, and not an hour had passed before she'd mock-reluctantly agreed to help.

"I had not planned to return to the desert for at least a year," she lied, "but I'm so outraged by the murder of such a splendid man that I gladly offer you my services at once. I have excellent informants among the local population, and shall surely be able to come up with some productive leads. Of course I shall need something to work with, some money on account, but since you tell me your heart is set . . ."

"Stop, Si Mahmoud! Not another word! Name your figure —I shall write you out a check at once!" And as the old marquise reached for a pen, she inadvertently dropped her fuming pipe.

Watching it shatter to a hundred pieces on the marble floor Isabelle was seized by a surge of enormous power. She would take this hideous old moth for all she was worth, send her fantastic reports, and, when the woman demanded results, she would be told that the "murderers" (whom, in her mind, Isabelle had converted into Arab saints) had already met ghastly deaths.

Power was what she felt then, sheer power, the power to take, to dissimulate without remorse, to fool and then laugh at those poor idiots who preferred the moist, plush hothouse of the salon to the dry, crumbling gulley ruined by the sun. In short what she enjoyed at that moment was the pleasure of being ruthless, which was the most important thing any person could learn in Paris at that time. And, feeling this, the broken shards of the marquise's meerschaum became transformed into a symbol of the fragility of this same civilization which she despised, and upon which she was now determined to turn her back, once and for all.

The Spahi in the Garden

In the end Isabelle's check from the marquise was not so grand as she would have liked. The old lady's effusiveness quickly turned to shrewdness, and Isabelle felt fortunate that she'd bargained her out of a thousand francs, enough to live on for a year, and to provide her with a bitter-sweet memory of Paris—which she promptly left.

At dawn on July 23, 1900, after spending the entire night on the deck of her ship, she arrived at the port of Algiers where she was met by Eugène Letord.

They set out to walk, talking of all their feelings and thoughts. In the middle of a sentence she suddenly stopped, widened her eyes and hugged him to her chest.

"I'm so happy, Eugène—so glad to be back. Look— Moslem women in veils! Men in turbans and robes! The language! The smells!"

Delighted by her exuberance Eugène put his arm about her waist and guided her on.

"I'm done now," she told him, "with the corrupt and

hypocritical social comedies of Europe. Now I never want to leave this precious Moslem earth."

They settled down for breakfast in a teeming café, and there she told him of her disillusionment with writers and with Parisian literary life.

"But it doesn't make any difference," she said. "I'm not destined to be a writer—I see that now, and it doesn't bother me at all. My experiences, my feelings—these things are more important to me than anything I could possibly write down. I've decided to abandon literature, Eugène. From now on my life will be my novel, and in it I shall play an heroic role."

They walked through the deserted love markets, peered into the narrow shops of artisans, stopped while she bought herself a kif box made from the udder of a camel.

"I have a fantastic vision of my life. I will buy myself a horse. I will sit around fires and talk with Berbers. I will take wild lovers and lie with them beneath the stars. I'll sleep all day and ride the dunes all night. I'll have passions, adventures. I'll explore."

"But why," he asked, "why El Oued?"

"Because it's so hard to get to. It takes days to travel there—it's like going to the end of the earth."

"Yes, I see that . . ."

"And the beauty, Eugène! The stars. The sunsets. The buildings with their domes; the paths all made of sand; the faces, too; the tents, the skies, the mornings, the sound of the winds. It's an island, far away, lost among the dunes. In El Oued I can be myself. I never have to pretend. No one expects anything of me. Everyone accepts me as Si Mahmoud. In El Oued I'm completely free."

They talked of the twentieth century—what it would be like, what it would mean.

"Already," he told her, "it feels clean. Like a new beginning. Maybe a great new heroic era, where we can all realize our dreams."

"Yes," she said, "I feel that, too. I feel my future is open, a clean tablet, and that upon it God will write me a life unlike any other before."

He left her at sunset to catch his train for his garrison near Oran. As he sat in his compartment and watched the light fade from the sky over Algiers, he marveled that he was the friend of such a person, and knew he could bear whatever unhappiness might occur in his life because she was in the world, and he would see her again.

She left the station to wander off, found herself drawn at the time of the evening prayer to the Djemaa Djedid mosque. Here, deeply moved by the hush and gloom, the praying multitudes illuminated by hanging oil lamps, she thanked God that she'd come home.

She traveled south as quickly as she could, by train and mule, camel and horse. The heat was as intense as she remembered, the nights as frigid, the guides as solemn. The smell of the campfires of dried dung, the poetry of the nomads, even the fevers that came and went were all the same. And at night, when the ripples of sand were lit up by the stars, she thought how greatly she loved the emptiness and made up a song:

Sahara, O treacherous Sahara—how well you hide your somber heart beneath your silent folds of solitude.

At nightfall on August 4, precisely a year and a day since she'd completed the same trek, she mounted the great dune to the west of El Oued, picked her way past the bones of fallen camels fixed in poses of supreme abandon and looked down once again upon the city of a thousand domes.

Descending toward this town, to which she'd felt herself so powerfully drawn, she resolved that here she would re-create herself, become the "Si Mahmoud" of whom she dreamed.

After renting a good house that belonged to the caid, she bought herself an excellent horse. She called this affectionate animal "Souf" in honor of the territory she intended that it roam. Then, after only a few days of rest, she began to ride off at night to visit the outlying settlements, sunken palm groves and wells. She made friends quickly, and when her Arab neighbors inquired why she'd come to El Oued, she replied that she'd been sent to find the assassins of Morès. She'd laugh, then, as if this were a joke (which it was to her), but word traveled fast, and soon the interest of the Arab Bureau was aroused.

She'd been amused the year before at being taken for a spy. But upon reflection she realized that, since Morès had been murdered and his killers were still at large, she was foolish to broadcast the story and make enemies for the sake of a man she despised. So when the local commandant, a stiffer and even more proper version of De Susbielle, called her in for a talk, she told him she hadn't the slightest intention of carrying out her mission, and that as far as she was concerned Morès had met his deserved end.

The captain, shocked at her pleasure in her fraud, wired his superiors, who in turn found a discreet means of informing the old marquise. Thus, within a month of her arrival, Isabelle received word that she was sacked.

By this time she didn't care, for though her funds were dwindling she'd embarked upon her dream. She was prancing out upon the sand each night, searching out strangers, spending hours around nomad fires discussing religious points. She was learning the local dialects, befriending guides and studying an old medical textbook so that she could minister to the sick. She galloped about like a rushing spirit, urging Souf over dune after dune, raging across the sand. Since the desert belonged to no one, she felt that it was completely hers, a place where she could seek the annihilation of what she'd been and forge herself anew.

At last, she knew, her life had become extraordinary. She was beginning to live at a pinnacle of sensuality, open to anything, completely free.

It was in the garden of Bir R'arby that she met Slimen. She came often, at dusk, to this lush sunken grove, to prowl among the palms. At darkness the apparatuses of the primitive wells would loom into black brooding shapes that made her think of the ancient torments, the savage history of the Sahara. Then, at night, these forms would be transformed to softness, and beneath a heaven full of stars she would feel satisfaction in the cool and meditate.

She was not the only one who came to this place. Many men and boys came, too, in the early evening, each to sit alone. The reveries of Bir R'arby were private; the flutes played and the songs sung merged with the cool wind and became part of the sublime soft hush.

A few weeks after she discovered the place and had gotten into the habit of visiting it before one of her tempestuous night rides, a slender man with large moist eyes and a profound and gentle face approached her where she sat, arms curled about her knees, and asked if he might sit near.

They spoke together for a while, their conversation soft and loose, divided by long spells of silence, the sounds of their breathing, an occasional verse from the Koran. Though no one was near they spoke in whispers, for Bir R'arby had the aspect of a mosque.

After a while the man moved closer, brought out a pipe and offered her kif. They smoked and spoke again.

"Do you come here often?" he asked.

"As often as life permits."

"And do you pray?"

"I pray and then I ride."

"Your horse is very good."

"He is, and he knows it."

"I've seen you in El Oued. Your horse follows you about on the street."

"He relies on me. He thinks he's my brother."

"He loves you, perhaps."

"He loves himself more. He brings me here so he can drink, and then, after a few mouthfuls, he stares down at his reflection and nods at his handsomeness."

"Ah—like a young man."

"That's his trouble. He thinks he's human."

"You go well together. You are both good-looking."

"Thank you—or do you mean I look like a horse?"

"You are both handsome, and so fortunate that together you've found love."

She laughed gently.

"I have a horse of my own," he said. "Would you like me to fetch him? Perhaps they will like each other, go off behind some trees and have some fun."

"What sex is your horse?"

"A boy."

"Hmmm."

"Why not? Human boys can make love. Why not boy horses?"

"It would be very difficult, I think. With the four legs and everything."

"It's better that way. They also have the advantage of a tail. The tail tickles the parts and stimulates."

"It's hard to imagine."

"Let me show you. Come, get down like me, on all fours. Yes. Like that. Now we are horses. All right! Now we must go over there."

Amused, she took up the role, and scampered after him, toward the bases of the trees.

He wrestled himself out of his cloak, whinnying all the while, then spread it upon the sand. He trotted to her.

"What a slender pony you are," he said.

"No, a gallant stallion," she replied, rolling upon her

back, kicking at him with imaginary hooves. They played at fighting horses for a time, neighing and whinnying, neither holding onto the other for very long. Soon she felt a tingling all over her skin, a tingling she hadn't felt in a long while. He must have felt the same thing, for he proposed that she stand still on all fours so he could show her how one boy pony could enter another from behind.

"But I am not a *boy* pony," she told him.

"Ha! That's why they call you Si Mahmoud!"

"I call *myself* Si Mahmoud," she said, "but I am not what I seem to be."

"I think you are playing with me—one horse teasing another."

"Come find out for yourself," she said, and lay down on her back, her knees up, her arms stretched above her head.

He stopped playing a horse then and reached gently toward the division of her legs. He quickly withdrew his hand as if it had been stung.

"Praise be to God!" he said. "You are not a boy!"

"How does that strike you?"

He thought a moment.

"It's good," he said. "Better a mare than a stallion any time."

"Ah! Arabs!"

"And you are not!"

"Not me."

"But you speak . . ."

"I speak many things."

"What are you then?" he asked, confused.

"A Russian whore!"

He laughed.

"Come," she said. "Show me how a boy horse can make love to a mare."

He stared, bit his teeth into his lip, then pounced upon her. They fought each other as they made love like savages, and she was exhilarated by the fighting, for it warmed her body up. Afterward he told her he was happy she'd turned out to be a woman, because, though he could not understand why she went about disguised, he found it enormously appealing to have the best of the worlds of women and men.

"I have dreamed," he said, "of a brother and of a European woman, too. With you I have them both."

She stood up fast, arranged her clothes.

"You have nothing," she told him, "and certainly not me. No one has me, except myself. Anyway, the way I look at things, it's been I who's had you!"

He gazed at her with admiration, then spoke softly, meaning to show that he was being careful with his words.

"You are so good I would not want to let you go."

"But I am willing to let you go, like that!" She snapped her fingers, watched him wither at the crack.

"I'm in love with you."

"That's a problem you'll solve in time."

"You don't love me?"

"I don't know your name."

"Call me 'Mohammed Horse.'"

"Very amusing. Yes, I shall call you that. Good-bye, Mohammed Horse. I'll probably be seeing you again."

"Then you *don't* love me?"

"Of course not."

"But you must have liked me a lot—to lie with me . . ."

She reached down, pulled him to his feet.

"You don't understand," she said. "I wanted your body, and now that I've had it I want to thank you very much. Thanks for the use of your goods."

"But this is impossible!"

"I'm sorry if it puts you out."

"No, not that. But you can't be serious. Who ever heard of a woman saying a thing like that?"

"Why not? When you thought I was a man, you thought it likely that I would have fun using your ass. Well, I didn't want that; I wanted your nice *zib*. You have a pretty good one and I thank you for it."

She laughed, turned, walked back toward Souf.

"Where are you going?"

"To ride," she said. "Thank you and good-bye."

"No! Wait! Come back!" He gathered up his cloak and chased after her, reaching her just as she was mounting up.

"Wait, please. I want to ride with you."

"All right," she said. "We'll race."

As she urged Souf forward and cantered out of Bir R'arby, she decided she rather liked the slender young man who had declared his love with such sincerity and was now, doubtless, fumbling with his reins. Once upon the dunes she galloped less furiously than usual, to give him a chance to catch up. But as soon as she saw him kicking madly at his horse's flanks, she broke forward as fast as she could. She wanted to appear like a phantom galloping on top of a ridge of sand, highlighted by the moon, a silhouette against the sky.

Let him chase me for miles, she thought; *let me be an allusive horseman always just beyond his reach, and then when he's exhausted, and flings himself down upon the sand to bash his head with his fists and weep, I shall quietly circle back to gentle his heaving chest.*

She had great pride in her horsemanship, thought of herself as one of the best riders in the world. And she had confidence, too, in Souf. But the young man who pursued her was a persistent knight. He charged out on the sand with a determination that added to her liking of him, though she thought that if he should catch her he would be unbearable in his pride. So she pushed harder until she was flying along the crests, and Souf's legs were stirring up a storm of sand.

They raced along like this, pounding the sand with rapid soft thuds, she ahead but he gaining, though still a hundred meters behind. Crouched in their saddles, their bodies sloped, they were like a pair of urgent messengers tearing up the desert to carry news to an Arabian conqueror of a great triumph or else a terrible defeat.

On the sand their horses could not sustain a frantic pace too long. After some minutes they were forced to slow, and then, when Isabelle began to shiver from the cold that chilled her perspiration, she signaled Souf to halt. She dismounted, looked back at "Mohammed Horse" and cupped her hands.

"Praise be to God," she shouted across the top of the dune. "You chase me like a madman. From this I deduce your love for me is great."

She listened while her hoarse and rasping words pierced through the hushing wind. He stopped, dismounted, cupped his own hands and shouted back his reply.

"My love for you is as great as the Sahara."

"As empty?" she growled.

"As full," he answered, "as the desert is of grains of sand."

She pondered his declaration, found it satisfactory.

"Come to me," she shouted again. "I want to see your face."

He came toward her then with a careful stride that reminded her of a soldier in the desert on march. Then he stopped five meters away.

"Come," she beckoned, "I have a candle."

He stood still and for a moment she was afraid. Then with a gesture so quick she had no time to feint, he brought out a knife from beneath his robe and plunged with it toward the sand near her feet. She heard a sound, a soft thump, and then he sprang back up and kicked the sand.

"A snake," he explained. "I saw it ready to strike."

She was filled with admiration. He was a man of action, had probably saved her from a terrible wound.

"Thank you."

"Light your candle."

She did, then placed it in a small lantern and held it up.

She found him beaming, his face smooth, his moustache soft.

"Tell me your name."

"Slimen."

"Slimen?"

"Slimen Ehnni."

"And what do you do, Slimen Ehnni?"

"I'm a calvary corporal in the French army."

They sat, after searching carefully to be sure there were no more snakes.

"So, you're a Spahi," she said to him, running her fingers along his cheek. "You ride well. I might have known."

"I'd have told you, but I didn't want to ruin the game."

"Good. You understand. I was pretending to be a spy who'd escaped from an enemy camp. I'd left all my pursuers behind but one, and he—that was you, of course—was relentless, was going to follow me till I fell. Eventually we'd both stop—our horses would fail us, and then we'd be off on foot, you tracking me through the night. At daybreak I would have disappeared, or so you'd think, until suddenly I'd leap out from behind a dune, wrestle you down and stab you to death."

"And what then?" He was fascinated. Like all Arabs he loved a story of action.

"Oh, then I would take your goatskin and start across the sands. I would try to conserve the water, but by the afternoon I would have finished it off. Then there would be the misery of searching for a well."

"Yes, yes . . ."

"I would be panting like a dog, crawling on the sand. Finally, the sun would strike me down. And there I'd lay, broiling, my lips blistering, my skin shriveling on my bones, until . . ."

"Tell me—go on."

"I would wake up in a nomad's tent, and there would be an old woman nursing me, and she wouldn't tell me where I was. And at night a man in a dark cloak would come, his face covered, and he would be silent, too. He would take me away into the desert on his horse, and then I would find myself on the sand, my arms and legs tied to stakes, and he would ravage me and ravage me, and I would grovel and moan, until, finally . . ."

"Yes?"

"Until, finally, he would tear away the cloth from his mouth and I would see . . ."

"Yes?"

"I would see a skull, a gleaming skull, shaped like your face—the face of the man I'd stabbed the night before."

She stopped, lowered her eyes.

He gasped, put his hand to his cheek.

"But this is a fantastic story. I have never heard a story like this."

"It was one of my dreams when I was running away from you."

"And there were others?"

She nodded.

"Tell me. I want to hear them all."

She talked on, into the night, weaving tales for him, tales of herself alone in the desert, made out of bits and pieces of Russian nursery stories and parts of novels and even things she invented at the moment she said them, and he listened, fascinated, amazed, his large moist eyes growing big, his pupils reflecting the single flame of her candle until the candle burned out and she stopped. Then he grasped her, kissed her, held onto her for warmth on the cold black sand.

The next day Slimen Ehnni moved into her little house. Here they lived like husband and wife, he going off each morning to join his regiment, she to the markets of El Oued to shop and then to a café to chat with people for hours.

At night they lived a rapturous life. They would ride out into the sand, practice their horsemanship for a time, gallop this way and that, and then explore until, after a month, they knew every garden within a radius of twenty kilometers. Then they would settle near a well, share a pipe of kif, and Slimen, by mutual consent, would ravish her several times with his sturdy *zib*. Afterward they would lie together like brothers beside a fire of dung. She would run her hands over his hard wiry body, fondle the curly hairs on his chest, play with the ends of his moustache and tell him stories.

At first his demand for good tales was easy to meet—she invented them, or else framed imagined happenings from their future into romantic sagas in the style of Loti. But as he became more sophisticated and demanded more intricate plots, she relied upon her memories of the *Arabian Nights*, giving him hours of pleasure with elaborate renditions of Ali Baba and the Forty Thieves, Aladdin and his Magic Lamp, and as many as she could remember of the rest. Finally, breathless and hoarse, she would stop, they would fall into sleep in each other's arms, and, at dawn, ride back to El Oued where they would pray and then revive themselves with shots of cheap absinthe that seared their throats.

Isabelle wanted Slimen to take her roughly, and though this was contrary to his gentle nature, she forced him to it by climbing astride him and daring him to fight. Then he would mount her and ravage her with the hard strokes she liked the best. She wanted to be mastered, ground down, though it was often necessary for her to remind him that this was her desire. Then she would pretend he was a stranger, dark and strong and mean, who used her body to flog the sand, making her scream out beneath the stars.

"I *want* to be hurt," she would shout to him, and though he would protest, she would claw at him until he had no recourse but to pound her to submission with high-pitched cries. Then she would scream, as if with agony, kick about with her feet, writhe beneath him, roll her head, and gulp at the clean cold air. For a time he was mystified by this behavior, but soon learned what she liked and found that he liked it himself, especially since it was only necessary for him to be forceful when they made love. The rest of the time, when they rode or talked or ate, it was she who decided everything.

Their nocturnal expeditions did not go unnoticed. The French in the Arab Bureau, horrified enough to see a European woman sharing her lodgings with an Arab male, suspected that she had not given up her pursuit of Morès' murderers, and was using Slimen to help track them down. The Arab community was even more suspicious. Her visits to nomad tents, where she taught people to clean wounds, and nursed enflamed eyes, were misunderstood. People said she was a spy, and a few fanatics said she was a kidnapper looking for babies to sell in the Sudan as slaves.

Isabelle and Slimen made no attempt to discourage these rumors. They welcomed the strange searching looks of their neighbors, and enjoyed deflecting curious questions. They savored their roles as outcasts who shared forbidden pleasures, though their only indulgence was alcohol, in defiance of the prohibitions of the Koran.

They spoke often of religion, the perfect beauty of their shared faith, and then of the future they would share in El Oued. Slimen had a dream of retiring from the Spahis and running a small grocery. He intended to do some minor smuggling on the side as well. Isabelle was amazed at the modesty of his vision: his imagination, which she treasured for its purity even as she deplored its miniscule size, could conceive of nothing grander than a caravan ten camels long.

Perhaps, she thought, *I love him because of his inferiority*. But still, she harbored a great dream for herself: to explore the Sahara as no European had before, ranging in ever-widening circles from her base in El Oued.

She saw herself riding into oases out of the dawn, materializing in little settlements with science for the sick and sagacity to settle disputes, then riding off again, chased, perhaps, by a few stray children who shouted for her to come back from the fringes of the sand. As the years wore on she would become a legend, and no one would know that in another life she was the wife of little Slimen—ferocious lover, gentle brother—who waited for her always, and to whom she never failed to return.

At first she believed she possessed everything necessary to accomplish this dream—everything except money, which she was certain the sale of Villa Neuve would gain her in time. But the longer she remained in El Oued, the more clearly she realized that being Islamic was not enough. She needed another key to open the door to Saharan mystery—membership in one of the closed religious sects.

That no outsider had ever been admitted only hardened her resolution to try. Si Mahmoud, she vowed, would be the first.

The Sheik

In late autumn, when the great summer heat has passed, and it's possible to ride on the dunes during the day, Isabelle learns of the arrival of Sidi Mohammed Lachmi, sheik of the Kadrya sect. She urges Slimen to join her on a ride to the village of Ourmès where the great holy man is to be met by a multitude of followers and escorted back to El Oued. But Slimen is hesitant, and the night before the arrival, they quarrel for the first time.

"I'm sorry, Si Mahmoud," he says. "I have my obligations to the army."

"Send word that you're sick."

"And then be seen in the procession?"

"Why not? Are you afraid?"

"Not afraid. *Never!* But I can't afford the risk."

"You're too obedient, Slimen. And your obedience shows a small nature."

He rises, furious. "And you, Si Mahmoud, you are *so grand*. How fortunate you're a woman. How sad for me that I serve the French."

"So," she says, ignoring his sarcasm, "you refuse to go."

"I will report to my regiment."

Isabelle, disgusted, rides off before dawn alone.

She broods over their quarrel the whole distance, telling herself that soft Slimen is an insufficient man, and she is foolish to think he is someone to whom she can devote her life. *He's not of my style*, she thinks, but then, when she sees the first glimmers of the fires of the Kadrya camp, she is so thrilled that she forgets everything and hastens toward the glow.

A cold breeze rustles the palm leaves and the black tents of Sidi Lachmi's encampment. Beautiful fringed flags, like the wings of huge prehistoric birds, flap upon their staves. She lingers about the camp, wandering first among groups of spectators, then sitting close enough to smell bread baking in the ovens, and the aroma of coffee boiling in kettles on the fires.

At first light the camp is quickly packed onto camels, and when Sidi Lachmi's escorts begin to mount their horses, Isabelle mounts Souf, too. Fumbling, she lights a cigarette, incapable of removing her eyes from the great pavilioned tent in the center. Four black Tunisian musicians, dressed in silks that glow in the dawn's light, begin to pound upon huge drums made of camel skin stretched taut. Other musicians come forward, shaking tambourines above their heads. Finally, with a grand gesture, a man throws open the flaps of the tent, and the sheik appears, dressed in a long robe of green silk, his head wrapped in a turban.

Isabelle is struck at once by his posture, noble and erect, his dark skin, his jutting beard, his hooked nose, his weathered face. His wise black eyes glisten, and there is a hint of cruelty in the arch of his brows. Suddenly out of the crowd comes a cry—trembling, immense:

"Greeting, great son of the prophet!"

The sheik, calm, unreachable, grave, acknowledges the salutation by a slight expansion of his chest.

It is repeated, over and over, faster and faster, while the musicians beat their drums to climax and the tambourines shake madly in the air. Horses rear up, their eyes fearful, their mouths spewing foam. And still the great man stands in the portal of his tent, gazing forward with immunity to praise.

An aide brings forward a white horse—a horse so fine that Isabelle cries out at its beauty. The sheik mounts his saddle, barely altering the angle of his head, and, as the magnificent animal prances to the cheers of his followers and the music which has now become a deafening roar, he raises his arm and thrusts it imperiously toward the east. The procession begins.

She rides with those on the wind-swept flank, parallel to Sidi Lachmi and his aides. The advance is stately, slow, aimed at the rising sun which is still hidden by the enormous dunes that shield El Oued. As they make their way out of the blue shadows of Ourmès, beams of golden light suddenly appear. Then, at the same instant, the silent empty dunes all around give birth to mobs. Entire tribes come riding out to join and wait in a great half circle far away.

As the procession approaches, Isabelle begins to hear their chant, at first nothing but a barely audible murmur, but becoming, the closer she rides, a thunderous savage song of war. Suddenly a thousand horsemen appear scattered on the heights of all the dunes, standing at equal intervals, rearing on their horses, shaking long-barreled muskets in their arms.

Then a great whoop below as a hundred men break from the center of the circle and charge toward the sheik at full gallop, twirling their rifles around their heads and discharging them in attack. The luminous air fills with smoke, but the column of Sidi Lachmi continues its march, while the men who have taken part in the circle behind join the other followers on its flanks. Now the vast circle parts, giving way to Sidi Lachmi's column, and as it passes through the center, the chant of war becomes an obeisant hail:

"Welcome, peace, O saint of God, Sidi Mohammed Lachmi, son of the prophet, great sheik of all the Kadrya, whose name shines east and west across the sands."

And looking to the holy sheik, Isabelle sees that still his countenance is without expression, hard and strong, showing not the slightest sign that he has heard.

She admires him most of all for this, for though she is moved by the great spectacle of his welcome as she has never before been moved by any human gathering, still the ultimate grandeur of the day is that its hero accepts everything as his due.

Later, before the gates of the Kadrya monastery in El Oued, Isabelle watches the ceremonies in honor of Sidi Lachmi's return. He sits upon his magnificent white horse, watching acrobats, singers, riflemen and an exhibition of equestrian skills.

Isabelle cannot restrain herself, works up her courage, then goes to one of the Kadrya officials and begs to be included in the competition. Her wish is granted and she plunges out on Souf, a fine lithe figure, galloping and halting, turning around in her saddle, twirling a borrowed saber like a mad Cossack. She knows that her riding style is different from the others, filled with boldness and risk, but the spectators like her, begin to applaud, and for her creditable performance she is chosen to be among those presented to the sheik.

Then, so close to him that she can smell the perfume on his beard, she kisses his hand and asks, with perfect equanimity, if he will grant her an audience alone.

The men around are shocked, but Sidi Lachmi seems amused. He stares her in the eye, and then, after what seems to her the longest moment of her life, he asks the reason for her request.

"So that I may enter the brotherhood of the Kadrya," she

says. The men around click their tongues, and murmur disapproval at her effrontery, but the sheik gravely nods.

"Perhaps," he says, "perhaps, my son. It may be possible."

"When may I come to you?"

"Tomorrow night. And be prepared to be examined by the wisest of my men."

She nods and moves to the side, thrilled at her boldness, for she knows that if she'd applied the normal way, her request would have been rudely denied.

That night at dinner, when she tells Slimen what she has done, he turns away and frowns.

"Be careful, Si Mahmoud. Sidi Lachmi is ruthless. He will never accept you once he discovers you're not a man. And then you'll be his enemy."

"Nonsense. He's a great sheik. Not the sort who splits hairs over a petty matter of sex."

"When he was young and there was fighting in the Souf, he skinned his captured enemies alive."

"Ah," she says, "I might have known—that's why you refused to come. You Spahis fear the sects. You know that if there's an uprising you'll be considered traitors to the French."

"I'm not a traitor and I'm not afraid."

"Good, Slimen. Good. I wouldn't love you if you were. But take care, dear brother. From what I've been told the tortures begin with castration. I would not like that to happen to you!"

Slimen shudders, then they embrace and laugh.

Later, when they are smoking kif by the small dome on the roof of their house, he asks again if she's determined to join the Kadrya.

"I want to *know* the desert, Slimen. So, if they'll have me—*yes*."

He nods then, and seeing that he understands she reaches to him, meets his liquid gaze and fondles his moustache.

The next evening she dazzles her examiners, a trio of old men with long beards. Her knowledge of Koranic science and law, her deep interpretations of scripture confound them, for she has lived in Tunis and Bône, talked of religion with the finest minds in the Maghreb. Unused to such erudition, the wise men declare themselves satisfied. Then they usher her into Sidi Lachmi's court.

He reclines, in his green silks and white veils, upon a pile of sheep hides lit on one side by a single thick candle set on a brass tray. The room is huge, the floor and walls covered with fine carpets. Black servants squat in dark corners. A brazier provides a modicum of heat.

Sidi Lachmi confers with his wise men, then motions Isabelle to sit down. While a servant pours tea he studies her face.

"My examiners give me good reports," he says in French. She is surprised that he has chosen her language, and also by the elegance of his accent which reminds her of the best she's heard in Parisian salons. She starts to speak but he raises his hand.

"Say nothing until I am finished."

She lowers her eyes.

"We must be frank. Otherwise nothing is possible. On the other hand, if you are honest, then many interesting things may occur."

She looks at him and nods. He grins, for the first time displaying warmth, though she feels it's blended with craft.

"You are European, of course."

"I am a Moslem."

Sidi Lachmi waves his hand again.

"Never mind about that." He stares at her most closely, his lips curling to a strange smile.

"Tell me, my child—why do you dress like a man?"

For a moment Isabelle is afraid.

"You see that?"

"I saw it instantly."

"But how?"

"It is my business to read faces."

"Then others see it."

"Perhaps. And then, perhaps, many are deceived. But that doesn't interest me. You must answer my question."

"I don't know."

"The truth," he demands. "Otherwise we have nothing more to say."

"I disguise myself so that I may live here as I like."

"And for no other reason?"

She shakes her head.

"Then you do not spy for the French?"

"Of course not. They loathe me. Most likely they think I'm mad."

He strokes his beard.

"Yes—that is what I've heard."

"You've heard of *me?*"

"Who has not?"

"But, I . . ."

"My daughter, you are not a fool. You have a deep understanding of our religion, and are devout besides. Surely you realize that your presence in the desert has been observed. The problem with a disguise, especially one as shallow as yours, is that when it's uncovered people wonder at its purpose. In Touggourt I was approached with the proposition that you be killed."

"But why?"

"Because you wear two faces, and are therefore presumed dangerous. But none of that matters to me. Other women have been admitted to the brotherhood, though not very many, I confess. It depends on the person, you see. A good human is a good human just as a good horse is a good horse. In the end the only thing that matters is quality."

Again he grins, and she finds herself taken with him, though frightened a little, too. Clearly he is no primitive, but a man of subtle sophistication. He has an ulterior motive—she is certain of that—and that he speaks in French so that servants will not understand.

"Do you play chess?"

She nods.

"Good. We will play."

He snaps his fingers, a servant creeps forward on his knees, and the sheik growls something into his ear. A moment later an inlaid board is set between them, a box of carved pieces, and a fresh pot of tea.

"Help me set them up."

They arrange the pieces and begin, Sidi Lachmi immediately preparing a strong defense. Isabelle feels he is testing her, and wonders if etiquette demands that she should lose. But she plays as well as she can, and soon they are embroiled in a complicated position with dozens of possibilities, and no clear sign of victory on either side. She decides to clarify—Vava's favorite strategy—and starts a series of exchanges which he cleverly turns to his advantage. Then he begins to attack, his game full of duplicity and tricks, poisoned pawns, deceptive sacrifices, lines of attack suddenly revealed. Soon she is decimated and gives up the game.

"Your play is clever," he tells her, "but you lack experience."

"Even that would not aid me against so great a lord."

"If I may characterize your game, it is much like the way you ride your horse. Direct, without caution or tact—plain and strong and wild."

"I'm sorry."

"You needn't be. It's the way you live. But don't expect longevity."

Isabelle, shaken, recalls his earlier remark.

"Why," she asks suddenly, "would anyone want me killed? I bother no one. I do no harm."

Sidi Lachmi strokes his beard.

"I'm not sure. There are always people who fear what they cannot understand. And you are difficult to understand."

"But I don't do anything, except ride the dunes, and sometimes tend the sick."

"Perhaps that's the problem. You don't *appear* to do anything, and that raises the question, what do you really do?"

She thinks for a moment, then asks for his advice.

His face turns blank, as if the silk veil that frames it has been pulled across. A silence—she can hear the snores of men asleep in distant chambers.

"You shall become a Kadrya," he says, finally, "and enter my protection. Then those who wonder what you do will know that you serve me."

"You accept me?"

He nods.

"The rites are simple, the rituals are for fools, and the secret signals will amuse you. But you must know that the sects are political parties, the members soldiers in a long and devious war that makes chess seem like a children's game. Right now the French favor the Tidjani, who acquiesce to their rule. We are weak because we are divided, and the French use this to manipulate us, keeping strength from a single group. My aim, of course, is to gain dominance, control of the desert. But the days of armed uprisings are over, and now everything is politics, trickery, deceit. In my youth I was like you—reckless, direct. But now, in middle age, I've become crafty, for that is the only means I know to accomplish my ends."

He stares into her eyes, she into his. She sees caldrons that glisten like black mica, a pair of furnaces where history will be forged. For the first time since she's been in the desert, someone is speaking to her with a vision that goes beyond the next well. The man's dominance reminds her of Vava, and she feels the same weakness before him that her father once inspired. Impossible, she thinks, to resist a man who is obsessed. But Sidi Lachmi's obsession is grand, not some petty scheme to manufacture perfume. It's a will to power, a dark instinct to rule and revenge. He has everything she ever hoped to find in a Saharan sheik—greatness, ruthlessness, strength.

"Why," she asks finally, "do you take me?"

The sheik closes his eyes, is quiet for a long while.

"I like you," he says, and waves his hand to dismiss.

She stands, backs away from his throne of piled sheep-skins. Sidi Lachmi does not look at her again.

A few days later, at her initiation, she learns the special way of reciting "there is no God but God," with heavy breathing and a contortion of her body, and also how to handle a string of beads placed about her neck so she will be recognized by her "brothers" everywhere. She recites a pledge, gives ritual answers to catechistic questions and is finally embraced by the three wise men.

She finds the ceremony boring, though she suspects that if Sidi Lachmi hadn't told her it was devised for fools, she might have been thrilled.

He has use for her. She drafts his letters in Arabic and French, sits behind him at meetings with his counselors, takes notes as they discuss their strategies against the Tidjani and the French. If the religious purposes of the sect seem cynically contrived, the political machinations of a desert sheik are a fascinating revelation.

Sidi Lachmi treats her sternly, always maintains his reserve. But she often feels he is watching her, thinking about her, and she cannot forget that he knows people who have wanted her killed. She is, as he promised, under his protection, and though this gives her some comfort, she wonders occasionally for what purpose he will finally decide she should be used.

They play chess often—he finds relaxation in the game. But she is never able to defeat him, no matter how hard she tries. For a time it seems important that she gain at least one victory, if only to raise his estimation of her worth. But his duplicities are without end, and always, when he has checkmated her or forced her to resign, he repeats his remark that she is insufficient in deceit.

"That's one thing," he tells her, late one evening after a particularly strenuous and protracted game, "that the Europeans have never understood. They know all about how we dress and pray and speak, even how we wage war, but they don't see the principle of deception that lies behind everything we do. It's the single great principle of survival in the Sahara. Here mirage is everything, and we who rule in the sands not only know how to make mirages, but also how to recognize them as our enemy's deceits."

She is surprised at his monologues, unexpectedly delivered in the most lucid French. Also by their aftermath—the manner in which he shuts his eyes and waves her away. It is as if Sidi Lachmi is speaking to himself, and her purpose is to be a mute witness, an acknowledgment that his mighty words do not fall with silence like a landslide in an uninhabited gorge.

Slimen is not forgotten, for though she spends much time with Sidi Lachmi, often staying with him late into the night, she always returns to the house in El Oued, and then, no matter how late, she and Slimen ride out upon the sand. She has two separate lives now, almost as she dreamed. She divides her time between her medical ministrations and the politics of the desert, between her role as wife and brother to

Slimen, and secretary to the sheik. Often she asks herself which role she prefers. But the answer, always, is that she loves them both.

For a time after she joins the Kadrya, Slimen's mood is depressed. But he regains his good humor when he sees that his possession of her is not impaired. By then they have explored all the outlands of El Oued, and so devote themselves to revisiting places they especially like. Here they play their various games of love, games in which they enact the roles of horses, camels, gazelles.

For her there is still nothing better than feeling that some violent creature, far stronger than herself, is crushing her, annihilating her in the empty wastes of sand. There is tragic poetry in this, an escape from being remarkable and strong. She knows that she is extraordinary, but there are times in the desert when she wishes she were dust.

Slimen shows little interest in the intrigues of the Kadrya, perhaps because as a French soldier he knows it is best to remain aloof. But on one occasion he thanks God that Isabelle has joined the sect.

In late November they depart for a journey of several days. They ride south, to the great emptiness east of Touggourt, and here set up their tent in a small valley between high dunes. The air is clear, made brilliant by the winter sun. All sorts of strange plants have sprung out of the sand on account of violent autumn rains. They wander in this thwarted scrub, chasing Saharan rabbits, pausing often to stare at the vast horizon of monotonous sands. Isabelle is struck by the intensity of the calm. The silence of the desert is so strong that it lulls her, and then Slimen complains. He misses her energy, even her diatribes. He is bored and wants to return to El Oued.

On their third night, while they are sleeping, wrapped in

burnooses against the cold, a violent south wind rips across the sands. Suddenly a gust destroys the tent, which nearly smothers them as it collapses about their heads. They crawl out, only to have their faces lashed by sharp blowing sand.

Since it is impossible to go back to sleep, they huddle together until the storm subsides. Then, at dawn, disgusted at the wreckage of their little camp, they ride off at a gallop to clear their heads, leaving everything—their revolvers, their goatskins, even their compasses behind.

The winds have slightly changed the dunes, new curves and ridges confuse them, and after a while they realize they are lost. They have only their belt flasks full of water, and just as their horses begin to tire, the winds blow again.

No refuge now, no place for them to huddle. They wander for hours, their faces covered with cloth, their eyes squinting against the wind that increases slowly until it reaches gale force. The storm of the previous night has deposited dustlike sand everywhere, and now the new storm blows it furiously so that all the air is filled with fine powder and they can see nothing, not even the outlines of the dunes.

They wander in circles, frightened, unnerved. They are in a limbo and Isabelle feels surrounded, oppressed. She begins to fear the desert, and, at the same time, to feel sorry for Slimen who, mumbling frightened incoherent prayers, reminds her suddenly of Augustin.

When she is finally ready to dismount and lie face down and wait for some horrible dehydrating death, the wind stops, the dust falls back upon the earth, and she sees they are on a great empty plain, without even a tuft of weeds in sight.

"We shall die." Slimen's sand-crusted face is streaked with tears.

"No, brother, we have luck."

"It's all over. We've been stupid, and now everything is finished."

She looks with pity at his stricken face and marvels at how weak he is compared to her.

"Gather strength, my brother," she says. "Better to struggle until the end."

They wander on, and then, turning behind some dunes, they see a valley, and in its center some scraggly trees. They descend and find a well.

Bent over, in the act of filling their empty bottles after laughing, embracing, dancing about, they hear the sudden click of rifles being cocked.

They turn to find three men, faces almost black, wrapped in multi-colored robes, approaching from three sides.

"You cannot use this well!"

"We are thirsty," Isabelle replies. "We are lost."

"Stand back!" The man in the center motions with his gun. "This is a well of the Rebaia tribe. You are not Rebaia. I forbid you to drink."

The two men on his flanks inspect their horses. Isabelle feels she is going to be killed. She begins to mumble the recitation of the Kadrya, "there is no God but God," breathing the special way she's been taught.

"You are Kadrya?" asks the leader.

"Thanks be to God!" she says.

The tall black man pulls roughly at the collar of her robe, strokes the rosary beneath. Then he peers into her eyes.

"We are brothers," he says. He lowers his rifle, throws it to the ground and embraces her with both his arms. "You will spend the night with us. Then, in the morning, we will show you your way."

She does not sleep, but listens all night to tales of life in this desolate quarter, learning much about the mysteries of shifting dunes.

For weeks she broods over the incident, asks herself what it means. She knows the odds against stumbling across a well, though Slimen is more impressed by the coincidence of meeting Kadrya.

"Thirst or a bullet," he tells her, "it's the same death in the end."

But still she wonders if God has saved her for something, some destiny yet to be revealed. She decides to ask Sidi Lachmi, the most cynical man she knows. She finds him with his retinue hunting gazelles in the desert with a fierce-looking falcon perched on his wrist.

"It is interesting that you began to pray," he tells her, releasing the gigantic bird. "I'm not sure that I would have done the same. Perhaps your salvation is a sign. Perhaps you are a mystic, or even a saint."

To his surprise she takes him seriously.

"Do you think so?" she asks.

"Already," he says, laughing, hoping to deflate her with ridicule, "I see the signs in your face. *Fanatic's* eyes!"

The next morning she rides west to the great dunes which she crossed the first time coming from Touggourt. The air is still and cold, the bones of fallen camels bleached a chalky white, and each grain of the desert seems etched by the brilliant winter sun. She stands at the crest for a long time, waiting for a revelation, some sign that she has a destiny, that God has saved her for something great. But there is only silence, and after a while she shrugs, falls to her knees, kisses the shimmering sand.

Suddenly, in January—disaster. All the money from the marquise is spent; her letters to Eugène, Samuel and Augustin are unanswered; the café refuses to extend her credit; she has not even enough to buy absinthe. For a moment she considers selling Souf, but knows this is impossible, that without him she will not be able to ride at night.

And then, just as she is grasping the awful reality of her financial condition, Slimen comes home with the news that he is to be transferred to Batna in two days. There is not even the possibility of a postponement—his pleas have already been rebuffed.

"But why?" she asks. "Don't your officers understand our hardship? Don't they understand what this will mean?"

"They understand very well. I was led to believe that the transfer is deliberate—that the Arab Bureau doesn't like you and wants us kept apart."

"They hate us, of course."

Slimen nods.

"So much so that they said I would have to live inside the garrison—just in case you were thinking of coming along."

"Oh, they hate us because we are free."

They discuss desertion but it is impossible for Slimen, and, besides, they would have no way of earning money to live. Over the next twenty-four hours they become possessed by a kind of madness. Anxious, depressed, they ride around the dunes discussing alternatives, realizing that all they have together is soon to be lost.

"There is always suicide," says Slimen, cheerfully. "We could make a pact."

"Oh, how stupid . . ."

She stops herself, looks at his fallen face, is seized by an enormous fondness for his romantic heart.

He shrugs and bows his head.

"Then it is written, Si Mahmoud. It is God's will. We have no choice—we will be separated. That is our destiny, and we must submit."

"Oh, brother," she cries, dazzled by the depth of his resignation. And then she begins to weep.

She can think of no other man, no other kind of marriage than theirs. That he never tries to dominate, except when she insists; that he offers her total freedom and total friendship without jealousy or cant; that she can be both brother and wife—these are things she doubts she will ever find again. Faced with separation and utter penury, she tells herself her life is ruined, though she is not yet twenty-four years old.

On the morning of their last day together Slimen's hand trembles as he lifts his tea. There is a strange hysterical look in his eyes, red from crying, that moves her to pity.

"Don't worry," she tells him, "somehow we'll survive. I'll find some money, pay our debts and move to Batna. They'll never be able to keep us apart. We'll find some way to end your enlistment, and then move back here and ride the dunes."

"It's a dream," he says.

"All right, we'll see. Tonight I will bring you to Sidi Lachmi. We'll throw ourselves on his mercy. Perhaps something will come of that."

They arrange to meet by the cemetery of Ouled-Ahmed. She waits for hours, but Slimen does not appear. She rides out to find him and then hurries back, afraid he will come when she is gone and think she has given him up. Finally he arrives long after midnight, swaying on his horse. He has been smoking kif and guzzling absinthe. His face looks terrible, and he shakes like a man who's been condemned.

Inside the monastery Sidi Lachmi looks at them. He is impassive. Suddenly Slimen begins to weep.

"What is this, Si Mahmoud? You bring me a man who cries like a child."

She begs to explain, to tell her saga of troubles. Sidi Lachmi shows no emotion as she speaks. His eyes betray nothing, and when she rambles on about her love for Slimen, he seems implacable, like a mountain of rock.

Finally, when she's finished, he asks what she wants him to do. She is silent.

"Is it money?"

She nods.

"Money means nothing," he says, reaching into his purse,

bringing out several pieces of gold. "This will help, and God will pay the rest."

Slimen, his nerves strained beyond control, breaks into laughter. While Isabelle comforts his shaking body, she and Sidi Lachmi exchange a lengthy glance.

"Tomorrow I am riding to Nefta," he says. "I will need you to accompany me, and take notes."

She kisses his hand.

This last night she and Slimen decide to ride out to the sand, gallop and roam from garden to garden, revisit all the places they love. Sentiment soon draws them to Bir R'arby where they nestle among the palms and laugh over the strange way they met.

"Do you remember," he asks, "how I was going to show you how one boy horse could enter another boy horse from behind?"

"How," she laughs, "could I ever forget that?"

It is too cold to take off their clothes. They make a little fire of foraged twigs and dung, wrap themselves in their cloaks.

"Believe me," she says, "now that Sidi Lachmi has given us gold, things are going to change."

But he is too tired to speak, prefers to rest in her arms, and soon falls off. She holds him for many hours, but is unable to sleep herself. She listens to his breathing, regular and strong, and stares at the stars. Then a sweet sadness descends upon her, a mood of longing and sorrow that brings back the memory of an October evening long ago in Meyrin. She feels the same melancholy that pressed upon her the night Augustin left home. Then, with a smile, she remembers how she spent that night sleeping in his sheets.

She wakes Slimen before dawn, brings him his horse and stands quietly while he wraps his things. When he is mounted she goes to his side.

"I will come to Batna as soon as I return. I must go now to Nefta with Sidi Lachmi—you understand."

He bends to touch her lips, they each touch their hands to their hearts, and he rides off alone.

When he is gone from sight she mounts Souf and rides to the Kadrya monastery. The morning light is dazzling, the air still. She finds Sidi Lachmi preparing to leave with a small retinue of aides. They begin the ride to Nefta.

They stop for food at Behima, a small oasis on the road to the Tunisian frontier. Sidi Lachmi is greeted by an enthusiastic delegation, and they are taken to the house of a man named Si Brahim Ben Larbi where they are served a sumptuous tagine of camel meat and dates. There is much talk of desert politics at the meal, and Isabelle, fascinated by the intrigues, forgets her sorrows for a while.

After the feast the sheik retires with a few men to another room, to smoke and continue discussions which she is not trusted to hear. She waits in the banquet room with the local notables while a curious crowd mills about outside. Then, when the muezzin calls for the afternoon prayer, she kneels with the rest.

Afterward the host introduces her to a merchant who begs her to translate a commercial telegram from Algiers. She is bent over, trying hard to make out the faded words, when she hears a sound and glances up.

Something dark is rushing at her out of a doorway filled with sun. She cannot make it out, then sees a flash of metal, hears something cleave the air.

Instinctively she raises her arm and turns her head aside. Suddenly she is stunned by an enormous blow that falls upon her shoulder and knocks her to the floor.

Writhing there she sees a man with wild eyes slashing a saber down from above his head.

She cries out and rolls, then is cut again. This time it is her elbow, and watching it gush out blood, she begins to murmur frantic prayers.

Loud sounds now. Frantic curses. A struggle.

The man with the saber is being held by one of Sidi Lachmi's bodyguards, while another chops at his arms until he drops the knife.

Screams from the crowd outside. Shrieks. Cries she cannot understand.

A terrible dizziness comes to her. She rolls her head from side to side, sees her assailant break loose and start toward her on the floor. She thrashes frantically with her good arm, searching for a weapon, a stick, anything to defend herself. But the wild man halts and she catches a glimpse of bloodshot eyes.

"I'll get a rifle and finish you off!" he screams, spittle shooting from his mouth. Then he rushes into the mob that throngs against the door.

Sidi Lachmi runs into the room. Chaos, now, as people push forward through the door, and others come from all corners of the house, attracted by the screams and noise. Isabelle, trying to stand, slips, falls, slides back into a warm thick liquid she knows is blood.

"There is no God but God . . ."

She gasps, turns imploring eyes upon the sheik who kneels beside her, fondling the instrument that has split her shoulder, sliced her arm.

"The pain," she whimpers. Her head falls back to the bloody floor. She repeats the Kadrya prayer.

"Who did this? Where is he?" Sidi Lachmi is furious, bellows at his aides.

"Abdullah ben Mohammed ben Lakhdar!"

"Yes. It was Abdullah!"

Others, crowded against the windows, repeat the name.

"Find this man! Bring him here!" Sidi Lachmi turns to the caid of Behima, but the old bearded man shakes his head.

"Abdullah is a sherif," he says. "We cannot touch him."

"*I* am a great sherif, idiot! He's a Tidjani dog. And so are you!"

The caid is silent. Isabelle, from the floor, sees Sidi Lachmi's face turn threatening.

"If you don't want a religious war, bring him to me fast. I'll denounce you to the French. If Si Mahmoud dies, you are the accomplice!"

Isabelle is fascinated by the struggle of wills, at the same time aware of her enormous pain.

For a moment it looks as though the caid will stare Sidi Lachmi down. But there is sweat on his forehead and his hands tremble. Suddenly he leaves the room. The sheik returns to Isabelle.

"I feel weak," she tells him.

"You will live, my daughter," he whispers in French. "Lie back. Rest. Your wounds are not serious, but the pain will soon be great. Pay no attention to the blood." And then to the others: "Stand back. Let Si Mahmoud breathe. Bring him water. Bring a pillow and a blanket . . ."

This time she closes her eyes. She feels no fear; rather, a great confidence she will survive. She cannot understand why her body has begun to shake.

She dozes for a few minutes, calm, courageous in the face of mounting pain. Passionate men crowd around, try to make her comfortable and mop the blood from her cheeks. She wakes to a chorus of exclamations as the man who attacked her is brought into the room, tied to an iron bed. He twists against his bonds, speaks nonsense, rolls his eyes.

Someone cries: "You are faking, Abdullah!"

"He is pretending to be a madman," says the caid, "but we know him well. He was never like this before. Yesterday he sent his wife and children back to his father's house. He knew what he was going to do."

"You do not fool us, Abdullah!"

Others agree his exhibition is a fake. Abdullah listens, then lies still. When he speaks again his voice is normal.

"It was God who told me to do this," he raves. "I am not responsible."

Isabelle looks at him. The bed has been set down near her. Their faces are but a meter apart.

"Do I know you?" she asks, searching her memory. And then, wincing with pain: "I can't remember seeing you before."

"You have not," he says, "nor have I seen you." Abdullah meets her gaze.

"Why did you try to kill me?"

"God instructed me."

"No!"

"If they untie me, I will try to kill you again."

"Why? Tell me why. What have I ever done to you?"

"I have nothing against you," he says, struggling against the ropes. "You have never done anything to me. I don't know you at all. But I know I must kill you and that is true."

Helpless, weak, she looks around.

"Si Mahmoud is Moslem. Do you know *that?*" Sidi Lachmi has crouched between them. Others press forward to listen. Isabelle feels the strangeness of the scene—they talk as though discussing a rational event. Calmly, methodically, they search for a motive, and in the meantime she bleeds to death.

"Yes, I know."

"God would not tell you to kill a Moslem."

Silence.

"Si Mahmoud is a Kadrya. You know that, too."

Abdullah turns his face.

"He is Tidjani!" Sidi Lachmi shakes his head. "And he is lying about everything. This man is a political assassin. He attacked you because I was not in the room. He could not know you would come here, but yesterday, when he moved his family, everyone in Behima knew I would be here today!" Then to Abdullah, lying submissive in his bonds, face clear of all feeling, all sense of remorse: "Tell the truth, my son. You wanted to kill me. Tell us who paid you to do this."

"It was God's will."

Again he turns away, and though they ask him the question many times, he refuses to reply.

For a long while Isabelle stares at his mute profile.

"I pity you, Abdullah," she whispers finally in Arabic. "May God forgive you for your crime."

She faints.

Hours later French officers arrive. A lieutenant takes depositions from witnesses, orders Abdullah taken off in chains. A doctor examines Isabelle, sets her shoulder, cleans the wound on her elbow, comforts her as he warns of greater pain to come.

"You are lucky," he tells her. "The saber hit a beam on the first slash. That slowed it enough to save your life."

She turns to the ceiling, sees a portion of woodwork deeply gouged.

"Yes," says the doctor. "If it weren't for that piece of wood you would now be split in two."

She smiles. She knows it was God, not the beam, that deflected the blade. Already she has heard murmurs in the room. People are saying she has *barraka*—holy luck, a sign she is blessed. Someone is telling the French lieutenant that when Abdullah attacked, a fog surrounded her, a sparkling haze that confounded him, shielded her from sight.

That night she cannot be moved, is too weak, has lost too much blood. In the front room of the house of Si Brahim Ben Larbi, on the same iron bed where Abdullah was tied, she drifts in and out of sleep, awakened often by new stabs of pain.

In the morning she is loaded onto a stretcher, drawn by mule cart to the military hospital at El Oued. Here, in a narrow white room, she is placed on a high bed and left alone. Souf, at her request, is tied outside the window. He stares at her sadly from the shade. She hears nothing for hours but the interminable silence of the desert, and then, late in the afternoon, the steps of soldiers, a perfect mechanical beat, the thud of rifle butts against the earth, a cold command. The guards at the gates are being changed. And then again—silence.

She needs Slimen desperately. If she is to die—and the thought obsesses her—then she must see him now, must be allowed to die in his arms. To die alone in this cold narrow room, attended by medics who look upon her as a freak, to die without love—the thought makes her shiver with fear.

All night she is torn by pain, and, at dawn, hurting even more, she asks herself what this awful wounding means. She wants, more than anything, to find purpose in the event. Impossible for her to accept Abdullah's crime as a gratuitous act. For if there is no reason, if she can be struck suddenly by a man without cause, then existence is pointless, pain and death hold no grandeur, and the value of her life is diminished.

Days pass, boring days, broken only by the sound of the changing guards, the sorrowful stares of Souf, an occasional visit by a nurse. The nights are filled with fever, unexpected pain, fear that she will move too suddenly in her sleep and reopen the stitching that binds her up. Often she thinks of Abdullah, his somber declaration that his hand was guided by God. Why? She is tormented by the question. She broods and ponders, becomes flushed as new, strange motives flow into her brain.

It is possible that he meant to kill Sidi Lachmi, and not finding him, struck at me instead.

But she has learned from Sidi Lachmi that in the Sahara things are never as they seem.

Perhaps the French were behind it and paid this man to strike me down.

They have always suspected her as a spy.

Then, thinking back over the past six months, she remembers Morès. Everyone in the Souf knew she was sent to find his killers. Perhaps they've been tracking her all the while, mysterious, silent men, assassins, waiting for Slimen to go away, then sending Abdullah to finish her off.

The most terrible thing, she thinks, confused by so many possibilities, is that Abdullah will somehow be let off.

If he goes unpunished then I am condemned. It will be a signal to all the Tidjani, to every madman, every fanatic, every discontent in Algeria: "Si Mahmoud is fair game. Kill Si Mahmoud! Succeed or fail, you have nothing to lose!"

She dreams of a life of a thousand attacks, mad cloaked creatures rushing at her out of mosques; smiling strangers with daggers hidden in their sleeves; killers disguised as beggars; headhunters converging on horseback to cut her down. She dreams of storerooms of weapons all destined for her flesh: knives, rusty sabers, gleaming daggers, bayonets. She dreams of fights and close escapes, evasions and dangers, sees herself growing old, her body carved so many times that not a portion remains unscarred. And then, finally, resignation, submission to her fate—a long walk through a dark overgrown oasis, the sky bruised purple and gray, giant black cobras slinking among the palms, each step possibly her last. She walks on, waiting, and then, finally, release: her killers appear in silence from behind the thwarted trunks, surround her, raise arms, plunge knives, stab. Sinking, she looks up, sees the same countenance on them all—Abdullah Ben Mohammed, raving, angry, staring at her with fanatic's eyes.

On her twenty-fourth birthday, regaining her spirit and her strength, she emerges from her fevers with a new view of her predicament, which she considers with gloom. Slimen writes that his commander has refused permission for a visit. Sidi Lachmi sends word that he is still in Tunisia, and will be there for several weeks more. Newspapers from the north —Algiers, Constantine, Bône and Oran—carry extravagant accounts of the incident in Behima, which are so distorted she must devote a day to writing letters to set them straight. Eugène Letord telegraphs his concern, and the captain in charge of the Arab Bureau at El Oued visits her in her hospital room, tells her there will be a trial in Constantine and takes her deposition with a clerk.

She lies back. A sense of mystery envelops her. She feels a bond with Abdullah, some mysterious connection between their fates. Assailant and victim—both their lives have been changed by a few seconds of contact she cannot explain.

Behima, 3:00 P.M., January 29, 1901.

If only she could unravel the lines that intersect.

$\mathscr{French\ Justice}$

Toward the middle of June 1901, people begin to gather for the trial of the year. The better hotels in Constantine are filled with officers and their wives, curiosity-seekers from all corners of the colony and journalists from as far as Marseilles. The cheaper rooming houses are host to an assemblage of stern bronze-faced men who flaunt brilliant robes and speak in the strange dialect of the south.

Isabelle and Slimen arrive on the evening of the fifteenth. Since leaving the hospital she's spent the months in Batna being interrogated by officers and trying, with infrequent success, to meet with Slimen. His request to live outside the garrison has been denied, so cohabitation must wait until his enlistment expires. In the meantime she's become convinced that certain officers in the Arab Bureau will use the Behima Affair as a pretext for forcing her out of the south.

As soon as they are off their train, relaxing with absinthes in the Ksouma Café, they become aware, for the first time, of the notoriety now attached to her name. A young French couple seated at another table—good-looking, exuberant girl, and stiff blond boy whom Isabelle takes for a junior officer and his visiting fiancée—are loudly discussing her case.

"But, my dear, she's disgusting." The boy looks like a young De Susbielle. "She lives like a tramp, and then, you see, it turns out she's one of those Russian millionaires."

"Everyone knows the Russians are eccentric."

"And we certainly don't need them here!"

"But I don't understand. Why is everyone against her?"

The boy squints, shows small contemptuous eyes.

"She's damaged European prestige. Naturally we want to see this criminal put to death, but one can't help but think she got what she deserved."

"What's she like?"

"No bosoms at all, and at least fifty years old."

"Fascinating!"

"... sleeps with anything in a robe ..."

"My dear!"

"... licentious as a strumpet—the most utter trash ..."

"How absolutely marvelous!"

A beggar approaches the table. The boy waves him away. But when the beggar comes at him again, muttering in a droning Arabic, the boy flies into a rage.

"Get away you filthy pig!"

He throws some coins on the table, yanks the girl up by her arm.

"Beggars! Vermin! This is what you get when you sit in a native café."

Sidi Lachmi arrives the next day with a retinue of aides. Seeing him step off the train in his magnificent robes, Isabelle's heart is warmed by his crooked face, his deep liquid eyes and subtle smile. She rushes to him, offers a firm embrace, but feels he is distant, somehow distracted, as if they were playing chess. There is trouble, then, at the Hotel Metropole—the management is not pleased by this invasion of a sheik's entourage. Sidi Lachmi and his men find rooms at the Ben Chimou, and Isabelle and Slimen, disgusted by the quarrel in the lobby, go off to dinner alone.

That evening they wander the medina, find a café, settle back to smoke a mixture of chira-enriched kif. Musicians wander the narrow streets of the quarter, playing for the patrons. Isabelle is thrilled by the high-pitched singing in the night, the delirious beat of tambourines.

They retire late but she does not sleep well. The months in Batna have worn her down. She is haunted by the past year—her double life, the strange way she has stirred up so much admiration and hate. She looks at Slimen, asleep beside her, finds him beautiful, lays her fingers upon his dark furry chest and wonders what will become of their lives. So many changes have come so fast. They have fallen from ecstatic heights to penury and despair. It will be eight months before his enlistment expires, before they will be free to live their dreams. *But perhaps*, she thinks, *the trial will clear the air, open up something new and great.*

Before dawn a messenger brings her a telegram from Oran: "All my love and hopes with you today. Eugène."

She will get through the trial, she knows, if only because of friends: Slimen, Sidi Lachmi, the men of the Kadrya and the warm encouragement of Letord.

On the morning of the eighteenth she dresses, for the first time in her life, in Arab women's clothes. She senses the trial will be a spectacle and chooses to play an unexpected role. At 6:00 A.M. she presents herself at the door of the Conseil de Guerre, is shown to the witnesses' room and served coffee from a steaming pot. Awhile later she hears noises in the hall, peers out and sees Abdullah, hands chained in front, marching between guards. People in the corridor see her and stare. She ignores them, returns to her seat, waits while the room fills slowly with faces from the past.

All the horrors of Behima come rushing back as the other witnesses appear: Abdullah's father, who glares at her with pain; the caid who claimed Abdullah was a sherif and because of that could not be touched; Brahim ben Larbi whose house has been sullied with her blood; the men who held Abdullah; the one who took the saber from his hand. Finally Sidi Lachmi arrives, guided in by the prosecutor, Captain Martin. He nods to her and sits apart. Then Martin crosses over to shake her hand.

"I promise, Mademoiselle, that you will see Justice served today." He speaks loudly, in a courtroom voice, but then stoops, whispers into her ear: "My wife and daughter are just outside."

She follows him to the hall, bows to a pinched-faced woman dressed for an Easter promenade, accepts the nervous curtsy of an awkward girl who wears pigtails and a sour frown.

"Thank you," says the captain. "Antoinette is absolutely thrilled."

She returns to the witnesses' room, smokes and waits. At precisely seven o'clock the bailiff appears to call them into court.

The room is huge, much larger than she'd supposed, signifying, she has no doubt, the power of colonial France. Already the air is close, for the benches below (she thinks of this place as "the pit") are choked with Arabs, and the balcony is packed with Europeans in fancy dress, women fanning themselves with the morning's *La Dépêche Algérienne*, officers in stunning uniforms and civilians in immaculate white suits waving to personages below.

Her entrance is greeted by craning heads. People whisper and point. She hears the words, "The Russian!" echo in the room. Looking around she is struck by a vision of colonial rot—the natives below, crowded, sweating, draped in their tattered robes, and, above them, the masters from France, cool, detached, suited in finery, thirsty for a bloodletting to avenge their suffering beneath this merciless North African sun.

She follows the bailiff proudly to a seat beside the sheik. She is moved by the costumes—Sidi Lachmi resplendent in his sherifian silks, green and white; the caid of Behima in a fez and red burnoose; the other southerners with their expressive heads, bronzed faces and robes.

The tribunal which faces them is equally decorous: five officers, chests festooned with medals and decorations, polished buttons, uniforms immaculate and sharply pressed. Their faces are rigid, impenetrable. She studies them and sees no compassion. The president, a colonel of artillery named Janin, seems made of stone.

Suddenly—a stir. All faces turn to the back. A man with thick gray hair and a magnificent moustache, epaulets on his shoulders, stars on his kepi, takes a roped-off seat in the first row. Janin gives him an ingratiating nod. It is General Laborie de Labattut, commander of the Sud-Constantine, known for his precise etiquette, legendary for his ruthless suppression of insurrections in the south.

The general, however, interests Isabelle far less than Abdullah and his coterie, the blank-faced guards who stand behind him, the stooped interpreter by his side and his counsel, a hawk-faced Frenchman with knitted brows who stares at her with devastating eyes. She turns to Abdullah, tries to meet his gaze, but he is focused on Sidi Lachmi, who stares straight ahead without expression. She feels tension, then, as if the four of them are working themselves up for a bout.

A presentation of arms: A herald announces the case; a clerk stands to read the accusation. He recounts the incident much as it took place—the facts are not in dispute, and Isabelle is satisfied. But then he reads on, and she can hardly believe her ears.

"Mademoiselle Eberhardt," he drones, "has been observed

since her coming to the Sud-Constantine by officers of the Arab Bureau. They have found her behavior exceedingly eccentric, and likely to give offense to the indigenous population. She is known to be a rich Russian, though she claims she is a Moslem and poor. She obtained permission, in 1899, to travel in the military zone on the basis of a false statement that she was writing a book about Saharan customs. She stayed a short while, returned to Europe and then came back in August of last year, at which time she proceeded to live a lascivious life in a squalid fashion, cohabiting with a Spahi corporal in an Arab house, and then becoming involved with the Kadrya sect and its sheik—the witness Sidi Lachmi—a sherif, with whom she has often been observed in intimate consultation at late hours of the night.

"Shortly after her arrival a coded message was received by the bureau's annex in El Oued. It had been discovered through informants that Mademoiselle Eberhardt had been sent as a private investigator on behalf of the Marquise de Morès. Her mission was to identify the murderers of Antoine de Vallambrosa, killed by unknown persons in 1896.

"The annex kept a close watch on Mademoiselle Eberhardt and had her followed many times. A large dossier was compiled, containing reports of mysterious nocturnal rides, covert meetings with nomadic tribesmen, conversations with prostitutes in cafés, attendance at religious ceremonies, and numerous other activities whose purposes could not be explained.

"The annex did not disrupt these actions, hoping that by them she might attract the killers of Morès whom the Bureau had been seeking for some time.

"After a long investigation it has been determined that the accused, Abdullah ben Mohammed ben Lakhdar, was not one of these, but a member of a sect rivaling the one to which Mademoiselle Eberhardt became attached. She had become a cause of religious strife, and was attacked by the accused, according to his deposition, on purely religious grounds.

"Though her behavior is not an issue in this case, except insofar as it may have been the cause of the alleged crime, the investigators are recommending a separate process at which Mademoiselle Eberhardt, because of her disruption of stability in the region of El Oued, be brought to account."

Murmurs, chattering in the balcony. Janin calls for silence. Isabelle rises from her chair.

"I protest the accusation. It is filled with lies."

"That," says Janin, "is something this court-martial has been convened to decide."

"The statement that I'm rich is completely false."

"Silence, Mademoiselle. We are in France here. Not in Russia!"

She hears giggling in the balcony and turns to face those who dare to laugh. She opens her mouth to speak but is cut off by the clerk who begins to read the witnesses' names.

"The witnesses are excused."

After much testimony by others, she is called back. She takes an oath before the president who questions her from notes.

"You find fault with the indictment?"

"Nearly everything that has to do with me is incorrect."

"The Arab Bureau watched you for a long time. Are you saying they've falsified their reports?"

She thinks a moment.

"The past two summers have been extremely hot. There are many mirages in the Sahara. That may explain their errors."

From the balcony a massive intake of breath. Janin is furious.

"Are you trifling with this court, Mademoiselle?"

"Certainly not. But it seems odd to me that I should have to defend my conduct. I thought someone else was on trial today."

Janin coughs into his fist, asks the government commissioner to question the accused. The process is long. Each query and response must be translated. Isabelle listens and waits.

Abdullah admits to the attack, but insists he was guided by a divine impulse. An angel appeared to him, ordered him to kill this woman who wore masculine dress and made trouble in his religion.

His attorney rises, the hawk-faced Maître de Laffont.

"Please, Abdullah, speak precisely. Tell the court the troubles this woman caused?"

"She dressed as a man. Also, she was the mistress of the Kadrya sheik."

A stir in the chamber. Janin calls for silence. Sidi Lachmi stares straight ahead.

The commissioner speaks to Isabelle: "The accused maintains that you caused a disturbance in the Moslem religion."

"I *am* a Moslem. In any case, that's something he thought up after the fact."

Janin: "But isn't it true that you wore masculine dress?"

"I did."

"And is that an insult?"

"Unusual, perhaps, but not insulting."

"Why did you dress that way?"

"It was practical for riding."

Laughter.

"I think this might be a good time for you to explain what you were doing riding around the dunes?"

"I was studying the local ambience. I'm a writer and have been preparing a book for some time. It also happens that I have a small knowledge of medicine—conjunctivitis and a few other diseases. I often treated tribesmen and their families who had no access to medical care. So you see, rather than earning the disfavor of people, I was trying to make their lives a little better than they were before I came."

"Do you have anything to say about the statement of the accused?"

"Only that I forgive him. I believe he's mad. It's not him I want to see at the bar, but those behind him who pushed him to do what he did."

Abdullah gives her a quizzical look. Sidi Lachmi shakes his head. Maître de Laffont rises and immediately assumes a sarcastic stance.

"You refer to other people. Please tell us who they are?"

"I don't know."

"Then we're supposed to believe that certain individuals whom you cannot name are responsible for this crime and should be brought to trial?"

"Yes."

"But Mademoiselle Eberhardt, how can we bring them here if we don't know who they are?"

She shrugs. "I'm the victim of a crime. It's not my job to solve it."

"But you have definite views?"

"Of course."

"A serious accusation has been made—that you were the mistress of a religious sheik."

"It's a lie."

"But suppose it weren't a lie . . ."

"Impossible because . . ."

"But just *suppose* it were true. Wouldn't that be sufficient cause for a deeply religious man to feel that it was up to him to remove this affront to his faith?"

"This is an ugly rumor and has nothing to do with me."

Janin: "But you evade the issue, Mademoiselle. Suppose the rumor is true. Would it constitute an extenuating circumstance? I am asking you because I understand you're an expert on Koranic law."

"I can't imagine any circumstance, in Koranic law or even

in the law of France, that could possibly justify a murder."

"You are speaking as an expert?"

"I am speaking as a woman who was slashed with a saber. And I resent the way you try to force me to justify that act."

De Laffont: "But you don't deny that you wore the clothes of a man?"

"Of course not."

"Would you agree, then, that your behavior has been—to use the word of the indictment—'eccentric'?"

"Perhaps, but I don't see that my preference for the burnoose has anything to do with this case."

"It does, Mademoiselle, because the accused claims that he was provoked, and I'm trying to get a clear picture of just how provocative you've been."

"There is no way he could have been provoked by me. He said he never saw me before January 29."

"But your reputation, Mademoiselle! You were well known! He'd heard of you. We have evidence here of widespread rumors. Some of them you deny and others you don't."

De Laffont pauses for effect.

"Tell me—just what is the meaning of the expression: 'Si Mahmoud'?"

"It's a name."

"I know it's a name. But why do you use it? Why would someone with a perfectly pleasant name such as 'Isabelle Eberhardt' deliberately choose to call herself 'Si Mahmoud'?"

"That's a personal decision. Surely I have the right to travel under an assumed name."

"Perhaps, perhaps—but then we have the *right* to find that rather odd. And, if you refuse to explain yourself, we also have the *right* to draw conclusions about your personal life."

"What should I say to that?"

"Tell the truth!" De Laffont smacks down his hand upon

the bar. "Here we have a man, a commercial trader and a sherif, well respected in his community, a man who never raised his hand against anyone in his life. All of a sudden he runs at you with a saber and tries to cut you in half. There has to be a motive. He says he was motivated by religious anger. He was a member of a rival sect, and you provoked religious dissension. Now I think that's very much to the point."

"My conscience is clear."

"How nice for you! But how unfortunate for those poor people whom you claim to love so much! What did you think you were doing? Who gave you the authority to meddle in their lives? Frankly, Mademoiselle, it seems to me that a woman of your education might have found something better to do with her time than to ride about the Saharan dunes, dressed like a man, involving herself in religious intrigues!"

Laughter broken by applause and cheers. De Laffont beams. Janin calls for an hour's recess.

Slimen joins her in the corridor. Reporters crowd about, ask a hundred questions at once. Isabelle brushes them away.

Outside the Conseil de Guerre she gasps for air. The courtroom's been stifling. She longs to be away, anyplace else, riding the dunes, prancing across the sand.

People part before them, then stare. It's as if she carries some disease.

Yes, she thinks, *we are objects of disgust.*

They flee around the corner to an obscure café. Afraid to be seen smoking kif, she lights a cigarette, gulps down three coffees in a row. Slimen is in anguish and cannot find words to comfort her. He can only grip her hand.

She holds herself solid and brave. She resolves she will not show her hurt, will never hide her face. But she cannot understand the brutality of the trial. It's as if she's the criminal and Abdullah only an excuse.

Slimen is silent. The hour passes long. She has no desire to return to court, wishes she could rest forever in this café. But she knows she must see the process through, even if she's going to be ridiculed more. She grasps harder onto Slimen's hand. Their eyes meet. She can tell by his face that he understands, respects her dignity, her refusal to admit to pain. He loves her—she sees that and feels a great rush of love for him.

Just inside the Conseil de Guerre, as she is about to re-enter court, a young lieutenant blocks her way. He is soft-spoken, assiduously correct. He has a communication for her, an official government note. He hands her a sealed envelope, wishes her luck, honors her with a gracious salute. She nods, expressionless, but quakes inside. She has a notion of what this means, and afraid she will not be able to suppress her tears, she leaves the seal intact.

She barely listens as Martin sums up his case.

" 'God commanded me,' " he says, "is not a viable defense. This is France and French law must be supreme. We cannot allow religious fanatics to attack Europeans simply because of some imagined affront."

De Laffont is ruthless when he speaks of her, but his remarks pass over her like desert wind. He says she brought the attack upon herself. "To Abdullah this woman was a devil who lashed him to fury because she threatened that which he loved more than anything else—his faith. We must construe his actions as self-defense."

Captain Martin replies: "The testimony makes it clear that this was a premeditated crime. We must demand the death penalty for that."

De Laffont pleads for mercy, and then the judges retire. Minutes later they return. Janin reads the verdict in a stony voice:

"We find the accused guilty of attempted premeditated

murder. Due, however, to certain mitigating circumstances, we have decided to show him mercy. He is sentenced to hard labor for life."

From the gallery a mixture of hissing and applause. Isabelle is stunned. She turns to Abdullah, tries to read his eyes. But he is glaring at Sidi Lachmi who turns away, then gathers up his robes and quickly leaves the court.

How strange, she thinks, *that he does not even give me a nod.* And then, suddenly, she understands.

It rushes at her, smashes like a bullet against her brain. Motives, explanations—everything is clear. Sidi Lachmi—of course!

He was so quick, so glib when he told her it was a Tidjani plot, that Abdullah was an assassin who'd struck at her simply because he was in another room. She thinks back to the evening before the attack, when she'd gone to see him with Slimen. There was cunning, then, in his smile as he enticed her to ride to Nefta. He knew she couldn't refuse, not after he'd given her gold.

She is sure—all the loose ends fit. He'd warned her in many subtle ways, had told her the first time they talked that people wanted her killed, had proclaimed his ruthlessness a thousand times, had even hinted at his plans to alienate the Tidjani from the French. Certainly if a European had been killed by a fanatic member of a favorite sect, some of that favoritism would have been wrenched away.

So she'd been set up for that, a pawn in a human game of chess. No wonder his coolness at the station, his distant smile in the witness room, his refusal to meet her eyes in court. It all made sense.

And Abdullah—he'd been nothing but a dupe. Perhaps he'd been paid, or promised blessings upon his line.

She looks at him again. The guards have hold of his arms, are about to march him off to a dungeon where he will spend the rest of his life breaking rocks.

Suddenly her days in El Oued seem to her a sham. It's as

if she's done everything wrong—pursued her impossible dream like a fool, while all the time she's been nothing but a tool in ruthless hands.

Sitting in the courtroom, staring at Abdullah's empty chair, her year in the desert turns to bitter ashes in her mouth.

General de Labattut is among the few who congratulate her in the hall.

"You cannot say that French Justice has not thoroughly avenged you." He bows, then turns his back.

Captain Martin, wife and daughter clinging behind, shakes her hand.

"I trust you are satisfied, Mademoiselle. It was not an easy case."

Even De Laffont has a few well-chosen words:

"You understand, of course, that my antagonism wasn't personal. I had to save my client's life. Speaking personally, however, I must confess to an admiration for your style. I certainly wish you good luck."

Walking back to their hotel, she feels drained, dazed. Slimen remembers the envelope.

"What is it?"

"Read it for yourself."

He breaks the seal, looks at the paper, passes it to her.

"What does it mean?"

She glances down, then back into his eyes.

"It means, dear brother, that I have become a pariah—that now I am cast out. The governor-general has seen fit to expel me from Algeria, and all French North African possessions as well. The act of expulsion is final and cannot be appealed. I have forty-eight hours to pack up and leave."

"But why?" he asks.

"They say I'm a troublemaker, but the real reason, Slimen, is that they hate me because I'm different. That's the worst crime of all—to be a vagabond, without a permanent address."

In the morning they sell Souf to pay for her passage to Marseilles. Then she sends a telegram to Augustin, asking him to meet her boat. At the ticket office she discovers that only men can travel at the steerage rate. In line she improvises a new name. "Pierre Mouchet, day laborer," she calls herself, savoring the coarseness of this identity which suits her wish to withdraw for a time, to hide.

The crossing is rough, the worst she's known. The winds are ferocious, and the enormous waves make the little ship *Le Berry* tremble on the sea. She finds a curious sort of splendor in the stink of the communal hold, and eloquence in the awful groans of the men. She has the feeling of sinking, losing herself in filth, wallowing in the mud.

In the night she makes her way to the pitching deck, and, standing there with feet spread apart, she screams out her rage at the injustice of her fate.

Part Three

For the mob I put on the borrowed mask of the cynic, the débauchée . . . No one has yet pierced this mask and seen my soul, so much purer than the degradations that please me, allow me to spit upon convention and indulge a strange need to suffer, debase my body. . . .

Mes Journaliers,
January 1, 1900

"Pierre Mouchet"

When Eugène Letord arrived in Marseilles in the middle of August 1901, he was struck at once by the humidity and the smell of rotting garbage that littered the streets. He quickly made his way to a tenement at 67 Rue Grignan, where he found a soiled business card attached to an apartment door. "Augustin De Moerder," it read, "Private Lessons in Russian and German."

Admitted to an ugly little drawing room where all the furniture was draped with frayed lace doilies, and a malfunctioning cuckoo clock hung on the wall, he looked for the first time upon Isabelle's brother, a young man of whom he'd heard a great deal and with whom he'd had a brief correspondence some years before.

Eugène was surprised, for Augustin De Moerder bore no resemblance to the handsome, tortured Russian youth he'd pictured in his mind. He found himself facing a balding man with a paunch, uncomfortable in a seedy business suit, patronizing in manner, who seemed, unaccountably, on the verge of rage. Beside him sat his wife, the former Madeleine

Joliet, a plain little woman with distant worried eyes and black curls that were waxen and tight.

"Oh, yes," said Augustin, "she stayed here with us awhile, until she found a garret of her own. Really she was impossible—rude, insulting, especially to poor Madeleine. She flicked her cigarettes all over the floor, never helped with the housework and sat around drunk in a horrid tattered sailor suit, calling herself 'Pierre Mouchet.' It was unbelievable. I didn't recognize her; we had nothing in common at all."

"But surely," said Eugène, "she had reason to be depressed. You must know that she was nearly hacked to death by a madman, then expelled, separated from her fiancé."

"Oh, yes, we know all about *that*. She could hardly speak of anything else. But the more we learned the more clear it became that the whole ugly business was entirely her fault. And I must say we received a rather disagreeable impression of her precious Slimen—the 'fiancé,' as you call him. His letters were practically illiterate, though the way she moaned about him one might have thought he was the Prince of Wales."

"You can't imagine," said Madeleine, "the way she carried on, hanging around Arab cafés, scavenging cigarette butts for kif, then borrowing money from Augustin in the middle of a lesson so she could go out to some bar and drink herself sick. She was absolutely disgusting, and I wasn't the least surprised—all of them in that family were mad, except for Augustin."

They both stared at Eugène to show their outrage, and he stared back, distressed by their lack of sympathy, deeply worried about Isabelle's state of mind. But when he got up to leave, Augustin grabbed at his arm.

"There's something I want you to see," he said, motioning toward a corner and a battered steamer trunk. Augustin threw it open, exposing a mass of papers which he began to grasp up in wild flourishes and fling down upon the floor. "See! The rubbish of my family! The residue of my crazy stepfather's estate! Look at it! Letters from that crook Samuel, claims by the Russian attorneys, documents of contests, offers of settlement, transcripts of all the hearings at the Court of Vernier. And look! Thousands of francs of unpaid bills! If only we could get our hands on that damn house, we could move out of this hole and live in a decent style. But it's hopeless. You have to be a lawyer to understand it. The whole thing's a spider web that's entangled us all."

"Terrible," said Eugène, retreating from the clutter of molding documents, aghast at the thought that the tropical garden of which he'd heard so much was now reduced to this. "But surely you can salvage something. As I understand it Trophimovsky left you and Isabelle everything he had."

"Salvage something? Do you think I haven't tried? When Isabelle came I talked to her for hours. I had a scheme, you see." His eyes began to enlarge. "We'd borrow enough to go to Russia where we'd confront Vava's widow and come to terms. But she wouldn't listen. She refused. My own sister! She said she didn't care—that she loathed the house and would be just as happy if she never saw a cent: That was the last straw. I had to throw her out!"

As Eugène climbed the stairs to Isabelle's attic *garçon-nière*, the stink of cat urine made him flinch. She was not in, but her door was unlocked. He pushed it open and looked around.

There were few possessions: a cooking pot and a plate, and over the ratty cot a crude drawing affixed to the wall. *Miserable Eden*, it said. Eugène laughed and sat down.

Some hours later he heard her clumping up the stairs. When she appeared in the doorway, he was certain he'd made a mistake. Then he recognized her, though she was dressed in the filthy costume of a matelot, and her face and hands were black with soot.

"Pierre Mouchet, I presume," he said.

"Eugène!"

Her blackened face burst into a smile. She came to him on the cot, planted a great masculine kiss against his cheek. "So long since I've seen a friend—at last, *at last!*"

She began at once to peel off her clothes, which she threw into a corner as fast as she could get them off. Without any modesty at all, she stood before him dirty and naked to the waist.

"Look," she said, "look at what they've done."

He stared at her scars and shuddered at the marring of her flesh.

"See how angry they are," she said, running her fingers along the ridges on her shoulder and her arm. "This is what comes of going to the desert with a head full of illusions. I thought I'd find freedom—I found madness instead."

She wrapped her arms around herself to cover her nakedness, and he was moved by the pain in her face. She went downstairs to wash, and when she returned she was wearing a burnoose, had a black band wrapped around her forehead and a necklace of desert corals hanging from her neck.

"Now tell me everything," she said. "Tell me first of all about my dearest Slimen."

"He was getting a hard time from his officers for a while, but I spoke to them and now I think things will settle down."

"Poor darling—he doesn't know how to cope with those vicious colonial types."

"The trial was a scandal, as you know. People still talk about it. Your defenders are few, but we're extremely vociferous. There's even been some mention in the press that you were unfairly treated."

"Good! Good! And the transfer?"

"I think it'll happen soon. I've been in touch with a colonel here who's sympathetic. He'll have Slimen transferred to his regiment, and when he comes he'll give you permission to marry. Then, as the wife of a French soldier, you'll be French yourself, the expulsion order will be voided, and you can go back to Algeria again."

"Eugène, you bring me miracles. How good to see a kind face!"

"I went to see your brother this afternoon. He and his wife were hostile. They said some strange things."

"I'm sure they filled your head with tales of my miserable deeds. God, they make me sick—phony-proper, self-righteous, *petit bourgeois* worms. They're everything Augustin and I used to laugh at and despise. He made a bad marriage, and is horribly changed. You wouldn't believe their bickering—the pettiness in their voices—ugh!"

"So—how do you survive?"

"I have a job. I'm in the sanitation corps. I work on a garbage scow shoveling muck all day long."

"That's horrible! How do you manage with your injured arm?"

"It's a kind of hell, yes, but I enjoy it all the same. They're a few other women, and we work as hard as the men. Everyone's quite kind. Between the stops they share their wine with me. They think I'm a real character because I keep insisting they call me 'Mouchet.' "

She laughed then, put her arm around him, hugged him, rumpled his hair.

"Where, for God's sakes, did you get that name? 'Si Mahmoud' was quite adequate, and I rather liked 'Nadia' who used to sign all your letters, and 'Isabelle' who's nearly forgotten now, beneath all these layers of disguise...."

She laughed again, then explained.

"Si Mahmoud was badly wounded at Behima, Eugène, and for a time it was necessary for him to rest. So Pierre Mouchet came along and took his place. Now let me tell you about Mouchet—he's a real rat, ugly and mean, and a hell of a drunk. . . ."

He took her out to a decent restaurant; she asked him a thousand questions about Slimen. He answered them all, but studied her at the same time—she amazed him; he couldn't make her out.

"You know," he said finally, "your whole condition here is too extreme. I don't understand this horrible job."

"Yes, yes, you probably think I'm mad. But really it's what I want—to roll around for a while in the mud. I want to inspire people's disgust. I want them to cross to the other side of the street when they see me. I feel loathed and unhappy, miserable and alone, and I want to proclaim that to the world."

"But nobody cares, except a few friends like me."

"*I* care," she cried. "I *have* to do it. And now I know what it's like to be an Arab in French Algeria—to be ridiculed and despised."

"Ah, Pierre—Pierre Mouchet!" He whistled the words to her, as if they were beautiful music that melted his heart.

"It's a good name, isn't it? Of course everyone knows who I am. But it gives them something to talk about. They can go home and tell all their dull friends that they know a Russian girl who was stabbed in the desert, and now wears a sailor suit and calls herself 'Pierre.' What the hell! I told you last year that I'd decided I wouldn't write—that I was going to live my life like a novel, be a passionate character swept about by fate."

"I remember."

"Well this, my dear Eugène, is the blackest of the chapters—the one where the heroine is dumped onto the dung."

That night he spent hours caressing her scars, saddened by the hardness of her manner, her cynicism about life.

"No," she told him proudly, "I'm not cynical at all. The only thing I regret is being deprived of Slimen and my precious Moslem earth. But it doesn't matter. He'll come here soon, we'll get married, and then, when his enlistment expires, we'll go back and try again. I have great plans for him, and every confidence that he'll carry them out. The only thing that bothers me is the speed at which everything rushes by. When I'm having a good time, I always pray that it'll last. But it always seems to pass quickly, and then the whirlwind spins me around again. Why is that, Eugène? Why aren't the great moments long, and the bad ones quick? Why can't it be the other way around?"

She bent over him, planted kisses all over his face, but he lay rigid, deep in thought.

"You're like a camel," she said suddenly, giggling against his chest.

"What?"

"Yes, a camel."

"Why do you say that?"

"Because male camels don't like sex. In the desert there are men who specialize in arousing them. Camel-stimulators. They do things like *this*."

She reached down and tickled him in a private place. He was furious at the distraction, and amused at the same time.

"Come on, Eugène. I've had enough of garbagemen. They're brutes in bed, and they stink like hell. Make love to me. I crave the embraces of a French officer—the class that hates me and has cast me out."

He complied with pleasure, and when they were finished, she stared up at the peeling ceiling and smoked a cigarette.

"Admit it—I confuse you a lot."

"Oh you do, Mouchet, you do, indeed."

"Tell me why."

"I don't know. You're kind and good-natured and you have a marvelous presence. You're full of passion and energy and you're brave when things go wrong. You don't pity yourself, and you do what you want. But the way you live seems so misguided. Of course I'm just a French officer, and in no position to judge, but it seems to me that you're living a romantic illusion of sensation and adventure and self-made myth. What do you really want? If you could tell me, then I think I could help."

"Don't try, Eugène. I'm too fatalistic. That's a classic Russian fault."

"And you're Moslem, too."

"Yes, and so I must submit. That's the great consequence of my faith, you see. I must submit to my destiny, for everything in my life has been written, and there's nothing I can do to change the words."

"But you can't just let life wash you about, as if you were some flotsam on the sea."

"Listen," she said, sitting up on the cot, crossing her legs beneath her, brushing away some loose feathers that escaped from the quilt. "All my life people have told me I'm extreme. But to me only the extreme forms of life are worth living. All the greedy colonialists in Algeria, and their stupid, spoiled society wives, would envy my miserable rags, this wretched garret, the awful food I eat—if they only *knew*. They'd envy me for the love I have with Slimen—a love completely untainted by any question of advantage—and the way I took possession of the desert, and the way I feel about the wind and the sun and the stars. And they'd envy me most for the way I've let myself be possessed by my life, and have reveled in it more fully than any king ever reveled in his power. Listen—when I think of people in Paris making witticisms in brilliant salons, when I think of them laughing in boxes in the theaters and talking nonsense at spectacular balls, I'm filled with pity for their useless, unfeeling lives, and I crumple the stuff of all their dreams in my fist."

Suddenly she took her cigarette and started to grind it out against the back of her hand. Eugène wanted to stop her, but he found himself paralyzed, fascinated by the horror, and the smile that never left her lips.

"You see—I can enjoy even *that*." She brushed away the ash and showed him the scar. "Because it's real, and I can feel it. I'd rather be a garbageman in the port of Marseilles than those silly fools in Constantine who mock me even now. I'd rather roll in the gutter than live at the norm. Give me pain or give me ecstasy, but don't ever let me become like my poor ruined brother Augustin. Now do you understand? Do you see it now, Eugène? Do you? Do you understand me now?"

The next morning when he escorted her to the docks for the form-up of the harbor sanitation crews, saw her standing straight and proud in the mob of burly, heavily muscled men, he was still not sure he understood her, but he was no less determined to try.

His last glimpse was of her poised at the square end of a retreating barge, waving at him with a shovel which she held like an ensign above her head.

A month after Eugène Letord left, Slimen was transferred to a Spahi regiment near Marseilles. Isabelle was done then with the role of "Pierre Mouchet." She threw out the costume of the matelot, left her job and began to walk again in burnoose and boots.

On October the first Slimen was released from the army— earlier than expected on account of ill health. On October 17, 1901, he and Isabelle were legally married in the Hôtel de Ville of Marseilles, and, immediately afterward, under Islamic law, in a decrepit carriage house that the Algerian workers on the docks had turned into a mosque.

Isabelle wore the clothes of a European woman, and a tawdry and quickly purchased yellow wig to cover her close-cropped hair. Augustin stood beside her, wincing at the grotesquerie of her garb, while the strange guttural language and the mysterious atmosphere of the mosque made Madeleine afraid.

It was sunny and cool when the four of them walked back to the De Moerder apartment for a wedding feast of grilled bass and a toast of Beaujolais. There were no gifts, but afterward, as she and Slimen walked home, Isabelle stopped at a store and convinced its Corsican proprietor to give her a bottle of absinthe on account.

Back at the *garçonnière*, Slimen was anxious to make love, but Isabelle was solemn, made him sit down, then lit the candles and poured them each a drink.

"It's time to be serious," she said. "No nuptial rites for us."

Slimen swallowed the liqueur, began to unbutton his blouse.

"No, brother—no games tonight. We must talk about the future."

"But, Si Mahmoud—tonight of all the nights . . ."

"Yes! Tonight! Tonight we begin." She pulled out a batch of papers, spread them out on the cot. "I have great plans. There are books you must read. You're going to apply for a position in the Algerian administration. With my help you'll pass the exam, and then you'll have a *career!*"

"But, Si Mahmoud . . ."

"No 'buts.' This isn't just for you. It's for all the Arabs, all our brothers. We're going to show the French that the Arabs can perform. No more useless uprisings in the desert. Arabs must learn to beat the French at their own game. You're going to be an administrator. By following my course you'll take the first step, and no one will ever call you an Arab halfwit again." Her eyes widened. "Look at me, Slimen. You'll be just the first. Others will follow, hundreds, thousands, until you strangle the French with your numbers and your skills. This is how we shall serve Islam, and we start tonight!"

She poured him another drink, drank off a glass herself, scoffed when he protested he was too tired. Roughly, she handed him a list of words.

"Above all else the French respect a man who can talk. You must learn to dazzle them with your language, smother them with your lucidity. First you must learn pronunciation. No more nigger accents. Start at the top. Say '*Gouverneur Général.*'"

He tried. She laughed. He tried again. She gently slapped his face.

"No, no. Listen to my 'r's, and 'l's. Work up a pompous expression. Let the syllables roll and give a little quiver at the end. Yes—better. But you must *work!*"

They worked on through the night, reviving themselves with the bitter searing absinthe until they collapsed in the morning, exhausted, drunk. But she had him up at noon, drilled him more, encouraged, cajoled, showed irritation, anger and disgust. She used all the techniques that Vava had used with her, making him work to please her because only then would she let him rest.

The work went on, every afternoon and night, day after day, until Slimen began to control the words. She did not allow him a free moment, forced him to read aloud to her from Balzac and Montaigne, Descartes and Charles Baudelaire. Though she fell asleep at times when he was reading, she was careful always to face away, and to wake herself every so often to catch him in a fault or compliment him on a well-read line.

They worked hard, hour after hour, until she forgot her misery, thought only of the man she was making of this friendly mediocre boy she'd met in an oasis and told herself she loved. Though she wondered at times if he ever would pass the exam, she kept at him, pleading, correcting, giving complaints and praise, never allowing herself to show her doubts.

They were interrupted only once. In the middle of December Augustin came bursting in, waving a letter, ranting insanely of betrayal and revenge. Villa Neuve had been sold for thirty thousand francs. This money, all that was left of the Trophimovsky estate, had been distributed in accordance with a formula devised by a Swiss court. After the deduction of all legal fees and other attendant costs, including Vava's debts, their own notes and the interest that had accrued, they were informed by notaire Samuel that each of them owed him sixty francs.

His letter urged them to pay this debt at once. Otherwise, he warned, he would be forced to seek remedy in the courts.

Madame
Slimen Ehnni

The town of Ténès is situated on the Mediterranean coast halfway between Algiers and Oran. When the Slimen Ehnnis arrive by stagecoach on the afternoon of July 7, they are struck at once by the serenity of the place. Cultivated terraces mount the hills. Wild pine forests sweep down to the sea. There are fishing villages along the coast, an old town with ancient ramparts, an occasional Roman ruin, a bucolic sense of peace. They explore until sunset and are well satisfied, but within forty-eight hours Isabelle turns to Slimen and says:

"We are trapped, my brother. This place is a ball of snakes."

And to that he most sadly agrees.

They have come so that Slimen can take up his position as a functionary in the city hall. But Isabelle quickly feels oppressed by a web of small-town gossip, and the sneers and frowns of colonialists' wives. At the market strangers turn to one another and hiss out epithets:

"Wife of an Arab!"

"Russian transvestite!"

"Adventuress!"

The stigma of Behima, the stain upon her name, are still evident, though it has been a year since the trial in Constantine. She shudders at the insults and turns away, fearing less for herself—she can endure the jeers of fools—than for poor Slimen, so unsophisticated in the cruelties of European gossip, so innocent in this nest of petty intrigue.

Oblivious to the stares she struts the streets dressed like a cavalier in snow-white burnoose and her treasured boots. Preceded by two newly acquired Alsatian dogs, she walks to the beaches, the forests and back into the hills slashed by gorges and cascading streams. The region is beautiful, but reminds her of the Haute-Savoie—it is too rich, belongs to the romantic period of her adolescence when Alpine woods and valleys could move her soul. She recognizes that she is harder now, and craves the Africa of great deserts and dazzling light. She misses the mystery of bewitching Saharan towns which can move her by their savagery and the splendor of their pain.

Slimen has been appointed *Khodja*—the official link between his people and the French. But he is used only as an interpreter, and soon finds he has no function at all.

"You must push for power," she tells him. "Find an injustice, make an issue out of it and create yourself as a political force."

"I must bide my time," he says. "No point in risking a thousand francs a year!"

She looks at him then in wonder, asks herself if all her training for his exams has reduced him to the state of a fearful bureaucrat.

"I detest the way you kowtow to these Philistines," she tells him one day. "Do you think these French officials are important because they wear tight trousers and ridiculous hats?"

"I do my job."

"And you do it much too well."

"It was you who wanted me to be the link."

"The link—yes. Their servant—never!"

In October, when harsh winds blow in from the west, and the people of Ténès turn even more sullen and mean, she finds herself seized by fits of melancholia, and spends long hours brooding on the beach. She feels stifled by the pernicious atmosphere of the town, has trouble sleeping and begins to quarrel with Slimen. He looks back at her without comprehension, proud that he has a job, hurt by her irritation, her dark moods.

"Can't you see," she asks him, "that these French treat you like a fool? They want you to imitate them—which you do—and then they laugh at you behind your back. The more you slobber over them, the harder they laugh. Don't you see?"

"It was you who taught me to imitate."

"Just the pronunciations, my brother—not their high and mighty airs."

"France has the greatest culture in the world."

"Ridiculous!"

"It's true!"

She looks at him hard, can't believe her ears.

"There's nothing sillier," she says, "than an Algerian who apes his masters' manners and leaves behind his Arab soul."

"You brought me this far, Si Mahmoud, and now you're angry that I want to go further on my own. I may have been a savage when you met me, but now I want to become a civilized man."

"Oh," she cries out, "poor beloved savage—you're not becoming civilized. You're becoming a docile little clerk!"

She decides, then, to leave him for a few days, to make a trip to Algiers, where she can be alone and think out the meaning of what she's done.

When her name is announced to Victor Barrucand—editor of *Les Nouvelles*, the only paper in the colony to protest her expulsion the year before—he prepares himself to meet an arrogant Amazon—beautiful, Russian, rich. Instead a pale, slim young woman in a turban and an Arab robe strides into his office and begins to mesmerize him with her nasal, rasping voice. Throughout their interview she leans forward, supporting her head between her fists while her elbows rest upon her knees. She chain-smokes cigarettes and stares at him with piercing hazel eyes which do not waver for a moment, remaining fixed with burning intensity upon his own.

"I'm desperate," she tells him. "I'm looking for a job."

"I'd hire you at once," he says, "but I'm resigning next week to start a journal of my own. Would you be interested in writing for me there?"

"What do you pay?"

"Not a cent—for a year at least, until I can get the thing on its feet."

She studies him, carefully inspects his handsome face. Then she laughs.

"I shall always be poor—it is written. Tell me about your new review."

Barrucand describes *Akhbar* in which libertarian articles will be printed on facing pages in Arabic and French. The paper will publicize injustices and become the voice of the voiceless illiterate mass. Its purpose will be to transform Algeria from a society of oppressors and oppressed into a land of interracial brotherhood.

"I like it," she says, and then slapping her knee: "I believe what you say. What do you want me to do?"

"Seek out injustice and name names. Investigate the scandals and pillory the ones who exploit the country for themselves."

"And how do you know I can write?"

"It doesn't matter. I'm a good editor. What I like is the

look of your name upon the page. Isabelle Eberhardt! That's a scandal in itself. And with Victor Barrucand, the most hated man in Algiers, we have a combination that will make them sweat."

"They'll have diarrhea every morning at the Palais du Gouvernement."

"The very effect I wish to inspire."

She thinks a moment, then shakes his hand.

He invites her that night to dinner at Villa Bellevue. She likes his house, finds its shining white terrazzo floors, its glassed-in arches framing the sea, a pleasant change from Slimen's lowly apartment in Ténès. And she likes Barrucand, too—he's warm and decent, the first Frenchman she's met in the colony who doesn't hold the Arabs in contempt.

"I should be exploring the south," she tells him, gulping down her drink, "not suffering the taunts of little people in a horrid provincial town. There's nothing they can do to me that hasn't already been done, but where—where is my youth? I'm twenty-five years old!"

Barrucand laughs, offers her another drink, then listens in amazement as she tells him the story of her life and goes through a bottle of his best cognac in two hours and a half. At the end of the evening, when she is finally done, she falls down fast asleep on his best Berber rug.

The next morning they begin work on *Ahkbar*, outlining stories, planning the format and the point-of-view.

"Once I wanted to write novels," she admits to him, "but I didn't have the talent, and I despised all the writers I met. But journalism's different. It would give my travels a purpose. I hate the system here and long to tear it down."

He lends her a horse and in the afternoons she roams the countryside around Algiers. One day, on one of her rides, she comes into a town and stumbles upon a disquieting scene. A third-rate European, with an arrogant interpreter on one side and an armed gendarme on the other, has set up a table in the village square. All the peasants in the district are waiting before him in lines for compensation for their expropriated land. While the European dispenses centimes for the ancestral acres, Isabelle observes closely and takes careful notes. Then back at Bellevue she unleashes all her outrage in a stinging short piece she entitles "*Criminel.*"

Barrucand loves it and decides to publish it as a broadside to publicize his forthcoming *Ahkbar.* "*Criminel*" creates a sensation, and in Algiers, once again, her name is on people's lips. She is pleased and returns to Ténès, where she is surprised to find Slimen in a rage.

"So this is what you've been doing," he shouts at her, his hand trembling as he brushes the broadside across her face. "You disappear to Algiers, take up with some new man and write rubbish that can ruin my career."

"Your career," she tells him calmly, "is a farce. It was my gift to you—a gift I'm beginning to regret."

"An Arab wife belongs in the home!"

"But I'm Si Mahmoud, your brother—not some Arab *wife.* I'm not Fatima or Zohra—you can't order me around. It's really terrible, Slimen, the way you've gotten yourself confused. You want to be a French pig and an Arab at the same time."

Furious he slams the door, but an hour later returns with tears in his eyes.

"If it weren't for you, Si Mahmoud, I'd still be a sergeant in the Spahis. I'm sorry for what I said. I had no right."

"Your trouble, Slimen, is that you've been corrupted by the French. Don't be a fool and fall into their nasty trap. They are nice to you in the hope that you'll control me and keep me off their backs. At the same time they remind you how easily you could lose your job. Well, I say screw the job! We can live without money, but without freedom I'm dead."

Ramadan, to which she's always looked forward if only because the bodily torment of the fast gives her a feeling of spiritual cleanliness and expiated guilt, falls, this particular year, in the somber rainy month of December. Between the storms she goes to sit on a rock overlooking the sea, and there, hungry and alone, she ponders for long periods the mess she's making of her life. The marriage with Slimen is clearly not working out, and she feels terror, too, at the neurasthenic melancholy that comes upon her frequently and which she believes is a symptom of a family disease. "The curse of the De Moerders" she calls it, thinking of the morose natures of Vava and her brothers.

She makes a pilgrimage with Slimen to the great mosque at El-Hammel where she stands in an alcove and becomes moved by the endless repetitions of God's name She finds her body, despite her will, begin to sway in time to the muted whispered prayers. As a trance begins to take possession, she feels she could happily submerge herself in monastic gloom, far from the civilized world that has caused her so much grief.

But later, on the way back to Ténès, she realizes how far she really is from that. Though attracted to stoicism and renunciation, she is always yielding to ecstasy and desire. Sex, absinthe, the heightened vision induced by kif, the feeling of burning sun and Saharan wind, sand against her flesh, the taste of water, after a lengthy desert journey, drawn from a deep cool well—these are her greatest pleasures, and she cannot imagine giving any of them up.

One morning, on her way out of the apartment, after Slimen has gone off to work, she finds an unsealed package pushed against the door. She opens it and finds a horrible, shriveled, stinking fish with a piece of paper clenched between its teeth.

"Ehnni," it says, "your wife is unfaithful! She and Barrucand are trying to topple the regime!"

Isabelle scoffs and throws the note and the fish into the street. But the next morning, when Slimen arrives at his office, he finds a drawing of horns glued to his desk. Overpowered by rage he dashes out of the Hôtel de Ville, rushes home and rips the covers from on top of Isabelle who is still asleep.

"Pig!" he shouts. "Whore! An Arab man has the right to kill his woman for less!"

Amazed by his outburst, and his reference to herself as his "woman," she demands to know what she's done.

"Don't lie," he cries. "They're mocking me in the town. I'm a cuckold! You're an adulteress! Tell me who he is!"

She stares up at him with stupefaction. "Poor brother," she moans. " 'He' does not exist!"

He shakes her. She is thrilled to see his passions so aroused, and for an instant remembers the savage whom she loved, and who has been lost to her for so long a time.

"Tell me—so I may kill him. Otherwise I shall kill myself!"

"And why not me—why not kill me first?"

"I love you too much!"

"Then choke it out of me! Squeeze my throat until I cough out his name!"

He stands back in anguish. "You mock me, too! Never mind! I shall shoot myself!"

He rushes from the room. She chases after him. *At last*, she thinks, *a scene worthy of my life.*

After a frustrated search he finds his revolver. They struggle over it, but he manages to get his finger around the trigger. Then, as they flail about the room, fighting, screaming, they hear a hard dry click that stops them cold.

"My God!" he cries. "It's empty!"

He goes back to the bedroom, throws himself upon the bed, sobs and weeps until she gently caresses his head.

"Poor brother," she says. "See what they've done. The jackals!"

"You promise there was no one," he mutters, his mouth pressed against the mattress.

"No one," she says.

"Not even Barrucand?"

"Not even him."

"Oh, Si Mahmoud, I was certain you'd betrayed me. I know what you think of me. I know I fill you with contempt. You should have married a brilliant man—not a clod like me. Without you I'm nothing—nothing at all."

She is seized, then, suddenly, with a great ennui, a deep feeling of uselessness and self-disgust.

"Oh, Slimen . . ." Her eyes fill with tears. He reaches to embrace her, but she turns away.

Later, when he is calm, and has prepared himself to go back to work, he finds a note beneath a vase of flowers on the table where they eat:

"There's a full moon tonight—let's die beneath it. Bring the revolver (loaded!) and a bottle of absinthe. I'll meet you at midnight on the beach."

She comes to the rendezvous fully prepared to die. She has no further use for life, feels she is destroying both of them by her misery and her drink, and that they will be better off with a quick romantic death. A double suicide seems the perfect solution, *and then*, she thinks, *the animal who sent those notes will see what he has done.*

She is touched, when Slimen arrives, by his white burnoose. She imagines how nice the blood will look against the nubby wool.

He sits beside her, his face grave.

"It will be beautiful," he says. "I have often dreamed of a melancholy death upon the sand."

"The beach is not the desert, but it will do as well."

Slimen, enraptured by the thought, begins to recite an

ancient desert verse. He sings of night and death, and when he finishes he quotes to her from the Koran.

It is her turn now, and she wishes to show him that though she's a European she knows Arabic even better than he. After a deep swig from the bottle—which is a sacrilege and which she prays God will forgive—she launches upon a long improvisation in a rich, florid, Tunisian style.

Slimen, ashamed at being outdone, tries again, and she taunts him when he makes a bad rhyme. They drink more, then continue the contest, but soon Isabelle gives up, lying back, preferring to listen to Slimen's deep Saharan growl.

By 2:00 A.M. they are drunk, and she's begun to stomp about the beach.

"Tell me a story, Si Mahmoud—a good one before we end our lives."

"No," she snaps, marching this way and that, sometimes stumbling in the sand.

"I love you, Slimen, and I don't love you at all. I love what you were, and I hate what you've become. Our marriage was a mistake. I only did it to become French, so that I could get back here. No—that's not true. I *did* love you. I suffered over you. I thought of you every moment I was heaving garbage in Marseilles. That's what kept me going— the thought that I had a great love in my life. Ridiculous! The whole time in El Oued I was mad. All those rides we made across the dunes—they were wonderful—do you remember?—but we didn't know what we were doing, we were infatuated, and it was all like a dream. Yes—we must kill ourselves. It's the only way. We must end our misery; let God reclaim our souls. We suffer too much, my brother— the world is too harsh for us, and we can only find happiness in dreams."

After that they drink more, and then fall asleep. At dawn, awakened by the first rays of the sun, they search about for the revolver, finally find it buried in the sand then make their way back shamefaced to town.

After this adventure, which she admits to herself has been absurd, she flees once again to Algiers and the Villa Bellevue, where for months she devotes herself to *Akhbar*, writing articles, making brief trips into the *bled*.

On April 23, the Association of Algerian Journalists gives a banquet in honor of Émile Loubet, the president of France. Barrucand, wangling an extra ticket, takes her as his guest.

From the moment they alight from their carriage at the door of the Hotel St. George, Isabelle causes a stir. The other women, in their flowing Parisian gowns, are scandalized by her brilliant tarboosh, white Arab robe and red Spahi boots. While everyone mills in the lobby, waiting for the visiting president and governor-general Jonnart, she feels herself the cause of delirious buzzing on the part of the other guests.

"We're a sensation," whispers Barrucand, and she grins at the thought.

Visiting newsmen who have accompanied the president from Paris ask their Algerian colleagues who she is.

"A Russian eccentric," she hears one of them reply, and then, *sotto voce*, "Her morals are widely impugned."

They stare at her with even greater interest, and pretending at first to be oblivious she finally responds to their attentions with a devastating smile.

The dinner, marked by empty speeches and numerous obsequious toasts, makes her feel strange.

"What am I doing here, dining at the table of my enemies?" she asks Barrucand.

"Not an unpleasant sensation," he replies.

She grins and nods. Then, after the president has left, several of the Parisian reporters come over and beg to be introduced.

In front of the hotel she holds an impromptu press conference, fielding questions with a combination of disdain and charm.

"Is it true you're anti-French?"

"Nothing could be more ridiculous. I'm a French citizen. The interests of France are always uppermost in my mind."

"But you have spoken out often against the colonial regime."

"Of course. The regime is sick. Victor Barrucand and I are in favor of a more benign colonialism under which my Arab brothers will be equal and not oppressed."

"What did you think of the president?"

"Unfortunately we were not introduced. But I received a favorable impression. Perhaps this trip will open the eyes of many people in France who think of Algeria as a barbarous land. It's up to you to make them see us Moslems as we are—a great brotherhood of civilized men whose sensibilities can no longer be ignored."

She and Barrucand finally escape, ride back to Villa Bellevue where they throw themselves on lounges on the terrace, open a bottle of whiskey and laugh.

"How do you feel?" he asks her.

"Delighted. What's scandalous in Algeria, in Paris can earn a great name."

Barrucand sips his drink carefully.

"I have a mission for you, Si Mahmoud—something worthy of your talents."

"What is it?" she asks with a smile. "Tell me at once and save my wasted life."

"In a moment, my dear, but first you must do me a favor."

"Name it! Perhaps you'd like to sleep with me. Everyone else has. Come—we can see to that at once. . . ."

"No, no," he laughs, "but something personal nevertheless. What are your intentions vis-à-vis Slimen?"

"Ah," she murmurs, "poor Slimen. When I made him into what I thought I wanted, I looked at him closely and found I was filled with disgust."

"And now—?"

"Now it's over. I suppose there's a part of me that will always love him, but after what we went through in Ténès . . ." She shrugs.

"Then you're free?"

"Yes."

"Good—that's all I need to know." He takes another careful sip. "You know why Loubet is here. It's much more than a ceremonial visit. The stage is being set. France is going to gobble Morocco up."

Isabelle sits straight. She is intrigued, has caught a whiff of what her adventure might be.

"There's trouble in the Western Sahara." Barrucand speaks with the precision of a man who spends his life analyzing affairs of state. "The rebel Bou-Amama is wreaking havoc, and now French troops are massing, and a certain Colonel Lyautey has been called in to clean things up. He's no fool. Jonnart requested him because he's the kind of soldier who knows how to play at politics as well as war. Very soon we're going to hear of 'incidents.' Contrived or actual, there will be provocations, and then a rearrangement of the forts on the Moroccan frontier. Some territory will change hands, which will inevitably cause more 'incidents,' which in turn will provoke still more, and then—conquest!"

He snaps his fingers.

Isabelle is excited.

"What do you want me to do?"

"Go to Aïn Sefra. You'll be the correspondent for *Ahkbar*, accredited to the French army. You speak the language, so you'll be able to uncover the truth. This is a fabulous opportunity for a journalist. History is going to be made. If you go, I can guarantee you'll be famous within a year."

"And what is your profit in all of this?"

Barrucand laughs.

"I will sell newspapers. With exclusive dispatches from the

front written by a personality who is—shall we say?—a *cause célèbre* all by herself, *Akhbar* will make money and I will gain influence in Algiers."

He looks at her carefully.

"Will you go?"

"The desert! The south! A war! Of course I'll *go!*"

She stands up and twirls with her arms outstretched. "Oh, I'm happy," she cries. "And now we must both get drunk!"

She prepares carefully, studies the customs of the tribes and the political sequence that has led to the latest crisis in the Sud-Oranais. The idea of a French Morocco has its thrill—even to one, like herself, who has seen the costs of colonialism upon the Arab soul.

Suddenly, at the end of the summer, after the rebel Bou-Amama's devastating attack against a French convoy at El-Mounghar, she sheds the sadness that has consumed her life for the past two years and strikes out with a boldness she has not felt since the early days in El Oued.

The Desert
of Black Stones

The military train from Oran
is filled with legionnaires. She is struck by their faces—
haunted eyes, lean cheeks. They have the look of men striving to forget their pasts by losing themselves in anonymous
ranks.

All night she presses her face against the rumbling glass,
watching the towns and villages rush by. At midnight the
train stops while an extra engine is attached. Then it seems
to pant as it climbs the tortuous route of tracks to the High
Plateau.

She is excited by the presence of the troops, the smoke of
their black tobacco that swirls around her, envelops her in
clouds, as they sing and chatter through the night.

She dozes for a while, then listens to their talk—of the
enemy warlord, Bou-Amama, the trickery of his attacks, the
way he appears with a hundred men at night, lays siege to a
lonely fort, massacres everybody, then retreats back to the
mountains before the dawn.

"He slips across the frontier," someone says, "and then
he's safe."

"Damn the politicians! We should hunt him like a dog."

"And take Morocco while we're at it," mutters an old sergeant beneath his breath.

The train rolls and shakes as they talk on, of how it's better to fight to the death than allow oneself to be taken alive. Horrendous tortures are described. A young blond recruit, obviously a German, shudders as the sergeant tells of finding a decimated patrol, chopped up bodies strewn about on the sand, blood baked black by the sun.

"My captain looked around," he says, "and he gave us the word right there. 'No more prisoners!' I bet I've killed as many Arab fiends as there are men on this train!"

Fascinated by the old soldier's tales, she presses her face back against the window and dreams of war. But when they start to speak of Taghit, and of De Susbielle's stand, her ears prick up again.

"Are you speaking of Captain Édouard De Susbielle?" she asks.

"The same," says the old sergeant bundling his neck in the collar of his legion greatcoat. "They attacked his fort for hours, thousands of them, screaming maniacs, wave after wave. They kept coming out of the night, but Susbielle held on, rallied his men till they were fighting them off with bayonets at the gate. His stand at Taghit will be remembered for as long as the legion lasts."

She sits back then and lights a cigarette, incredulous that her loathsome little captain is now a hero of France.

The train rushes on. An occasional settlement blurs by, and at dawn the distant mountains become distinct. The men who've been talking fall off to sleep, but she cannot keep her eyes off the blue ranges of the Atlas that have begun to loom. Morocco, so forbidding, so mysterious, so full of violent passion and feudal power, is but a few miles to the west.

The train hurls through a region of fantastic red and golden dunes. Then she sees forts with notched towers on

the heights. It is Aïn Sefra, headquarters of the expeditionary force. She dismounts amid dust and wind and looks
around.

Horses and men march back and forth—companies of
Arab scouts on strong lean ponies, men of the camel corps
in black burnooses with cartridge belts crossed upon their
chests. She sees infantrymen in blue, Spahis in red cloaks,
and finally the legionnaires—tall, blond, Nordic, their faces
bronzed by the sun in colonies far away. She hears shrill
commands, curses in German, Danish, Dutch, smells ma-
nure and sweat and the oil used to grease guns.

She pushes her way through a throng of milling Arab
irregulars to a row of military canteens crowded in the dry
riverbed below the forts. Here, amidst cardsharks, pickpockets and spies, she drinks an absinthe, eats a piece of
bread and watches mules climbing the sides of the ravine
carrying trunks and whores.

She wanders out again and explores. The whole place
seems full of adventure, tensed for alarm. In a square in the
African village she finds a great black market of military
goods spread out in the sun. Soldiers bargain over Berber
jewelry while behind, in stalls, workmen pound out addi-
tional "antiques."

She makes her way, finally, to a tent set up for the convenience of the visiting press. Inside she finds a middle-aged
Frenchman repairing a camera spread out in pieces on a
Berber rug. Another man, young and bearded, is frantically
arguing with a lieutenant who sits passively behind a desk.

"What can I do for *you?*" The lieutenant and the bearded
man give her ironic looks.

She hands over her papers.

"Ah, a new correspondent. Mademoiselle Eberhardt rep-
resenting *Akhbar* in Algiers. This is Jules Bresson, of *Le
Matin.*"

Bresson shakes her hand.

"Bresson, here, is a complainer," says the lieutenant.

"We've only one telegraph, and of course he wants full use of it even if that means throwing the colonel off the line."

"I know for a fact, Mademoiselle, that the Foreign Legion here is being torn to bits. This little lieutenant is trying to black out the news."

The man working on the camera curses under his breath. Isabelle stands awhile, listening to the argument, then, ignored, she slips out of the tent.

She deposits her bag with the proprietor of a café, goes to the military hospital atop the ravine. She passes through its crenellated walls of red mud into a courtyard where wounded men rest in the warm shade of the arcades. These are the survivors of El-Mounghar, and she spends the afternoon with them, listening to stories of the ambush, and the brave deeds of the ones who've died.

Beyond tales of Arab savagery, and the horrible pain of their wounds, it is the blazing desert sun they most vividly describe. One survivor can speak of nothing else.

"It's the worst, most devilish sun I've ever seen, and I was in Indochina for ten years. You broil by day and freeze all night, and the thirst can kill you faster than a stomach wound. In the morning when it rises, you think you'll be glad for the warmth, but as it clears the horizon you feel it burning out your eyes."

That night the entire town goes on alert. She makes her way back to her café where Arab irregulars huddle in the shuttered darkness speaking of the weakness of the garrison, Bou-Amama's hordes and the consequences if the rail and telegraph lines are cut.

The night is full of unexpected dramas. A woman delivers a baby in the open air out back, her screams giving way after many hours to the cries of an infant child. At midnight a courier rushes in, gulps down a whiskey and asks all to pray for him since he must carry a message to a distant isolated fort.

Resting on the mats, with her pipe full of kif, she is

intoxicated by her impressions and writes her first dispatch. But still she cannot sleep. She is too thrilled at being in a place where she can test herself anew, lose herself in the silence of the desert, seek oblivion in its pain.

She buys herself a horse. It is a magnificent animal, a thoroughbred Arabian stallion, the best and most expensive she can find. Caressing its flanks, admiring the muscles rippling beneath its pure white flesh, she names him "Karim," then realizes she's spent every cent of Barrucand's advance. But she doesn't care. Her horse will be her single luxury, and upon it she will go to war.

Equipped, then, with a huge black revolver and a flask for anisette that dangles from her belt, she rides with the troops, sleeps on verminous mattresses in cafés, writes her articles and files them with exotic datelines to Algiers.

Deciding she must experience for herself the dangers of the men, she encamps with four teen-age Arab soldiers who occupy the blockhouse above the rail line at the pass at Hadjerat-M'Guil. Mustapha, Mohammed, Ahmed and Ahkmed are their names, and on the first night they seem to her a sorry lot, standing with their rifles at their notches, trembling with fear.

"Why are you frightened?" she asks them.

"We are here to protect the tracks."

"Yes, yes," she says, "but why—why do you fight with the French if you're afraid?"

They look at one another and shrug.

"We are conscripts. The French pay us. And our orders are to hold this place."

They sleep during the day bundled together in a heap. She watches as they absentmindedly hug one another, make random love.

On the second night, sometime after twelve, there is a huge eruption of barking from a pack of wild dogs scavenging below the cliffs. The boys all start to fire at once, pivoting about, spraying the moonlit scenery with bullets until she finally shouts at them to stop.

"You'll use up all your ammunition."

"Yes," says Ahkmed with a laugh. "Then we can go home."

In the morning she goes down to the village for food. When she returns she finds all four of them eyeing her in a peculiar way.

"What's the matter?" she asks.

"We know who you are, Si Mahmoud."

"Who am I?"

"You're a Moslem, but you're not a man."

"Oh," she says, "how did you find that out?"

"I watched you this morning," says Mustapha. "I saw you pee."

"Listen," says Ahkmed, who seems to be the leader of the pack, "we've been talking things over. Now we have a proposition which we sincerely hope you'll accept."

"What's that?"

"We've been counting up all our money, and between the four of us we have nine francs."

"So?"

"So—we're offering all of that to you—everything we've got."

"And what am I supposed to do in return?"

"We'd like you to teach us how to fuck."

She laughs.

"It's a good bargain," he says. "The whores in Aïn Sefra don't get as much."

"So why offer all of it to me?"

"We are very impressed with you."

"Why?"

"We've seen that you can write."

Their eight eyes are all centered on her face, gleaming, eager, moist.

What prestige, she thinks, *to be offered more than a whore—surely some sort of summit achievement for having led the literary life.*

"Listen," she says, "has any of you ever slept with a girl?"

They all shake their heads.

She is amused, then strangely touched.

"All right. But I won't take your money. You can take what I offer you as a gift."

They all four jump up, stomp their feet and cheer. She opens up her flask, takes a deep swig of anisette, wipes her sleeve across her lips.

"You must all wash," she tells them, "wash yourselves very well. And then you may draw straws to see who comes in first."

Ahkmed is the winner (he has cheated, she is sure), and when he comes upon her the others group around to watch.

"It's the same as with each other," he counsels them when he's done. "But juicier, and not so tight."

Mohammed discharges on his second stroke, Ahmed is the roughest, Mustapha is gentle and slow. When they're done, they dress quickly and resume their positions with their guns. They say nothing to her, but turn their backs.

Arabs are wonderful, she thinks. *Love to them is nothing but a body function.*

Lying back on the clay floor of the blockhouse, her legs still spread, her burnoose still hoisted above her waist, she thinks back and scoffs at the dream she forged on her first visit to El Oued. There she cast herself as a romantic, who would be as mysterious and as undulant as the dunes. Now on this desert of boulders, raging with war, she finds herself grown hard, but without regret. Her old dream, struck down at Behima, finally met its death with Slimen in Ténès. Now looking at the frightened backs of her quartet of lovers, she finds her heart as impenetrable as a stone.

Back at the Étoile Du Sud canteen in Aïn Sefra she meets up again with the correspondent, Jules Bresson.

"I'm just back from a week in the field," he tells her, ordering them each a drink. "You can't believe what's going on. At least a platoon of legionnaires is being killed every day. They deny it here, of course, but every time they send out a patrol, there's an ambush and the men are massacred like rats."

"Doesn't surprise me a bit," she says. "I've been making the rounds of the posts. The Arab irregulars are incompetent —they're even afraid of dogs."

"Listen," he says, lowering his voice, "this whole town's riddled with spies. Bou-Amama knows about every column that goes out, and he knows about it in advance."

"But don't the French realize . . .?"

"If they do, they're not willing to talk. Tomorrow I'm having dinner at the garrison at Duveyrier. Come with me. We'll throw them some tough questions. Maybe we can make them squirm."

When Captain Lascaux, in command at Duveyrier, receives word he's to be visited by a lady journalist, he and his officers become greatly excited and arrange a candlelight dinner in her honor at the fort. Lascaux, himself, prepares to offer her his personal quarters for the night. But their excitement gives way to stupefaction when Isabelle swaggers in, unwraps her turban and reveals her short-cut hair.

"What an Amazon!" Lascaux whispers to Bresson.

The journalist smiles. "Give her a chance."

At dinner she gobbles up her food like an Arab, using her hand to transport it to her mouth. A number of officers, clearly repulsed, excuse themselves and wander out. But a hard core of fascinated Frenchmen remain—Lascaux, another captain named De Jonghe and a Lieutenant Legrand who, Bresson tells her, is Colonel Lyautey's aide-de-camp.

"Well," she says after dinner, setting down her coffee to which she's ostentatiously added a tumbler of anisette, "you're strung out here for a hundred fifty kilometers in a line of little forts." She winks at Bresson. "From what we've seen, your railway is attacked every night, and every one of your patrols is torn to bits. Now isn't that a fair summary of the facts?"

De Jonghe clears his throat. "You exaggerate the situation, Mademoiselle, and you forget that we control the wells."

"Bou-Amama doesn't seem very thirsty to me. He attacks you all the time, but, then, perhaps he has wells of his own, or his men don't need so much to drink."

Under pressure from her sarcasm the conversation soon becomes intense. Isabelle begins to chain-smoke cigarettes, and, alternately to gulp down glasses of liqueur. She is fierce in her criticisms and forces the officers to put up a spirited defense.

"Bou-Amama has a phantom army," says Lascaux. "It's hidden somewhere in these rocky hills. He strikes out of the night and retreats God knows where. Impossible for us to search out and destroy. We must wait for his attacks, hope to win in the defense."

"The colonel," says Legrand, "believes that Bou-Amama cannot survive without the support of the local tribes. But how can we French convince these nomads they'll be better off with us? That's the crux of the question, and we don't have an answer for it yet."

"Someday I'd like to have a word with your colonel," she says, grabbing up another bottle, then placing it on the floor within easy reach. "If he'd deign to see me, of course."

"I've asked for an interview a half dozen times," says Bresson. "Apparently Colonel Lyautey doesn't like the press."

"Nonsense," says Legrand. "He's up in Oran bargaining for more troops. When he returns I'm sure something can be arranged."

"More troops—more shit!"

They all turn to her amazed, then watch as she yawns and pours herself another drink. "Even with fifty thousand men you'll still be prisoners in your forts."

As the evening progresses she becomes increasingly obscene, drinks herself to a stupor until she finally collapses in a pile beside the intelligence officer's dog. When she breaks into a husky snore, the three officers and Jules Bresson look down at her in dismay.

"What do you make of that?" asks De Jonghe.

"A rather tough young lady," says Legrand. "A little unbalanced, of course. But she does have interesting views."

"Listen, Bresson," says Lascaux, "we're delighted to entertain lady journalists, and we'd be pleased if you'd bring us more. But next time, dear fellow, could you kindly find us someone a little less *extreme*."

Jules Bresson returns to Paris at the end of September, leaving her alone in Aïn Sefra to cover the autumn campaign. From her sources in the ranks she learns of vast troop movements to the border opposite Figuig. A small but ancient settlement, Beni-Ounif, has become the focal point for this latest show of force. One day she watches as a train, covered with armed men, machine gunners on the roof, sweeps by without stopping toward the south. On it, she is told, is the commander of the Sud-Oranais, Colonel Louis Hubert Gonsalve Lyautey, come personally to orchestrate "incidents" that will make it possible to pursue Bou-Amama across the frontier.

She has heard too much of this Lyautey in the canteens where the men speak of his grandeur and marvel at his magnificent style. Anxious to meet him she departs for Beni-Ounif, riding with a mixed crew of camels, replacement legionnaires and a gang of dance-hall girls imported from Sidi-bel-Abbès.

She immediately seeks out Legrand and asks for an interview with his chief. The next day he tells her it's arranged.

"The colonel wants to meet you," he says. "He invites you for coffee tonight. But leave your notebook behind. He's interested in you as a personality, not as a reporter for some rag in Algiers."

That evening Legrand meets her at the gates of the French camp, escorts her past the sentries toward a cluster of Berber tents. A dozen horses are tied nearby. Flags wave on their staves in the gentle evening breeze.

Legrand leads her to a large tent in the center. The flaps are open, and, as she comes around the side, her eyes meet an amazing sight. The whole vast octagonal space, built around a central pillar of polished wood, is lined with white silk, and on the ground are piles of fine carpets, laid one upon the other as in a Turkish mosque. Flowers are everywhere, arranged in copper pots, while lanterns cast a soft even glow on a huge canopied bed, an ebony chest with brass fittings and a splendid Empire desk.

She thinks: *This colonel lives like a great sheik.* Then staring in at a group of men sitting at a conference table covered with maps, her mind flashes back to El Oued. She remembers Sidi Lachmi and is struck by a sense of *déjà vu.*

Legrand motions for her to wait, steps inside. He goes up to a man whose back is to the flaps and whispers in his ear. He, in turn, says something to a servant wearing a satin jacket monogramed with a large "L." While this man brings up two more chairs, Legrand returns to escort her in.

"Colonel Lyautey; Mademoiselle Eberhardt."

Lyautey stands and turns, revealing himself for the first time. He is gray-haired, balding, with a kind open face and a magnificent and elegant moustache. His tunic is buttoned at the top, he wears a cummerbund of black silk, a row of medals, fitted riding pants and a pair of shining black boots.

She is taken at once by his proud, smooth, aristocratic face and the friendly curiosity of his eyes. There is an aura of openness about him, and, in his greeting, something curious and sensitive that provokes her desire to win his esteem.

He, in turn, seems taken with her, for she is dressed like a costumed cavalier, in clothes one might see on an actor in an opera, but with a sense of pleasure in herself, and the allure, the desirability of a thoroughbred horse.

Graciously he introduces his officers who click their heels as he says their names.

"Though this is the first time that Mademoiselle Eberhardt and I have met," he tells them, "I've heard wondrous tales of a lady journalist who rides the best horse in the Sud-Oranais."

"And you, Colonel," she replies, "who has not heard tales of the man summoned all the way from Madagascar to deliver Morocco up to France?"

"Excuse us, gentlemen—please." The officers gather up their map cases, bow to her again and stroll out.

Legrand whispers to the servant who brings them coffee in octagonal cups. Then he lights a pair of silver candelabra beside a tray of cognacs and liqueurs.

"May I smoke?" asks Lyautey.

"Of course," she replies. "May I?"

He nods, amused, but she notices that his eyes widen slightly when she brings out her kif pipe and camel's udder box.

Filling their respective pipes, each waits for the other to speak. When Legrand can no longer bear the silence he interjects.

"Mademoiselle Eberhardt calls herself Si Mahmoud," he says. "She has some interesting ideas which correspond to things you've been saying to the staff."

"How good of you," Lyautey says with a smile. "I've been waiting a long while to meet someone who shares my eccentric views."

They laugh and then Isabelle begins, saying she does not think he will prevail with a rigid line of forts.

"Of course," he says, "I agree. But tell me why."

"I know nothing about war," she says, "but I understand these people and the problems of this land. Here Bou-Amama is not regarded as a bandit, but as a holy man embarked on a crusade. This region has always been a land of gunpowder. There's no clean line between Morocco and Algeria—the people have no notion of nations or frontiers. But there is Islam." She says the word with an intense intake of breath. "Islam—it is with them all the time. Now Bou-Amama represents the faith, and because of that he gains their help."

"Then what is my solution?"

"That depends on what you want to solve. Pacification is one thing—Morocco something else."

Lyautey's eyes narrow with fascination.

"Let's speak of pacification . . ."

"Fine. For that you must not think in terms of holding land. One or two oases—so you have water and resting places and depots for your supplies. But the rest is desert and has no value. It's not the land you must fight for, but the affections of the people. If they like you, then Bou-Amama cannot survive. And if they don't, you'll have more nightmares like Taghit and El-Mounghar. His men can always mass to attack your weakest point. You must move as much as he, change your headquarters every day, be everywhere at the same time, come out of nowhere in the night. But don't set up all these little forts and expect them to hold the line. I've slept in them, Colonel, and I can assure you that the men inside are scared. What can you expect, when they know Bou-Amama can appear at any moment and smash them to dust?"

"You're right. Legrand—she sounds like me. But she doesn't go quite so far."

Isabelle smiles. "I'm not a soldier, Colonel. I'm a writer, for an obscure Algerian rag."

"You're Moslem?"

She nods.

"And you speak the languages?"

"Of course."

"So you know the people?"

"Better than I know the French."

"Tell me—what do they think of us?"

"Nothing—nothing at all. They think of God, fervently and all the time. They cannot grow food or eat it or sleep or fight or make love without evoking his name. They—and I include myself—are obsessed with submission to His will."

"And the leaders—the caids . . ."

She shakes her head. "The caids keep civil order—nothing more. The real leaders are the Marabouts—the religious men, the sheiks with *barraka*, the descendants of the saints who rest in the domed tombs. They interpret the will of God, and by the power of their interpretations they lead."

"Bou-Amama is a Marabout."

"Yes, and there are many others who could influence even him."

Lyautey smiles, satisfied.

"We *do* think the same, from slightly different angles, of course. My interest is to make this region safe, and then expand to the west. The sultan of Morocco is a mental defective, a child sitting in a decaying court. What little power he has left is felt only in the cities, hundreds of miles away. But this land—of 'gunpowder' as you call it, this land of Marabouts and tribes—it must be played cleverly, without great frontal attacks and valiant last stands at the gates of forts. I must win the people over through the Marabouti sheiks. Yes, we see things the same way, though I suspect you've come to your conclusions through an interest in exotic tribes, while I've come to mine out of my duty to serve France."

She nods, locked to him by his probing eyes.

"You say you're a writer. Is that really your profession?"

"Yes. And I'm a drunkard, too."

264

They laugh.

"I can see it in your face," he says. "You're the sort who feels compelled to chase the sun, to bury yourself in some strange and empty part of the earth where you can forget who you are and blend with nature—perhaps with God."

She puts down her pipe, astounded at how deeply he has seen inside her soul. In only a few minutes of acquaintance he has put his finger on the force that has driven her to this desert of heat and pain.

"Perhaps," she says, "you're happier—serving France. Perhaps it's better to be pushed by something one can understand than by some mysterious force that drives one to extremes."

"We shall not know, Si Mahmoud, if we are happy until the moment when we die. But I can envy you riding about on your magnificent horse, feeling free because you have no home and can wander where you like. For me happiness lies in changing the world, not my inner self. I enjoy leading men and rather dislike being led. If you knew what problems I have doing these things, you would understand why sometimes I'd rather be free like you."

Legrand, embarrassed by these revelations, clears his throat.

"Perhaps," he says, "Si Mahmoud's activities are not incompatible with our own."

"Yes," says Lyautey, "I've thought of that. But we shall speak of it some other time. Are my singers ready?"

"Yes, Colonel—they are."

"Good. Bring them in. Stay, Si Mahmoud, and listen to the best voices in my command. These German legionnaires love to sing, and their fine sad lieder give me pleasure at night."

Six young men, all tall and deeply tanned with gleaming blond hair, appear in the shadows outside the entrance to the tent. Lyautey greets them, they light candles, and then they begin to sing.

The colonel and Isabelle refill their pipes, smoke and sip liqueur from huge fragile goblets. The serenade wafts to them across the silk-lined tent, dying in the deep-piled carpets at their feet. It is sorrowful, soft, a song of Nordic love, requited but then destroyed by an untimely death. Though it seems to contain the tragic mystery of a castle built upon a frozen peak, here, in this gently billowing tent, set upon the ground of a Saharan oasis, it blends and lulls and becomes sublime. Isabelle looks over at Lyautey, watches him resting with closed eyes, swaying to the melancholy lilt.

Much later, after many songs, and many more goblets of liqueur, she feels a soothing bliss. She is not intoxicated, feels no miseries within. It is like the early days in Bône when she first experimented with kif and found a still and subtle joy. And here, with an intelligent, powerful man, she feels something she has not felt in years: admiration, the sense that at last she has met someone great.

Over the next few days their friendship blooms. Legrand comes to find her often, to take her to the great tent for feasts on silver plate. Once Lyautey asks her to brief his officers on the confraternities. He sits like a gently smiling Buddha as she tells the startled men of the power of the sects. Another time he spends an hour with her carefully tracing his plans upon his maps. And still another time he calls her to help him question a prisoner.

Until his talks with her, he had been giving lavish feasts for the caids. Now he begins to entertain the Marabouts. He sits quietly at these banquets, listening gravely as she interprets, asking an occasional question, always showing respect for their beliefs. She notices that he does not degrade the conversation with threats against the enemy or promises of the benefits that will flow from France. He wants to convey an impression that he is a great sheik, too—that he has riches beyond count, can entertain in lavish style and possesses such awesome power that he has no need to boast.

Her admiration grows at each meeting until finally she's so dazzled she forgets her rejection of Europe and all it represents. Lyautey is a superior being, but there is something more that attracts her, a sensitivity to people and to life. When she compares him to the other men in her life— Vava, the mad Russian; Archivir, the passionate Turk; Sidi Lachmi, the scheming sheik; Slimen with his primitive Berber traits—she believes he comes closest to Eugène, but with a forcefulness and a self-possession that her dear friend does not possess. He's about to become a general—there's talk in the officers' mess of that—and she hears much of him there, sees him through the eyes of his adoring men who speak with awe of the grasp of his mind, his cleverness, his grandeur, the expert way he draws the best out of each of them.

"We grow when we are with him," says Legrand. "We love him for that."

He is warm and gallant with her, makes it clear that he respects her and is intrigued by the way she lives. But there is always something guarded—some delicate wall she cannot breach. He shows her neither temperament, weakness, impatience nor the slightest hint of dishonesty or guile. But though she senses he has many sides, she always leaves him feeling he's not allowed her to explore his depths. Beside him Sidi Lachmi seems a mere pretender to strength. Lyautey is unique, a sort, she thinks, one is lucky to encounter in a lifetime. She treasures their friendship, begins to live for his summons to the tent.

"What does he think of me?" she asks Legrand one day.

"That you're one of the smartest people around."

"And my personality?"

He pauses a moment, as if judging how much to tell.

"I must be discreet," he says, "but I'll tell you one thing."

"Yes?"

"Though he adores your rebellious spirit, he believes you use it to bring misery upon yourself."

"Oh," she says after a long silence. "I never thought of that."

❖

One evening after too much to drink, she enters the area around Lyautey's tent, learns from the sentries that he's alone and asks his batman if she may pay him a call. A few moments later he steps outside.

"How nice to see you, Si Mahmoud. How good of you to stop by."

He does not invite her in.

"I had to come," she tells him. "I was sitting alone, confused, and when I began to long for clarity I thought of you."

Lyautey smiles.

"I think of you often," she says. "At night, especially, I think of you a lot."

"I could be your father, Si Mahmoud."

"In age, perhaps, but not in your heart."

"Thank you."

She purses her lips, maddened by his innocuous phrase. *Doesn't he realize,* she asks herself, *that I've just made him a declaration?* She's about to blurt out something, words she's not yet framed but already knows she'll regret, when he takes her arm.

"Do you drink because you suffer, Si Mahmoud?"

She nods. Suddenly tears form in her eyes.

"Your life has been extraordinary and strange," he says. "I think the desert is your studio—a place where you suffer, are alone and work to form your soul. And you emerge from it strong, stronger than you know. There's great power in you—the aristocratic force of life. You're so much better than those fools in Paris who run about like ants."

She looks up at him, his gentle fatherly eyes. She wants to fall at his feet, thank him for this compliment which is the best she's ever received. She feels that something is happening between them, something that will bring her to his arms.

"I was just going down the hill to make a round of the canteens," he says. "They belong to the men, of course, but I don't think they mind if I step in for a minute or two. Come—let me walk you back."

Expertly he guides her out of the officers' section of the camp. She stumbles, still drunk—blushes when he helps her to her feet.

She looks at him again, sees something distant in his face. He is thinking, she is sure, of whether to turn and take her back. Suddenly she goes soft, holds her breath, feels some intention coming from his arm. But then there's a tightening up, a signal he's decided to resist.

"Yes, come," he says. "We'll look in at the dance hall. I enjoy watching the girls there myself."

As they move among the tents, down a narrow walk, past campfires and sentries who raise their rifles in salute, she knows their moment has passed, that for some reason he has steeled himself against taking her as a lover in his tent.

Another minute and this sad silent thought is broken by a faint hint of music that hauntingly pierces the Saharan night. They move closer to the dark mud building, transformed into a dance hall for the troops, and hear laughter, the thump of stamping feet.

They move to the windows, smudged panes, and peer inside. Hundreds of soldiers are cavorting with two dozen girls who look worn out. Isabelle recognizes faces from the convoy that brought her to Beni-Ounif. In wigs and frills they twirl among the men, splashes of color in a monotonous sea of tan, lit by carbide lamps that hang from ceiling wires and fill the top half of the room with yellowish smoke. Standing outside in the bitter desert air, Isabelle feels apart and turns to the tall presence at her side.

"I used to go to places like this," he says, "when I was a young officer in Saigon. But we didn't have many French girls there—the Annamese were so splendid, so petite."

He seems almost wistful to her, and she holds her breath, hoping he'll let down his shield, give her a glimpse of the man within.

"It's hard to imagine you dancing like that."

"Why? Because now I live like a feudal lord surrounded by an adoring court? I was gay when I was a lieutenant—now I must be grave. That's the cost one pays for high command. Now I must be a stern father to the men, mete out discipline and rewards. Still I miss the days when I led patrols, and then, happy to be back at camp unscathed, could dance away the night."

A pair of legionnaires passes by. They don't see the colonel or his friend standing in the shadows by the wall. They are speaking in German, laying plans for one of the girls inside. When they're gone Lyautey laughs.

"I don't know how many times I've overheard talk like that. Yet for all the brilliant seductive traps well laid, only one in a thousand ever catches the prey. It's the same in war. Still I must keep sending out patrols, even though I always lose some men. I never know, you see—by some majestic stroke of luck one of those boys in there might manage to shoot Bou-Amama through his heart."

They turn back to the dancing, more riotous it seems to her, building toward some explosion of flesh and sweat. She watches as one of the girls comes near the window for a breath of air. Her face is exhausted, lined, the eyes blood-shot, the lashes limp. And beside her, on the smudged glass, is a reflection of herself.

Isabelle narrows her eyes, examines her face—weary, turbaned, moody, scorned. *Is there some bond*, she wonders, *are she and I the same, both worn out by too much ecstasy, so hardened by life that we can no longer stimulate desire?*

The whore on the other side winces and turns away, leaving only the reflected image of Lyautey and herself as a faint stain on the smoky scene inside.

"A soldier like you, Si Mahmoud, is worth a thousand

patrols. There are important things I would like you to do. Tomorrow I'm going back to Aïn Sefra. Will you come and see me next week?"

She nods, and he withdraws without a word. She stands alone then, watching the dancing, and a few seconds later sees him enter, sees the men cheer, the dancers strut, the musicians stand and play the anthem of St. Cyr. Lyautey raises his right hand, gives a royal wave. Then he slips out and the crushed pursuit turns frantic once again.

A few days later she visits him in the commander's house at Aïn Sefra—even more lavishly decorated than his field tent. The furniture is gilded; there are flowers everywhere in Oriental vases; his ancestors' portraits hang on the walls along with tapestries and imported *boiserie*. These things— so inappropriate in this dusty desert outpost, especially in this voluminous house of baked red mud—are strangely impressive, like props in a set. With them, he creates a setting of irresistible splendor by which he magnifies his power and announces that even here France exists.

"I've had some indications," he tells her, "that Bou-Amama wants to talk peace. What do you think?"

"Be wary," she warns him. "I know these people and how they work. They open a hundred different lines, start rumors, set up diversions, talk peace and attack at the same time. They also take great pains to infuriate their enemies by unforgivable deceptions which, they hope, will inspire rash acts."

"That's very interesting. The question is whether my intelligence is correct."

She shakes her head.

"When Bou-Amama wants peace, he'll stop the attacks. And he'll do that only when he thinks he has no more chance. Then he'll lie low for a while, send you sweet letters, even sign a treaty if you like. He'll wait for the proper moment and then he'll attack again. This is his land. He thinks that sooner or later, next year or a century from now, you French will finally get tired and leave."

Lyautey stares at her a long time. "As always," he says finally, "you and I think along the same lines."

"So," she asks him, "how do you hope to win?"

"I don't."

"Really?" She is surprised.

"You've said it yourself—sooner or later we'll have to go. Or else move these troops when there's a flare-up somewhere else."

"Then . . .?"

"Then we forget about conquest. Instead we pacify, as inexpensively as we can."

"I don't understand."

"It's quite simple really. I have been developing a new approach. I have decided I must study the tribes, keep them apart, exploit their rivalries, turn them to advantage for France. There's no point now in conquering Morocco. The point is to control it, and that's more easily achieved by a protectorate than an outright conquest by arms. Divide and control—that'll be my method. What a waste to send out columns on attack, when I can more cheaply neutralize Bou-Amama through the rival Marabouts."

She looks at him, struck by his clarity, and the strength of his political grasp. At this moment, to her, he seems like a god, leaving her with no other wish than to serve him, learn and obey.

"Tell me, Si Mahmoud, do you suppose the local sheiks know that you and I often talk?"

"I'm sure of it—Arabs know everything."

"In that case I could use your help."

"How? Tell me what I can do."

"Many things, Si Mahmoud," he says fixing her with kind strong eyes. "So many things."

He excuses himself and leaves the room. When he's gone

she stares at the ancestral portraits, excited, mystified, intrigued. Many show the same high forehead and finely drawn chin. All wear uniforms, medals, sashes, epaulets.

He returns with Lieutenant Legrand who eyes her strangely, then sits down.

"You're Moslem, Si Mahmoud," Lyautey says. "You speak the language like a native. More important you understand the people—there's much sympathy between you and them. You're the only European, thus far, to become a member of an Islamic sect. In short you have all the qualifications necessary to deal directly with the sheiks."

"As your intermediary?"

He nods. "As my agent—a source of information, too. We need intelligence. My *deuxième bureau* isn't equipped to penetrate the sects. Our own Arabs are suspect, and Arabs, anyway, have a tendency to tell one what they think one wants to hear. Really, Si Mahmoud, you'd be invaluable— just the man we need."

They both are staring at her, waiting for her to agree.

She wonders, then, if she really wants to help, and whether to do so will be to betray the Arab cause. She needs to consider whether Lyautey, for all his magnificent stature, represents the sort of benign colonialism she can bring herself to accept. She decides she must divert them, give herself some time to think.

"This could compromise my status," she says. "I'm here as a reporter, don't forget."

"I'll write Barrucand. Don't worry about that."

"You're French now by marriage," says Legrand. "This is a chance for you to show your loyalty."

She laughs hilariously, and they both stare at her perplexed. She pauses again, then decides. Of all the Europeans she's met, Lyautey is the only one she can bring herself to help.

"Well," she says, "maybe . . . perhaps . . ."

"Good!"

"Excellent!"

Lyautey sends Legrand for a bottle of champagne.

When he returns they drink a toast.

"To our new agent, Si Mahmoud!"

"To France," she replies, a touch of bitterness in her voice.

She asks for more to drink while they settle the details of the bargain. Legrand is dispatched for another bottle while she and Lyautey talk.

"I insist on reporting directly to you."

"I wouldn't have it any other way."

"And later, perhaps, you'll do something in return."

"Anything you wish."

"Will I be paid?"

"You'll receive a small allowance to cover the costs. Also a pass that will allow you to eat in the messes and will give you priority on the trains."

When she leaves, finally, reeling with champagne, happy that her talents have been recognized and are at last being put to use, Lyautey turns to Legrand.

"What do you think?"

"I think she'll be magnificent."

"Yes," says the colonel, "for a while at least. But eventually she'll get restless. We'll have to keep her on a tight leash."

"Don't you trust her?"

"I trust her, certainly. But she has no discipline. She enjoys her suffering, and is susceptible to the most destructive forms of excess."

For several weeks, then, she shuttles back and forth between Aïn Sefra and the towns on the rail line to Beni-Ounif, visiting the monasteries, meeting the Marabouts, discussing the advantages of collaboration with the French.

When she gives Lyautey her reports, embellished with

meticulous descriptions of the personalities she's met, she has the sense he's using her as part of a master plan which he alone knows and holds secretly in his head. He is like a juggler with a hundred balls in the air, exploiting the Marabouts, playing on their rivalries, using them, his men and even herself to accomplish his grand design.

One night at his quarters she finds a stranger. He is young and dark with a brutal handsome face and a smile that seems more like a sneer. Lyautey introduces him as Lieutenant Antoine Desforges.

"He's from the Camargue," he says, "a land of marshes and wild horses. Desforges feels at home in the desert. He's used to horizons with a sharp edge."

As she gives her report she feels the lieutenant making a feast of her with his eyes. When she's finished, and Lyautey begins his questions, she becomes distracted by the intensity of his gaze.

"Is it necessary for this young man to stare?"

"What's that?" asks the colonel, looking around.

"Forgive me," says Desforges. "I forgot myself. I was so fascinated by your report."

She gives him an abrupt nod, continues with her reply. Later, when Lyautey goes to his desk to sign a stack of orders, she and Desforges begin to talk.

"Have you been here long?"

"About a year. I command a company. We're patrolling south of Beni-Ounif."

"Spahis? Camel Corps?"

"No." He laughs. "Irregulars—a terrible bunch. Bandits, deserters—anyone we can find. They spend more time fighting among themselves than anything else."

"Lieutenant Desforges is being discreet," says Lyautey, returning from his desk with a decanter of wine. "Tell her what you really do."

Desforges lowers his eyes, then raises them and shows his teeth.

"Oh, lots of things, Si Mahmoud. Patrols, of course, and armed propaganda, and then sometimes we pretend to be part of Bou-Amama's army and wreak havoc in the towns."

"What's the point of that?" She finds him arrogant, doesn't like him at all.

"To drive a wedge between the enemy and the people who help him to survive. If 'Bou-Amama' means pillage and rape, then they'll welcome the colonel when he moves south next year."

"What nonsense! But then, perhaps, rape is something you enjoy."

Desforges grins. "I follow my orders."

She turns to Lyautey who tries to conceal a smile behind his glass.

"So—you're playing it both ways. I might have known."

"Now, now, Si Mahmoud—I'm not a man to stake everything on a single card. Like yourself, Lieutenant Desforges is doing an excellent job. I gave him a nasty task and the worst scum around—people who'd ordinarily be locked up. He's done well, actually molded them into a first-class force."

"I'm sure he has. You must be an amazing officer, Lieutenant. How do you account for your success?"

"Discipline. That's all there is to handling men."

"I see. . . ."

"I don't think Si Mahmoud approves, Colonel. Please assure her I'm not a beast."

"I can assure you that Lieutenant Desforges is an exemplary officer in every way. I believe he even plays the violin."

"The cello, Colonel."

"Yes, the cello—I forgot. No, Si Mahmoud, don't underestimate the uses of brute force. Your civilized encounters with the Marabouts and Desforges' havoc in the towns are two arms of the same beast—me!" They laugh. "Each of you has much to teach the other. As a matter of fact I think it might be a good idea for you to ride with the lieutenant's company for a time. You could write about it, subject to my censorship, of course. Would you like a few days off? Desforges can put you up, in disguise, naturally, and then you'd see what it's all about."

She turns to Desforges, finds his eyes fastened on her, feels she's being presented with a dare.

"You've been telling me you want to live with the troops, write about their lives *en marche*. This would be an excellent chance."

What does he want me to find out? she wonders, suspecting duplicity, suddenly feeling that she's in contest with a most devious sheik, another Sidi Lachmi, whom she might do well to fear.

"You'd be welcome, Si Mahmoud. Perhaps if you rode with us you'd understand what we do, and we could redeem ourselves in your eyes."

"You understand, Desforges, you'd be responsible for her safety—personally responsible to me?"

"Understood!"

"Well, Si Mahmoud, what do you say?"

She hesitates a moment, then she agrees, thinking how well she'll be able to skewer this animal after observing him awhile at close range.

❖

Outside Lyautey's house Desforges invites her to join him for a drink.

"Couldn't we go to your quarters? I'd like to hear you play your cello."

"Unfortunately I broke it over a sergeant's head."

"Oh," she says, "what a pity. Now I'll never know if you can play."

As they follow a path into the ravine, she stumbles and he reaches for her arm. She jerks away.

"I can manage very well."

"You don't like me, do you?"

"Not especially."

"That's too bad, because I like you a lot."

"How sad for you."

"I've seen you before, you know. I was in the courtroom in Constantine. I wondered then what you were really like."

"Now you have a chance to find out."

"Yes, I'm looking forward to that."

She pauses, looks at him, sees the faintest sign of a sneer on his moonlit face.

"And I shall find out about you, Desforges. Perhaps more than you'd care for me to know."

They walk the rest of the way in silence, then stroll in the African village among drunken legionnaires toward the Oasis canteen. Over a drink they discuss the war and make arrangements to meet in Beni-Ounif. When she leaves him she's certain it will not be difficult to keep him in his place. He's younger than she and his Camarguin toughness will not be a match for one who swung a shovel on the garbage scows of Marseilles.

The autumnal light is pale against the sulfurous dunes. There is an immense sadness about the desert south of Beni-Ounif, where the company makes its camp. In the mornings she's awakened by the moans of camels, then by the sounds of the men around who rise slowly to stir the fires.

Desforges, as an officer, has the luxury of a tent. She sleeps among the men rolled in her burnoose, her rifle, like theirs, beneath her head. This time she takes great pains to maintain her disguise. She's an Arab—Si Mahmoud. Only Desforges knows her real name.

They seldom speak, though on the first night, when he strides about inspecting the camp, he invites her, in a whisper, to join him for dinner in his tent.

"No," she tells him. "If I do that they'll suspect."

He nods gravely and walks away.

But when they are *en marche* the next day, at a slow desert pace, he circles back from his position at the point and rides by her side.

"Everything all right?" he asks, and when she assures him that it is, he asks if there's anything she needs.

She grins then and shakes her head. He stares at her, confused, and rides away.

She has resolved to have nothing to do with him, to live among the men, listen to what they say, record the texture of their lives. Late at night, after feasts of stewed camel meat and dates, she retires to a place near one of the fires and makes notes on all she's seen. She's fascinated by the tribal disputes, the tales of vengeance, the insults happily exchanged.

As the days pass in a monotony of rocks and dunes, relieved only by the incredible luminosity of the air, she feels a building up of tension in Desforges. Then she enjoys a fantasy of him alone and smoldering in his tent, thinking up ways to gain her attention, grinding his teeth over her insufferable chill.

Each day he tries a different tack, devised, she has no doubt, the night before. He's in search of some delicate means to win her confidence without giving offense. Sometimes he implores her to join him for a talk after the march, and on other days demands her presence with a barely concealed anger she answers with contempt. She observes him when he inspects the camp, walking moodily, his hands thrust deep into his pockets, puffing with distraction on his pipe. And in the mornings, while eating her bread and *tangia* made in a communal earthenware pot buried the night before in the embers of the fires, she observes him snarling at his sergeants as though he's suffered a tormented night.

She finds herself becoming interested against her will. He becomes a specimen she watches, and hopes to see explode. But she conceals her interest beneath a contemptuous disdain, hoping to drive him to a fit.

"Where's that famous toughness?" she asks one morning.

"I don't know what you mean."

"I've been with you a week, Lieutenant, and I've yet to see you break something over someone's head."

He snorts and rides off, but an hour later is back by her side.

"What are you doing? Trying to drive me mad?"

"I'm too busy with my work."

"You know I desire you, so why do you resist? I need company. These men are animals and this terrain bores me to death."

"I'm sorry," she says, "but the truth is I don't like you at all. Wouldn't it be more civilized if we'd just stay out of each other's way?"

They ride in silence, then he mutters something and canters off.

For the rest of that day he stays apart, but after dinner he sends a sergeant who orders her to report to his tent. She goes, feeling she has no choice. But once inside, she taunts him.

"So," she says, "you've gotten me here at last. How clever and how sad that you couldn't manage it by yourself. You know I couldn't refuse without giving the game away."

"You can't refuse in any case. An order is an order, and I'm in command."

"Come, come, Desforges, I have special status here. You have no control over me."

He gives her a serene look.

"Your trouble, Si Mahmoud, is that you've lived your entire life without any discipline at all. You're the most willful, self-indulgent woman I've ever met."

"Ho-hum, the famous disciplinarian speaks."

"He does. Tomorrow we turn toward Béchar. The colonel wants to extend the rail line, and we're going to survey the route. I'm only taking a few men. You'll have to stay here."

"What? I absolutely refuse! I wasn't sent here to sit around your boring camp. I've been waiting a week to see some action. You have no right..."

"Shut up! I'm responsible to the colonel. For some reason your safety's important to him. So—you stay!"

"Now listen, Desforges..."

"That's an order. Do me a kindness and obey."

Then he turns his back.

That morning at parade he calls out the best of his men. The rest are assigned to guard the camp. Isabelle is given sentry duty at his tent. The order is formal, given in Arabic before the men.

She decides to follow him as soon as his troupe is out of sight. Without thinking of the risk she takes of being shot for desertion of her post, she sneaks off, mounts her horse and following the footprints in the sand, tracks him to the settlement of Bou-Aïech.

That evening she's discovered by a scout who notices her lingering on the fringes of the camp. He jumps her from behind, wrestles her to the ground, then holds a knife against her throat. Recognizing her at last as she squeals and squirms, he grasps her up and pushes her roughly into the lieutenant's tent where Desforges, stripped to the waist, is studying his maps.

"Look what I found outside!" says the scout. "It seems Si Mahmoud's a spy!"

"I shall question him myself," says Desforges. "You can return to your post."

When the scout's gone he shakes his head.

"I'm sorry you did this, Si Mahmoud—very sorry, indeed. I have no choice now but to send you back, with a report to the colonel besides. He doesn't like quarrels between his men. This time I think he'll agree you overstepped. It's a pity. You've acted like a woman, a very silly woman indeed, and now I must treat you like a woman in return."

"That's not fair. If there's danger I want to experience it. I'll write a letter to Lyautey now—explain everything, absolve you of all responsibility."

"You really want to be a soldier?"

"I told you that last night . . ."

"But you deserted your post, Si Mahmoud. A soldier can be shot for that."

She shrugs.

"No, Si Mahmoud, you can't have it both ways. If you're going to pretend to be one of the men, you're going to have to follow orders the same as they. I'm sorry. Tomorrow you go back."

Silence. She sees he's serious.

"Please, Desforges, be reasonable. Let me stay. I promise I won't disobey you again."

"It's too late for that—the whole camp knows you're here."

"Couldn't you overlook . . . ?"

"Impossible. One exception and discipline breaks down. The slightest hint of favoritism and I lose authority with the men."

She stands, silent, realizing that he's right.

"Look, Desforges, I'm sorry about everything. I admit I was playing games with you. Couldn't we—isn't there some way . . . ?"

"There is *one* way," he interrupts. "But I don't think . . ."

"*What?*"

"No." He shakes his head. "Impossible!"

"Tell me, Desforges. I'll do anything."

"Anything?" He smiles. "Well, in that case there may be a chance." He scratches his head. "If you stay, you see, you'll have to be punished in front of the others so they'd know what would happen to them."

"Punished?"

"Yes. For what you've done a man would be punished."

"I don't quite see . . ."

"Yes, I'm afraid that's the only way. Either go back, because you've acted like a woman, or stay here and get treated like a man."

"What do you want to do—have me shot?"

"No," he laughs. "Not for a first offense. You'll follow us tomorrow, on foot, with your hands tied to the stirrup of a guard. That's how we teach a man to obey, and that's how we'll teach you. Think about it—make up your mind, but let me know before we ride." He calls for a sentry. "Dismissed!"

She leaves the tent furious, goes to one of the fires, tries to eat but discovers her hunger has gone away. She finds a place to sleep, rolls herself up in her burnoose and is shocked to find she wants to cry. It's been years, she thinks, since she's truly wept, not since Old Nathalie's death. And after all she's suffered—Behima, Constantine, Marseilles, Ténès—she's surprised at this urge that comes upon her, unleashing tears that sting her cheeks.

How can this be? she asks herself. *There is nothing on earth that can make Si Mahmoud cry.* Wiping her eyes with her arm she knows that this is not Si Mahmoud at all—it is Isabelle who weeps, a girl of twenty-six, alone among men in an obscure corner of the earth, forced to decide who she is going to be.

She spends an anguished night over the choice, knowing that Desforges, in his uncanny way, has found out her weakness, plunged in his knife and now threatens to divide her soul.

She thinks: *If only he'd not given me the choice.* Then, she knows, she could accept his sentence, endure it as she's endured so many things much worse. If Si Mahmoud must suffer then suffer he must—but to be forced to decide between suffering and staying Si Mahmoud, or leaving and reverting to Isabelle—that is torture worse than any punishment Desforges could ever devise.

If I go back as Isabelle, then Si Mahmoud is dead. This, she suspects, is something Desforges, in his brooding, has found out. He's testing her, testing the strength of her role, knowing that if she refuses his sentence, he will have broken her and won. Knowing that to be sent back would be a worse humiliation than the forced march, she decides to endure the pain rather than the scornful laughter of this man who wants to rip away her mask.

But how cruel, she thinks, *how devilishly cruel of him to leave me with the choice.*

At dawn she presents herself at his tent.

"Well?" he asks coolly.

"I want to stay."

His lips form a narrow smile that broadens as she stares directly back.

"Very good. I'll give the orders. And if things become too difficult along the way, then, Si Mahmoud, just shout for me."

He snaps the flap shut, but in the moment before she sees a glimmer of satisfaction in his insolent eyes.

Her wrists are tied tightly with a leather thong in front of the men, and then attached to a long rough rope. A man dressed in black, his mouth covered, his high dark Berber cheeks bitten deeply by the pox, attaches the rope to the stirrup of his horse. He comes to her, holds his goatskin bag of water to her lips, then turns and mounts. *My executioner,* she thinks, *my man in black.*

Soon the rest are on their horses—she sees Karim tied behind the camel that carries Desforges' tent. The lieutenant mounts last, but his horse is restless. She watches as it rears, halfheartedly trying to shake him off. She hopes he'll be thrown, but he's an excellent rider, leans forward, speaks to the animal and strokes its neck. Then he is off to the front of the column without giving her a glance.

The march begins, and for the first hour she's surprised at its ease. She moves proudly, trying to find a pleasant, sliding desert gait. Her only annoyance is the thong that binds her wrists. Her hands feel awkward, tied before her body; she longs to swing them by her sides. However, this is nothing but an inconvenience which she forces herself to forget. *I must think of this as a promenade*, she thinks, and catching sight of Desforges, she fixes her eyes on his back so as to be ready to meet his when he finally turns.

Not so bad, she thinks, *not so harsh. The winter sun is bearable enough.* And she welcomes it when it comes, hitting her full on the right side of her face, giving pleasure as it takes the morning's chill from off her cheeks.

An hour later she is praying for a solar eclipse. This gentle sun is fast becoming a cruel monster in the sky, rising and steadily increasing its heat, until the growing pain in her feet and the numbness in her wrists seem insignificant compared to its infernal gaze.

Her guard stops, drinks, then dismounts and gives her water. Relief, then, for a minute or two, but after that the pain begins again, the beating down, hard, blinding, which starts a dull thudding tom-tom in her brain. Quarter hour by quarter hour it gets worse, until it takes all her strength to keep from crying aloud.

The next time her guard drinks, he does not bother to dismount but motions for her to walk beside his horse. Then with a gesture that is more weary than mean he pours her ration upon her face. Most of the precious liquid splashes away, and she must dab about desperately with her tongue. She catches little of it, finds salt caked around her lips. She opens her mouth again, squinting at him, whispering a plea for more, but brusquely he motions her back, and then enrages her by a harsh jerk he gives the rope.

They are moving toward the base of the Antar Mountains, through what the French maps call "the Desert of Black Stones." This is a place of uneven rocks that bite into her boots. She keeps her head down, afraid she'll stumble, but raises it often so she'll not miss Desforges if he should look back. What she hadn't realized before is that, winter sun or not, it is one thing to sit on a horse, barely moving, lulled by the animal's gait, keeping one's face to any glimmer of a breeze, and quite another to move one's body, take step after step, at a pace set by others, with no choice but to follow or be dragged. *It's the moving that's killing me,* she thinks, *having to move my whole body at every step.* For she knows this law of the desert well: wasted motion means a depletion of moisture, that every movement is agony beneath the sun.

As it rises higher she is struck by an increase in her pain. Now her wrists, her feet, her eyes, her lips, her face and legs and back all ache; an entire torment wracks her body, threatening to make her cry and fall. There is a temptation, then, to call out for Desforges—she's proved her point; surely now she can be released. She knows better—that he has set the terms, and she must meet them or else admit she's Isabelle and not Si Mahmoud.

She turns her face up to the blinding whiteness of the sky, can tell by the position of the sun that it's not yet eleven o'clock. The worst, she knows, is still to come—at least two more hours of marching, finally broken by the midday rest. After that the sun will not give so much pain, but the ground, the stones, the thongs, the rope—they will take their turn.

She decides to divide her punishment into segments, see each one through and decide then how to go on to the next. Maybe this way, she thinks, she'll manage to survive the day. The first segment will last until the shadow of her guard's horse falls directly beneath its belly; the next, at the midday stop. Her skin feels as if it's being ripped away by white-hot solar tongs. She gives up waiting for Desforges to turn, decides to concentrate on the stones beneath her feet. Just then her toe, connecting with a rock, gives violent pain. She hops on one foot, stumbles and a moment later feels the rip of the rope against her wrists. Both shoulders are pulled out hard, stretched until she screams. Her black guard turns, stops his horse, halts and when she's up, starts again. *How compassionate he is*, she thinks, for she knows how little such men care about another's pain.

He gives her water then, poured more carefully than before, and smiling she nods her gratitude. For a moment her guard looks into her face, and then he turns away his eyes. It occurs to her that she may not be presenting a pleasant sight.

By noon, when the sun is directly overhead and her own shadow is concentrated to a moving puddle at her feet, her suffering reaches a new and heightened pitch. Everything is pure pain, and the worst of it is that she cannot lie down and find relief in coma or sleep. She must march on, step after step, or else be dragged and bruised upon the stones. No question now of giving in, crying out for mercy, begging pity and relief. She hasn't even a voice for that, as she learns the second time she falls and tries to call to her guard for a moment of respite. Her black horseman is sleeping in his saddle, lulled by the monotony of the terrain. When the rope goes taut he simply removes his foot from his stirrup and nudges at his horse. Somehow she pulls herself up, then stumbles after him to slacken the rope.

Pulled along now, across a field of pointed stones, her wrists numb, her arms sore, her shoulders wrenched, her lips scalding, blistering, her whole face and head resounding with a beating ache, she searches for some inner power to help her to endure. Other men, she knows, have suffered worse. It takes, she thinks, some kind of mental magic, some interior adjustment to blank out the pain. *I must submerge myself, forget, seek oblivion, become like these rocks, these mountains. I must disappear, bury the part of me that feels, become a thing, a wheel, perhaps, that merely rolls where it is led.*

But no matter how she tries she does not know the way to self-annihilation; she doesn't yet possess that mystic power that comes so easily to primitive desert men. She has no notion of how to make herself an unfeeling stone, and it is not possible, she knows, to learn such a thing in a single day. But then, as she falls forward again, this time opening cuts in her knees, a new thought suddenly occurs.

I must try to seek out the pleasure in this pain. She feels a trickle of warm blood rushing from her knees. *I must begin,* she decides, *by forcing the agony off my face. Smile, smile, laugh if I can.* And at that she manages to let out with a dry unhappy gasp. *Think of ecstasy, think of joy.* She fastens on the torment in her shoulders. *They feel good.* Then, like a litany, she begins a dialogue with herself. *Do my arms feel light? Yes, they feel light. And my shoulders—are they sore? No, they are not sore. My whole body—it's in ecstasy. Oh, God, help me find the pleasure in this unbearable pain. Help me find the will to turn it around. Smile, laugh. Make each step a pleasure. Let the bite of every rock become a sweet caress.*

Her guard unties the rope from his stirrup but leaves her hands bound. Ignoring her eyes, he leads her to the shade of a boulder, drinks, gives her water, helps himself to bread, then breaks up small pieces and puts them one by one between her lips. He says nothing to her, but before he sleeps ties the other end of her rope around his waist. She looks about. The rest of the men are spread in the shade of other boulders in a vast amphitheater of basaltic rocks. Sentries are posted, and she sees Karim resting with the camels beside a well. She doesn't even look for Desforges, doesn't even think of him. Trying to recall the last hour of marching before the halt, she can remember nothing at all.

By midafternoon the worst rage of the sun is past. She marches three more hours, smiling the whole time, serene in her accomplishment, her defeat of pain. At the camp her wrists are finally untied and she collapses in a heap.

Later she sits apart, with her hands still pressed together, watching as the men prepare the fires and the food. She eats

a little and afterward runs her hands over her face. Her skin
is badly scorched, her lips are puffed, the sockets of all her
joints are sore. She removes her boots and examines her feet.
They are blistered, cut in many places, and the caked blood
on her knees is black.

As she is contemplating her wounds, marveling at her
martyrdom and the fact that she's survived, a sergeant
comes to fetch her to Desforges' tent. Wearily, she replaces
her boots, then follows him toward the black hexagon lit up
strangely by the fires of the camp.

She stands before the closed black flaps, willing up an
anger at this man who has caused her so much pain. In her
mind, now, he is more than a man—he is a font of power,
absolute, a dark force whose field she can feel even in the
cold night desert air. The sergeant opens the flap, she stoops,
enters and rises to face her enemy at last.

He inspects her strangely. She watches as his eyes roam
her baked-out face, her ruined lips, then search her torn
knees and feet.

"You look like you've been barbecued, like a piece of
roasted lamb, a *mechoui*. Did you like it?"

His sneer, his vile choice of words, conjures a rush of
hate. With all her force she spits into his face.

"Cunt! Whore!"

He slashes at her with the back of his hand. She falls
before the blow, and then turns to see him standing above
her quivering with rage.

She lowers her eyes, has lost all interest now in meeting
his menacing gaze. She feels his hard body come upon her,
feels him ripping at her robe. His strong fingers tear at her
djellaba, snatch it away to bare her breasts. She turns her
head as he takes her on the stony sand with savage strokes.
She is conscious of nothing except the image of the sentry
outside, a silhouette against the dark wool wall of the tent.
When Desforges grinds her down against the rocks, she does
not even flinch. She is amazed. It's as if the Desert of Black

Stones has made her so hard she's become immune even to annihilation by a lover—a sensation she's always craved.

She spends the night beside him, curled up upon herself against the cold, her back, bruised and marked, in touch with his dark warm skin. He wakes up several times to caress her absently, brush his lips against her neck and cheeks. But it is as if he is not even there. In her numbness, she thinks that *nothing* is what she is, that love and torment are the same, that pain is good, that submission is conquest, and that he who has tortured her is now her slave.

Before dawn she creeps over his sleeping body, arranges her clothes. When he wakes up she is sitting on his stool, staring down at him, smiling, smoking a cigarette.

"I'll be riding back to Beni-Ounif today," she says.

"You want to leave—now?"

She nods.

"But I can show you action, anything you want."

She shakes her head, pitying him with her smile.

"We can be friends now. Comrades. I respect you. You can sleep with me or outside if you like, as one of the men."

Again she shakes her head.

"Si Mahmoud!"

She grins, reaches for his hand, gives it a hearty shake.

"Thank you, Lieutenant Desforges. Thank you for your time and everything else."

Then she stands up and walks out of the tent, down to the fires where she helps herself to coffee and bread.

Awhile later, when she is watering her horse, an armed Berber tribesman appears at her side.

"I am your escort, Si Mahmoud. The lieutenant has ordered me to guide you back."

She nods and a few minutes later they start their trek across the silent Desert of Black Stones toward the camp at Beni-Ounif.

Visions of Isabelle

A few days after her return to
Aïn Sefra, Isabelle is summoned to Lyautey's house.

"How did it go?" he asks. "Any interesting adventures?"

"Yes," she replies. "Now I can write about the lives of our
soldiers *en marche*. I'm very happy to have had the experience. Thank you."

Lyautey smiles.

"But I'd heard—oh, well . . ."

"Yes?"

"It's just that I received a report. Nothing important. A
small unpleasantness. But since you don't mention it,
well . . ."

She looks at him, sees him searching her face.

"Oh," she says. "*That!* It's not worth mentioning—a small
unpleasantness, as you say."

"It must have been frightful. If I'd known, then of
course . . ."

"Don't even think about it."

"But, my dear, you must have suffered."

"Yes," she says, "but in the end I rather enjoyed it, too."

He shakes his head.

"Poor Si Mahmoud."

They talk awhile longer, about his progress with the Marabouts. There have been some setbacks, but generally he's satisfied.

As she leaves she's struck by a sudden thought: that he might have been behind the entire episode with Desforges, might have set him up as a proxy lover to discipline and seduce her at the same time.

But a moment later she knows this is impossible. Lyautey is too civilized a man. Though he's as ruthless as Sidi Lachmi, and as cunning, he is not the sort to turn upon a friend.

At the Foreign Legion canteen in Beni-Ounif, a mixture of infantrymen, Spahis, Camel Corps soldiers and legionnaires have been drinking through the night. They are shouting good-natured insults, boasting of the exploits of their units.

Isabelle sits at a table in the center, dazed by a night of absinthe and several pipes of potent kif. She feels miserable, tired, disappointed with her life. As the brawling becomes louder and the insults of the soldiers more obscene, she suddenly swipes her glass onto the floor.

Someone kicks it away and it breaks against the wall. The brawling continues while she lies with her head upon the table, oblivious, ignored.

At dawn the soldiers disappear. She is alone, asleep, in the smoky room.

In the souk at Tirkount everything is dusty and brown: the earth, the clothes of the inhabitants, the pottery they make and sell. Donkeys stand about unfettered. The people crush the sellers. Their bargaining is not intense or shrill; it blends into the hushing wind.

Beside the women seated on the ground are pieces of orange rind, squashed dates, potatoes bearing the stamp of heels. Before one of these women, selling goats' milk, there suddenly appears a pair of scarlet boots.

The woman looks up, sees Isabelle in a white burnoose, searching the horizon with her eyes.

"Some milk?"

Isabelle does not reply.

From a distance her boots are two red flames in a sea of brown.

At the correspondents' tent at Aïn Sefra, Isabelle has spent the day drinking anisette and by late afternoon has fallen to sleep. Jules Bresson of *Le Matin* sits talking with an artist who's been sent to paint a portrait of Lyautey for a corridor in the Ministry of War.

"This is a puny little war," says Bresson. "Give me Indochina anytime. At least there are women, and you can bear the heat."

"I'd like to make love to a Tuareg," says the artist. "I like the idea of blue skin."

Their eyes fall upon Isabelle. She's waking, slowly—peering around. Suddenly her eyes glaze and she begins to shriek.

"Bring them on! Bring on the soldiers! I want them all!"

The painter is embarrassed, tries to hush her up.

"Calm down, Si Mahmoud. You've had a bad dream."

Later, when she's fallen back to sleep, he turns to Bresson. "Is she always like that?"

"Sometimes she is, and sometimes she's not."

Night, near the stables at Aïn Sefra. Isabelle is wrapped against the cold in a black burnoose. Her head is wrapped in a black turban which she's drawn around her face to cover her mouth. She sits on the ground. Her horse, head down, stands a few feet away.

After a few moments she stands and strokes his neck. Tears form in her eyes.

"I'm sorry, Karim," she says. "I'm sorry I can't afford to buy you better food."

At the canteen in Duveyrier, Isabelle has spent the night trying to make an advantageous deal. She has approached a group of legionnaires with a proposition: she will find them an Ouled-Naïl prostitute whom they can share through the night, and in return they will pay her ten francs. She thinks she can get the girl for three and pocket the difference for herself. Her problem is that the legionnaires are drunk and will not commit themselves. In the meantime the girl may make another arrangement.

She leaves the canteen and walks back through the alleys of the village to assure herself that the girl is still there. When she returns, one of the legionnaires has dropped out of the group, and a new one, who has taken his place, asks the same questions she's answered many times.

Finally she is disgusted and issues an ultimatum. They must bring her the money in fifteen minutes or the deal is off. She steps outside for a cigarette. A German legionnaire she's met several times is leaning against the wall.

"You're the talk of the camp tonight," he tells her. "The boys can speak of nothing else."

She is silent.

"They're making fun of you, Si Mahmoud. Surely you know better than to get yourself involved in something that will bring you shame later on."

"What can I do?" she asks. "I haven't got a cent."

"There must be something," he says. "Meantime let me give you this."

He hands her a few small bills, walks away.

Later that night she loses the money at cards.

She is sitting in the officers' mess at Aïn Sefra when a young lieutenant comes bursting in. He grabs a plate of food, brings it over to her table.

"I've just been with the chief," he says. "I'm excited as hell. His plan is fantastic. We'll soon have Bou-Amama on the run. What I can't get over is the precision of his mind. Lyautey's a genius—no question about it. In twenty years he'll be a marshal of France!"

For three nights she's been wracked by a terrible fever, the same sort that has recurred since 1899. The garrison doctor says it's malaria, and she can look forward to attacks for years to come.

After she leaves him she visits the garrison dentist. He tells her her teeth are in terrible shape. He extracts three of them and tries to patch up the rest.

"In a year or two you'll lose them all."

"What should I do?" she asks. "How will I be able to eat?"

The dentist shrugs.

"Perhaps in Algiers someone can make you a false set."

That night she notices that her hair is coming out. She can pull it out in clumps. In the morning she goes to the garrison barber and asks him to shave her head.

"Yes," he says, as he lathers her up. "It's better this way. Takes care of the problem of fleas and lice."

Sometimes at night she toys with a loaded revolver. It is huge and black. With her finger on the trigger she raises it to

her head and holds her breath. Then she puts it down and
smiles.

She adopts a dog she calls "Loupiot," a shaggy creature
who reminds her of Dédale. Loupiot has a habit of running
around her as she rides or walks, making larger and more
distant circles until he is out of sight. Then, suddenly, he
reappears at her heels.

She is happiest when she writes. She loves to transpose her
notes. Her handwriting is precise and she enjoys embellish-
ing the backs of the pages with beautiful Arabic script.

When she writes descriptions of the little settlements
around Aïn Sefra—the oasis of Figuig, the ksars, the souks
—she becomes totally enraptured by the words and reads
them over to herself, marveling at the music. As much as
she loves the sound of Arabic, she is equally enamored of
French.

When she reads over her pieces, before posting them to
Barrucand, it seems to her, sometimes, that they were written by someone else.

Outside Lyautey's headquarters she encounters Captain
De Susbielle.

"You are a big hero now," she says.

"You are famous, too."

"Once you tried to destroy me. Why?"

"It's a soldier's life," he says. "Destroy or be destroyed."

She looks at him closely. He looks better now in his field
uniform, much better than he ever did behind a desk. At the
Arab Bureau he looked like a big baby. Now he looks like a
hero with a row of medals on his chest.

"I hope we can be friends," he says.

"Of course," she answers. "See you in Rabat."

In Figuig—a place that thrills her—she is invited one night to watch an esoteric dance. She is the only European in the whitewashed vaulted room whose walls run into the floor and remind her of melted ice cream. Candles are set about in niches. The room is packed with men. Despite the chill outside, Isabelle feels hot.

Two women, supple and black, are sitting facing one another on the sandy floor. Using their legs as scissors, they grip each other's waists. A pillow is placed where their bodies meet. By thrusting their bodies in unison to a booming drum they make the pillow bounce.

It jumps, faster, faster, while their black skins become slick with sweat. When the drumming turns to a continuous throb, the pillow is levitated in space.

Often, when she goes to talk with Lyautey, he surprises her with an extravagant gift: a bottle of fine champagne cognac, or a carton of good English cigarettes. She can't understand why he doesn't give her decent pay, but under no circumstances will she allow herself to ask.

It would ruin everything, she thinks. *The moment he becomes my patron, then our friendship will be lost.*

Early one morning Legrand comes to her shack. He wakes her up.

"What is it?" she asks.

"Bad news."

"You've come to tell me I'm under arrest."

"Desforges is dead."

She stares at him, sees it's true.

"How?"

"An ambush. He was on the route to Béchar, chasing snipers who drew him off. He led his entire column into a trap."

"There's more," she says. "Tell me."

Legrand shakes his head.

"His body—they cut it up?"

Legrand nods.

"Yes," she says, after a while, "they like to do things like that. It proves something—their manhood, I suppose."

Winter comes to Aïn Sefra. The mountains around are whitened by snow. The desert is cold long before dark and the light is crisp and pale. Lyautey moves his headquarters to Beni-Ounif. Isabelle decides to return to Algiers for the winter.

On the morning of her last day she makes a tour of the town. It is nearly deserted now—most of the soldiers and camp followers have left, and the crenellated forts are like empty shells.

At noon she saddles her horse and rides to the rocky plains in the north. Here, finally out of sight of any habitation, she dismounts, spreads her black burnoose on the ground and lies upon it, her knees drawn slightly toward her waist.

The sun is hot, its face blank, without pity. She thinks of all the hours she's spent like this, curled to a crescent upon rocks or sand, staring out at nothing, immense emptinesses, immensities of sadness.

The route to Géryville is harsh. She must ride through mountain passes, sometimes dismount and lead her horse up frosty rocky trails. Each afternoon she must find a camp, someone who will let her share a tent. Sometimes she finds nomads who have lit up an entire field of esparto for warmth.

She spends the evenings sitting in tents, warming herself with tea, listening to tales, jotting down poems and songs.

In the mornings she rides into landscapes that remind her of the Alps. She thinks of herself as an eternal vagabond and savors the mystery of the unmarked roads.

White on white: Isabelle as she crosses the Djebel-Amour toward Aflou. There is snow on the ground, Karim is white, and she wears a white scarf and a white burnoose.

In Algiers she writes a letter to Maître de Laffont, her old antagonist in Constantine. She asks for news of Abdullah ben Mohammed ben Lakhdar, and also whether it is possible for her to adopt him.

When there is no reply, she wonders whether her letter is lost or whether she may have forgotten to take it to the post.

Eugène Letord has been looking forward to their meeting for a year. She chooses a café overlooking the port, near the terraced arcades. They speak with great admiration of Lyautey, the frontier war, the digestion of Morocco. Then they lapse into silence.

The next night she takes him to dinner at Villa Bellevue. Several prominent colonialists are there. She drinks too much and monopolizes the conversation.

"The Foreign Legion!" she says. "I know the Foreign Legion! I've slept with them all!"

Later, apropos of nothing, she says, "I'm a Russian at heart—I love the knout."

The party breaks up early. Isabelle goes to bed. Letord and Barrucand remain on the terrace to talk.

"What do you think?" Barrucand asks.

"It's a pity to see her like this," Eugène replies. "She evidently feels she must shock people—that this is what they expect."

Silence as they listen to the sea.

"Strange," he adds, "the way she's aged. She's only twenty-seven, yet she seems—burned out."

Walking the quais of Algiers in the rain, her shoulders hunched, a cheap cigarette clenched between her teeth.

Two of Barrucand's maids discuss the neatness of her room:

"He always arranges his boots—the heels are always together."

"His pens, too—they are always lined up on the desk."

"If I move the prayer rug a little, he moves it back."

"He keeps his kif in a camel udder box!"

She is sitting on a stone bench in the garden at Bellevue, staring at the sea. Victor Barrucand, twenty feet away, studies her unobserved. From the back she appears bent over, her elbows resting on her knees, her fists supporting her head.

What is she thinking?

He moves closer, inadvertently breaks a twig. She turns around, gives him a look of anguish, then quickly composes her face.

Barrucand will never forget the few times he has caught her off her guard.

To
Rend the Veil

In early May she receives a summons from Lyautey:

"Need you for important mission. Please meet me in Beni-Ounif."

The cloud of depression in which she's been mired for months quickly falls away. With a new rage to live she throws her clothes into a suitcase, says quick good-byes and travels to Oran to join a troop train bound for the south. She stops a day in Aïn Sefra, sensing a different mood. It is a depot now, a place for tending wounds and sorting troops. There is no more talk of an imminent collapse. Lyautey, who's been made a general, has moved his headquarters to Colomb-Béchar.

Waiting for him at Beni-Ounif she frequents the canteens where she finds the conversation as sophisticated as in Algiers. The officers talk endlessly about the implications of the *entente cordiale*, by which Britain, in return for a free hand in Egypt, has agreed not to interfere with the Moroccan designs of France.

Lyautey arrives a few days later in an elegantly appointed railway car. There are fanfares at the station, an honor guard, the unfurling of his personal ensign. When she meets him finally at the fort, she feels she's being ushered into the presence of a Bonaparte.

"So," she says, looking him up and down, "now you're *General* Lyautey!"

"You like my uniform?"

"Very much."

He smiles. "You'd be surprised at how much difference it makes. Now the Marabouts want to kiss my ring."

She bows, takes his hand, kisses his ring and gives him an ironic look.

"Algiers was boring. I missed the war."

"Cities are bad for you, Si Mahmoud. You need the desert —you really don't look well at all."

"I know. It was a bad time for me. But never mind about that. Tell me about yourself."

"Bou-Amama is quiet, and pacification is going well. Right now I'm considering another 'frontier correction' at Berguent."

"May I wire Barrucand?"

"Absolutely not! The foreign minister will be down here personally to hang me from a tree."

"So—you are really softening Morocco up."

"It's only a matter of time." Then he shakes his head. "Still, I wonder sometimes. These people give us no quarter, but when we finally tame them, I shall feel sad and maybe a little ashamed. They're so magnificent in their barbarism. They have the passion of wild stallions, and when we seize Morocco—as I'm sure we shall—I hate to think that all of that will end."

"Don't worry," she says. "In a hundred years the European conquest will be forgotten. On this desert only Islam can survive."

"Ah, Si Mahmoud, you always have an answer. You help me because you love adventure, but you don't believe at all in the French cause."

She laughs. "How well you understand me."

"But you're not a hypocrite."

"No. And this time I've come a long way to help. I hope this mission you have for me is good."

"It is. About twenty kilometers west of Béchar there's a holy town—Kenadsa. It's built around a monastery of the Ziania sect. The Marabout, Sidi Brahim Ould Mohamed, is an extremely powerful sheik whose influence extends to Fez."

"I've heard of him."

"I was sure you had. But he's no ordinary tribal Marabout. No, Si Mahmoud—this man is a completely different experience, a Moroccan first of all—and they're a different breed. A deeply devout and truly mystical man. It's not possible to put on a banquet, call in some musicians and expect him to be impressed."

"You want me to talk to him?"

"Yes. But your dealings with the others were mere rehearsals. I want you to go to his monastery as Si Mahmoud, a Tunisian student searching for enlightenment and spiritual truth. He'll be expecting you—my people will see to that. No question, of course, of fooling him with the disguise. He'll know who you are and that you've been sent by me. But you will both act out the pretense. You can expect to stay with him for weeks, even months, and it's possible you may rarely speak. I ask nothing more than that you study the character of this man. Then you can advise me at the proper time."

"I take it he's important to you."

Lyautey nods. "With him I could stabilize the south and move on to other things. Without him I tie up nearly all my men. But neither of us is ready for the other yet. When we are, Si Mahmoud, I want to know who I'm dealing with, and I want you to help me make all the meanings clear."

"You realize," she says, after lighting up her pipe, "that you're giving me the opportunity of my life."

"I'd hoped you would see it that way. That's one reason I called you. Another is that there's no one else. Think of it, Si Mahmoud—I'm sending you to spend the summer in a holy place where you need think of nothing but Sufism and religious truth."

On her way out of his quarters she gasps with delight. Suddenly there are possibilities, an adventure that will take her to the heart of Islam. *And,* she thinks, *with luck I may find tranquillity and peace.*

With a Spahi scout as guide she passes through the gorges of Ben-Zireg, black arid gulleys screaming with flies. The hills on either side are sharp as saw's teeth, but after Hassi-el-Haouari the stones end, and the metallic basalt gives way to a sinuous caressing terrain of red dunes.

Here the heat is even more intense than on the infamous Desert of Black Stones. After hours of staring at an oscillating horizon, she is relieved to see a stripe of blue mirroring the sun. But riding closer she discovers it's only a mirage mocking at her thirst.

It takes her five days to reach Colomb-Béchar. She rests and then begins the trek to Kenadsa, guided by a tall black slave named Embarek, sent by the monastery as a courtesy to an honored guest. They leave before dawn and after several hours mount a small hill strewn with chips of flint and slate. There, spread before them, wrapped in a pinkish haze, is Kenadsa, holy city, Moroccan and unknown, marked by a crumbling minaret.

Descending from the dunes they move into a vast cemetery. This is her welcome to the dusty brown mud town, closed upon itself, untouched, offering no compromise to the traveler coming from the sand.

They pass through gates to a small square where women flutter away like nuns and a few squatting men look grudgingly up. They enter the walls of the ksar, move through the winding passages of the Jewish mellah, and then into a labyrinth toward the mysterious monastic ancient heart.

She feels a building up of tension as they pass beneath covered alleyways, a sense that there is something that will change her life at the center of this maze.

Finally they dismount, enter the monastery by an ordinary door, and once inside she is immediately suffused by an impression of otherworldliness and peace. Several gentle, mute slaves armed with curved daggers, moving with a refinement that suggests an elegant culture of the past, lead her to a chamber where a gigantic black man approaches to kiss the cords that bind her turban to her head. He leads her, in turn, through an empty silent courtyard to a small cell-like room where a rug is spread, perfumed water is poured upon her hands, she is served with coffee and left by herself to rest.

When she opens her eyes she finds Sidi Brahim watching her carefully from another corner of the room. She is struck by his aura of health and strength. He is vigorous, middle-aged, with a strong Berber face framed by a graying beard. His clothes are pure white, and when he speaks, she notices his Moroccan lisp. As he asks discreet questions about her journey, she feels him measuring her with a kindness she cannot resist. He welcomes her to his monastery and then withdraws, suggesting she refresh herself with a walk in the garden and then a long night's sleep.

Days pass and she falls into a languorous life, observing the people who live in the *zaouïa*, watching the work in the graineries, enjoying the calm rhythms of this paradise where life flows gently and time stands still. She meets with Sidi Brahim every day, listens as he explains that the Sufistic mystery, the attainment of vision, is not some trick that can be quickly taught. It can only come through a long process of silent meditation which in time will lead her to the ecstatic moment when she will rend the veil that separates herself from God.

This veil, which alternates in her thoughts between a soft mist with the opacity of smoke, and a thin membrane which can be split by a single insightful slash, becomes, as she ponders it, a compelling mystery whose solution she hopes will finally free her from her pain. It is the cloud of confusion that surrounds her life—the mystery that has driven her for so many years to take refuge in disguise. She must pierce this taut fabric, tear it away, for she knows that if she can see the face of God she will also, in that instant, see herself.

She explains her need to Sidi Brahim who hears her with sympathy, then tells her she has a long road to traverse.

"You *will* see God, Si Mahmoud—one day you will see Him, and then you will understand everything about yourself with all the clarity you dream. It's possible, for a moment, the ecstasy is sublime, and the insight will never fade. Come—come to the window."

He leads her to a slit looking down upon a courtyard. Men are unloading bags from donkeys' backs.

"Do you see that man?" He points to an old man staggering under a heavy sack of grain. "He came as a novice in my father's time, the wandering son of a great family in Meknes. And he's remained here ever since, learning, working, striving for the vision that will give him peace. He's a great man, perhaps a saint, though no one knows that he is. He's been silent for thirty years."

She peers closely now. He moves like a peasant, with a graceful blend of resignation and strength.

"Look at his face. Make your face like his, Si Mahmoud, and you will be happy. God is in him and he is rid of nearly everything else."

"How? How do I change my face?"

"You must begin by purifying yourself."

Time seems to stand still. She rises, eats, walks, thinks and sleeps in a cell with a slave lying before the door. Very quickly Lyautey and the practical world he represents become lost in the meditations that consume her days. He and Sidi Brahim are totally opposed, the one concerned with conquest, power, manipulating men, the other with the nature of being, submission to destiny and fate.

One day she receives an urgent summons to Sidi Brahim's room. This is the only time he speaks to her of anything but the road to spiritual insight. He greets her with trembling hands and an agonized face, hands her a letter and watches as she reads. It is from a Marabout in Fez and tells of the murder of another sheik.

"Our lands," he says to her, when she hands him the letter back, "are convulsed by hate. With honest holy men being killed by fanatics, and impostors like Bou-Amama inciting ignorant hordes, I doubt that Morocco can long survive. The infidels will conquer us, and if that is our destiny then we must submit."

Is this, she wonders, *his way of telling me that he is willing to cooperate with the French?* It is too delicate a point, and she hesitates to ask. She looks at Sidi Brahim and lowers her eyes to show her compassion for his pain.

Weeks pass and she receives his permission to leave the monastery to explore the town and the surrounding dunes. She wanders the Jewish quarter, discovers a place where kif smokers congregate to share their fantasies and dreams. She learns about a mystical place, a dune named Barga that dominates the town, where the colors are like a kif dream, and where, in a cell carved out of rock, there lives an "illuminated one"—a man with an emaciated body and a burned-out face who continuously murmurs certain mystical invocations which have held him in a state of ecstasy for twenty years. She peers into the face of this Saharan hermit, sees a look she knows from the portals of Gothic cathedrals in France—a gaze of joy at having seen eternity, a sight from which there is no return to earthly things.

That night, returning to her cell, she spends hours pondering the meaning of her life. She has a wish now to stop the war inside, the struggle between sensuality and stoicism, the longing for adventure, the strange obsession with disguise and erotic pain. The calm of Kenadsa has softened the tempest, and she longs to become, as Sidi Brahim has advised, a still cool lake, deep and clear, reflecting truth.

It seems to her that she has been wandering all her life in search of something that she can only find within—that the force that has pulled her down so many roads has only diverted her from this journey she must make into herself. It is time, she thinks, to live in stillness, away from corporal pleasures, away from kif and alcohol and sex. No point in using intoxicants to relieve the pain—it must be faced and pierced, just as she passed through the physical agony when she marched across the Desert of Black Stones.

In the middle of August fever strikes her. It is malaria again, but with a new force—more virulent and withering than before. It ravages, convulses, then subsides, only to reappear a week later, and send her to her bed where she alternates between heat and chill with a frightening rapidity that leaves her weakened, awaiting the next attack. During shivering, perspiring, delirious nights, she loses her sense of time, often waking to find Sidi Brahim's soothing presence by her side. He speaks to her, whispers encouragement, and his words are like a cool hand upon her burning face.

She keeps a mirror by the side of her bed, and every so often between the fits, she snatches it up. She peers at herself, looking for the clarity Sidi Brahim showed her on the old man struggling with the grain. Is that look of willfulness, that stare that shows expectation of being hurt, is all that now beginning to fade?

At times, in her deliriums, she believes the veil of mystery that hides God from her eyes is turning diaphanous in her feverish heat, that she can glimpse something beautiful, although still vague, on the other side. A delicious and perhaps dangerous numbness comes. These many weeks at Kenadsa, in which nothing has happened, seem now the most important of her life. She can feel desire and regret begin to vanish from her soul.

She knows that simplicity in being and resignation to fate are the most important things she must learn. Though they come naturally to nomads on the sand, they are most difficult goals for her. She takes to murmuring prayers, repeating them over for hours, hoping to lose all feelings of desire. She wants to be able to face the shining incandescent horizon of the desert without a flinch.

One night, emerging from a fit, covered with sweat, she rises from her bed, grasps a piece of charcoal and scribbles upon the wall. The next morning, clearheaded but weak, she gazes with amazement at her trembling serpentine script:

"My life is creeping toward its tomb as inevitably as night curls toward dawn."

Suddenly she is frightened, realizes that she's dangerously sick. Alone, perhaps forgotten in this lost corner of Morocco, she is too far from help among these mystic people who impassively look on at the ruin of all that surrounds them, cross their arms before sickness and death and say: "It is written—*Mektoub*."

She knows she must leave, must wake herself, return to the world, struggle to survive. And she knows, too, that her monastic interlude has been a turning point, that Sidi Brahim has shown her the way to end the tumult in her life.

Mektoub

She enters the hospital at Aïn
Sefra on October 1, 1904. Among the waiting letters are
several from Slimen. She cannot resist his pleas for a meeting and sends him a cable inviting him to come. A few days
later she receives a reply. He has arranged a leave and will
arrive on the twenty-first.

A few days later a photographer visits her room. Barrucand needs a new picture—her fame as Lyautey's confi-
dante has begun to spread, and there is demand in Algiers
for a recent photo of her face. She poses against her cylindri-
cal pillow with a tarboosh jauntily tilted on her head. Later,
when the photographer examines the print, he is struck by
her expression. It seems to say: "By what devious route has
my life brought me here?"

By Lyautey's order the military doctors give her special
care. They cannot believe that this feverish, emaciated
woman is only twenty-seven years old.

Looking forward to Slimen's visit she arranges to rent a
house in the African quarter of the town. It's a simple mud
building set among the shacks of the camp followers on the
farther bank of the dry river El Breidj. From her window in

the hospital, she can see it among a nest of laundries and canteens.

Early on the morning of October 21, she leaves the hospital, goes to the village, buys a shopping basket, then
marches to the souks to purchase vegetables, meat and a
couscousière. At noon, when the train arrives from Per-
régaux, she is at the station to greet Slimen.

Tired from her walk she sits on a bench, watching the
soldiers disembark. When Slimen steps off he peers around,
his eyes sweeping her face. *He does not recognize me*, she
thinks, amused, as she watches him on the platform, turning
this way and that, searching for his missing wife.

She calls to him, he turns abruptly, sees her and rushes to
her arms. They hug among the new recruits formed up
by their sergeants for the march up to the forts.

He takes the shopping basket, she leans against his
shoulder and they go off to find a mule. She mounts and he
walks by her side as they make their way to the little
house.

He sits beside her as she cuts up the meat and vegetables
and prepares the couscous grains. He wants to make love to
her, but is put off by the evident weakness of her body and
the tone of their conversation which is awkward and
strained.

"It's just three years since we were married," he says. "Do
you remember the day?"

"Of course. We had great plans."

"I've disappointed you."

"No," she says. "I've disappointed myself."

Shyly he runs his finger across her cheek.

"Are you sure you're all right?"

"I'm fine. The fevers are past, and now all I have to do is
gain weight and ride in the sun."

Silence as he peers about.

"I brought some good kif."

"Thank you, Slimen, but I don't smoke it anymore."

"What?" He laughs. "I don't believe you. I can't imagine you living without kif."

"I'm going to try," she says.

He goes off to unpack, explore the house. Stirring the couscous with her hands, she wonders what has become of their great tempestuous love, asks herself why now she feels only fraternal affection for this wiry dark man with liquid eyes and such a sad resigned face. Was it all an illusion—her mad passion for the Spahi horseman in the red cloak who took her on the dunes? *I must be careful not to hurt him,* she reminds herself, setting the steamer on the coals.

They eat late in the afternoon, then go to the roof of the house to lie in the dying sun. He touches her again, and this time she responds, partly out of friendship, partly because she feels cold. Afterward they bundle themselves in burnooses and Slimen begins to smoke.

As she settles back to watch the stars, beginning now to come out in the darkening sky, she thinks back upon the tempests of her adolescence and the fury of living that has consumed the past five years.

Yes, she thinks, *I have lived furiously, and I regret nothing of what I've done.* But now, on this roof, comforted by the company of her brother, Slimen, she looks forward to a calm future as a simple woman, away from tormented striving and disguise.

Slimen smokes on, through the sound of distant bugle calls, the echo of commands shouted in the fort.

"Tell me a story, Si Mahmoud."

She thinks a moment, nods, and begins.

"A lone cavalier met a woman on the dunes between Béchar and Beni-Ounif. The woman was picking out little stones from the sand. 'What are you doing?' the cavalier asked. 'I'm cleaning the desert,' she said. 'But that's absurd,' he told her. 'It will take you and all the people in the world a million years to clean the desert, and then, when you're finished, the desert will be dirty again.' 'Yes,' the woman replied, 'I understand that, but anyway, I try.' The cavalier watched her for a long time, and the longer he watched the more certain he was that he had fallen in love. But he did not know how he could take such a woman away—a woman who loved the desert so much she wanted to clean it with her hands. . . ."

She turns to Slimen, sees delight in his face. A curl of kif smoke lingers before her. The air is still.

She shuts her eyes, trying to regain her story's thread, but then she's distracted by an unpleasant noise. It's a deep, rumbling growl, and when she turns to look, it is louder, much louder, as if a whole mountain were rolling toward her cutting off escape. Someone runs by the house. She hears a cry. Suddenly Slimen stands up.

Lyautey is in the private dining room of his residence, taking coffee with his staff. Suddenly one of the German legionnaires bursts into the hall.

"Come, quick! Something terrible is happening in the town!"

Lyautey and the others jump up from the table, rush to the terrace that overlooks the ravine. By the moonlight they can make out the riverbed and a gigantic tidal wave that seems to have come out of nowhere and is rushing through smashing everything in sight. The entire village is being torn to bits. Trees, animals, people and the tops of houses are being swept in a torrent downstream.

Lyautey, standing helpless, quickly understands. It's one of the great curiosities of the desert—a flash flood that comes out of the mountains, without even the warning of a thunderclap, to rip through gulleys with devastating force.

Isabelle and Slimen stand on their roof watching the ruin all around. Children are screaming, dogs and sheep are struggling against the ferocious tide. The sound is terrible in the still night air. And then bits of their house begin to melt.

"We'll have to swim," yells Slimen. She shakes her head, motions that they should try to climb to the neighboring roof. The water is rising higher. Suddenly she feels the house collapse beneath her feet.

Slimen leaps into the water, disappears. Then he rises again, far away, and she watches in wonderment as he turns, lost in the maelstrom, trying to find her as he's swept from sight.

She peers around, then lowers herself into the rushing stream. Holding onto the terrace wall to keep herself from being swept, she suddenly feels something heavy crush her down.

There is an enormous pain across her back as she begins to sink. She struggles against the weight, frantically trying to fight her way back to air. But she cannot make the water yield. The pain begins to spread.

After a few seconds her strength gives out. Water begins to fill her lungs. Fear gives way to resignation. But then, sinking into oblivion, there comes a feeling that something important is very near.

Now the struggle is within, to rend the veil, to see the face of God. Sinking beneath the water, drowning in the mud, she is struck by an illumination, a blinding insight in which all the confusion of her life fits with perfect symmetry into a dazzling design.

It is light she sees—clear, white and hot. She smiles as she sees she is but a grain of sand in God's limitless desert. She is in tune with all the universe, the music of the stars, and though only a speck of the immense weight, the totality of everything, she is also a part without which the whole cannot be whole.

❖

When Lyautey's men find her body the next day, crushed beneath a heavy beam loosed from her house, she is curled like an embryo, her arms raised in front to protect her face.

Afterward

Slimen Ehnni survived the flood and died two years later of a respiratory disease.

In 1914 Augustin De Moerder committed suicide in Marseilles.

General Louis Hubert Gonsalve Lyautey gradually tightened the screws against Morocco until the establishment of the French Protectorate in 1912. Lyautey became the first resident general of Morocco, was later made a marshal, and in 1917 served briefly as war minister in France. He was elected to the French Academy and died at the age of eighty in 1934.

Much is known of Isabelle Eberhardt's life, but there are great holes which only fiction can now fill.

The best sources are her own writings, and it should be noted that many passages in this book paraphrase her descriptions of events, her own psychological states and desert terrains.

Particularly valuable are her journals, published as *Mes Journaliers* (Paris, 1923) which cover several years and are especially detailed on the period 1900–1901—the Souf, the stabbing and its aftermath.

The three books which were put together and heavily edited by Victor Barrucand are also useful: *Dans L'Ombre Chaude de L'Islam* (Paris, 1905), rich in material on her stay in Kenadsa; *Notes de Route* (Paris, 1908) which deals mostly with her impressions of the Sud-Oranais; and *Pages D'Islam* (Paris, 1908) containing many short journalistic pieces and her moving defense of vagabondage.

Au Pays des Sables (Paris, 1944) contains some of her short fiction and also documents that illuminate various periods in her life. As for her novel, *Le Trimardeur*—it is best forgotten.

It would take pages to separate the blend of fact and fiction in this book. For example, though she did write a letter to Augustin on Christmas Eve, 1895, the letter quoted here is not the same, but a composite of several letters, with the addition of fictional material as well. The same is true of the dialogue at the Constantine trial, and events such as her first meeting with Eugène Letord which actually took place under other circumstances at another time.

But some of the more amazing things happened much as they are reported here: the saga of her brothers who *were* mixed up with anarchists and opium (according to Trophimovsky, Vladimir *was* tortured by Prozov); the attack at Behima; the suicide pact in Ténès; the flash flood; and even the incident with the fictional "Desforges."

There have been many biographies, mostly bad. René-Louis Doyon was the first serious writer to deal with her, and in his *Précédés de la Vie Tragique de la Bonne Nomade* (Paris, 1923) he established the first accurate chronology of her life. Another good book is Cecily Mackworth's *The Destiny of Isabelle Eberhardt* (London, 1951)—accurate, well-written, though lacking in footnotes to the many sources from which the material has been drawn. Of the recent French biographies, Françoise Eaubonne's *La Couronne de Sable* (Paris, 1968) is quite good, but unfortunately marred by an absurd speculation: that Isabelle was the illegitimate daughter of Arthur Rimbaud.

Though there are several streets named after her in Algeria, very few young people in France have ever heard of Isabelle Eberhardt, and she is virtually unknown in the English-speaking world. But there was a time when she was something of a legend, a sort of French T. E. Lawrence with a feminist dimension. Now I hope interest in her will be revived, both because of this novel, and also the publication of some of her stories, excellently translated by Paul Bowles.

❖

In the autumn of 1974 I traveled to Algeria to retrace her footsteps. The country has changed enormously, of course, but one gets a sense of the desert as it must have been at the turn of the century simply by turning down any one of a thousand ragged *pistes*. Then one must stand in awe of her bravery and her love of the road.

I had no trouble getting to Beni-Ounif, Figuig (in Morocco), Kenadsa, El-Hammel or any of the rest of those hidden places in North Africa where she spent her time. One sees young people wearing granny glasses and Che Guevara T-shirts in El Oued today, but there is still sand in the streets, and the palms are still grown in deep basins called *cuvettes*.

I met there with the local writer-historian whose grandfather had been caid in Isabelle's time. "She was strong and svelte, built like a gazelle," he said, and then showed me the ruins of her house, the hospital, the Arab Bureau (now the prefecture) and the house in Behima where she was stabbed.

Ténès, like so many of the coastal towns in Algeria, has the shuttered decayed look of a place hastily deserted by the French. There is a small private beach around the mountain to the east where I imagined Isabelle and Slimen trying to fulfill their suicide pact.

As for Aïn Sefra, I was there seventy years to the day after the famous flood. The river was bone dry and the Algerian army now occupies the old barracks and hospital on the heights (not so high as I had thought). Aïn Sefra is set in a stunning country of red earth and sand, and at sunset the light coats the mountains with an indescribable glow.

After a long chain of complications I found her tomb. It is a simple raised monument set apart from the other graves. "Si Mahmoud," it says in Arabic, and then in French: "Isabelle Eberhardt, wife of Slimen Ehnni, dead at 27 in the catastrophe at Aïn Sefra, October 21, 1904." Nothing else, but the tomb faces Mecca like the rest, and is extremely eloquent in this weed-choked cemetery facing the dunes.

After she died Lyautey wrote: "She was that which attracted me more than anything else. A rebel." She rejected Western culture—the virtues of logic, lucidity, science, proofs. She was attracted to mysticism, poetic leaps of the soul, disguise, erotic love, mad rides across the sand. She was the quintessential wanderer, a troubled, moody vagabond who tried to live in total freedom, re-creating herself according to her dreams. She was fearless in pursuit of what she was, afraid of nothing except that she might harm someone else. Once I learned of her I found it impossible to put her out of my mind, and thus this fantasy, in which I have tried, like other historical novelists, to use fiction as a means of approaching truth.

Tangier, 1973–1975